Sign of the Times

Also by Susan Buchanan

The Dating Game
The Christmas Spirit
Return of the Christmas Spirit
Just One Day – Winter
Just One Day – Spring (coming 17 May 2022)

Sign of the Times

Susan Buchanan

First published in 2012 by Susan Buchanan

Copyright © 2012 Susan Buchanan

Susan Buchanan has asserted her right to be identified as the author of this Work in accordance with the Copyright, Designs and Patents Act 1988.

A CIP catalogue record of this title is available from the British Library
Paperback – 978-0-9931851-7-5
eBook – 978-0-9931851-0-6

Dedication

For Mum, Dad and Tony
With much love
Susan xxx

About the Author

Susan Buchanan lives in Scotland with her husband, their two young children and a crazy Labrador called Benji. She has been reading since the age of four and had to get an adult library card early as she had read the entire children's section by the age of ten. As a freelance book editor, she has books for breakfast, lunch and dinner and in her personal reading always has several books on the go at any one time.

If she's not reading, editing or writing, she's thinking about it. She loves romantic fiction, psychological thrillers, crime fiction and legal thrillers, but her favourite books feature books themselves.

In her past life she worked in International Sales as she speaks five languages. She has travelled to 51 countries and her travel knowledge tends to pop up in her writing. Collecting books on her travels, even in languages she doesn't speak, became a bit of a hobby.

Susan writes contemporary fiction, often partly set in Scotland, usually featuring travel, food or Christmas. When not working, writing, or caring for her two delightful cherubs, Susan loves reading (obviously), the theatre, quiz shows and eating out – not necessarily in that order!

You can connect with Susan via her website www.susanbuchananauthor.com or on Facebook www.facebook.com/susan.buchanan.author and on Twitter @susan_buchanan or Instagram @AuthorSusanBuchanan.

Acknowledgements

Thanks go to Fi Broon for editing

Claire at Jaboof Design Studio for the amazing cover –
claire@jaboofdesignstudio.com

And BB eBooks for formatting –
www.bbebooksthailand.com

Chapter One
Holly – SAGITTARIUS

Fun-loving, friendly, philosophical, intellectual, straightforward and optimistic. Blunt. Dislike being tied down and love travelling. They require freedom of thought. Traditional, conventional.

'Would passenger Jameson, flying to Pisa, proceed immediately to Gate 84. Your flight is fully boarded and awaiting departure. Passenger Jameson, flying on BA 2600 to Pisa, Gate 84, thank you.'

Holly rolled up her sleeve to study her watch. Damn! Eleven o'clock. Her flight left at eleven twenty. No wonder they were calling her name. She always lost track of time in the shops. She couldn't walk past a cosmetics counter. Laden down with Clarins tinted moisturiser, body crème and an eye gel, she hurried towards the cash desk. She was confident the flight would wait. There would be up to another two calls before they told her that they were offloading her luggage, leaving her just enough time to snap up these bargains and hightail it to the gate.

The tannoy burst into life again, demanding Holly's presence. Even Holly was becoming anxious now. Unfortunately, the girl was having trouble with Holly's credit card.

'It's asking us to ring for authorisation,' she explained.

'Damn,' Holly swore. 'Look, I'll just pay cash. I'm in a bit of a hurry.'

'If you're sure.' The head cashier eyed her suspiciously, as if Holly had just presented a stolen card.

'Yes, yes!' muttered Holly, willing them to hurry up.

Transaction completed, Holly thanked them, flew out of the shop, glanced at the signs to see in which direction the gate lay and sprinted towards it. About halfway there, an announcement came over the tannoy. 'Notice for passenger Jameson, travelling to Pisa, your luggage is now being removed from the hold, and she will no longer be able to travel on this flight.'

'No!' Holly said. She quickened her step to Olympic pace and almost sped straight past the gate.

Unable to catch her breath, she pulled out her passport and thrust it towards the ground staff member at the gate, gesticulating wildly at her name. The woman smiled, waiting for Holly to regain her breath and *then* speak.

After several attempts, Holly managed to blurt out, 'I'm Holly Jameson, I'm ready to travel. Please don't unload my bags.'

The woman's lips curved upwards, not unlike the Wicked Witch of the West's, and she said, 'We can't let you travel now. You're too late.'

'But you haven't unloaded my luggage yet,' exclaimed Holly.

'Yes, but it's being attended to. As soon as they locate it, it will be removed from the hold and the flight will depart. That way at least the aircraft will only have suffered a slight delay.'

Her words were intended as a direct dig at Holly for having held up the flight. OK, so some of the blame lay with her, but not all of it, as without Tweedle Dum and Tweedle Dee serving her in the shop, there wouldn't have been a problem. But how many times had Holly had to wait for flights that were delayed? Spurred on by this thought, she said, 'But if I board now, it'll save them having to look for my bags. Then the flight can leave even sooner.' She cast an imploring look at her tormentor, but in the same crisp tones as before, she informed her, 'There's another flight at four o'clock.'

She was wasting her breath with Miss Iron Knickers. Defeated, Holly said wearily, 'Don't suppose I have much choice.'

'Not really,' replied the woman, with the same fixed smile, which Holly would have loved to wipe off her face.

Holly watched on as her flight rose into the air. At least she'd managed to secure a window seat for the next flight. It would be a treat for her not to be squashed between two strangers. There really was nothing worse than being jammed between an obscenely overweight man who burped and farted all the time and an arrogant one, full of his own self-importance.

She searched in her bag for her compact, checking to see if she looked as hot and bothered as the rivulets of sweat running down her back told her she was. To her relief her creamy complexion bore no tell-tale signs, and her black shoulder-length, naturally curly hair wasn't as unruly as she had imagined. Taking out her mobile, she called Tom.

'Hi, sweetheart. How are you?' Tom's lilting voice asked.

'Great thanks. You?'

'Fine, thanks. Shouldn't you be on a plane to Pisa?'

'It's a long story, but I'm still at the airport and now fly out at four. I decided to give you a call since I have three hours to kill.'

'Ah.'

They chatted about trivial matters and then Holly said, 'Well, take care and I'll talk to you in a few days.'

'Have a good flight. Love you.'

'I love you too,' Holly said, before flipping the phone shut.

As Holly waited for her flight, she called her friend Jennifer. She wasn't home and unfortunately Jennifer didn't have a mobile, so she left a voicemail. Bored, Holly took out a notebook and started ticking off some tasks on her to-do list. She wished her parents were alive to see her now. Successful travel writer, engaged to be married, happy. The one thorn in her side about next year's nuptials was that her father wouldn't be there to give her away.

She and Tom had been together four years. She'd met Tom when she was looking for a new flat, and had ended up moving into one not far from the town centre. It had been a real wrench to move from that flat, as she had great neighbours, but she was hardly ever there. She missed Jennifer and of course, proximity to town. Their ramshackle farmhouse wasn't within walking distance of a supermarket, which killed her, but Tom's master plan included six kids, ponies, dogs and plenty of room for all of them. Fortunately, his DIY skills were excellent, or they could never have taken it on. The house needed an incredible amount of work.

They muddled along together pretty well. He was easy to please and they rarely argued, not like with her previous boyfriend. Tom was always there for her and she knew he always would be. He had lived through some of the terrible times she had, each of them having lost both their parents young.

'Flight 2602 to Pisa now boarding at Gate 84.'

This time Holly didn't miss the flight. She sat back in her seat, fastened her seatbelt as tightly as it would allow and skimmed over her notes. She hadn't been satisfied with what she had written about Viareggio and Fornacette after her research trip earlier in the year and was determined to improve upon it or shelve it. She preferred not to write only about *places* she had visited; instead, she immersed herself in the culture, picking up on the idiosyncrasies. It seemed to work. She had written several travelogues, which had been published in magazines and adapted for TV, and had her first travel book published last year. Since then several TV programmes had featured her book and she had been hailed as 'an exciting new voice in travel journalism'. She wasn't so much writing as a Brit, but almost as an Italian who had moved abroad a long time ago and was returning home. *Secrets of the Neapolitan Riviera* had provoked a lot of interest and had soon reached the top ten in the non-fiction charts.

Now there was the pressure of making the second book as successful, if not more. It had to be sharp, avant-garde. Holly had chosen Tuscany as it had always fascinated her. From the hope of catching a glimpse of the elegant sunflowers in the fields swaying in the light breeze, to the mules carrying sand up from the beach for the cement mixers; from the bartering at the market, to the bend-over-backwards-to-help-you attitude, she loved it all. She had been attending evening classes in Italian for around three years now and took every opportunity to practise the language when she was in Italy, as she knew it was the only way to become proficient.

When she emerged onto the concourse at Pisa Airport, she noticed how much busier it was than when she had visited in March. She would have come back sooner, but was so busy trying to placate her publisher's constant demands on her, that time had simply disappeared. So here she was nine weeks later, only now returning to Tuscany. Over the next few months, she would stay in a couple of hotels, and travel back and forth to the locations she would include in her book. As she passed through the terminal heading towards the car hire office, a hotchpotch of nationalities thronged past her. Evidently Tuscany was becoming a more popular holiday destination, as she heard several voices speaking, in what she was certain was Arabic, whilst some Russian gentlemen were heatedly debating something. Cries of '*Niet*' boomed over the usual level of chatter encountered in airports. How times had changed. Europe really was a melting pot nowadays.

After waiting half an hour for the Chinese group in front of her to be served, Holly had the chance to see if her improved Italian and frequent visits could gain her the much-desired free upgrade. It looked like she was in luck. The blonde-haired assistant didn't appear to have much grasp of English and seemed grateful that Holly had more than a passing knowledge of Italian. Holly inwardly sighed with relief, and pleased with herself, collected the keys for an Alfa Romeo, instead of the small Fiat she had been expecting.

Holly reversed out of the parking space and headed out of the airport at a steady pace.

Normally she hated driving, but ironically, in Italy she loved it. She liked the *autostrade* and the tolls. It was all so organised. The crazy Italian driver was a thing of the past. Since the law had been brought in, adopting the British system of applying penalty points and handing out fines for speeding, the Italians had slowed down considerably. They really did not like being hit in the pocket. She didn't enjoy driving in the dark, but that couldn't be helped.

The road from Pisa to join the A1 Firenze to Milano motorway was a winding, narrow one. It would take her forty-five minutes to reach the *autostrada* and then perhaps another hour and a half to the cut-off for the road to Arezzo, which was still another thirty miles away. She wished she had abandoned the Clarins counter and made the original flight. Now, she wouldn't arrive until at least midnight. She should phone ahead and let the hotel know. Suddenly, she heard a loud crash and then a thumping noise. The car listed to one side.

Oh no! I must have a puncture. She tried to think of where she could stop to have a look. Not that she had the faintest idea what to do. She had never changed a tyre before. She wasn't even sure where the spare was, nor did she know who to call.

About a mile down the road, she saw a light. A hotel? She squinted and tried to make out where the entrance was. She passed it, cursed, reversed and pointed her car up the driveway towards it. Putting her handbrake on, she rummaged around in the glove box for the car's manual and finding nothing, switched on the overhead light. She checked everywhere. Zilch. *Bollocks!* There was nothing for it, she'd have to go and ask for help. Uncertainly, she approached the large portico of what looked to her like a residence, now that she was up close. Even in the all-encompassing darkness she could see it was a beautiful building with limestone walls and terracotta roof. She had glimpsed a little of the perfectly landscaped gardens as she had driven up. The dimmed exterior lights cast a soft glow on the various cherubs and little fountains which adorned the perimeter of the garden. Having rung the bell and heard it peal out somewhere beyond the ornate decorated panels of the oak front door, Holly stepped back. No answer. She was about to leave when a voice called out, '*Arrivo.*'

Brushing back her curls, Holly tried to compose herself and prepare what she had to say. She stretched herself up to her full five feet four. She didn't know exactly how to explain her situation, as although her Italian was good, she'd never had a puncture in Italy before.

The heavy door opened. Standing at a little over six feet was a well-built, muscular, but not bulging, Greek god. With dark brown floppy hair, brown puppy-dog eyes and eyelashes that any girl would kill for, he took Holly's breath away. It didn't help that he was wearing only a towel and had obviously just come out of the shower. His dark hair complemented his deep tan, in stark contrast to Holly's Celtic pallor.

'*Si?*' said the man, with a smile, glancing down at his semi-naked state.

In her best Italian, Holly said, 'My car has a puncture.

Could I use your phone to call a garage, please?'

His smile increasing, showing off very white teeth, the man said, 'That won't be necessary. I can change your tyre for you.'

He couldn't have made himself more attractive to her if he tried. 'Thank you so much.'

'No problem. Would you like to wait in the lounge whilst I go upstairs and dress?'

She followed him into an austere-looking hall with oak panels and what appeared to be real paintings on the walls. Doors led off in all directions. Holly trotted behind him until he stopped, so suddenly that Holly almost bumped into him. She could see the droplets of water on his skin and sense the heat of his body. She gulped and stood back as he showed her into the lounge.

'I'll be back in five minutes. Please take a seat,' he said, in his Tuscan sing-song accent.

Holly sat gingerly on the edge of an armchair. Everything in the room looked antique. The gold brocade curtains, the finely polished credenza, the oil lamps which lit the room. Rows of bookcases were stacked high and crammed with books. An avid bookworm, Holly found herself drawn to the first bookcase, and her eyes slid over the titles. Verga, Lampedusa, all the classics were there, interrupted every so often by contemporary novels. Moving to the second bookcase, she recognised some Bill Bryson travel books and a few about Tuscany written in English. Intrigued, she continued along, until with delight, she found a copy of *Secrets of the Neapolitan Riviera*. Holly felt hot all over. He had bought her book. Well, perhaps not him, but someone who lived here had bought her book.

'*Le piacciono i miei libri?*'

Holly started at the sound of his voice. 'Ye-e-s.' He clearly didn't know who she was and who could blame him, as she looked an absolute sight and the photo her publisher chose for the book cover portrayed a glossier, shinier Holly. Maybe he would realise later, once they'd spent more time together. What was she like? How long did she think it would take him to change her tyre? She turned to face him. He was now dressed in Levi's and a cream fisherman's jumper. He smiled down at her, his handsome features crinkling.

'*Andiamo.*'

Whilst relaxing in his lounge, it had started to rain. It had been so warm when she arrived. Cursing her light jacket and skirt, she jumped when he enveloped her in a large waterproof jacket. It was as if she'd touched a high-voltage fence when his hands brushed her shoulders. She approached her car and unlocked it, then he was beside her, a torch shining from beneath his waterproof. He slowly circled the car and whistled, then dug the jack out of the boot and worked away in silence. After five minutes, he glanced up at Holly, who hadn't dared interrupt him.

'I'm sorry. It's no good, it's not only the tyre that is punctured, the wheel is buckled too. It will have to go to a garage.'

Holly was at her wits' end. What the hell was she meant to do now? She realised she was standing staring open-mouthed at this complete stranger. Eventually, she latched on to the idea of finding a hotel nearby.

'Thanks for trying anyway. Could you possibly recommend somewhere to stay?'

In typical Italian fashion, he gesticulated with his arms

and told her that the nearest hotel was Il Giardino, but unfortunately it was twenty miles away. She couldn't drive twenty miles with her wheel like that, and besides the garage was only two miles away. She must stay the night here. There were many guest rooms in his house. Holly started to protest, but he silenced her, saying he would be offended if she didn't accept, and anyway, what was the alternative? Smiling at her, he leaned forward slightly and said, 'No need to be afraid. I am not some crazed madman.'

Holly followed her host inside. She didn't even know his name. As if it had dawned on him, too, he said, 'Dario Barsacchi.' He offered his hand to Holly, which she accepted, saying, 'Holly Jameson. Pleased to meet you. Where am I anyway?'

'This is Rosetto. It is around thirty kilometres from Pisa. And the house is L'Uliveto.'

The olive grove. As Holly didn't ask him anything else, he turned, passing the lounge, and indicated a room on the left.

'That is where you will find me once you have settled in. Are you hungry?'

Holly was starving but didn't want to impose further. As if reading her mind, Dario said, 'It's no trouble. I am cooking for myself and it is always more pleasant to have company.'

Acknowledging his generosity with a barely discernible smile, Holly followed as he ascended a marble staircase. Alabaster busts were positioned at intervals along the staircase. Holly tried to appear nonchalant, but was dying to see if they were members of Dario's family. Some of the inscriptions were so worn it was impossible to read to whom they belonged. At the top of the staircase, Dario swept towards the left wing. It was dark in this corridor, but he pulled an object from behind a hidden alcove then scrambled around a little more, and the next moment, there was light. It was an old oil lamp, encrusted with semi-precious stones.

Who is this guy? Holly found it odd that he should be knocking around in this stately home all on his own. She couldn't deny it, the size and grandeur of this building made it obvious that this was the home of someone of standing. Dario leaned across her and turned a key in the lock. He stepped into the room and laying the oil lamp down, beckoned Holly to enter.

Wow! She wasn't sure what was more impressive, her host or this sumptuous room. In front of her stood a huge four-poster bed, the ruby red hangings of the canopy ridiculously opulent. An enormous cast-iron bath occupied the middle of the room. She glanced round, surprised to note how feminine the furnishings were. A mahogany dressing table, several replica Louis XVI chairs – at least she imagined they must be replicas, they couldn't be real, could they? – a credenza, a roll-top writing desk as well as a chaise longue. How decadent. She had always imagined having a chaise longue, although she knew they were terribly impractical, much better off with a squashy sofa. She'd have a little lie on it later.

Dario pointed to a room off the main chamber, which housed a bathroom with power shower and a dressing room.

Such a strange mix, power showers, but oil lamps. And no electric lighting. After inviting her to use the telephone, Dario excused himself.

Holly thanked him for his kindness and he left. She

really must start being more articulate. She would be spending the evening with this drop-dead gorgeous man and she couldn't string two words together. It wasn't even speaking Italian which was making her tongue-tied, more the fact that Dario was stirring emotions in her that she didn't want stirred, because of Tom. She loved Tom. Dario probably had a beautiful wife or a girlfriend who was a sultry sex goddess. It was true how much women let themselves get carried away: one date and they were planning the wedding. She hadn't even been on a date with Dario, nor was ever likely to be, yet was already picturing their dark-eyed, perfectly tanned children, with her flawless complexion and green eyes. Snapping back to reality, Holly called the hotel in Bibbiena.

Wonderfully relaxed after a soak in that bath, Holly lay down on the four-poster. This was the life. She assumed the four-poster was genuine, as the frame itself was pretty worn. It was too tempting to lie there for long though, as she would drift off. Pulling herself up, she threw on the clothes she had taken off less than an hour before.

Chapter Two

Holly found the door Dario had indicated, hesitating briefly before pulling it open. The aroma of herbs and meat assailed her senses.

'*Ciao.*'

'*Ciao, vieni.*' Dario invited her in. He was standing in front of the hob, flipping the contents of a small saucepan. A larger saucepan held aubergines, peppers and courgettes. She joined him at the hob. He seemed very au fait with what he was doing, as if he was no stranger to a spot of cooking. At the far end of the kitchen was what she guessed to be the dining room.

'Please, take a seat.'

As he cooked, he asked Holly questions and she opened up to him quite freely. It was a lot easier to hold forth on topics she was used to discussing. She told him about her childhood in a little village near Edinburgh and how she had started to write at the age of twelve. It had then become an obsession. He was a good listener, so she shared tales of her life back in Ayrshire, in the south-west of Scotland, of the farm she lived on. She didn't mention Tom, and Dario didn't ask if she had a significant other.

Dario smiled in amusement at his real-life damsel in

distress. He spoke perfect English, he had to for business, but this signorina was making such an effort speaking Italian that it would have been churlish to switch into English.

Holly positively glowed. She was so animated and truly beautiful, unlike some women he met, with their fake eyelashes, Botoxed lips and more make-up than a Holly-wood actress, and she seemed unaware of how lovely she was, which only made her more attractive. Her forest-green eyes shone out from beneath her loose raven curls. She was smaller than the women who usually surrounded him; it would be nice for once to tower over someone, to be able to act protectively towards them. She was slim, with an impressive cleavage. Curvaceous, he supposed you would call her, sexy. He had found her striking when she had first rung his bell, but now, as she sat here chatting away as if they had known each other for years, he was warming to her even more, too much. Tomorrow she would be out of his life again and there was nothing he could do about it.

Oblivious to the inner turmoil she was causing him, Holly babbled on. She was nervous, but at the same time exhilarated to be in the company of such a...gentleman, was the only word she could think of to describe Dario.

After Dario finished preparing the meal, he led Holly through to the dining room. The food was divine. Holly hadn't realised just how hungry she was, until Dario tempted her with his special bruschetta. He explained that the ingredients were all fresh from his garden and the olive oil from the olive groves his family owned. *So that's where the money comes from.*

When they finished the Chianti, Dario went off to the

cantina. Bearing a Brunello di Montalcino 1997, he pulled out the cork and poured a small quantity into a glass. Holly thought it was OK. She wasn't a wine connoisseur, but what she did know was that the more expensive a wine, the more acquired the taste. The Chianti was more to her taste, even if it was a classier and older version than that drunk in the UK. She wagered it wasn't Chianti from Tesco at seven quid a bottle. The Brunello, however, didn't do much for her.

'Tell me, what do you think of the Brunello?'

Holly said, 'Sorry, but I prefer the Chianti.'

Dario let out a belly laugh. 'Your honesty is refreshing.'

'Perhaps we should let the wine breathe,' he suggested.

He spoke of his family, his business and Rosetto with such pride. Holly had an image of him as a kind of Italian laird.

He talked of the re-enactments they held at the beginning of June, of the *Ferie delle Messi* — the jousting ceremony and craftsmen showing off their art, teaching the younger generations how to carry out the ancient arts of bookbinding and arrow-making. He told her of the determination of the locals to beat their neighbouring Carduccio. To Holly it was like Highland Games, but far more interesting and romantic, as befitted twelfth-century Tuscany. He smiled as he told her his friend was undefeated in the archery tournament since 1997. People came from the length and breadth of Italy, to see if they could beat him. The festivities lasted a week, but with the anticipation before the events, and the enthusiasm and good-natured sense of belonging which permeated the whole village, it seemed more like a month. He adored it.

The weather improved as the evening progressed. Only the odd tiny puddle remained here and there, so Dario suggested they sit outside. An old-fashioned lean-to canopy clung to the side of the house. Dario switched on the lights and stepped outside. Picking up a long wooden pole, he pushed the water-laden sections of the canopy upwards. However, he wasn't quite quick enough to move out of the way and managed to almost drown himself with the water which spilled over. Holly grinned, as, soaked through, he looked up at her. She had no need to ask what his cry of '*Cazzo*' meant. Dario pulled out a wicker chair, inviting Holly to sit, and said he would go and change.

A blanket lay on a shelf next to her. Holly picked it up and wrapped it around her. Dario had only just left the room and already she missed him. Even though she wasn't doing anything wrong, guilt stabbed at her conscience. She didn't want to sleep with him, but found it hard to believe she could form such a connection with someone she had just met, especially when she already had a wonderful boyfriend. This was torture.

Dario returned wearing a white T-shirt, which showed off his physique to perfection. They continued to chat, anticipation hanging in the air. Holly was aware of the sexual chemistry which was playing out, but she wasn't sure if it really was reciprocated or if it was one-sided. She needed to knock this on the head. It was getting late and Holly yawned.

'You must be tired. It has been a stressful day for you. We should go to bed now,' said Dario.

Holly's heart leapt. She knew he meant separately but those words leaving his mouth had unleashed something in her. Had Dario noticed her reaction? Had he been able to read the desire in Holly's eyes?

Dario turned out the lights and escorted Holly to her room. Outside, he stopped and said, 'Goodnight,' then he leaned in and kissed her. Holly kissed him back, expecting the kiss to last a few seconds, but he placed little kisses tenderly around the edge of her lips. She couldn't breathe. She shouldn't be doing this, but was powerless to stop herself. All evening she had imagined this happening and now it was. She hadn't even known for sure he was interested. Dario flicked his tongue gently inside her mouth, across her teeth, finding her tongue, until Holly moaned softly beside him. Suddenly, she pulled back.

'I'm sorry. I can't do this.' She took hold of his arms, to distance herself from him. 'I really like you, but I have a fiancé and I shouldn't have kissed you.'

'I kissed you,' Dario said quietly. 'And can I just say that your boyfriend is very lucky. Lots of women are not so faithful. I am sorry if I offended you.'

'Not at all. If things were different...'

A brief silence ensued.

'What time would you like me to wake you?' Dario finally broke the uncomfortable silence.

'Whenever suits you.'

'Eight o'clock then.'

'Fine. Thank you, for everything.'

Dario lay in bed and wondered if 'for everything' included his kiss. He hoped so. It took him a long time to fall asleep, but when he did, his thoughts were of this captivating Scottish woman.

Holly also had trouble sleeping. It was too quiet. Crickets chirruped in the garden. She felt *so* guilty. She had let Dario kiss her. In four years, she had never kissed anyone but Tom. She loved him. They were getting married. Maybe the fine wine had gone to her head. Exhausted, she drifted into a restless slumber.

'*Buongiorno, signorina.*'

Holly opened her eyes to see a wizened old lady standing in front of her, bearing a cup of coffee.

'*Ha dormito bene?*' the old woman asked.

'*Si, ho dormito benissimo, grazie,*' she lied.

The elderly lady, seemingly happy Holly had slept well, turned to go, but as she was leaving, she said in Italian, 'The mechanic will be here in an hour to collect you. Breakfast is ready downstairs.'

'Thank you. Is Dario up yet?'

'Yes, but he has gone over to the vineyard. He left a note.'

Holly barely touched her breakfast. When she reached the breakfast room, she picked up Dario's note eagerly and after reading the single line, turned it over to read the back, but it was blank. Dismayed, she reread the line, hoping to translate it into something with more substance, but the bland, 'Sorry. I have to work. I have asked the mechanic to collect you' wasn't any easier to read second time around. It was with a heavy heart that Holly left L'Uliveto an hour later.

'*Grazie, signore.*' Holly bid farewell to the mechanic, happy that her car was roadworthy again. A bit of a dent in her credit card, but the insurance would reimburse her.

Holly had been unable to think of anything all day, but Dario. Dario and Tom. She tried not comparing them, but in vain. Tom was a bear of a man. He was reliable and provided safety and security, but Dario had awakened feelings of passion in her that she wasn't sure she'd ever felt for Tom. Holly tried to blot out the disloyal thought. With a sigh of exasperation, she realised she was heading in the wrong direction. Glancing briefly at the map, she dropped it on the passenger seat and navigated a U-turn.

Chapter Three

'*Benvenuta,*' greeted the owner of the three-star family-run Hotel di Piazza S Paolo. Sig.a Tagliaferri had spoken several times with Holly on the phone and welcomed her as if she were her long-lost daughter. With true Tuscan hospitality, she bent down and picked up two bags which Holly had dumped next to the terracotta urns at the entrance when Sig.a Tagliaferri had enveloped her in her embrace.

The signora ushered Holly through to the simple breakfast room and offered her an espresso. Holly smiled at this institution of Italian culture and couldn't help but draw a parallel with the Brits offering cups of tea the moment anyone entered their home. As she sipped her espresso, Sig.a Tagliaferri chatted to Holly as if they were old friends.

Two almost identical men, with black hair, dark eyes and deep tans appeared. Holly assumed they were brothers. Her guess proved correct when Sig.a Tagliaferri launched into a fast-paced exchange with them.

'Hollee,' she enunciated, 'these are my sons, Emilio and Guido. Aren't they handsome?' she asked, brimming with pride.

Embarrassed, Holly quickly answered, '*Sì.*' They were attractive-looking men, but they didn't do it for her. Not now, not after having met Dario. The two 'boys' sat at the table, as their mother fixed them espressos. Guido complimented Holly on her Italian, Emilio practised his English with her, which Holly usually found so sexy. Italian men seemed to elongate the words. This time, although it still sounded sexy, it didn't melt her insides.

After promising to let them show her around, Holly excused herself. With Guido and Emilio fighting over who would carry her bags to her room, she headed off to take a shower. Her room was surprisingly large, with two shuttered windows. Although it was only May, it was stifling. There was no air conditioning that she could see. Anxious to catch a glimpse of the view her bedroom offered, she risked opening the shutters and immediately a whoosh of heat struck her. Peering out, she gazed upon the valley below.

Two villas stood nearby; one almost conjoined to theirs and one about a mile away. The one next to her exhibited large wrought-iron gates, and she could just see into its garden, which encompassed perfectly tended lawns, with a large fountain in the midst of a few strategically placed shrubs.

Tearing her gaze away, she studied the house on the hill. It seemed a far grander establishment. Some rich tourist had probably bought it and didn't even appreciate it. It appeared to have a vineyard to the right of it. She could explore later. Gulping in some unwanted, fetid air, Holly closed the shutters and went to shower.

Steaming jets of water poured over Holly's tired body. What a bonus to have a power shower in such traditional premises. The modernity surprised her just as much as at L'Uliveto. She poured a generous dollop of shower gel onto her bath mitt and vigorously rubbed her aching limbs. She decided she could do with a little snooze after her shower. Surely she must be entitled to a siesta in this heat?

Holly woke with a start. She could hear a phut, phut, phut noise. Sleepily, she opened the shutters to see a tractor trundling through the fields. The land to the left of the villa must be farmland. Then she noticed Guido astride the tractor, waving. She grinned and waved back. Revived, she arched her body and shook herself out. That was better. Turning on the cold tap, she splashed water on her face and reapplied her moisturiser. Her skin became so dry, with the heat here. *It must be around thirty-two degrees and it's only May.* She pulled a fresh T-shirt over her head and studied herself in the mirror. She still looked a bit tired and her hair resembled a bird's nest, from having fallen asleep on it whilst it was still wet. Picking up her satchel and her notebook, she headed downstairs.

'I'm going to explore,' Holly told Sig.a Tagliaferri.

Her hostess smiled. 'Holly, will you join us for dinner later?'

'That would be lovely, thanks.'

She passed through the automatic gates and sauntered down the dirt track, her flip-flops soon filled with tiny pebbles. Cursing, she switched swiftly to the grass.

The sun shone high in the cloudless sky. Holly's thoughts returned to Dario as she padded down the windy road and up the hill to the centre of Bibbiena. It was a little as she had expected: bumblebee-striped canopies and green chairs stacked on top of tables, at what she could only assume was one of the restaurants on closing day. A group of teenagers stood around chatting and flirting. Holly strolled past them and spied twenty or thirty stalls with canvas awnings ahead of her. *So, there* is *a market.* Continuing, she passed a bar on the opposite side of the road, where four elderly men were playing chess. Holly watched them for a few minutes and then, conscious they had stopped chattering and were looking in her direction, waved then moved on.

She crossed the road a little further along and turned up into the village centre, following the sign for the church. The reddish-brown buildings were of rough-hewn stone and Holly guessed they were eighteenth century. Today she wanted to absorb the atmosphere, without having to remember she had to write about it. She passed a *tabacchi*, a lawyer's office, an accountant's, until finally she came across a *bottega*. As she peered through the glass in the door, the owner sprang to open it, and she fell forward into the shop, almost colliding with him.

'*Scusi, signorina.*'

Holly waved away his concern and then picked up jars and bottles, examining the contents and ingredients. The *bottega* was filled with mouth-watering goodies; pickled vegetables, zucchini, red peppers and cherry tomatoes filled with anchovies. The upper part of one wall consisted only of wine and the lower half entirely of olive oil. Holly had never seen so many different kinds of olive oil. Next to the *cassa* and the beaming shop owner lay a wide assortment of cold meats and cheeses. Holly wanted to buy up the whole shop. Then she clapped eyes on the counter of fresh pasta...mmm. Ricotta-filled ravioli, pumpkin *stracci*... Little wonder some women deemed food better than sex, although perhaps they simply hadn't met the right guy. Had she? Or, had she met not one, but two? That was unfair. She couldn't possibly equate the four-year relationship she had with Tom with the lust she had felt for Dario. She genuinely liked Dario. She wasn't sure how to deal with it, but then again, would she ever have to? She would never see him again. That made her feel worse. She tried to convince herself things were better this way.

'*Le piace qualcosa, signorina? Quell'olio d'oliva ha vinto il premio del quartiere quest'anno. Guardi. Porta il sigillo.*'

The shopkeeper's words brought Holly out of her reverie. '*Scusi.*'

He asked her again if there was anything she liked and said the olive oil she had been looking at was the district prize-winner. Holly studied it. It was very expensive. After hearing a history of virtually every bottle of olive oil in the shop, Holly gave in and bought that year's prize-winning oil. She seriously hoped it had earned its prize, as it had cost her a small fortune.

As she approached the wine racks to choose something suitable for dinner, the shopkeeper, who by this point had introduced himself as Giampiero, asked, 'Is the wine for a special occasion?'

'The *signora* has invited me to dinner.'

'*Perfetto.* Do you know what Sig.a Tagliaferri is cooking?'

'Unfortunately not.'

'No problem. We will find out.' He picked up the telephone as Holly looked on bemused. Surely he wasn't calling Sig.a Tagliaferri?

A few seconds later Giampiero said, 'Giuseppe. *Ciao!* Has Viviana been in this morning? Yes? What did she order? *Bistecca? Grazie, a dopo.*' He replaced the receiver then turned and gave Holly a knowing smile.

'I hope you are not vegetarian. You're having *bistecca alla fiorentina*, so I would suggest a Chianti Classico.'

The accuracy of their grapevine impressed Holly. She bought two bottles and Giampiero bustled around wrapping them for her. She would come back here for sure, if simply to use Giampiero as a case study. Goods safely in a bag, she thanked Giampiero and set off to explore the rest of the village.

Holly was walking downhill from the village to the little stream which heralded the start of the climb up out of the valley and the steep ascent to the villa, when she heard a car behind her.

'*Ciao.*'

She turned to see Emilio puttering towards her in a beaten-up Fiat Punto. He grinned and beckoned her over. 'Would you like a lift?' When she hesitated, he said, 'If you want to walk, I can take the bags.'

Holly, sweating and red in the face, gave him a warning look. 'No, I'll hop in too, thanks.' Dumping her bags on the back seat, she then eased herself into the passenger seat. Emilio clunked the car into first and it groaned and spluttered over the bumpy, unforgiving road for the rest of the journey.

'Thanks,' said Holly, when Emilio drew up outside the villa. He lifted her bags out of the car and carried them inside. No sooner did she cross the threshold, than Sig.a Tagliaferri appeared. '*Tutto bene, cara?*'

'Yes, thanks.'

Emilio passed her the bags and juggling them, she made her way upstairs. As she turned the key in the lock, her mobile rang.

Damn, why do these things always go off at the most inopportune moments? She dropped her things on the floor and unearthed her mobile. Her face lit up immediately. 'Tom! How are you?'

'Good. Just thought I'd see how your trip's going.'

'Fine. I had a bit of a hairy start with the car breaking down, but things are going well now.' Holly neglected to mention the part Dario had played in her maiden-in-distress situation, as she regaled Tom with her tale of woe.

'So, what are you up to?' he asked.

'I'm having dinner with the landlady and her sons. What about you?'

'I might get to grips with that mountain of paperwork on the dining room table. Have you written anything yet?'

'Not yet. I was just gleaning my first impressions today.'

'I'm sure it'll be another bestseller.'

'Not that you're biased or anything.' Holly laughed.

A shrill ring pierced her laughter. 'Is that your mobile?'

'Afraid so. I'd better get that. Love you.'

'Love you too.'

Chapter Four

'These are for you,' said Holly, handing over the bottles of Montalcino.

'*Ma che cosa fai? Che ragazza!*'

The signora scolded Holly for bringing wine and told her in future she should just bring herself. A cream lace tablecloth, with tiny hearts cut into it, adorned the oak table, where Guido and Emilio already sat, hungry looks on their faces. Holly hoped they were simply in need of sustenance and that steak would put them to rights. She didn't think she could cope with any romantic overtures. It was bad enough explaining she had a fiancé, never mind the added complication of Dario appearing in her head. Sliding into the seat adjacent to the signora's, she pretended not to see Emilio's offended look. The table was laden with simple terracotta earthenware, and silver cutlery which Holly was certain Sig.a Tagliaferri only brought out on special occasions.

Sig.a Tagliaferri placed one of the bottles of Montalcino on the table. A large salad bowl and servers soon followed. Olive oil and balsamic vinegar already sat in the centre of the red-and-white chequered tablecloth. Emilio and Guido wolfed the salad down as if it were going out of fashion. She could never get Tom to eat salad like that. It was as if it would have compromised his masculinity. Most men she knew still abhorred the very idea of eating salad, unless it accompanied a Big Mac and even then they probably threw most of it away. Finishing hers, she glanced at Guido, who was mopping up the remaining juice on his plate with some crusty bread.

The two boys cleared away and Sig.a Tagliaferri struck up conversation with Holly whilst she served the *primo*: *ravioli di zucca*, in a creamy pumpkin sauce.

Holly explained the reason for her stay. The signora was impressed and asked Holly if she had written any other books. Holly related some of the anecdotes in her first book, *Secrets of the Neapolitan Riviera*. She told her how happy it had made her writing about a subject so close to her heart, about a people she held in the highest regard, and how much fun she had had in the process.

She recounted the wine tastings, her introduction to grappa and limoncello, savouring *bistecca alla fiorentina* for the first time. At this Sig.a Tagliaferri wailed that that was what they were having for their *secondo* and went on to enumerate the qualities of the high Florentine cut. Fortunately, Holly liked her steak medium, so she was looking forward to it, if she didn't completely fill up with this amazing ravioli. She adored pumpkin. She smiled as she remembered Tom attempting to make pumpkin pie. Not known for his culinary skills, he had been determined to make the perfect pie for Holly, since she was always cooking for him. Holly had entered the kitchen and seen her fiancé surrounded by an assortment of pots, pans and plates, sweaty and swearing.

'I've made an absolute mess of this. Do you want to get a Chinese?' he had asked.

Holly had managed to salvage the ingredients and handed Tom the pumpkin and a knife and asked him to carve her a Halloween lantern, in exchange for dinner. The pie had turned out to be mouth-watering and she had frozen the leftovers so Tom would have something to live on whilst she was travelling. He was hopeless and would subsist on takeaway if he could. Likewise, the lantern was an artistic masterpiece. They each had their strong points, Holly reflected. Snapping back to reality, she realised Guido and Emilio were telling their mother about the four old men she had spotted playing chess. She was thankful that her temporary lapse in concentration had gone unnoticed.

'And what will you do in the next few days, Holly?' Emilio asked.

'I thought I'd go to Poppi Castle and possibly La Verna to see the monastery. There are a lot of connections to Cardinal Dovizi around here. I'd like to include those in my book.'

'So, do you write stories about your travels or do you write travel guides, places to see, to stay, that sort of thing?' Guido asked.

'No. I write stories about my experiences and about the culture of each place, traditions, history and how understanding it all has impacted me,' Holly explained.

'So, will we be in your book?' Emilio asked eagerly.

'Possibly.'

'Oh please,' he begged.

'I haven't even started my research yet.' Holly laughed.

'We'll help, won't we, *Mamma*? Guido?'

'*Certo*,' came the reply.

Holly assured them they would be mentioned in her

book, although not necessarily by name. 'If I need help, I know where to come.'

The *bistecca alla fiorentina* was heavenly. Holly licked her lips as the signora carved a piece for her. It didn't ooze blood, but it was pink. It was so succulent and melted on the tongue. *I should live in Italy for the food alone!* Dario came unbidden into her thoughts, but she immediately banished him.

'Do you like the *fichi d'India*?' Sig.a Tagliaferri asked her.

'Yes, they're delicious.'

They were certainly very unusual, like fried courgettes, and Holly had really enjoyed the first one, but two was enough. They were a bit bland. The grilled vegetables, sun-blushed tomatoes, red onions and baby mushrooms, were cooked to perfection. Holly couldn't understand how she, a good cook, could never get her Mediterranean veg to taste quite like those she ate in Italy. She used olive oil, the same spices and preparation methods, yet some vital ingredient seemed to be missing. She vowed to ask the signora's advice.

The *pièce de résistance* was the *tiramisu*. Sig.a Tagliaferri revealed it had taken only five minutes to make. It was like heaven to Holly's taste buds. They rounded off the meal with a selection of cheeses and some more of the Montal-cino which Giampiero had recommended; it had gone down well, too well. The evening continued until they were all replete and slightly sozzled. Holly was glowing, partly from the red wine, but mainly because she loved being in Italy and in the company of Italians. Swaying slightly, she bid them goodnight. Today she had felt like one of the family, exchanging escapades and imparting tales. She flopped onto her bed and was asleep in seconds.

Her dreams were confused. One moment Tom was there, her knight in shining armour, the next Dario was alongside Tom, replacing him in his vintage sports car. Holly wasn't sure if Dario *had* a sports car, vintage or otherwise. For all she knew he drove a Fiat 126. No, he wouldn't drive that kind of car, not with such a house. Maybe he was a Ferrari man. Holly awoke feeling headier than when she'd gone to bed, and it wasn't all down to alcohol.

As she had slept late, Holly passed on breakfast, hungry to go out and get some ammunition for her book. She spent the next few days visiting Sestino, Stia and Chiusi della Verna. The audio tour of Poppi Castle impressed her. She also purchased some of the *Lamponi la Verna*, a raspberry alcoholic drink distilled by the monks at La Verna.

Guido and Emilio showed her the surrounding area. They introduced her to Zita who ran the *salumeria*, where the Tagliaferris bought their cold meats. Zita was ninety. It was customary to spend thirty minutes in Zita's when you had only gone in for a hundred grams of prosciutto. Like the chess players and Giampiero, she knew everything about everyone. Whether it was how Carlo's goat was coming along, or that Natalia had been spotted in Arezzo with Sig.a Lazzerini's husband having lunch, or that Alfonso's nephew had graduated from an English university, Zita's kept the gossip moving.

Emilio even let Holly ride the tractor so she could experience life in the fields first-hand. She'd never taken so many notes. Guido and Emilio seemed to have resigned themselves to not being Holly's type and had become good friends.

Today Holly had decided she would go to the market,

to see what it offered. The signora told her to try the home-made pastries stall which Pina ran. Holly was eager to set off as she didn't want to miss out by arriving late.

The market was already thronging with people, some milling around chatting, others perusing the wares on the various stalls. Holly passed the butcher's stall, where fresh duck and chicken vied for position with the venison and veal. Moving on, she came to one of several fruit and veg stalls, where she spotted the *fichi d'India* she'd tasted for the first time a few days ago. They looked rather different in their raw state. Everything was larger, juicier, more misshapen – no European directives had affected these. As she turned away from the stall, a shadow flitted past. She stood stock still and stared. She could've sworn that was Dario. Was she going mad? Had she been thinking of him so much, she'd even managed to conjure him up? Giving herself a shake, she moved on to the next stall.

Holly pottered through the remainder of the market whilst the sun beat down mercilessly from its pole position. She came across a stall which sold fans, and although she didn't quite fit the prerequisite ninety years of age for using one, she bought herself one anyway. As she rested against the edge of a stall, fanning herself with her new purchase, she saw the man again. Practically launching herself from her resting place and quickening her pace, egged on by curiosity, she followed him. She rounded the corner, just in time to see him disappearing into a silver Alfa Romeo. Her pulse racing, Holly asked herself if she was going loopy. Was it him? Tortured by uncertainty, she thought about little else as she trudged back up the hill towards the villa.

Chapter Five

'Hollee!' shouted Emilio. Holly, who had been relaxing in the pool, shot upright and then swam to the edge.

'What's wrong?' she asked.

'I have some news, and I think it will be good for your book. I wanted to tell you before Guido,' he admitted, lowering his eyes.

'It's not something bad?' Holly was confused.

'Noooo. It's very good. Our friend Alessandro is getting married next week. I asked him if you could come to the wedding and he said yes!'

'Oh, thank you! I've never been to an Italian wedding before.'

'Well, you'll have to eat nothing for two days before.'

'Are you saying I'm fat?'

'Fat? *Ma sei pazza?*

'No, I'm not mad, but why shouldn't I eat for two days?'

'OK, maybe not two days, but it's like a marathon eating event, eight courses. Last week you couldn't even manage dessert.'

Holly sighed. 'I know. I love food, but I fill up quickly.'

'So, we have eight courses usually, and there is lots of

dancing, singing and many speeches. And probably at least two hundred people.'

'Two hundred guests! Evening or day guests?'

'What do you mean? The wedding is during the day.'

'No, I mean, of the two hundred guests, how many are invited for the whole day and how many just for the evening?'

Emilio looked aghast. 'No! We do not do things this way. Everyone comes for the whole day. It is a day for celebration.'

'I have nothing to wear!' wailed Holly.

'I am sure you'll find something. I would like you to be my guest, Holly. I know you have a fiancé, so don't worry, I have the purest of intentions.' He winked, letting her know that if Tom hadn't been on the scene, his intentions would have been less than pure.

That night at dinner, the four of them talked of little else. Guido explained that Alessandro owned the large house on the hill, which Holly had so admired on her first day.

Holly's creative juices were flowing. She had already written eighty pages in three weeks, which was a lot, as she was a perfectionist and drafted and redrafted to within an inch of her life.

On Tuesday afternoon she decided she really did have nothing suitable to wear to the wedding. She asked the signora if she knew anywhere to buy a dress in Arezzo. Sig.a Tagliaferri was delighted to be of assistance. She even went as far as to suggest that Holly might want someone with her to approve her choice. So, they set out after lunch and within half an hour were scouring the shops in search of the perfect dress. The assistant couldn't have been more helpful, rushing to do Holly's bidding. Holly wondered if this was because she was foreign and therefore more likely to spend vast sums of money, or because she had a local as a companion.

First, the assistant brought out a red flowery dress which horrified Holly. The assistant must have seen the terror on her face, as she disposed of it quickly. Next was a pale green floaty number. It was pretty enough, but left Holly looking somewhat washed out. The third dress brought a sharp intake of breath from Sig.a Tagliaferri when Holly emerged from the cubicle. She'd been struggling with herself, as to whether to even show Sig.a Tagliaferri this dress. It was *so* revealing. The top was cut like that iconic Marilyn Monroe dress, and it was made of voile, with silk underneath. Holly felt fabulous. Her main preoccupation was the colour: it was cream.

Certainly in the UK it was considered poor etiquette to wear a white or cream dress to a wedding, so as not to upstage the bride. The signora, also a wedding guest, dismissed this problem and insisted Holly buy the dress. Holly hesitated and the assistant said she'd give her a ten per cent discount. So she bought it.

The days leading up to the wedding flew by. The villa had more guests than Holly had seen in previous weeks, so the signora wasn't around to chat as much. Guido was busy in the fields, Emilio was helping with the wedding and Holly was working on her book like a woman possessed. She had befriended the four old chess players. Salvatore, who seemed to be the ringleader, happily recounted to her as many tales as she could listen to. She'd also made time to call Tom the day before the wedding, guilty that she hadn't phoned him for several days. It didn't occur to her that he hadn't contacted her either.

The day of the wedding was a glorious one. The sun was the colour of primroses, the sky couldn't have been bluer and the birdsong couldn't have been more melodic. Many of the villagers had been invited to the wedding ceremony, which was at two o'clock. In the morning, the whole village bustled around, collecting flowers for buttonholes, having their hair styled, nipping into each other's houses to see if one approved of the other's outfit or make-up.

They had all agreed to meet in the villa reception at one thirty and Guido would drive them across. They would then return by taxi later or one of their friends could drop them off.

Both Guido and Emilio gasped when Holly entered the room, in her magnificent dress, her hair up in a French roll and delicate, loose tendrils framing her heart-shaped face. The new shoes added a few extra inches in height.

'Wow!' said Guido. 'You look amazing.'

Holly smiled and said, 'Thanks.' She had given up not accepting compliments graciously a long time ago. Plus she knew she looked good.

Guido drove up the windy, scenic route to Il Castagno, named after the many chestnut trees in the area, whilst Holly took in her surroundings. Rows of wild flowers blossomed along the hillside, but they were so uniform that it seemed they had been specially planted for the wedding.

She drank in the smells of cut grass and poppies, wisteria and roses. Guido negotiated the car to the buzzer in front of the gate and pressed it.

'*Pronto?*'

'*Siamo noi,*' shouted Guido, and the gates opened.

Guido opened the car door for her. It was a simple gesture, but polite, and Holly appreciated it. She looked in awe at the villa, which was about five times the size of the Tagliaferris'. The signora cut into her thoughts. 'It's beautiful, isn't it?'

'It's incredible. How long has it been here?'

'It has been in the family for at least nine generations, so more than two hundred years.'

'That's a lot of history.'

'Hollee,' shouted Emilio. '*Andiamo?*'

Holly followed the brothers through the house to the garden, where the ceremony would be held. As she passed through the villa, she was reminded of Dario's house, although this was much more rustic and relaxed. Even though this villa was equally grand, it was less formidable. She gasped when they entered the garden. It was enormous, lined on both sides by acacia trees and dotted with flowers in an astonishing array of colours. She was marvelling over the beauty of it all, when she caught sight of the vast marquee where the meal would be held. Its flaps were closed, but adjacent to it, she could see several hundred chairs and a raised wooden dais. She walked towards the seating area, to admire the archway, which was made of wrought-iron, but painted white, completely wound around with carnations, peonies and white lilies.

How lucky the bride and groom are to be married in such a place, on such a glorious day.

She stood lost in thought, until a hand touched her arm. Without turning around, she said, '*Arrivo subito,*' assuming it was Emilio come to look for her. When he didn't answer, she turned around and found herself face to face with Dario.

'Jesus!' gasped Holly, flushing scarlet. 'Wh-wh-what are you doing here?'

Measuredly, as if trying to find the right words, he said, 'I'm a guest at the wedding. Alessandro is a very good friend.'

'I came with Guido and Emilio.' At Dario's raised eyebrow, she continued, 'They live in the villa across the valley, and are good friends with Alessandro.'

Dario's amused expression didn't falter, but his voice altered slightly. 'Guido and Emilio?'

'They are my landlady's sons. There she is!' Holly waved at a surprised Sig.a Tagliaferri. Her stomach had what she'd always termed 'flutterbies' in it. She wasn't much enjoying feeling like a gauche, sixteen-year-old. Pulling herself together, she said, 'You didn't say goodbye.'

Before Dario could reply, Emilio appeared, '*Scusatemi,* but Guido wants to introduce you to someone.'

'*Certo.*' Dario shrugged. 'Speak to you later,' he said to Holly, as Emilio dragged her away.

After making polite chit-chat with Guido's friends, Holly's gaze returned to where she had left Dario. He was standing watching her. When she looked over, his eyes met hers and a frisson of excitement shot through her. Smiling to herself, she turned back to reply to a question about her book.

The string quartet announced the imminent start to the proceedings, and as the guests made their way to their seats, the incessant chattering died down to a hush. The groom and the best man took their seats. Eventually, Holly glimpsed the bride, on her father's arm, at the end of the little path with the floral archway. The musicians began playing Monteverdi and all the guests stood up. The bride's dress was a virginal, white satin, fussy, meringue affair, which wasn't to Holly's taste, but it wasn't her wedding and she didn't have to wear it. It was a shame, though, as the bride was beautiful, although un-Italian looking, with her flowing golden tresses. The groom stood at the platform, waiting to receive his bride. He was dressed simply in a well-cut black suit as befitted tradition. The beam from his smile would have given the sun a run for its money, as he took in the sight of his bride-to-be walking towards him.

A lump formed in Holly's throat just as she spotted Dario in one of the front rows on the groom's side. As she watched him, she saw something glistening on his cheek. Were those tears? No, they couldn't be. Men don't cry. As the bride and groom exchanged their vows and rings, Holly risked another glance in Dario's direction. His face was definitely wet. No one had noticed except Holly, all eyes quite rightly on the newlyweds.

Everyone stood again as the happy couple made their way along the path to have their photos taken. Meanwhile, the guests were invited to drink aperitifs. Holly had just raised her glass to her mouth when Dario materialised in front of her.

'*Ciao*.'

'*Ciao*,' Holly replied.

'We never did finish that conversation.'

'No, we didn't.'

'I wanted to say goodbye, you know. It was just...' he searched around for the word '...difficult.' He looked so sincere and regretful that Holly couldn't chastise him any longer.

'I know,' Holly reassured him. 'The problem is, I didn't want to say goodbye.'

Dario's eyes widened. 'Do you mean what I think you mean?' he asked her.

Holly laughed. 'It depends what you think I mean. All I know is I enjoyed spending time in your company.'

'Do you spend time in Emilio and Guido's company?'

'Yes,' replied Holly, knowing where this was leading.

'And do you like spending time with them, in the same way you enjoyed spending time with me?'

'No, it's different.'

Dario smiled, giving the impression he was happy she felt more than just friendship for him, but he changed the subject and they were soon talking about the merits of Dante's *Divina Commedia* and whether Sciascia could be considered as the greatest Italian detective writer. They paused only when they were summoned for dinner.

Three hours and eight courses later, the speeches started. Dario and Holly had been placed at tables at opposite ends of the room. Their only occasion for conversation was when they bumped into each other returning from the toilet.

The speeches finally drew to a close. Then the music started and the bride and groom rose to dance their first dance as husband and wife. They were joined by two elderly couples, and gradually the other guests took to the floor.

Out of breath after dancing for what seemed like hours, Holly begged her current dance partner to show some mercy and let her get a drink. She hadn't noticed Dario dancing. In fact, she was sure he wasn't on the dance floor. She glanced over to where he'd been sitting during the meal, but his table was empty. She procured herself a glass of wine and sat for ten minutes before realising he wasn't coming back anytime soon. Where was he?

She asked herself this again at two thirty when she left to return to the villa with the Tagliaferris. Dario hadn't returned all evening. What was with that man? To leave her once without so much as a by-your-leave lacked etiquette, but twice was downright rude. Maybe she was already with the right man after all. Pushing Dario from her thoughts, she fell into step with the two brothers.

Chapter Six
Tom – CAPRICORN

Responsible, disciplined, practical, methodical, cautious, serious, sometimes pessimistic. Believe anything worth having is worth working hard for. Shy and sometimes awkward. Need security, especially financial.

Tom plonked his half-empty glass down on the table, missing the beer mat. He glanced at his watch and frowned. Mike was now forty-five minutes late. He wouldn't have minded, but it was Mike who had wanted to go for a drink. He sighed, and leaned forward in his seat so the barmaid might see him where he was buried in the darkest corner of the room. Naturally shy, Tom always sat in the deepest recesses of the pub, behind the pool table and the fruit machines.

Annoyed with Mike for being late, especially when he'd had to rush off site to meet him, Tom checked his watch again and decided to get another drink. Mike could get his own. Gesticulating to the barmaid to bring him the same again, he took out his mobile. With everything else in his life not exactly going according to plan at the moment, it comforted him that at least he had Holly. Or, rather he did, when she was here. She was often travelling, doing research for her books. He was immensely proud of her and never passed up an opportunity to let people know his fiancée was the renowned travel writer. With these thoughts uppermost in his mind, he called Holly. After ten rings, her voicemail kicked in. Frustrated, he replaced his phone in the pocket of his yellow builder's jacket and gratefully took his Guinness from the barmaid.

As he drank, he mulled over the day's events. He had lost another two tenders, big ones. O'Reilly's had managed to undercut him again. He didn't know how they managed it and was beginning to suspect foul play. No one could quote such cheap prices. He sketched some figures again on the notepad he always carried with him. Even allowing ten per cent less margin, he simply couldn't get near O'Reilly's price. Stumped, Tom put his notepad away and was relieved to see Mike approaching.

'Sorry I'm late.' Mike sank into a chair. 'Been here long?'

Tom welcomed the distraction of talking to Mike about ice hockey, the Grand Prix and their upcoming hillwalking expedition, rather than think about the continuing slide of his business. He hoped his company would still be operating months from now. Last year he had expected the business to continue to thrive, but this year, there had been nothing but failure. He had his fingers crossed that things would turn themselves around, but he didn't know how. It was just as well Holly wasn't around often enough to notice.

Over the course of the evening, they downed their fill of beer and shorts. Tom managed to convince Mike it really was time to hit the road. He tried several times to pour Mike into a cab, but eventually Mike admitted defeat and shared the taxi as far as Tom's farmhouse. Swaying slightly, as, although he was over six feet and built like an ox, he had downed a fair amount, Tom weaved his way up the path. After numerous attempts, he found the right key and slotted it into the lock.

Walking through to the bedroom he'd converted into an office, he flicked on his computer to check his email. He hadn't had much chance today, having spent the day troubleshooting. It was high time he promoted one of his assistant managers, as he couldn't oversee everything.

Even if they were losing more and more tenders, that didn't mean he had any less work. Au contraire, he had submitted proposals for two major tenders, a new-build site they were being considered for, and a government bid, a new secondary school. If he won those, he'd be laughing.

As the blurb came up on-screen, Tom helped himself to a Glenmorangie. He tapped in his password and, as his email started downloading, raised his glass to his lips, letting the malt glide down his throat. It burned slightly. He checked his work email; a few new enquiries, but nothing of note; a memo from his bank manager. He then logged on to his personal account. That should cheer him up. Maybe Holly would have emailed. She was somewhere near Arezzo. He had never been to Italy. Strange, that. Tom poured another glass. His fiancée, a highly successful travel writer, was writing her third book about Italy, and he'd never set foot in the place. Then again, it's not as if Holly had ever invited him to accompany her. Slightly miffed at this thought, Tom reflected that it wasn't Holly's fault if he never showed any interest in visiting new places. That was her department. Tom was happier with a two-week beach holiday. He worked so hard that on the rare occasion he did take time off, all he wanted to do was lounge around, do a bit of swimming and have a few drinks.

Still, he would have liked to see Venice. From what Holly told him it was like stepping back in time. He should have gone with her when she did her research trip, but he had claimed work was too busy. He'd always wondered what the floating city would be like. Oh well, the nearest he would get to it now would be the book launch for *Venetian Dreams*. It made him smile to think of Holly doing a launch for a book set in Venice when she would not long have returned from a research trip to Tuscany. How confusing. How did she keep it all straight in her head?

Tom's eyes were drooping, but he continued going through his inbox. Simon had sent him an email, giving him the details of the ridge walk they planned to do in a few weeks. Tom loved the outdoors and couldn't wait to kick back for a bit.

He was just about to close down his email, when a familiar banner popped up: Chat. Fighting sleep, he decided to have a quick look to see what this chat-room nonsense was all about then go to bed. It was more complicated than he thought. First of all, he had to register. He hated that, felt as if Big Brother really was always watching. Not that he had anything to hide, but it annoyed him; however, he decided to throw caution to the wind and input his data.

After what seemed an eternity of inputting his preferences, Tom was able to access the site. Wishing to remain anonymous, he called himself farmboy35, as would you believe it, farmboy up until 34 had been taken. Initially, navigating the site was rather daunting. Then he stumbled across something useful. A menu.

By this time, totally game, Tom went into the 31–40 section, where Sarah36, said, '*Hi, Farmboy, how r u 2day?*'

He typed back, '*Fine, thanks. You?*'

'*Gr8. Wot u do?*'

Tom had never bought into text message lingo. He wasn't capable of differentiating between real jargon and what he'd be making up as he went along, so had decided the best option was to steer clear of it altogether. But, what to say to this woman? Unless, she was really a man. You could be chatting to anyone on the internet. He'd read enough articles to know you had to be wary, so he simply put, '*Own business. You?*'

The answer came back swiftly. '*H/dresser, p/t. Wer u from?*'

At least he could understand her abbreviations so far. Not wanting to divulge too much, he simply typed, '*The North.*'

Several smiley faces appeared on-screen, followed by, '*Me 2. Leeds. U married?*'

Taken aback at her directness, Tom replied frankly, '*No.*' It didn't occur to him to explain he had a fiancée. They exchanged pleasantries for a while, Tom even becoming accustomed to the strange language Sarah used. When, twenty minutes later, Sarah wrote. '*Got 2 go. Hope 2 c u soon x,*' he was disappointed. On autopilot, he switched everything off and went to bed.

'What's your problem?' a voice yelled.

'You just ran into my car!'

Tom groaned, pulling the covers tighter around him. His head felt as if a wrecking ball had scored a direct hit on it. He should never have drunk so much. Whisky really didn't agree with him. He curled his body into the foetal position, wanting to die.

OK, he'd got the message. He wasn't going to get any more sleep. Sitting up, he shielded his eyes against the sunlight spilling into his bedroom. *Bloody motorists. What time of day is this to be having a confrontation?* He looked at the clock. *Shit. It's half nine.* He'd overslept. He jumped out of bed and then quickly sat back down, as the room swam before him and nausea overpowered him. Finally, Tom's brain kicked into action. He was meant to be seeing the executives about the new-build deal this morning.

Barely managing to avoid knocking over the leafy arrangement positioned outside the lift, Tom sprinted along to his office. His secretary told him the executives were already waiting for him. Tom tensed. *Shit.* He was late. That was *not* going to look good. Sweeping into the boardroom, Tom firmly shook the hands of the two executives.

'Would you like some coffee?' Tom gave a wry smile when they stared pointedly at the table to show they'd already been taken care of. Trying not to appear flustered, he set up his charts and handed out copies of his calculations. He really was rough today. He had better get a grip on himself.

Fortunately, Tom was excellent at presenting. Favouring the more personal approach, he never used confusing jargon, and many companies liked that. He was very well thought of, and it was widely known that the standard of work from Matthews Construction was second to none. They always used the best of materials, made an excellent job and also had a no-quibble guarantee, which mattered a lot to customers, particularly when there were so many cowboys around. Slipping comfortably into his presentation-giving persona, Tom rattled through the details, asking at intervals if they had any questions. By the end, he was confident he had given as good a presentation as possible. He only hoped his tardiness didn't go against him. Hopefully his secretary had said he was busy elsewhere and he would come across as, in demand, as opposed to, late and hungover. Certainly when he was showing them out, they appeared enthusiastic, even volunteering that they would let Tom know within the next six weeks.

His guests gone, Tom slipped off his tie, picked up a bottle of water and drank it in one go. He'd needed something to slake his thirst. Whether that was from the strain and pressure he felt, or if it was down to his hangover, he couldn't be sure. Buzzing his secretary, he asked if she could find him a bacon sandwich.

By the afternoon, Tom felt more human. He was due to visit two sites and was glad he'd perked up, as the men would wind him up and say he couldn't handle his drink. Although he was the boss, he didn't rule with an iron rod. He had started off as a brickie's apprentice not quite two decades ago, and years of hard graft and determination had got him where he was now. He craved the security that financial success could give him, something his family hadn't had when he was growing up.

His business had started off small, just him, but his reputation had grown, as people were impressed with the job he did, so he had taken on a few labourers. Six months later he'd needed to employ four more men and the success story continued. Thinking back to those halcyon days, he wondered where it had all gone wrong. Was there less competition then? He quoted a fair price for a good job and liked to pay his labourers fairly so they wouldn't want to move on. He shook his large blond head in despair, wondering how his fiercest competitor was able to quote such killer prices.

When he arrived at the site, Tom donned a hard hat, then flipped open his notepad to check the expected progress since his last visit. He liked to be involved, to still get his hands dirty, but he really must talk to Jamie about becoming Assistant Manager. They'd also have to look at advertising, to try to drum up more business.

Just then, he spotted Jamie striding out of the show home. Putting his hard hat back on, Jamie waved to him, and with his face set in a grim line, he made his way over.

'Hi, Tom. How's it going?'

'That's what I'm here to find out. Everything on schedule?'

'Sort of.'

'What do you mean sort of?' Tom asked, surprised.

'One of our timber deliveries has gone missing. The truck seems to have disappeared off the face of the earth. Derek and Nigel are off sick. Nigel fell out of his loft and broke his leg, so he's going to be out the game for a while. Joe says his wages were short. He hasn't been paid any overtime, so he's like a bear with a sore head. He wants to talk to you about it. We're a wee bit behind, but we should make it for the twenty-ninth. What do you want to do about Nigel? Should we bring someone over from another site? I reckon he'll be out of commission until this site's complete.'

Tom took all this in and said, 'Ask Admin to put an ad out and I'll take Ray off the Mollinsburn site. We're less stretched there, although I'm not sure Mike will agree. It'll only be temporary. I'll drop into Nigel's on the way home, see how he is.'

'Right, boss. Anything else?'

'No, I just needed a status update. I'll have a walk round the site and then check in with Cynthia about Joe's wages. See you Wednesday.'

'Yep.' Jamie turned and walked back to plot number eight. Tom strolled around the site, making notes and praising the guys on the good job they'd done so far. Once he was satisfied, he headed back to the office.

'Cynthia, can I see the time sheets for Joe Nash, please?'

With a few clicks, Cynthia printed off copies of Joe's timesheets. 'They're on the printer.'

Comfortably ensconced in his office, Tom checked Joe's sheets. It was like reading a doctor's handwriting. It looked like Jamie had signed off his usual forty hours and another five for Saturday, but then it seemed the totals had been altered. He checked against the records. He had been paid for forty-five hours, but here he was claiming an additional twelve. Tom frowned, trying to remember if he'd authorised more overtime. He didn't recall doing so.

Retrieving his messages, he heard Holly's voice, 'Hi. Just wanted a chat. Give me a call later.'

Tom glanced at his watch. It was half three. He still had to go to Mollinsburn and nip in to see what that daft bugger Nigel had done to himself. He had just enough time to call Holly.

The phone trilled three times before Holly answered, 'Hi, gorgeous. How are you?'

Tom hoped she didn't expect an honest answer to that. Swallowing down the truth, he told her everything was fine. 'So, where are you today?'

'I'm in Bibbiena. It's a lovely little village about twenty miles from Arezzo. Everyone's so friendly. Already they call me *la ragazzina scozzese*, the wee Scottish girl. I have so much copy for my book. You'd love it here. The hotel I'm staying in is fantastic too. It's really just an old family home, a massive villa with a pool, in among the vineyards. I've landed on my feet here.'

'So, where else have you been?'

'Well, I've visited the monastery at La Verna and I spent quite a bit of time in Arezzo seeing how they prepare for *Le Giostra*. You remember the medieval festival I told you they have all over Tuscany? But mainly I'm just scoping out the locals.'

'That's my girl. Just keep writing and then we can retire on the proceeds.'

'Ooh, listen to the big construction mogul. *You'll* soon be able to keep me in the style *I've* grown accustomed to!'

Not wishing to be reminded that there was no chance in hell of that happening, if present times were anything to go by, Tom fell silent.

'What are you up to tonight?' Holly asked.

'I've some paperwork to do, and one of the guys has broken his leg, so I'll take him a bottle of whisky. What about you?'

'The people in the villa next door are having a get-together and they invited me. I thought it might be nice, and I might get some material for my book.'

'You really are wicked, Holly Jameson.'

'Isn't that why you love me?'

'It isn't the only reason, although it helps.' Tom laughed. Aware of the time, he said, 'Look, Hols, I'm sorry, but I've got to go. Enjoy the party.'

'So, everything's OK here then, Mike?'

''Cept me. I had the hangover from hell this morning. What did you give me last night?'

'Yeah, that's it. Blame me! You just can't handle your drink,' Tom ribbed his site manager and friend. 'I need a favour.'

'In my current state? This should be good.' Mike laughed.

'I want to borrow Ray for a week, two weeks tops, for Castlecary. Nigel's broken his leg and Derek's off sick. One man down they could cope with, but not two, and we can't afford to be behind schedule.'

Although Mike was a good friend, Tom hadn't discussed the company's financial situation with him. That was his business, plus he never liked to burden anyone else. So Mike didn't know just how crucial it was they meet the deadline.

'If you can authorise me overtime, I'll put it to the guys. Some of them are going on holiday soon, so they should be up for it. It's the only way I could afford to give you Ray. You know he works at twice the speed of anyone else.'

'You're not wrong there. I'll authorise twenty-five hours for now, so pick your best workers.'

'OK. That should work. I'm sure we'll get the bodies to do the OT.'

'Great. Listen, I need to go.'

'No probs. Catch you next week,' said Mike as he walked away.

Chapter Seven

Finally home, Tom switched on his laptop. He loved this house. They'd poured a lot of time and energy into it. When he bought it, it was a wreck, but he'd managed to purchase the shell of a farmhouse for a song. If you were any good at DIY, it really was worth buying a house requiring a bit of TLC and making it your own. Houses were like people: they needed care and attention.

He and Holly had decided to knock down the walls separating two bedrooms and create one larger room and an en suite. It was handy too, as when Holly was home, she spent ages in the bathroom, making it more of a necessity than an extravagance.

The kitchen, however, was Tom and Holly's favourite room. Ironically for Tom really, as he hadn't a culinary bone in his body and didn't know one end of a fondue set from the other. An antique oil stove was already installed when they viewed the property. It was still in good condition and dominated the twenty-foot room, but what Holly and Tom adored were the original wooden beams, which vaulted the ceiling in a graceful arc. The whole house sported similar beams and some rooms boasted slanting roofs. It was love at first sight and they had immediately put in an offer. Making it habitable took a gruelling nine months.

Tom padded through to the kitchen, popped a beef casserole into the microwave and went to check his email. There was another from Simon, asking if Tom knew anyone else who wanted to do the ridge walk. So far eight of them were going. His sister, Francesca, had sent a brief note, reminding him he had promised to come for dinner.

His sister fussed over him so much. Their parents had been killed when they were young. Since then, Francesca became anxious over the slightest thing. Tom wished she would settle down, find someone who'd make her as happy as Holly made him, someone who could perhaps ease the pain Francesca so openly displayed. It was as if she blamed the whole world for their parents' death and not just the drunk driver who had collided with their parents' Austin.

Scrolling down, Tom saw an email from his bank manager, requesting a meeting. That sounded ominous.

Disheartened, Tom closed his email and was on the verge of shutting down, when he noticed it was still early. He logged on to Chat and surveyed the copious choices before selecting Sportaholics. There were hundreds of people there and a chat unfolded between Chelsea and Man U fans regarding an upcoming game. Deciding he wasn't interested in their point-scoring, he moved on, coming across a conversation about the World Athletics Championships, before noticing there was a menu subdividing the various sports. Tom clicked on Walking and entered the room, which currently held eleven guests.

Ed421: *'I climbed Buachaille Etive Mor last year. Conditions were appalling and afterwards I was told we'd gone up the wrong side. Apparently, even the* *goats would be lucky to get up that way.'*

Climbinggirl: *'It makes all the difference if u get a good day. Never did see the point if the weather isn't in ur favour, as u put in all that effort and then u don't even have a good view at the top to make it worthwhile.'*

Ed421: *'I know what you mean and sometimes it can be dangerous. I did the Aonach Eagach ridge walk a few years back and the weather changed on us. We'd to call out the mountain rescue.'*

Climbinggirl: *'I've been meaning to do the AE for years.'*

Farmboy35: *'Hi. I noticed you're talking about the Aonach Eagach. I'm doing it in a few weeks. Can you tell me any more about it?'*

Ed421: *'Sorry, already late for work. See you.'*

Climbinggirl: *'Bye, Ed.'*

Tom waited to see what would happen next. Then Climbinggirl said, *'I can tell u about the AE. My friends have done it.'*

Farmboy35: *'That would be great.'*

Tom and Climbinggirl chatted for ages. When he finally shut down the computer, he was exhausted. Belatedly, he realised he had forgotten about his dinner. Stifling a yawn, he stood up from his desk and headed for bed. As he passed the clock, he started. It was after one! He'd logged on about half nine, which meant he'd been chatting for more than three hours. They'd talked about walking and climbing and then about the cinema and books. Now he came to think of it, what hadn't they talked about? She was very easy to talk to, this Climbinggirl. As Tom drifted off to sleep, he found himself wondering what her real name was.

The next few days Tom got up at six, as usual, went to work, checked on the sites, did his paperwork, ate his TV dinner and logged on. He spent longer and longer online. By this time, Climbinggirl, or Shirley, had given him her email address, and he would write long emails to her late at night, after they'd finished chatting. She'd introduced him to the delights of Facebook and Bebo. He was a bit of an amateur in this respect, and when Shirley first mentioned them, he had no idea what she was talking about. Since then he'd registered, and even started a blog. It was good to have another friend to talk to. He wasn't sure if she was single. It wasn't important, as theirs was a platonic friendship. But Tom thought it significant neither of them had brought the subject up.

Tom had met with his bank manager the day before, and the news wasn't good. So, he felt justified in indulging in a little bit of light entertainment to help take his mind off his depressing state of affairs. The Chat thing was only harmless fun, after all.

As his computer booted up, Tom tidied up the excesses of the night before. He'd almost polished off the Glenmorangie. It was all too easy to knock it back whilst he tap-tap-tapped away at the computer.

Shirley wasn't online and Tom felt a twinge of regret.

This chatting was becoming an obsession for him, reeling him in like a deadly opiate. He checked his email: nothing from Shirley, only an email from Simon with definitive details of their trip. Just as he was about to reply, a beep alerted him he had new email. Shirley. Like a child ripping open his Christmas presents, Tom devoured the contents of the email. Dismayed when he came to the end, he then noticed the P.S. *'In case you want to chat…'*

Her phone number!

Suddenly, their chats and the emails they had exchanged took on a different quality. *Won't that be betraying Holly?* As he was closing down, Shirley logged on. Hastily, he turned off his PC and picking up the remote he scrolled to a movie channel.

Tom half-heartedly watched *Twister*. By ten o'clock he'd had enough. He switched his computer on again. Shirley was offline. He checked his email. No new messages. Tom opened Shirley's message, grabbed a pen and wrote her number on a Post-it. With a generous helping of Dutch courage, he dialled. A woman's voice answered. 'Shirley?' he asked.

'Tom, is that you?'

'Yes, sorry for calling so late. I had a few things to do.'

'No problem. How are you?'

'Fine, thanks. It's strange to hear your voice. Not bad strange,' Tom hastened to add, 'nice strange, like putting a face to a name. I'm not explaining myself very well, am I?'

Shirley laughed. 'Don't worry. You're doing fine. It *is* a bit strange hearing you too. You sound different to how I imagined.'

'How did you think I'd sound?' Tom was curious.

'Well, less… I don't know…this might come out

wrong. I suppose you have a more manly voice than I expected, deeper.'

A frisson of excitement shot through him. Bringing himself back down to Earth, Tom tried to concentrate on what Shirley was saying. She had a lovely melodic voice, quiet but strong.

How surreal was it to be on the phone to someone you'd met over the internet? Someone you knew so much about, but at the same time, so little. How did he know everything she'd told him wasn't a pack of lies? She could be a seventy-year-old woman or worse, a thirteen-year-old girl, or even a sixty-year-old man. OK, OK, he was getting carried away. She had said she was thirty-four, and his gut feeling told him she was telling the truth.

Tom let Shirley chatter on, participating every so often, but taken aback by how lively and vivacious she was. He supposed her emails always had been quite lengthy. Eventually, he overcame his nervousness and managed to speak to her with just as much ease as when they'd been online. When he finally replaced the receiver, he'd been on the phone for over an hour.

On Wednesday, Tom had dinner with Francesca. Shepherd's pie, his favourite. Francesca only ever made him three dishes and each of them she proclaimed to be his favourite.

As he shovelled another forkful into his mouth, Francesca wittered on about how perilous walking the Aonach Eagach ridge was. Zoning out, a light bulb flashed on in Tom's head. That's where he should meet Shirley. She had mentioned last night that she'd like to meet, and Tom, disconcerted but excited, had agreed. They were to think about when and where. Tom felt a little guilty about Holly, but justified Shirley's presence by the fact they were simply friends, although his conscience reminded him he was deliberately choosing to meet Shirley outside of his and Holly's social circle. As Francesca prated on, Tom decided Shirley should definitely come. He was sure Simon wouldn't have a problem fitting one more on the trip. It would save on petrol too. Convinced Shirley would be all for the idea, he let Francesca ramble on, safe in the knowledge he would go anyway. She couldn't stop him and what's more, Shirley might be going too.

His ringtone disturbed his reverie. Holly. A pang of guilt coursed through him, and holding the phone away from him as if it carried a deadly virus, he answered, 'Hi, Holly.'

'Hi, honey. How are you?'

'I'm fine, thanks. At Francesca's.'

'Ah, old misery guts still making you eat shepherd's pie then?'

'Something like that,' Tom replied.

'I miss you.'

Tom's heart lurched, partly with longing for Holly and partly with discomfort over his potential visit to Glencoe with Shirley. How would Holly react if she knew? She wouldn't be too pleased, even if it was all perfectly innocent.

He listened inattentively. Finally, even Holly noticed.

'Tom, are you OK?'

'I've just had a long day,' he fibbed. 'Can I call you back? It's just since I'm at Francesca's, I should really…' he chose his words carefully, his sister seated opposite him '…make the most of it.'

'O-O-K,' she stuttered. 'Bye.'

Damn, she's not happy and she has very good reason to be put out. I've never blown her off to talk to Francesca. I'll call her back later and…think of something.

Tom gave himself up, in body, to his sister's remonstrations, but his mind was elsewhere.

Home again, Tom checked his mobile; Shirley had left a message. The radio must have been too loud in the car. Lifting the receiver of his landline, he placed it between his chin and his chest, whilst he searched for the Post-it he'd scribbled her number on. Dialling the number, he'd just started twirling the cord between his thumb and index finger, when Shirley answered,

'Shirley?' Tom greeted her affectionately. 'I just got your message.'

'How you doing?'

'Fine. I was at my sister's.'

'Oh right. I was phoning to suggest somewhere to meet.'

'Actually,' Tom interrupted her. 'I have an idea I think you're going to love. But…if you've already thought of something,' he added quickly.

'Let's hear your idea first,' Shirley offered graciously.

Tom told her about the Aonach Eagach trip. No sooner had Tom finished speaking than Shirley agreed, 'That's an excellent idea. I'd love that. Next Saturday, you said?'

'Yes,' replied a relieved Tom.

He told her he'd have Simon book her a room at the Aonach Inn, the principal haunt of all hardened walkers, akin to climbers what après-ski offered the skiing community. Half the fun was in getting plastered after the arduous day's labours. The Aonach Inn was the perfect place to get sozzled.

When Tom awoke next day, his first thoughts were of the following Saturday. In the meantime, he had work to do. So, yawning and easing himself out of bed, as he'd have preferred to remain under his duvet, he started the day. It was shaping up to be a busy one. There was a problem over at Castlecary, so he had to reschedule a few meetings. He remembered he needed to resolve Joe's overtime issue. On reaching the site and asking for Jamie's whereabouts, he was shocked to learn Jamie had been rushed to A&E. A load of wood had fallen on him. And apparently he hadn't been wearing a hard hat at the time.

'Jesus,' said Tom appalled. 'Why didn't Cynthia tell me what the problem was before I came over? She just said there was a problem. Is he going to be OK?'

'Don't know. He wasn't conscious when they took him away. The paramedics said he had head injuries,' Willie added as an afterthought. 'Sol's at the hospital with him.'

'Which hospital?' was all Tom managed to blurt out, already striding back to his car.

'Falkirk Royal, but he might get transferred to the Southern General.'

'I'll be back later. Leave a message on the mobile if you need anything. I'll call you when I have news…and Willie?'

'Yes, boss?'

'Stand in for Jamie.'

Tom drove at breakneck speed to the hospital and was lucky not to have ended up in hospital himself. He swung his Mazda into the car park and barely pulled the hand-brake on, before he was marching through the door marked A&E. He glanced round for Sol, but didn't see him. Flustered, he spotted the triage reception desk, where a young couple were being attended to. Eventually his turn came and he was able to ask about his friend's welfare.

'I'm looking for Jamie Patterson. He was brought in earlier with head injuries. Accident at work.'

The receptionist scrolled through a few screens, then told Tom, 'He's been admitted. If you take a seat, I'll see what else I can find out.'

Whilst he waited, he listened to the booking-in procedure of the prospective patients. Twenty minutes later, the receptionist called his name.

'He's in the ICU. Are you a relative?'

'No. I'm his boss.'

'Is his family here?' the receptionist asked.

Dawn! He didn't even know if anyone had informed Jamie's wife. He'd better call her. The receptionist must have been used to dealing with situations like this, as she read his expression well, smiled kindly at him and informed him there was a payphone in the next block, or he could use his mobile outside.

Tom told Dawn to get a cab and meet him at the ICU. Meanwhile he found out where it was and tried to find someone who could give him information on Jamie's condition. Luckily he found the consultant within five minutes.

'Are you a relative?'

'Yes. I'm his brother,' he lied. 'Can you tell me how he is? I heard he'd had a nasty knock to the head at work.'

'I'm afraid he's in a coma at the moment. I can't really tell you much else until we obtain the results of his X-rays and his MRI scan. Once the swelling to the brain subsides we'll know more.' With that he excused himself and left Tom sitting in the relatives' room, feeling useless.

Dawn arrived with her sister in tow. Tom explained what the consultant had said. She listened, tears spilling down her face, streaking her mascara. After a few awkward moments, when Dawn sobbed against her sister, she regained her composure sufficiently to ask Tom what had happened. Tom admitted he didn't know, but assured her he would find out. It had just occurred to him what Willie had said about Jamie not wearing his hard hat. Jamie was a stickler for rules and safety especially and always led by example. Tom couldn't envisage any situation where Jamie wouldn't wear his hat.

'Dawn, I'm going to go back to the site, speak to the guys, see what I can find out. Please let me know if there's any change.' He hugged her and left.

Tom stormed blindly out of the hospital. He couldn't believe Jamie was in a coma. He prayed he would be all right. He'd known Jamie since he was ten years old. It put everything else in perspective. Ashamed, but unable to help himself, Tom's thoughts turned towards the business and the further setback it would take as a direct result of Jamie's no doubt lengthy absence. He called Mike to let him know the latest. Mike took the news in his stride, but was deeply sorry about Jamie. The builders' grapevine was such that Mike had already heard rumours of Jamie's accident.

'Tom, if you need to talk…'

'I'll phone you later.'

Tom arrived back at the site and sought out Willie straight away.

'Willie. Jamie's in a coma. We don't know yet how serious things are,' said Tom in despair. 'Earlier you said Jamie wasn't wearing a hard hat. You know Jamie, Mr Safety, why wasn't he wearing his hat?'

Willie seemed guarded, eventually stammering, 'I-I'm not totally sure.'

'What do you mean you're not sure?'

Willie finally blurted out, 'Just before the accident, Jamie was arguing with Joe.'

'Arguing?' Alarm bells went off in Tom's head.

'Well, a few punches were thrown and…'

'A few punches!'

Willie said miserably, 'Joe threw the first punch, but Jamie retaliated and Joe smacked him on the head and Jamie's hat flew off. Next minute the load fell. But everything happened so fast…'

'Where's Joe?' Tom's blood was boiling. 'You realise the implications of this? The police will have to be called in.'

'I haven't seen him since the accident.'

Tom went off in search of Joe. He would break his bloody neck. But, there was no sign of him. Tom called Cynthia and asked for Joe's address. He jumped back in his car and raced down the M77 to Ayr to see if Joe was home.

Chapter Eight

Tom knocked a second time and a third. The fourth time he hammered on the door, a neighbour came out. 'Can you cut that out?'

'I'm looking for Joe.'

'Haven't seen him, son. He's working at a site near Cumbernauld, though.'

Tom thanked the man and returned to his car, fuming. Where was the little runt? He sat, staring at the steering wheel, lost in his thoughts. Snapping back to reality, he picked up his mobile and called Mike.

'Mike? Tom. How about that pint this evening?'

By the time Tom made it to the pub, Dawn had called with an update. Jamie had been assessed and a brain scan had indicated a considerable amount of swelling. They were going to have to operate to relieve the pressure on his brain. The medical team would then continue with further tests, but couldn't yet confirm if he'd have any permanent damage. The next few hours would be crucial. Tom told her to keep her chin up, reminded her Jamie was a fighter and said he'd call her first thing to see if there was any further change.

Mike arrived shortly after Tom. Tom was just telling

Mike about Joe's involvement in the incident, when he spotted Joe entering the pub. Joe hadn't seen Tom, as he was headed towards the lounge and not the bar side of The Jolly Japes. Tom excused himself, pointing towards Joe. He crept up on him and was just on the verge of pouncing, when he reeled back as if punched in the stomach. Joe was sitting at one of the trestle tables, with none other than James O'Reilly. Dread clawed at Tom's insides. He wasn't aware Joe knew O'Reilly socially. He watched a brief exchange between the two men, heads huddled together.

Tom witnessed Joe hand O'Reilly an A4 envelope. O'Reilly opened it and leafed through the four or five sheets of paper enclosed. A sly grin spread over his face as the blood drained from Tom's. His worst fears were confirmed as O'Reilly, in turn, withdrew a small packet and handed it to Joe. He opened it, and by the way his lips moved, Tom could see that Joe was counting. But like a cuckolded lover in denial, Tom asked himself if it were really possible that Joe would betray him like this, accepting bribes in exchange for Matthews Construction's plans for tender. Yes – that would explain how O'Reilly was able to undercut him. He swallowed hard and returned to the bar in shock.

He didn't tell Mike everything, but let him know he hadn't spoken to Joe and had a very good reason for not doing so. He asked Mike not to let on they'd been in the pub tonight.

Mike and Tom continued their drinks but Tom was unable to relax. He wished Holly were here. Outside the pub, Tom turned down Mike's offer of a fish supper. It was a fine night, so he decided to walk. The moon was full and seemed to be smiling, or was it laughing at him? The sky was sprinkled with twinkling stars, so he would have no difficulty finding the path to the farmhouse. He hadn't had much to drink and the evening's events had sobered him somewhat. He wished the walk was *this* Saturday. He needed something to help him clear his head.

The next thirty-six hours flew by. Tom called Dawn. Jamie wasn't out of the woods yet, but the swelling had subsided considerably, which the consultant had indicated was a very positive sign. Tom's relief was palpable.

Tom spent Friday combing through the latest tenders lost to O'Reilly's. In the last three months, they had lost nine tenders, each time at prices Tom wouldn't have believed possible if his customers hadn't consistently relayed them to him. Tom wondered about the security of the files. Who had access? He'd ask Cynthia. She was the soul of discretion. He was certain only he and she had keys. By now he was a hundred per cent sure Joe was the reason he'd been losing so much money and why his company was in danger of going under. He wouldn't allow it to happen. Grim, but determined, he picked up the *Yellow Pages* and looked under the section for Private Investigators. He'd soon flush this particular rat out of its hole, but he needed proof. He still had to take Joe to task over Jamie's accident. He would be expecting to be pulled up about it. With a wry smile, Tom marvelled at Joe's audacity and sheer stupidity. He could easily have been discovered through clocking too much overtime. Foolishly Joe had put himself in the limelight, the exact opposite of what Tom imagined a small-time crook, such as Joe, should be doing.

A week later, Jamie was over the worst. Although his recovery would be slow, the doctors were hopeful he would make a full recovery. With a much lighter heart Tom closed his front door, trailing his camping gear behind him. He was nervous. So many things had happened recently. Exhausted and overwhelmed, he really needed this break. He had arranged to meet Shirley an hour before the others, so no one would realise they weren't really acquainted, and hopefully there would be no awkward moments. They had arranged to meet at the Little Chef, just off the A80, a midway point between their two home towns. Tom had suggested they leave his car at the restaurant and Shirley could drop him off there on Sunday night. She had told him her registration so he wouldn't make an idiot of himself by approaching someone else by mistake.

Tom needn't have worried. Shirley was bent over her boot, pulling out hiking boots and a waterproof jacket, when he drew up. Before she turned around, Tom had a chance to appraise her. She was petite, around five feet two and lucky if she weighed seven stone. Tom, at six feet four, couldn't help noting their height difference. Her hair was an ash-blonde bob and she wore hiking thermals and dark trainers. No Kylie Minogue, but she was cute.

Shirley whirled around. Looking up from beneath thick, unmade-up lashes, she smiled impishly. She was exactly as he'd imagined.

'Hi,' she said shyly.

Tom got out of the car.

'You're taller than I expected.'

Tom laughed. 'Hopefully I measure up.' He hesitated. 'Sorry, it's just I feel I should shake hands with you or something.'

'We can shake hands if you like,' Shirley replied, the ghost of a smile on her lips.

He shook her hand. Her hands were small, with perfect fingernails. To his relief she wasn't a nail-biter. He found her handshake firm, yet gentle. A spark coursed through him. *This weekend might be even better than expected.*

'Shall we go inside?' Tom asked, as they had both been standing like rabbits caught in the headlights.

They found a table and Tom went to get them some coffee.

Overcoming their shyness quickly, they were soon jabbering away. Tom finally exclaimed, 'What time is it?'

'Nine thirty. We'd better get a move on. Your friend will be wondering where we've got to.'

'I'll give him a call now,' said Tom, striding towards the door.

They were only five minutes late and Sam hadn't appeared yet, so they weren't quite ready to leave. Tom introduced Shirley to the guys.

'Am I the only girl?' she asked.

'You're not a girl. You're an honorary bloke. It's a great honour,' said Jed gravely.

'As long as I know where I stand. That must mean I get to drink twenty pints of Guinness, enough so's it puts 'airs on me chest and I need to find the ugliest females gorgeous after five pints.'

They all laughed. Tom looked at her with affection. It

was going to be a good weekend.

Tom and Shirley went with Jed, and Sam, when he finally turned up, and the others followed. It was traditional for them to stop off at the Stag's Head, at the top of Loch Lomond, for a spot of lunch, but they decided to motor on and save themselves for dinner.

The car park was busy. As it was a ridge walk, they had to walk seven miles and descend in a different part of the glen, so it made sense to drop one car at the finish. Tom and Shirley were in the only car which made straight for the starting point. The others soon returned and they set off at a brisk pace. The sun shone high above them, casting a golden glow across the heather-strewn glen. A welcome breeze stopped them feeling the real force of the sun. They walked on, laughing, prattling on and generally being lads and taking the piss. Shirley, Tom was pleased to see, gave as good as she got. They stopped several times to admire the incredible scenery. Some of the group were keen photographers and took the opportunity to capture the magnificence of the Highlands.

'I'm starving,' said Sam. They had been walking for a good two hours. Everyone laughed. He was always first to need feeding. Six times he'd told them since they set out that he was hungry, including once in the car park before they left. Simon took pity on him and granted permission to stop. Sinking onto some nearby rocks, they unpacked their lunches, munching away for ten minutes, before Simon announced they needed to crack on.

The rest of the walk passed without issue, but the path became more difficult to navigate and they were tiring. The breeze had dissipated and the sun beat down mercilessly.

Now came the tricky part. The Clachaig gully was universally accepted as the easiest place to descend from the Aonach Eagach, but it was deceptive. Too many walkers had suffered a grim death, or had nasty accidents here, so Simon warned them all to take extra care.

'I'm glad you and Simon are on either side of me,' Shirley whispered to Tom. 'I'm not easily put off or scared of heights, but this is something else.'

'You wouldn't be the first to baulk at this ridge. And it's better to be scared than cocky when it comes to these things,' Tom said.

They were fortunate it was such a fine day. When they arrived safely at the bottom of the rocky gully, a round of applause went up.

'Thanks, guys,' said Shirley.

Tom knew he and Simon weren't the only ones who'd noticed she'd been spooked by the steepness of the gully and had seen from her expression that she was daunted at the prospect of descending into the rocky ravine, where one misplaced step would mean almost certain death.

'Hey. We've mastered the Aonach Eagach,' Tom said to Shirley.

'I know. Isn't it great? Anyone for beer?' Shirley had to raise her voice to be heard above the chatter.

'Yeessss!' the shout went up, as they scrambled down the remaining few feet and walked towards the Aonach Inn.

'I'll get the beers in,' said Tom.

After the first drink, Simon and another of the lads slipped off to pick up Simon's car, whilst everyone else continued drinking in their honour. They soon returned and after sharing a beer with them, to cries of 'Sláinte,' they went to check in. Jed handed out the keys.

'Number nine for you guys, Tom,' said Jed. Mike looked askance at Tom.

Tom stared at Jed, alarmed. 'Jed, we're meant to have separate rooms.'

'Oh right. I'll have a word.'

The receptionist leafed through her reservations book. 'I'm afraid the best I can do is a twin.'

Tom was mortified. What if Shirley thought he'd intentionally booked only one room? Hardly daring to, he turned towards her. Her face was all smiles, as he apologised for the misunderstanding,

'Don't worry,' said Shirley, 'honestly.' And she took the key from Jed.

Chapter Nine

The room was basic but clean. Two single beds lay side by side. A door led to an en suite.

'Do you mind if I jump in the shower first?' she asked.

'On you go,' Tom said, glad to have a moment to marshal his thoughts.

Fifteen minutes later, she emerged, face flushed and hair combed back, with a skimpy bath towel not quite covering her. Tom gulped. A hint of cleavage was showing at the top of her towel. One hand gripped the towel, probably in case it slipped. Barefoot, she was even smaller. Again that protective urge rose in him, but that wasn't all. Embarrassed, Tom grabbed his towel off his bed, and holding it in front of him, asked, 'Are you finished?'

Shirley, no doubt aware of the reaction she had caused, said, 'Yep, all done.'

Tom remained in the shower for a good ten minutes, a myriad of emotions sweeping through him. When he walked back into the bedroom, Shirley was drying her hair. As he laid out his clothes, he sensed Shirley watching him. He padded back into the bathroom to get dressed.

'I could just avert my eyes, you know,' Shirley said.

'I don't know that I can trust you.'

'That makes two of us.'

Flustered, Tom gave a tight smile then closed the bathroom door, heart pounding.

When they rejoined the others, the bar was considerably busier. It was always mobbed in the evening. It had a great reputation and if you didn't enjoy yourself there, there was something seriously wrong. The live folk and rock music drew in the crowds, but the bar itself was nothing special. Some wooden benches and tables, a stone floor which was almost always sopping wet, usually from walkers and climbers who had come in out of the elements and dripped water, or carried in snow, which soon melted all over the floor. A large log fire stood to the right of the bar, but as it had been a scorcher of a day, it remained unlit, although in winter, it was a particularly warming sight. Next to the fire was a smattering of wooden tables and chairs and the back of the bar held a couple of booths. A little nook off the main bar revealed some beat-up old sofas, where patrons could take refuge from the noise.

Many people came straight off the hills, and if they were camping would pitch their tents before setting out and wouldn't go back until after closing time. It was a common sight to behold people with what appeared to be miniature miners' lamps on their heads, enabling them to see their way back in the darkness. Those who were unlucky enough to be staying in the youth hostel had to be under lock and key by eleven, so always missed the best the pub had to offer.

Tom pulled over two chairs, and sitting down, whispered to Shirley, 'We usually put a kitty in. Fifteen to start.'

'Cool.' She handed him fifteen pounds and Tom, pulling a wad of notes from his pocket, handed thirty pounds to Jed.

'There's our kitty money, mate.'

'Thanks. What you having?'

'Guinness for me. Shirley?'

'Vodka and orange.'

Tom was torn with indecision over what to have for dinner.

'I'm having scampi,' Shirley said. 'If you order steak pie, I'll steal some of that and you can eat some of mine.'

'You're on.'

Fed and watered, they sank pint after pint and soon had to add to the kitty. Sam met up with one of his friends, Ben, whom he hadn't seen for ages. Ben worked in Fort William and was a mountain rescue volunteer. Simon knew just about everyone, as he'd been going to the walkers' pub for years. By halfway through the evening, the bar staff was more than able to rhyme off their order.

The Nifty Drifters started their host of folk songs just after nine, by which time the friends were half-cut. The band played mostly popular songs. Where Tom and his group knew the words, they sang along and where they didn't, they tra-la-la-ed.

By the time the band had finished, some of the guys were hardly in a fit state to walk, the downside of cheap drinks. Various hillwalking tales were recounted and soon the Last Orders bell rang.

'It can't be time already,' wailed Sam. 'We only just got here.' Evidently he had incurred some short-term memory loss. He rose to his feet, but his lack of coordination made him fall down again. On his second attempt, he managed to remain upstanding, and swaying, made his way through the throng of people to the bar, to get a double round in.

Soon even their double round was depleted. Finally, the bar manager stood over them, interrupting their chatter. 'Right, folks. Drinking up time was an hour ago. Beat it.'

Everyone laughed at his straight talking.

'He's a right charmer,' Shirley said.

'We should go.' Tom picked up his jacket.

'You guys up for a walk tomorrow?' Simon, ever energetic, even after a good skinful, asked.

'Let's see how our heads are.' Tom wouldn't commit himself.

'Do you want to go into the residents' lounge or are you done in?' Shirley asked.

'What would you rather do?' Tom asked.

'I'm pretty tired. I wouldn't mind going walking tomorrow, but I'll need some sleep.'

Tom agreed. He was sozzled. He'd have to sleep until tomorrow night to be fit to drive.

They walked in silence side by side. There was a sense of anticipation in the air. Tom opened the door and Shirley turned the lamps on. Suddenly he felt very awkward.

'I'm just going to brush my teeth,' he told her.

As he put his hand on the bathroom door, a hand covered his. 'Don't. I like the taste of Guinness.' With that, Shirley stood on tiptoe and kissed Tom very gently, parting his lips with her tongue. His teeth were almost chattering with excitement. He realised he had fantasised about this happening. Shirley's tongue found his and met no resistance. Then they were kissing passionately, urgently. Tom felt himself grow hard. Then Shirley's hand was on him, stroking him, undoing his flies. Her mouth found his, where hungry lips awaited her. They took their time with each other and Tom pleasured her as best he knew. By the time she came, he was close, although he held himself back as much as he could, never wanting it to end. They made love twice more and fell exhausted into a deep slumber, their arms around each other, legs entwined.

Tom woke with a headache like none before. *Ugh, I need water.* He stretched out his hand for the glass he'd left beside the bed the evening before, but it grazed something sticky. Opening one eye, he squinted to see what it was. A condom. A used condom! He sat bolt upright. Three used condoms! Oh my God! It all came flooding back to him. He'd slept with Shirley. Oh Jesus! Finally, he worked up the courage to look across at the lumpy outline in the next bed. She was like a tiny porcelain doll. She hadn't behaved like one last night, he reminded himself. More like a Russian gymnast. *I've been unfaithful to Holly. What am I going to do? Although, perhaps last night was just a bit of fun for her.* Shirley stirred. It looked as if he were about to find out.

'Morning.' She yawned and pulled herself up into a sitting position, making no attempt to cover herself.

She's beautiful. Struck dumb, guilt gnawing at his insides, he gawped at Shirley, who was smiling at him. Forcing himself to speak, he said, 'Morning. How you feeling?'

'Absolutely fantastic.'

Oh Holy Jesus, what have I done?

After breakfast, the troops agreed they were in no fit state for another walk. Shirley and Tom clambered into Simon's Volvo. Gone was the easy camaraderie. Tom was unsure why Shirley was so quiet. Maybe she regretted the previous night too. The journey passed slowly, with Simon fortunately blethering away most of the time, to whichever of them would listen.

'Bye, Simon. Thanks,' Tom called with forced jollity, whilst Shirley fiddled with her keys. Tom watched her anxiously. What he had done was wrong, very wrong. He'd been totally unfair on Shirley too. He was just lonely. Lonely, with too much on his plate and happy to sleep with the first person who showed him some attention. Disgusted, Tom slipped into the passenger seat. He hadn't even had time to fasten his seatbelt, when Shirley broke the ice, 'So, Tom, do you want to tell me what the hell is going on?'

Chapter Ten
Maggie – AQUARIUS

Visionary, curious, open-minded, independent and eccentric, creative. Emotionally detached, but friendly and sociable. Often attracted to activism. Less concerned with practical and physical matters, than with intellectual pursuits. Have difficulty with personal relationships.

The clock struck three. The invigilator told them to turn their papers face down and remain in their seats until they had collected everyone's papers. Maggie had been doodling on the exam sheet. She thought she'd done OK, but who could tell? Politics was meant to be one of the easier subjects. But, she supposed you were actually expected to listen to the news and watch current affairs programmes. She asked herself why she'd opted for Politics. Perhaps it was because she *had* been fooled into thinking it was an easy choice. Whatever the reason, she wasn't sure she'd done enough and she certainly didn't want to repeat. That meant two months worrying about the results and then another two cramming for the resit. She should have studied. If only she hadn't spent so long preparing for that last demo.

Since the age of twenty-five, Maggie had been a protestor. The cause didn't really matter. Anything she believed in was enough for her to be out there brandishing a placard. The last one had been this weekend, entailing a twelve-hour round trip to Morayshire, returning exhausted and with not enough energy even to cram. History of Art was tomorrow. She would do better in that. Even as a toddler, she had always doodled, apparently very well. It was no surprise when she was accepted to Glasgow School of Art. Just a pity she'd had to give it all up. Gathering up her rucksack and coat, Maggie strode purposefully towards the exit.

Outside the exam hall, scores of students stood chatting, and the smokers who had been prohibited from puffing away for the past three hours, lit up, dragging gratefully on their cigarettes. Maggie joined them.

'Hey, Mags, how d'you think it went?' Josh, Maggie's best friend at university, came up behind her.

'OK.'

'OK? I thought it was a nightmare. I really should listen in lectures.'

'It usually helps.' Maggie grinned.

'So, how's the greenfield site campaign coming along?' Josh asked.

'Not bad.'

'Sorry to hear about the badger's sett.'

'Yeah, well, at least we made ourselves heard. It was even in *The Guardian*.'

'Really?'

'Yep. And guess who was in the photo?' She grinned smugly.

'You were not!'

'Yep. I'm just hoping whoever marks my Politics paper

doesn't read *The Guardian*, or they're a badger lover and understand why I didn't study.'

'You must have studied a bit.' Josh's jaw dropped.

'Not recently.'

'You're brave. I couldn't do that, badgers or no badgers.'

'Anyway, stuff it. Fancy a drink?'

Hidden in the darkness of the student union, Maggie and Josh chattered away about Josh's goings-on at the weekend. They made a funny pair; Josh, the camp gay guy who adored clubbing, and Maggie the rebel, champion against injustice. Josh would entertain Maggie with tales of who he had pulled at the weekend and Maggie would relay to him the minutiae of her campaigns. Next week was the Gay Pride march. Even though Maggie wasn't gay, she supported other people's right to be. This was one march where Josh could accompany her.

'Another?' Josh gestured towards the bar.

'Go on then.' Maggie smiled at him.

A couple more Millers down the road and Josh and Maggie were tipsy.

'Do you know, if I were straight, I'd want to marry you.' Josh hiccupped.

'I know, and you're the nearest I'd ever get to marrying again.'

'Why?' Josh was curious.

Maggie hesitated, then said, 'Why not?'

'Well, because I'm gay.'

'I just don't see the point.'

'Of what?'

'Of tying yourself down to one person.'

'But isn't that what all women want? Marriage, a five-bedroom detached and two or three sprogs?'

'That's a seriously sweeping statement! What happened to the new empowered woman? Did Emmeline Pankhurst teach you nothing?'

'Don't you want to get married and have a gaggle of children? I mean, no offence, but you're not exactly a spring chicken.'

'Thanks,' Maggie said.

'You know what I mean.'

'I can't,' Maggie mumbled.

'Can't what?'

'Have kids.' She lowered her eyes to her drink.

'Really? Oh God, I'm mortified now. Sorry. Why didn't you tell me?'

'I'm telling you now.'

'Yes, but before?'

'The subject never came up.'

'Well, no, but did you want to have kids?'

'Yes–' Maggie's voice was almost inaudible '–I did.'

Josh broke the uncomfortable silence which followed, saying, 'At least you won't have to fork out for them until they're eighteen.' It was the only way he knew how to deal with the awkward moment, Maggie realised, but it still made her wince to see her infertility made light of.

'Another beer?' Josh asked.

'No, I'm going to head off home.'

'No! Come clubbing with me.'

'I'm not really in the mood.'

'Are you sure?'

'I'm sure.'

'Let's get a taxi then and I can drop you off.'

'No thanks. I'm in the mood for a walk.'

Maggie walked along the river, the quickest way back to her flat. Although a student, she was past flat-sharing. She didn't want to become part of the mortgage-paying percentage of the populace, but valued her privacy. Tonight had been a lapse. She didn't normally discuss serious matters with Josh.

Fighting back tears, she thought back to her twenties and of the times she had tried so desperately to have Nick's child. Five times she had come close, only for each pregnancy to be snatched away. She even had to deliver her six-month foetus, stillborn. She had asked to see him. She wanted to hold him. He was beautiful, perfectly formed, with the most beautiful little mouth and ten little toes which would never wiggle for her. Then came the final straw. She needed an emergency hysterectomy. Nick held her in his arms as she tried to take in the news. She cried silently inside for months. Eventually the strain proved too much for both of them. They still loved each other, but it was too hard. She couldn't bear to see him, as she could read the sadness in his eyes. A clean break seemed the only way for them to keep their sanity.

That last night, they had clung to each other. They hadn't made love, but lay in each other's embrace, tears wetting their cheeks. If only things had been different. In the past thirteen years, she had spoken to Nick rarely. She hoped he was happy. Maybe he was a father. She really must stop torturing herself. On reflection, she hoped Nick *was* a father, as she had loved him intensely and he had been so broken each time her pregnancy bore no fruit. Shaking her head, as if to rid herself of these unwanted thoughts, Maggie stopped in front of the communal entry door to the flats. The bulb was out. She couldn't see a blooming thing. Where was the damned keyhole? It didn't help that her eyes were blurred with tears. She let herself into the tenement and was thankful for its warmth. Trudging up the two flights of stairs, she entered her flat.

Chapter Eleven

'Morning,' Akbar said.

'Hmm,' grunted Maggie. Not usually the most communicative, after a heavy session she was even less so.

'What can I get you?' Akbar beamed at her.

Maggie pointed to the poppy-seed loaves behind him and said she'd have a root around to see what else she needed.

'Right-o,' Akbar's sing-song voice rang out. 'Let me know if I can help.'

It never ceased to astound Maggie that an Indian had opened a German food store in Glasgow. An Indian delicatessen she could have envisaged, but German? She had once asked Akbar if he had German relatives, to which the reply was negative.

'So, how come you opened a German store?' she had dared to ask.

'Oh well, every other Indian family either has an Indian restaurant or an Indian deli. I wanted to be different.'

Now Maggie was one of his better customers. She was in here practically every day.

'So, how did your protest go?' Akbar asked.

'Not great,' admitted Maggie.

'Does that mean the poor wee badgers are homeless?'

'Akbar, it's not funny.'

'No, of course not, but if we worried half as much about people as we do about badgers, the world would be a better place.'

'I do worry about people,' Maggie said indignantly.

'Not you. Some of those wildlife lovers treat their own children as if they don't exist, yet they'll defend animals to the death.'

'I don't have to worry about that.'

'You'd make a fine mother,' offered Akbar. 'But I suppose you'll need to find yourself a good man first.'

'I think not.' Maggie's tone was cold. Much as she liked Akbar and saw him on a daily basis, she wasn't going to discuss her childlessness with him. Besides, he had six kids. Although Maggie thought six was a bit much, she would rather have had six than none. Dragging herself back to reality, she handed her basket to Akbar, who began totalling up her purchases.

'That's £14.67,' said Akbar. 'Where to today then?'

'I have an exam, so I'm going home for a bit of breakfast from this lot–' she held up her shopping '–and then I'm off to uni.'

'Which is it today?'

'History of Art.'

'No problem. Weren't you an art teacher?'

'Yes, hopefully I should pass. See you.'

Maggie headed out into the street, now full of schoolchildren. It must be nearly nine. With a pang of regret, Maggie thought back to Akbar's words, *Weren't you an art teacher?* Yes, she had been an art teacher and a damned good one. She loved working with kids, seeing their progress, encouraging them, even advising some to enter competitions. She really wanted them to do well, to make the most of their talent. But the toll of not being able to keep her babies had been too severe. Initially, she had simply withdrawn from the children a little. She wasn't sure if this was normal or not, as she had expected to become even closer to them, since it looked like she wasn't going to have her own. Up until then her classes felt like large family gatherings and the kids genuinely seemed to enjoy them.

She remembered the day she had to fail the best student in the year for all other subjects, as she was abysmal at Art. She should have given her an E, but couldn't quite bring herself to do it, so gave her a D instead. The girl was gutted, but what could Maggie do? She couldn't even draw a square, much less the still life she was to draw for the exam. In fact, it was almost impossible to tell if she *had* been drawing a square or a bouquet of roses. The girl was close to tears, explaining how disappointed her parents would be.

Maggie sat her down and told her she mustn't think like that. How could her parents be dismayed when she was the top student in her year? Not everyone was made for Art, she explained. In fact, it was the less academic who usually excelled at it. The girl appeared cheered by this and asked in a quiet voice, 'You don't think it will affect my plans of going to Cambridge then?'

'Of course not.' Maggie smiled at her. 'Anyway, next year you have to choose your options for third year. Were you intending to choose Art?' Maggie already knew the answer.

'No,' the girl admitted.

'That's settled then. Your mum and dad have no reason to be upset, and you can always back it up by saying you're dropping Art next year. Anyway, aren't you really good at Music?'

'I wouldn't say I'm good, but I play piano and a little clarinet and oboe.'

'You've nothing to worry about then. Not only are you the top student in your year, but you have a creative gift too. Do you know how many people I know who can play piano, oboe and clarinet?'

The girl shook her head and Maggie replied, 'One.'

'Oh,' the girl said. 'Who?'

'She's sitting right in front of me.' Maggie smiled and the girl smiled and she knew the girl would be all right.

It was a shame Maggie had blown it, not long after. His name was Paul. He was thirteen, always trying to play the big man and had no interest in any class, never mind Art, which he proclaimed was for poofs. Initially, it irked her that he just wouldn't try, as he obviously had an aptitude for the subject and indeed was an intelligent boy, but just didn't want to let it show. She had spoken to other teachers and they had all given her the same story. Undoubtedly bright, he just didn't want to apply himself.

However, as time passed and he didn't respond to any stimulus, she gave up. She *had* to concentrate on the rest of the class. Her priority became to ensure Paul caused as little disruption as possible. So, she ignored him. Then he started getting personal and several times, she had to consult the headmaster. Paul's taunts ranged from, 'You need a good shag,' to, 'Nobody would want to shag you,' to the last straw, when one day Maggie had kept him behind after class: 'You think you're something, don't you? What do you know about kids? You haven't got any. Thank fuck you aren't my mother. Thank fuck you aren't anybody's mother.'

Maggie, who had returned three weeks previously from recuperating after her hysterectomy, snapped. She slapped Paul hard across the face. They stared at each other in shock.

'You bitch!' He lunged at her, but Maggie grabbed his wrists, unable to believe she had struck a pupil. Unfortunately for Maggie, at that moment, the headmaster walked in, took in the situation and assumed Paul had tried to strike her. She released him and Paul started yelling at the head, 'That mad bitch hit me! She hit me! Look at my face!'

The headmaster, appalled by the boy's outburst, peered at him closely and saw the tell-tale marks of Maggie's slap.

'Paul. Go to my office. Talk to no one. Understood?'

Astonishingly, the boy complied and, glaring at Maggie, left the classroom.

For the first few seconds neither said a word. Then, calmly, the headmaster said, 'Maggie, what happened?' And out poured the whole sorry tale.

'I see. Maggie, I know you've been under a lot of stress recently.'

Maggie raised her eyes to meet his gaze.

'However, much as sometimes we may want to thump the little darlings, and God knows you wouldn't be the first to want to take a swipe at Paul, we can't. Ever. Maybe if he'd held a knife to your throat, you could get away with it, but not otherwise.'

Maggie had looked at him, fearful of what was coming next.

'Maggie. You know what to expect.'

Her superior had genuine sympathy in his eyes as he said, 'Maggie, I'm sorry, I really am,' before heading off to deal with Paul.

The hearing had been brief. It was an open-and-shut case. Representatives from the school had tried to paint Maggie in a better light, had talked of how she motivated the pupils. They explained about Maggie's delicate problem. The headmaster blamed himself, said perhaps they had let her come back too soon. But it was all to no avail. Her suspension officially became a termination of contract with the recommendation that she not be allowed to teach children again. This had been the final nail in her coffin. It was so unfair. She had never regretted anything so much in her life. First she had her potential to be a mother taken away from her and now her career.

Things were bleak for a while. Unfortunately, much though Nick wanted to, he was unable to offer the solace she required. Three months later they split up. She had thought about teaching adults, but it wasn't the same. She couldn't nurture them in the same way. So, she had tried to put it all behind her and spent several months trying to figure out what to do. One day she realised the only other time she had been truly happy was at university. She loved studying. She loved teaching. If she couldn't teach, she could study, but what? She was twenty-seven.

Psychology had been her first choice on her return to Higher Education. She had discovered that grants were quite good for a mature student. Not good exactly, it was still a pittance, but it was more than other students received. She applied for money from the Access and other funds to help her get by.

Her first year at the University of Glasgow had passed uneventfully enough. Of course, she had needed to adjust, but she took it in her stride. After Psychology came Philosophy, after Philosophy, English. Over the next few years she studied English Language, then English Literature, studying Keats, Milton, Shelley, as well as the obligatory Shakespeare. She learned not to take novels, plays or poems at face value. She learned the hard way by failing the first paper she wrote, basing it on what she thought the author meant. The tutors couldn't care less what *she* thought it meant. They wanted her to utilise the information available from the university library, the plethora of critiques on the various works, written by 'experts' and simply regurgitate their interpretation. After implementing this strategy, she started to do rather well. English was followed by a branching off into languages, Spanish, Portuguese and German to be precise. Now, at forty, she was taking things easy, doing Politics and History of Art, with European Business Management thrown in for good measure. She didn't intend to use it, but it came in handy for debates.

With a jolt, Maggie pulled herself out of her daydream. She hadn't even opened a book and was now hoping she hadn't been too cocky. But, she did have an excellent memory for artists and dates and their period and style, so after dropping her dirty dishes into a basin and with a glance in the mirror, she opened the door and was back out in the close again. *I really must do something about my hair. Pigeon-shit streaks went out a long time ago, and they have never suited me.* Nor did they bring out her hazel eyes, flecked with gold. It was time she started taking a bit of pride in her appearance. Since she considered herself unremarkable to look at, and flat-chested, not that *that* bothered *her*, she really had to make the most of what assets she did have. Her eyes were her best feature, although perhaps over-large in her thin face. She was taller than most guys she fancied, unprepossessing, the type of person you'd walk past in the street, although she could scrub up quite well when she put her mind to it. She'd go to the hairdresser after her exam. That could be her starting point.

Chapter Twelve

'Maggie!' Josh yelled to her. 'Over here!'

Maggie smiled at Josh bouncing up and down like an overeager lamb.

'Are we ready?' he asked.

'Think so.'

'Last one and then we are freeeeeee. Yippee!'

Sometimes Josh really did make Maggie think of what Tigger would be like if he took drugs. He was so full of energy, she envied him sometimes. This was his final year, being a conventional student and not a *lifer*, as she termed herself. He had gone to great pains to choose the supposedly easy courses: Psychology, Philosophy and History of Art so he could concentrate on his principal reason for going to university, getting laid. He seemed to have accomplished his objective, too, as he was often found with some gorgeous male wrapped around him. The tales of his sexual exploits were endless, but Maggie knew they were all true. Occasionally she envied her friend, simply because his sex life was so hip and happening and although her own wasn't drought-like, Josh did tend to end up with the finer specimens.

'So, what do you think?' Josh asked.

'A couple of Renaissance questions took me by surprise,' Maggie said, 'but otherwise it was all right.'

'I only knew the Impressionists and Renaissance ones, but who cares? We're frrreeeee!!! Let's go celebrate.' Linking arms with Maggie, murdering the tune to *Celebration* at the top of his voice, Josh dragged her to the student union, where a bevy of students exhibited various stages of inebriation.

Several hours later and with her ears ringing from all the noise, both chatter and loud music, they had been subjected to, Maggie drained her glass.

'Hic, hic, hic, Maggie, hic, how many, hic, of these, hic, Bloody, hic, Marys, have we had, hic?'

'In your case too many by the sounds of it.' She grinned. 'Same again?'

'Play it again, Sam,' drawled Josh. Maggie laughed at Josh's gobbledygook. She'd slag him tomorrow about being so drunk he was talking absolute drivel. No change there then.

'Maggie. Look at me!' Josh shouted.

Turning, Maggie groaned at Josh somersaulting between couches, spilling drinks and attracting as many jeers as applause. He always did this when he was plastered. Apparently the gay kingdom loved his acrobatics. She bet they did.

Maggie accepted her latest round of Bloody Marys from the barman and dashed off to turn Josh upright, as he'd crashed into a speaker. It was a miracle he hadn't ever been barred. She reckoned the manager fancied Josh, and she often wondered if they had some secret liaison, which meant the poor manager couldn't bar him, especially since he was newly married and his wife six months pregnant.

Propping Josh up on the seat opposite, she said firmly, 'This is your last one.'

She'd had to fork out a tenner to the table whose drinks he'd spilt and she'd never see that again. Josh was always broke. She wasn't flush, but she didn't plead continual poverty. She supposed all the Paul Smith and Ralph Lauren gear had to be paid for somehow, although he *did* receive lots of presents from his beaus. For someone with no cash he had expensive tastes. Maggie had never cared much about clothes, particularly not in the last thirteen years. You were more likely to find her gracing Oxfam, than Karen Millen. Her thinking was, if it was in good nick, you could wash it and it would be as good as new. If it was in poor condition, you didn't buy it. Simple. What she couldn't buy in charity shops, she bought off Ebay. Thank God for the internet. She flipped open her phone and rang for a taxi.

'I'll call you,' Maggie told Josh, as she dumped him on his bed. The taxi sat outside waiting for her.

Maggie awoke the next morning with a resounding headache. Why, oh why, did she do this? Straining to open her eyes, she searched for the light switch and suddenly everything was illuminated. She hoped she had some headache tablets.

After a reviving shower, she sat on the sofa, with a towel atop her head and a cup of tea in hand. A slice of toast and a glass of water containing soluble aspirin lay on the table. She was free, at least until September. She still had to work, of course. Usually she did bar work or waitressing to keep her solvent during the summer.

She was certain she had passed her exams, maybe not

top grades, but definitely passed, so she didn't have to worry about resits. Thankfully, she'd already received her acceptance for her next course, but she would need to fund it herself. The taxpayer couldn't be expected to subsidise her yearning for knowledge indefinitely. Pity. She'd decided to do a BA in Geography, mainly because it had interested her at school and she hadn't the foggiest where anywhere was in the world, unless she'd actually visited it. For years, she thought Florida and California shared a coastline, until she went to Long Beach on holiday. Now, as she sat there, on her first morning of freedom, she wondered if she really did want to go back to university. Perhaps it was time to stop being the eternal student. Laying that aside for now, Maggie picked up the phone and called her friend, Jennifer.

'Hello?'

'Hi, Jennifer. It's Maggie. How are you?'

'Busy.'

'Oh?'

'The usual. I've been up since five thirty running after Mum. I've just given her a bed bath and was about to jump in the shower.'

'Fair enough. I was phoning to see if you wanted to grab a sandwich. I'm coming down to Ayr.'

'I'd love to. It would get me out of here.' Jennifer sounded down.

'If you're sure you have time.'

'Yes. I need to go and pick up some more incontinence pads for Mum, so I can spare half an hour or so.'

'Great. See you in Caprice at half three.'

'Sounds good.' Jennifer rang off.

Maggie threw some clothes on, suddenly aware she was bored of the same grotty clothes day in, day out. Everything was faded. They were good for marches and demos, but she needed a few new clothes to update her look. A shopping trip after lunch would sort her out.

Maggie sat in the corner of the café tugging at her hair. What a mess. Josh had dragged her to the pub last time she'd thought of getting her hair cut, so it was even more of a bird's nest now. She really must do something about it. Now that uni had finished, she'd have to make time.

She liked the atmosphere in the pub, the banter. It was a real pub, unlike the faceless chains that were on the increase. Three Monkeys had character. Generations of families had been going there for years and their children would most likely do the same.

'Hello, you,' Jennifer broke into Maggie's thoughts, dropping onto the soft leather couch beside her and dumping her carrier bags on the floor. 'How's it going?'

'Better now the exams are over. I should have time to catch up on things.'

'Like Ebay, you mean?' Jennifer grinned.

'Among other things, but yeah, that's pretty high on my list. I've so much junk. How do we accumulate so much stuff?'

'We buy it on Ebay, I suppose.' Jennifer shrugged. That's how they had met, two years previously. Maggie was selling a beautiful burgundy-and-cream throw patterned with cream elephants. Jennifer had been looking for something to brighten up the lounge in her mother's house, after circumstances dictated she live there. She had won the auction and, not being flash for cash, since giving up her job at an insurance firm to care for her mum, had asked Maggie if she could come and collect it, to save on postage, as she lived nearby. Maggie agreed and was pleasantly surprised when she met Jennifer.

Maggie had made tea whilst Jennifer surveyed Maggie's other Ebay items. There were several Jennifer was interested in. Maggie showed her the condition of the books and the foot spa, which was still boxed and the TV, which made a slight buzzing noise, but had a reserve price of a fiver. They had talked for a good few hours before Jennifer, suddenly noticing the time, left to attend to her mother once again.

'What do you want to drink?' Maggie asked.

'I hear cinnamon lattes are good.'

'Can we have two cinnamon lattes, please?' Maggie asked a passing barman.

'I'll bring them over.'

'So, what have you been up to?' Maggie leaned her arms on the table.

'The usual. Mum's demanding as ever.' She rolled her eyes. To lend some levity to Jennifer's situation, they pretended her mother was just a nightmare to live with, instead of the incapable, broken woman she'd become, thanks to the myotonic dystrophy she'd developed four years ago.

'Are you still entering as many competitions?' Maggie asked.

'Yeah. I spend half my day filling out postcards to win holidays or cars. Imagine, me with a car. I don't think I'd remember how to drive, it's been so long.'

'You'd manage. Have you won anything yet?'

'A few things. A CD wallet, a pair of spyglasses, don't ask!'

'Anything useful?'

'No, although I did win a makeover session in London.'

'You're not going, are you?' Maggie was horrified.

'When would I have the time, or the money to get there?'

'That's true, but you know it's all a con to make you part with more money?'

'I suppose so, but you *do* get a makeover and a photo of the newly improved you.'

'Yes, but trust me, it's a scam.'

'This sandwich is delicious.' Jennifer changed the subject. 'What did you order?'

'Chicken tikka. It's not bad, but it's expensive in here for sandwiches. Six quid. How many loaves can you buy for that? You could probably buy a couple of chickens too.'

Jennifer almost fell off her seat laughing.

'Well, you can get enough for a meal for four for seven quid, and cafés want six quid for a sandwich with one paltry slice in it.'

'Good point,' agreed Jennifer. 'Anyway, when do you start back at Three Monkeys?'

'Tuesday. I told my boss I wanted a few days off first. I've so much to sort out. The flat's a bomb site.'

'I know how you feel,' said Jennifer, as Maggie concealed a smile.

Jennifer's house was spotless. She spent so much time in it, it had to be, or she'd go stir-crazy.

'So what are you up to for the rest of the afternoon?' Jennifer asked.

'I thought I'd go shopping.'

'Oh. Asda or Tesco?'

'No, clothes shopping.'

'Clothes shopping? What's the occasion?'

'I'm just fed up with the same old, same old. I fancy something bright.'

'Red?'

'Perhaps, or maybe green or yellow or purple.'

'Good for you. Top, shirt?'

'Not sure. I'll just see what jumps off the rail and says *Buy Me*.'

'There was a nice purple three-quarter-length shirt in Oxfam the other day,' suggested Jennifer. 'Might still be there.'

'No. Today I'm opting for chain stores.'

'You're what?'

'I need a change of image. I'm going to get this mess sorted out too.' Maggie pointed at her hair.

'Right, what have you done with my friend? Bring her back,' Jennifer said, laughing.

'Do you want another drink?' Maggie asked, as the barman weaved his way towards them. Looking at her watch, Jennifer sighed and said, 'Better not. I need to get back.' Reaching down, she picked up her bags, took ten pounds from her purse and handed it to Maggie.

'I'll give you a call soon, OK?'

'OK, good to see you.'

'You too. Bye.' Jennifer disappeared through the swing doors.

Chapter Thirteen

A week later

'Same again, Maggie.' A regular at Three Monkeys slid his pint glass down the bar. Maggie laid down the dishcloth she had been washing in soapy water, rinsed her hands and, grabbing a glass from below the gantry, placed it under the pump.

'There you go. Who's next?'

There had been an unexpected rush today. Sadie had called in sick so Maggie had been on her Jack Jones. She hadn't managed to carry out half the tasks she'd meant to; cleaning the gantry, washing the glasses shelves, checking stock. Three Monkeys had character all right, but it wasn't computerised, so everything had to be done manually. Maggie wondered, not for the first time, why so many men were in the pub at three o'clock on a Monday afternoon. She'd barely had time to serve them and wash glasses, never mind clean tables.

She was glad she was finishing at eight, and had agreed to go to her mum's as she hadn't seen her in ages. She'd gone to see her the day she'd met Jennifer for coffee, but she was out. Much as she loved her mum, Maggie found it difficult spending time with her these days, as no more than half an hour would go by before she would mention Nick, no matter that thirteen years had passed. Her mother had been Nick's number one fan. When he and Maggie announced they were getting married, she'd been delighted. She couldn't get over their break-up and would never understand why it had been necessary and how much pain it had caused them.

Afternoon soon became evening, and Maggie was so busy she hadn't realised it was nearly time for her to finish. It was only when Leo opened the pub door that she glanced at the clock and saw it was ten to eight.

'Hi, Maggie. It's busy in here tonight.' Leo lifted the hatch leading behind the bar. Relieving himself of his jacket, he said, 'Where's Sadie?'

'Sick.'

'Bollocks. So, you've had this lot to cope with on your own?'

'Yep.'

'Great. That means I'm in for more of the same. Any reason why nobody was called in to cover Sadie?'

'Not to my knowledge,' Maggie replied.

'So, how come so busy?'

'Bowling club's closed for refurbishment.'

'Ah,' said Leo.

The bowling club was the only place in the area which sold cheaper drink than Three Monkeys, unless you counted the trendy new gastro-pubs, which had sprouted up all over the place. But the more mature clientele of Three Monkeys didn't hold much truck with that type of establishment. As Leo started serving customers, Maggie dashed around wiping tables and collecting dirty glasses. She then sped back gantry-side and started washing the glasses in the specially designated sink. That done and the stocktake begun, Maggie left instructions with Leo of what was still outstanding and headed for the door.

Maggie rang her mother's doorbell, listening to the melody of 'Greensleeves', whilst she waited for her to answer. Mrs McWhirter was a sixty-five-year-old member of the blue rinse brigade, who fussed terribly over her daughter on the rare occasions she let her. She had too much time on her hands, despite being chairperson of the Women's Guild, an avid Rotarian and constantly manning stalls at the Salvation Army bring-and-buy sales.

'Why didn't you use your key?' her mother asked, embracing her.

'I don't have it with me.'

Truth was, she didn't like entering her mother's house without warning. She hadn't lived there for more than twenty years. She didn't like to barge in, even with her mother's permission.

'I've got your favourite warming in the oven.'

Good old Mum. Maggie could almost taste the stovies, as she followed her mother. The aroma wafted through the kitchen door to meet her and Maggie realised just how hungry she was. The heat emanated welcomingly from the oven, as her mother removed the casserole dish containing the sausage, potato and onion speciality. Maggie's mouth watered as her mum spooned a generous helping onto her plate.

'Is that enough?'

Maggie drew her mum a look. It would have fed about six people.

'Thanks, Mum.' Maggie was desperate to dig in.

She felt at home here, in this familiar kitchen. Her

father was no longer there, her parents having divorced when Maggie was ten; perhaps one of the many reasons Maggie was the rebel she was. Yet, the warmth of the kitchen and the companionship of her mother were balm to her soul. This would always be her home. No matter what happened she could always come back here. Somehow it was nice to know that. She munched away.

'You look tired, sweetheart.'

'I'm fine, really. No need to fuss.'

'If you're sure.' Her mother narrowed her eyes.

'Yes, Mum, I'm sure.'

'Oh, I meant to say, do you remember Mrs Lawson?' Jean asked Maggie.

'No.' Maggie glanced up from her munching.

'You do. She taught music at Ayr Academy and had the poodle with the permanent limp.'

'Oh yeah. I remember the dog. Wasn't it called Fopsy or something?'

'Flopsy,' her mother corrected.

'Funny thing to do, giving a dog a rabbit's name.'

'So, what are you up to at the moment?'

'This and that.' Maggie was evasive.

'What kind of this and that? Have you been on any more demos recently?'

'There's one planned for next Saturday up in Glencoe, protesting against the proposed visitor centre.'

'Oh yes. I heard about that. That would be awful. No doubt it would be the first of many, if this one goes ahead.'

'Exactly. That's why we're out to stop them.'

'So have you scheduled time off?' Jean asked.

'Yes. They owe me a couple of Saturdays. I've told them I'll settle for all of next weekend off and then we're even.'

'Good. Don't let them take advantage of you.'

'Don't worry.'

'Anyway, I was telling you about Mrs Lawson.'

'I gather she died.'

'Who told you?' Jean's eyes widened.

'You did.'

'No I didn't. I was just about to.'

'I know, but as you only ever finish your "Do you remember such and such" stories with, "he/she died on Tuesday and the funeral's on Friday," I worked it out.'

Maggie's mother looked put out. 'I was only saying. I like to keep you up to date with what's going on in the town. You're not here very often.' She huffed.

Maggie softened. 'I know, and I appreciate it. So tell me, who's had a baby or got married recently?' Maggie feigned interest as her mother spewed forth on her other two favourite subjects: births and marriages.

She couldn't help but think her mother would do well working for the Announcements section of the *Ayrshire Post*. She certainly knew everything that went in the paper before it was printed.

The problem was her mum had too much time on her hands. She needed a hobby. Wait. Her mum needed something to fill her time, and Jen had almost no time to herself. Eureka! She knew exactly how to kill two birds with one stone.

'Mum, I have to make a call. Back in a minute.' Maggie went outside and dialled Jennifer's number.

'Jennifer?'

'Maggie. How you doing?'

'OK thanks. You?'

'Ah, fair to middling.'

'Thought as much. I have the perfect cure.'

'Oh?'

'What are you doing on Saturday?'

'Hmm. Let me think. Usual round of Lidl and the pharmacy. Why, do you want to meet in Caprice again?'

'No, better than that. I'm going to Glencoe to campaign against this state-of-the-art visitor centre. I thought maybe you'd like to come. We could go to the Aonach Inn after the demo and we can camp, so it won't be expensive.'

'Camping?'

'C'mon. It'll be fun.'

'Can't.'

'Why not?'

'Mum.'

'Ah. I think I may have a solution to that. So, do you want to come? You deserve the break.'

'I could certainly do with it.' Jennifer sighed. 'So, what's your solution for Mum?'

'Mum,' Maggie said, re-entering the kitchen, where Jean stood baking.

'Did you get Jennifer?'

'Yes. Listen, I need a favour…'

Later, Maggie rang Jennifer, who was delighted to hear that Jean, an ex-nurse at Ailsa Hospital, had agreed to look after her mum whilst they were away. Their mothers had met only once, but Jennifer thought her mum would be fine. She was glad hers wasn't one of those whiny, hypochondriac, fetch me this, that and the other mothers. She would be more than happy that her daughter could go and have fun for once. Her mother felt a burden to her.

The only qualm she would have about this coming weekend would be guilt at her daughter needing to arrange for someone to sit with her. It was a shame they had no family to speak of; otherwise the burden could have been shared. They ironed out the details, then Maggie rang off to make their travel arrangements, leaving Jennifer to break the news to her mother.

Chapter Fourteen

Maggie was relieved her shift was over. There had to be more to life than this. She didn't know if she could be bothered doing bar work until term started, and although she was interested in geography, what was it all going to achieve? With that contemplative thought, Maggie set to finishing off the placards.

'Save our Glens.' 'No to Commercialism.' 'Beauty not Profit.'

The remaining days until Saturday flew by. Jeremy came to pick Maggie up from her mum's house in his people carrier. He was the nominated driver when any of their campaigns were outside of mainstream public transport distance. Plus it was easier transporting banners and placards by car than walking about with them before the demo. It gave the game away to the police, too, not to mention earning them glares from fellow passengers on the trains or buses. Jeremy chatted to Maggie until they reached Jennifer's. Maggie jumped out to rap on Jennifer's door, but just then the door shot open and Maggie's mother came out. She stepped aside to let Jennifer past and told them to enjoy themselves.

'Save our countryside! Down with commercialism! No to the Visitor Centre!' the thirty-two-strong group of protestors chanted. Apart from Jennifer, their group of six consisted solely of 'professional protestors'. The remainder were mainly locals. Others milled around, offering their support, but didn't get actively involved. Theirs wasn't quite the placard-brandishing level of commitment. Probably too concerned about the possibility of being arrested for breach of the peace. The Black Watch centre had seen better days, and yes, it needed a lick of paint, but it was the centre of the Ballachulish community. Throwing up a multi-million-pound visitor centre ten miles north in Fort William wouldn't help the village one bit. Rumour had it a well-known property developer was earmarked for the land. Maggie incited the crowd to rally behind them and not to give in to the capitalists trying to turn their village into a ghost town, by taking the heart out of it.

Maggie's rich, resonant voice carried across the glen, as she outlined why they should fight for this centre, what it signified. If they tore the centre down, tourism in the immediate area would fall, tourists heading instead to the new visitor centre in Fort William. Local jobs would be lost. It would set an unwelcome precedent. If the developers won this battle, where would it end? They would encroach upon other unspoilt villages and bring about their ruin too.

The crowd cheered as Maggie came to the end of her speech. Suddenly silence fell like a blanket over the crowd. The thunderous noise of a JCB could be heard coming ever closer. Maggie told everyone to hold hands and spread out in front of the centre. Those with placards shook them angrily at the driver with the wrecking ball. On Maggie's cue, they chanted, 'We will not, we will not be moved,' interspersed with, 'Down with the Visitor Centre! Save Black Watch!'

The JCB driver pulled at his skip cap and nervously scratched the back of his head. He looked down at his foreman, who was striding into view, a vein bulging in his neck, waving a piece of paper in front of him.

'Look, you've said your piece. Now let us do our jobs.'

'No way.' Maggie stood firm.

'I'm sorry it means so much to you, but it's been decided.'

'Over our dead bodies,' Maggie said. She was sure the foreman muttered something along the lines of, 'fine by me', but when she glared at him, he acted dumb.

'We're not moving.' Maggie was defiant. 'You can take your bit of paper and go tell them that.'

Despairing, the foreman tried another tack. 'Look, love, it's already been authorised, nothing's going to change that now.'

Maggie folded her arms, splayed her legs and literally dug her heels into the soft earth. It was bad enough that Black Watch was closed temporarily due to all this malarkey, but to allow them to tear it down would be unthinkable. An approaching siren could be heard over the idling of the JCB.

Shit!

The patrol car pulled into the lay-by adjacent to the Black Watch and two officers got out, donned their hats and walked over to Maggie.

'What's going on?' the older policeman asked, his voice as gruff as if he smoked forty Woodbines a day.

'We're protesting against the Black Watch centre being

pulled down.'

'Name?'

'Maggie McWhirter.'

'Address?'

'Number 46 The Quays, Glasgow.'

'Not exactly your neighbourhood.'

'No, but it doesn't mean I can't support the cause. I've been coming here for years and many of these people–' Maggie flung her arm out in a wide arc, to encompass her companions '–*are* residents and don't want to see the soul ripped out of their community.'

'I understand that,' said the policeman, trying to adjust the buttons on his jacket, perhaps to better accommodate his girth, 'but these men have work to do. It's not their fault. They're just following orders.'

By this point, the *Lochaber News* had turned up and were busy snapping away and interviewing bystanders. The younger policeman tried to disperse the crowd and persuade the press that there was nothing to see, but everyone remained rooted to the spot, although they ceased to link hands.

'We're not moving until someone from the planning department gets down here and realises what a mistake they've made.'

'If you don't move, I'll need to arrest you,' the policeman said.

'You're going to have to carry me, because I'm not moving.'

The policeman rolled his eyes and walked towards his younger colleague. They conferred for a few minutes and then returned to where Maggie was standing. The younger one said, 'Maggie McWhirter, I'm arresting you for breach of the peace.' As he tried to slide the handcuffs on, Maggie pulled away. 'And for resisting arrest.'

The sergeant helped the constable load Maggie into the back of the car, where she sat silently fuming. Jennifer tried to speak to Maggie, but the constable headed her off.

'Where are you taking her?'

'Fort William police station.'

'What happens now?'

'She'll be questioned and may have to stay in the cells overnight.'

Overnight? Cells? Jennifer was horrified.

'But she can't be. She hasn't done anything wrong.'

'She's caused a public nuisance and if you're not careful you could be joining her.'

With that, the constable walked along the line of protestors, encouraging them to disperse. All but a few complied, clearly concerned about suffering Maggie's fate. Jennifer was tearful. 'They've taken her to Fort William police station.'

Jeremy put his arm around Jennifer. 'OK then, pile in. We'd better go and get her. She'll be out soon, I'm sure. Maggie'll be all right. First time she's been arrested, mind you, but a miracle, given how many demos she's attended. We'll follow the police and maybe have a drink in The Lochaber whilst we're waiting on her being questioned. She may not have to spend time in the cells. It's her first offence.'

Hearing a tremendous clatter, they turned. The JCB had whirled into life and was trundling towards the Black Watch centre, wrecking ball swinging. The driver depressed a lever and the ball careered into the community centre, smashing the café section in half. Maggie, grim-faced, managed a tight smile to Jennifer as the car sped off.

The desk sergeant asked Maggie for her details and relieved her of her sunglasses, cigarettes, Zippo lighter and Swatch watch. She was then locked in a cell until someone was free to interview her.

'So, do you want to tell us what that was all about?' Sergeant Morris asked her.

'I told you earlier,' Maggie replied.

'If you could just tell us again for the benefit of the tape,' Sergeant Morris insisted.

Maggie relayed what she'd told him at the Black Watch centre.

'You can't go taking the law into your own hands.'

'Someone had to act.'

'The decision had already been made. You were causing a disturbance. Now, you've been arrested, and for what? It didn't solve anything, did it?'

Sergeant Morris' words hit home and although Maggie wanted to retort, 'Whose fault is that then?' she bit her tongue. 'I know.'

'Look, if you promise not to get up to anything like that again, I'll let you off with a caution, but if you do cause another breach of the peace, you'll probably face a custodial sentence.'

'OK.'

'Good. Interview terminated 15.47.'

Rising, Sergeant Morris ushered her out to the reception area and handed her over to the desk sergeant to retrieve her belongings. Maggie quickly texted Jennifer.

'Now remember, I don't want to see you again.'

She signed for her possessions. He was right. What difference had it made? Zilch. As she turned to leave, Jeremy and Jennifer burst through the doors.

'Oh, Maggie. Thank God. Are you OK? Do you have to pay bail?'

Maggie laughed. 'It's not quite *The Bill* you know, Jennifer, and yes, I'm fine, it's only my pride that's dented. I'm just upset about the centre.'

Chapter Fifteen

Maggie adjusted the groundsheet and reached for the poles, sliding them into the tent with ease. She gave Jennifer instructions on how to hammer the pegs in almost diagonally, otherwise they'd come straight back out. Maggie then slipped the flysheet over the frame and secured the first few pegs before letting Jennifer do the rest.

'Not bad for a first attempt.' Maggie appraised Jennifer's endeavours. 'We'll make a camper out of you yet.'

Jeremy came up to them. 'I don't know about you lot, but I'm starving.'

Lee, Henry and Susan mumbled their agreement, so, tents erected, they set off from the Grey Squirrel campsite towards the Aonach Inn in search of sustenance.

'Mmm. This gammon steak's delicious,' Jennifer said.

'Yep. The steak 'n' ale pie is pretty tasty too,' Maggie added, 'although it could just be because we're ravenous.'

'Could be,' Jeremy agreed between mouthfuls of cottage pie.

They spent a merry late afternoon, made all the merrier by the amount of alcohol they'd consumed. Suddenly, Jeremy shouted out, 'Ben, Ben! Over here.' He stood up and patted his friend on the back. 'I haven't seen you for, like, forever. How the hell are you?'

Ben grinned. 'I'm fine, Jez, and you? What you been up to?'

'Rescuing this one from being arrested.' He waved his hand at Maggie then turned back to Ben. 'Are you on your own?'

'Yes. I'm supposed to be at home in Glasgow. I wasn't meant to be working up here this weekend, but I'm covering for a mate who's gone on holiday at the last minute.'

'Well, why don't you join us?' Jeremy suggested. 'Budge up, guys!'

After Jeremy introduced him to everyone, Ben sat down on the end of a bench beside Jennifer and Jeremy. Maggie meanwhile was listening to Lee talking to Henry and Susan about his stay in St Vincent.

'St Vincent?' she said. 'You lucky sod! How long were you there, two weeks or just the one?'

'No. I was there six months. I was doing a placement teaching the locals about AIDS.'

'Really. That sounds really rewarding.'

'Oh it was. It is,' Lee corrected. 'I'm only home for six weeks and then I'm going back.'

'To St Vincent?'

'Possibly, but I never know for sure where I'll end up.' They carried on chatting and when Maggie checked her watch, it was already half past ten. Damn, they only had fifteen minutes before they'd have to leave to make the campsite curfew. She turned to Jennifer, but she was deep in conversation with the dark-haired chap Jeremy had introduced them to earlier. What was his name again? Ben. That was it. They looked pretty cosy with their heads close together. She'd have to ask Jennifer all about it later.

Maggie woke up on Monday morning more refreshed than she'd been yesterday morning, that was for sure. She'd had a hell of a hangover and as for Jennifer, she was seriously unwell. They'd had to stop the car twice for her on the way home. Maggie had decided she'd grill her at a later date about the luscious Ben.

She spread some low-fat cheese on brown bread and grabbed a handful of raisins from the packet in the kitchen cupboard. *Today seems like a Sunday.* So much had happened over the weekend. She was glad she had allowed herself the luxury of having the Sunday papers delivered. Fair enough, she was a day late in reading them, but so what? She always bought loads of Sunday papers and never bothered at all during the week. As she got older, her brain required more from a newspaper than which celebrity had had their boobs done, or whose Botox op had failed, so she'd started reading *The Sunday Times* as well. It had so many supplements and was very Tory biased, but it did have a lot of good stories and some pretty gritty journalism. Maggie nestled down into the contours of her sofa and began to munch away, simultaneously flicking through *The Sunday Times.* Suddenly she stopped. She read and reread the advert and said out loud, 'I wonder...'

Chapter Sixteen
Jennifer – PISCES

Sensitive, emotional, sunny, dreamy, creative. Great sympathy for the suffering of others. Vulnerable and delicate especially when under emotional stress. Capable of great strength, because of their adaptability, and cope well in difficult situations.

'Jennifer, darling. Jennifer!' her mother's voice called.

Jennifer finally heard and ran in to see what her mother wanted.

'Yes, Mum?'

'I need to go to the toilet.'

'OK.' Jennifer picked up the shallow stainless-steel basin and sat it on the edge of her mother's bed. She raised her mother's left leg until her foot was flat on the bed, with her knee bent, and placed her mother's left arm around her right shoulder, to gain purchase, whilst she manoeuvred the bedpan for her. She ensured her mother's right foot was close to her straightened right leg and then slowly rolled her onto her side. Placing the bedpan under her, she carefully rolled her back into place. Her mother's business done, she set the bedpan on the floor. She tore off some toilet paper from its roll, carefully wiped her mother's bottom and dropped the dirty tissue into a small polythene bag on the bedside table. Extracting a baby wipe from the packet, she cleaned her properly. The wipe joined the used toilet paper and Jennifer rearranged her mother's nightgown.

'Thanks, dear.'

'I'll get rid of this and then I'll make us a cup of tea.'

Her mum smiled. Jennifer lifted up the polythene bag, then stretched down for the basin. She walked through to the bathroom and chucked the contents of the basin's cardboard insert into the toilet, then flushed it away. The rest she disposed of in the outside wheelie bin. Returning to the bathroom, she washed out the stainless-steel basin and placed it on the lid of the toilet then turned on the taps and began to wash her hands, adding a generous dollop of antibacterial handwash for good measure. She re-entered her mother's room and took another cardboard insert from her stash on the shelf of the bedside cabinet and placed it into the basin, before pushing it gently under the bed with her foot.

'Here you go, Mum. Tea and chocolate digestives.'

'Thanks, love. Are you going to town today?'

'Yes. I need to get some shopping. That was the last of the milk and biscuits.' She gestured to the three digestives on the plate.

'Could you get my prescription? Remember the surgery called yesterday to say it would be ready after two.'

'Yes, I remember. What do you fancy for dinner?'

'Those beef olives you got were very nice.'

'How about I get those and make roast potatoes and peas, or would you prefer sprouts?'

'Sprouts if they're not too expensive. If they're more

than fifty pence a pound, it means they're out of season and in that case, peas will do fine. Garden ones though.'

'Sure. Do you need anything else?'

'Could you get me some Lily of the Valley?'

Her mother always liked to smell nice and had worn the same perfume since she was a girl. The fact she was now bedridden thanks to her myotonic dystrophy didn't mean she couldn't still make an effort.

'I'll see if they have it in Hourstons.'

Jennifer had dealt with all the finances since she had moved in, after her mother's diagnosis three years ago. Her mother's needs were simple, but they didn't have much money coming in. They lived solely on Jennifer's carer allowance and her mother's disability benefits. Unfortunately, it would have been no good asking her father. He'd cut himself off from them when she was twelve and needed him most. He'd got his latest floozie pregnant and decided he actually wanted to live with and, worse still, marry her.

The only contact her mum had had with him was regarding the divorce, and her mother shielded her from that as much as possible. Jennifer had her pride, plus she knew the answer would have been no. She knew he was aware of her mother's predicament. They still had mutual acquaintances, even after all these years, but he hadn't even phoned to enquire after her or her mother, never mind offer to help out financially. They could ill afford the relatively inexpensive scent her mother had requested, but she would not deny her mother this simplest of pleasures. In any case, she still had a couple of things left from their old lives, which she could sell on Ebay. Her savings had almost entirely gone, as she no longer worked.

Jennifer knew that many children wouldn't have been as unselfish as she had been, giving everything up. But her brother Tim lived in New Zealand and her sister Sara had moved out to be near him and enjoy the good old life he'd told them about on his last visit seven years ago. Sara had moved to Christchurch about three weeks before her mother's diagnosis. It was unthinkable that she could come back at such a critical phase. She had three kids to think about settling into a new continent for goodness' sake. Anyway, Sara said, everyone knew their mother preferred Jennifer's company. Her brother had suggested they put their mother in a home. Jennifer could not believe these people were her flesh and blood. Her siblings could be so heartless and were adamant their mother should go into residential care. So, it fell to her and only her, as they saw it, to look after their mother. Nor did they feel they could or needed to contribute financially. Where would they get the money? All of a sudden, the good life they were leading in New Zealand was made out to be a struggling existence, not the financial mecca Tim had boasted of a few years ago. But Tim's Jaguar and his wife's Mercedes were testimony to the fact they weren't exactly destitute, and her sister was just as bad. Sara had a house in the city and an apartment near the sea.

There wasn't exactly much work Jennifer could do from home, although she had been known to stuff envelopes to make ends meet. She had even tried a pyramid-like scheme, which had promised to quadruple her money in a month and then grow exponentially. Unfortunately, the products, although good, were expensive, and Jennifer didn't have the right personality to work in Sales. She couldn't bring herself to be as blatant at networking as the high-powered hotshots she was supposed to model herself on. The only products she'd really managed to sell were to close friends, and she'd decided she didn't want to alienate them by giving them a sales pitch every time they met. Her performance was lacklustre and their group leader had been most disappointed with her. She'd given up less than a month later and decided it was a lesson well learned.

Jennifer missed the camaraderie of the office. When she did go out, she had little to add to conversations, as the furthest she'd been was Kwik Save and the most riveting things she had to talk about were who was shagging who off *Big Brother* and if they'd seen the latest home makeover or other reality TV show that week. It seemed like all of her interests had been shelved when her mum became ill. She used to attend lots of evening classes; Advanced Cookery, Massage for Beginners, Feng Shui. Her lovely flat in Prestwick had overlooked the golf course and she'd feng shuied it to within an inch of its life. Shame it had turned out to be a load of old bollocks. Her love corner and her health corner, or rather her mother's health corner had become well and truly screwed up. Jennifer faced facts. She didn't live, she existed, and if she didn't have Maggie, she didn't know what she'd do. As she was leaving to go into town, the phone rang.

'Hello?'

'Hi, Jennifer. It's Maggie.'

Jennifer walked into town, elated at the prospect of seeing her friend again. Now that Maggie's exams were over, maybe they'd have more time to spend together. Maggie often used to turn up at Treetops unannounced, out of term time when she didn't have to be in Glasgow every day and could stay over at her mum's on Racecourse Road. She knew Maggie was going back to work at Three Monkeys, but hoped it wouldn't be seven days a week so she could come see her occasionally. Even watching soaps with someone was a luxury. Her mum was usually asleep by seven thirty and since she was bedridden, Jennifer was the only one who used the living room.

In some ways, this worked well as their flat had only one bedroom and there wasn't a lot of space for one person, never mind two. Jennifer slept on the sofa, which happened to be a very decent double bed, but after three years of it, her back was killing her.

The original idea had been for Jennifer to take time off work to look after her mum and then get a full-time or even a part-time carer in. Unfortunately, the insurance company she worked for wasn't particularly understanding about her situation, after she'd initially used her four weeks of annual leave to care for her mum. They said that if she didn't come back the following Monday, she was out of a job. It was too soon to leave her mum with anyone else as she was still coming to terms with the extent of her condition. So, Jennifer had lost her job. The rigmarole and the humiliation she had to go through to become an official carer for her mother was unbelievable. She'd lost count of the number of forms she'd had to fill in.

As she padded around the supermarket, she thanked the Lord for the day she met Maggie. Online, checking her email and seeing how her Ebay sales were going, she had decided they needed something to brighten up the living room-cum-bedroom. She was going through her terracotta phase and at that time didn't yet have too many money worries, but she enjoyed Ebaying and also thought it prudent to buy something significant, like a throw, second-hand, although to look at Maggie's throw now, you would still think it was brand new. Her shopping finished, Jennifer carried the wire basket over to the till.

Chapter Seventeen

'Hello, you,' Jennifer interrupted her friend's thought process and sat down. The attentive barman brought her a drink and she settled back to listen to Maggie. She reminisced for a very pleasant half hour with her and then, with an anguished look at her watch, said she had better get back.

When she arrived home, her mother was asleep, so she put the shopping away, checked the cooking instructions on the beef olives and switched on the kettle. Ripping open the packet of plain chocolate digestives, she demolished the first one in seconds, realising she was ravenous. She had made porridge for her mother this morning, but there hadn't been enough milk for two. The sandwich she'd had with Maggie was her only sustenance all day. Her stomach rumbled and she helped herself to a second biscuit as the kettle came to the boil.

Jennifer tiptoed through to the living room, peeking into her mother's room en route to ensure she hadn't woken up. Settling herself down, she picked up her magazine. She was addicted to entering competitions. She hadn't won much, just a measly CD case and some kids' film binoculars, but she lived in hope. Occasionally she won cinema tickets, but ended up letting them expire, as she was afraid to leave her mother alone for that length of time. A win of thirty pounds' worth of M&S vouchers meant they had some gorgeous food for a few days. She used to subscribe to several specialist competition magazines, but when she lost her job, she couldn't afford the subscriptions. Her favourite competitions were those you had to create a slogan or jingle for, as she assumed not so many people would enter, because they required a bit of thought and she would have a better crack at winning. She had treated herself to a competition magazine yesterday though, and she was looking forward to seeing what prizes were on offer. Sipping her coffee and picking up the magazine and her pen, she circled those of interest to her – £500 of jewellery in a Bond Street jeweller's, a BMW 5 series, a vintage 2CV, a fortnight in Tenerife all inclusive, a seven-day-trip on the Orient Express, and a villa in Spain worth £200,000.

As Jennifer went to get her box of postcards, a noise startled her. Her mother must be awake. She sighed and set down her magazine, jerked open the door and traipsed into the bedroom. Her mother lay with her eyes wide open, unable to pull herself up to a sitting position. Maggie adjusted her pillows and gently raised her mother's frail body.

'Thanks, dear. Can you check my pad?'

Jennifer nodded grimly. She felt so guilty, but sometimes she hated the fact this was her lot. Pulling the blankets aside, she hoisted her mother's nightgown upward and checked the incontinence pad. She knew from the smell of urine which emanated from her mother, even before checking the pad, that she needed changing. She took the pad away, bent down to get another from the bedside cabinet and grabbed a wipe too. When she stood back up, she realised her mother was widdling once again, totally unaware, over the sheets she had just changed that morning. Blinking back tears and not wanting to humiliate her mother further, she waited until she'd finished, then wiped her, as you would a baby, and put the new incontinence pad on. Thank God she wasn't doubly incontinent. Jennifer dumped the sodden pad in the outside bin, washed her hands and retrieved some clean sheets from the linen cupboard. She manoeuvred her mother around the bed, took away the wet sheets, cleaned the rubber sheet with antiseptic wipes, dried it off and then slipped the fresh sheets under her mother and over the mattress, all the while clasping her mother's skinny frame to her. Her mother relaxed against the pillows, then said, 'Could I have a cup of tea, Jennifer?'

Jennifer headed back to the kitchen, carrying the stinking sheets, which she bunged in the washing machine. Throwing some washing powder into the dispenser, she turned the machine on. Tea duly served to her mum, Jennifer retired to the living room to finish hers and enter some competitions.

'Here you go, Mum. Your favourite, beef olives and roasters.'

'Oh, thanks so much, dear.'

She sat companionably with her tray on her lap whilst her mother took dainty forkfuls of her meal.

'Can you turn on the TV? I'd like to watch the news.'

Jennifer got up from the rocking chair where she usually sat in her mother's room when they ate together, and switched on the TV. The headlines popped up on the screen, dead on six o'clock.

Jennifer cleared away the plates and, noting that her mother was already asleep, settled down in the living room. She flicked through the TV channels, finally plumping for *Who Wants to be a Millionaire?* and sat back to relax with a few chocolate digestives and her competition magazine. This was the only time she really got to unwind, when her mother was asleep. It was just a pity she couldn't do anything worthwhile, like go to a pub, or a disco, or the cinema, or anything really. She was stuck in here night after night. If she didn't find a solution to all of this soon, she would go stark raving mad.

'Twelve second-class stamps, please.' Jennifer handed over the money to the cashier, who passed her the book of stamps. 'Thanks,' she said, stuffing them into her purse. It was a beautiful sunny day. She had a little time before she would have to go back and prepare her mother's lunch. So she sat in the park, putting stamps on her postcards.

After soaking up the sun's rays and admiring some men out jogging, she picked up her shopping and dropped her postcards in the postbox. It had been a long time since she'd been with someone. She missed that affection, but when would she get the opportunity? It was hard enough to meet someone nowadays, even if you had a job and a social life and were used to mixing with new people. How on earth would she ever meet anyone if she never went anywhere? She mulled this over as she made her way home.

She was in the kitchen unpacking her shopping when the phone rang.

'Hello?'

'Jennifer?'

'Maggie. How you doing?'

'OK thanks. You?'

'Ah, fair to middling.' Jennifer carried a mug of cold tea through to the kitchen.

'Thought as much. I have the perfect cure.'

'Oh?'

'What are you doing on Saturday?'

When she came off the phone, Jennifer's heart was pounding with excitement and she prayed it would all work out. Maggie was going to Glencoe to campaign against a multi-million-pound visitor centre and had decided Jennifer needed to get out of the house, so she wanted her to come too. When she had protested she couldn't leave her mother, Maggie had the perfect solution: her mum would look after her. She was phoning her to check.

The phone trilled a few minutes later.

'Jennifer. Mum says that's fine. I'll call you tomorrow, OK?'

'Thanks. You have no idea how much I appreciate it.'

Jennifer wanted to skip, whoop and shout with joy. It was funny, she was going to a march, about what she couldn't give two hoots, but the point was, she was going *somewhere*. She would have to pick her moment with her mum so that she didn't offend her.

Later, she seized her chance.

'Mum?'

'Yes, dear.'

'Can I talk to you about something?'

'Oh? That sounds serious.'

'It's not anything bad. I wanted to ask how you would feel about it, that's all.'

'What is it?'

'Maggie asked me if I wanted to go to Glencoe with her this weekend. Her mum used to be a nurse at the Ailsa. She knows our situation and is happy to help out whilst I'm gone. Would you have any problem with that?'

'No, dear. If she's a nurse, then she'll know what to expect, won't she?'

'Yes.' Jennifer breathed a sigh of relief.

'That's settled then. Would you mind bringing me some choccy biccies to go with my tea?'

'Sure.' Jennifer would have given her the moon and the stars if she could have.

For the rest of the week Jennifer was like a nervous schoolgirl. She was counting down the days as if she were going on a long-haul holiday. To her, going to Glencoe was just as good. It was the getting away from it all that she was looking forward to, being able to pretend she led a normal life. The days until the trip were the longest four days of her life.

Saturday finally came and the doorbell rang. It was Maggie's mum, a sweet woman, still spry for her age. Jennifer showed her in, hung her coat on the pine coat stand behind them and gestured for Jean to follow her to her mother's room, where she re-introduced them.

'Thanks so much, Jean. You have no idea what this

means to Jennifer and me.'

'It's my pleasure. Let the young ones go away and wreak havoc for the weekend.' Jean chuckled. 'Now, Jennifer, why don't you show me where everything is. Hmm?'

Jennifer was showing Jean how to operate the sofa-bed mechanism, when the bell rang again. Jean took charge and went to answer it. Jennifer looked in on her mum again and raised her eyebrows questioningly, to indicate 'Well?' Her mum gave her the thumbs up. Relieved, she bent down and kissed her mother's cheek and thought once again how unfair their situation was. Jean was able to bustle around better than most her age, whereas Jennifer's mum was forced to lie in that bed every day. She tried to push these sad thoughts to the back of her mind and said goodbye to her mother.

After Maggie introduced Jennifer and Jeremy, they set off.

I've already met someone new today. She was sure Jeremy must think her mad as she kept beaming at him. They picked up Lee next, in Troon. He was a merry Jack-the-Lad character who never stopped talking. Jennifer instantly liked him, although she was sure his constant chattering would eventually exhaust her, but right now she *loved* chatter. Last stop was Susan and Henry's semi-detached in Kilmarnock, before heading up the road towards Glasgow and then branching off up the A82 to Glencoe. Of course, they had to stop off at the Stag's Head for some breakfast. The Stag's Head, as the name suggested, greeted you with the eponymous stag mounted above the bar, with another in the toilets. The carpets were Buchanan tartan, garish yellow, green, red and orange, covered in stains, best not to ask of what.

There was a crowd of regulars at the bar, who, you got the impression, had been waiting outside for it to open. The absolutely gorgeous giant behind the bar wore a kilt and looked like a younger version of the guy on the Scott's Porage Oats packet, a big, strapping lad with thighs that would… She flushed at the thought. As she took her plate of sausages, fried egg, bacon and black and fruit pudding, he said, 'I like a lassie who likes her grub,' and winked at her. Jennifer was mortified, wondering if he'd caught her scoping him out. The others, who had witnessed it all from their table, burst out laughing.

They chatted about their jobs and their lives and their hobbies, but Jennifer noticed that no one asked her about her occupation. She always wondered if she'd lie and say she worked in Insurance, or whether she'd admit she was a carer. Often people wrongly viewed carers as not particularly bright, with little or no qualifications.

Breakfast eaten, they bundled into the people carrier again and headed north. Jennifer wasn't sure what to expect at Glencoe, at the Black Watch centre, but they arrived to the sight of about fifteen protestors, brandishing placards, with a small crowd looking on.

Maggie soon rallied the troops and before long the numbers had swelled to more than thirty hardcore supporters. Jennifer didn't include herself in this number. She was, at best, a half-hearted protestor, only here for the social scene.

When Maggie lay down in front of the JCB, Jennifer stood open-mouthed. She had known Maggie was pretty radical, but she didn't really think she'd go to such lengths. A larger crowd gathered as events unfolded and Jennifer whispered to Jeremy, 'What's she doing?'

'Whatever's necessary.'

Meanwhile, he, Susan and Henry waved their placards in the air whilst Lee led the crowd in chants of 'No to the Visitor Centre' and 'Save Black Watch.' The villagers occasionally joined in with a 'Yay,' but you could tell some of them were uncomfortable. Perhaps some of the B & Bs and restaurants would see good temporary business from the very contractors about to tear down their beloved centre. The foreman's voice rose as he stood gesticulating at Maggie, and Maggie's own tone sharpened. He walked away, throwing one hand up in exasperation, flipping open his mobile as he did so. Maggie had the air of a zealot as she addressed the crowd, who half-heartedly yelled and jeered at the workmen.

Just then, a police car drew up. Oh dear. Jennifer stood, rooted to the spot, willing Maggie to move, but Maggie stood firm.

The older policeman spoke with the foreman, then headed towards Maggie. Jennifer couldn't hear what they were saying. Lee stood shaking his head and Susan watched the scene, her brow furrowed. Some of the onlookers moved away, clearly not wanting to get involved, if things were going to get serious. The policeman seemed agitated, but Maggie just smiled at him.

At that moment, a white van appeared, rounding the last bend at a higher-than-average speed. It braked sharply in front of the police car. The emblazoned logo of the *Lochaber News* meant that the press had come to join the circus. This would be big news around here, protestors for the centre actually protesting, but oh, how much better a story, a woman impeding the progress of the wrecking ball, as the police remonstrated with her. She wondered if Maggie hadn't engineered the press presence, and resolved to ask her later. Right now she was in a bit of a predicament. Horrified, she watched as the police removed Maggie by force and put her in the back of the police car. Jennifer ran towards the car but the younger constable stopped her.

'Where are you taking her?'

'Fort William police station.'

Jennifer gave Maggie a despairing glance across the distance that separated them, but Maggie, even in the back of a police car, handcuffed, was still smiling, albeit grimly. The car pulled away and the crowd dispersed.

'They've taken her to Fort William,' Jennifer told the others tearfully.

'OK then,' said Jeremy, 'pile in. We'd better go and get her. She'll be out soon, I'm sure.'

Jennifer hoped Jeremy was right. Had Maggie actually been arrested? Didn't they usually read you your rights? Had they and she hadn't noticed? She *had* been momentarily distracted by the arrival of the news team. Maybe they did that down at the station. You'd think she'd know after years of watching police dramas. Jennifer allowed herself a small smile. How dreadful that her knowledge was gleaned almost solely from TV these days. She clambered into the car along with the other four and they set off on the fifteen-mile journey to Fort William.

Jennifer went in to the station to find out what was happening. The kind sergeant at the desk checked and told her Maggie would be interviewed in an hour or so. Jennifer informed the others and they decided they'd be better waiting over the road at The Lochaber.

Chapter Eighteen

'Oh, Maggie! Thank God. Are you OK? Do you have to pay bail?' Jennifer whispered the last part as the swing doors she had burst through swung to and fro behind her before settling.

'It's not quite *The Bill*, you know, Jennifer, and yes, I'm fine, it's only my pride that's dented. They let me off with a caution and told me to behave a bit more responsibly, if I really have to protest. I'm just upset about the centre.'

'Thank goodness.'

'Yeah. Where are the others?'

'In The Lochaber.'

'Good. Let's go.'

'Hey. There's the heroine of the hour,' Lee called.

'Hardly. They've already started demolishing the centre.'

'You did your best, Maggie,' Jeremy consoled her.

'It wasn't good enough, though, was it?'

Nobody could argue with that.

'You can't win them all,' Susan said.

'I know. I really do,' Maggie said, 'it's just so frustrating. OK, let's get moving. I'd like these tents up as soon as, so we can head over to the Aonach Inn. I'm starving.'

'That was a top-class meal,' declared Henry.

'Yep,' agreed Jeremy.

A band played in the background. Jennifer rather liked the blend of folk meets blues. They'd just performed a cover of 'Hoochy Coochy Man'. Everyone was chatting, trying to decide on the next song to request. 'Irish Rover' was top of most people's list, not for the significance, but because everyone knew it and it had a good rhythm. They were voting on who would go up and ask for 'Irish Rover' when Jeremy shouted, 'Ben! Ben! Over here!'

A tall, well-built guy of about twenty-five to thirty glanced over, grinned in recognition and made his way towards them. Jeremy patted him on the back then said, 'I haven't seen you for, like, forever. How the hell are you?'

'I'm fine, Jez, and you? What you been up to?'

'Rescuing this one from being arrested.' He indicated Maggie. Turning back to Ben, Jeremy said, 'Are you on your own?'

'Yes, I'm supposed to be at home in Glasgow. I wasn't meant to be working up here this weekend, but I'm covering for a mate who's gone on holiday at the last minute.'

'Well, why don't you join us? Budge up, guys!'

As Jeremy introduced Ben to everyone, Jennifer's hormones went haywire. When she'd shaken Ben's hand, a jolt of pure lust coursed through her. She'd almost forgotten what that felt like. Whilst Jeremy and Ben brought each other up to speed, she took advantage of the fact that Lee had captured the others' attention, by some tale he was telling, to study Ben. He wasn't classically good-looking, but he had sex appeal. Presence, that's what it was. The way only people who're sexy but don't know it have. His hair, like his eyes, was dark brown, and cropped short. He also sported a significant five o'clock shadow. Jennifer hadn't known she liked rugged types until now. Her heartbeat accelerated and parts of her, long dormant, reawakened. Heat rose in her face; she had to get away from the table before Maggie noticed.

'Anyone for another?'

Unsurprisingly, everyone took her up on her offer.

'Ben, what are you having?'

'What are *you* having?' He smiled.

Jeez, he had the most incredible smile and fairly white, even teeth, with a tiny gap to the bottom left side. *God, what am I, his dentist?*

'I-I'm having vodka and Coke,' she stammered.

'Make that two.'

She smiled and fled.

'Three vodkas and Coke, a Baileys and ice, two pints of lager and a vodka and diet Irn Bru,' reeled off Jennifer.

'Coming up,' said the barman, appraising her in a way that creeped her out a little. She wasn't used to strange men eyeing her up. She wasn't used to anyone eyeing her up any more: man, woman, Martian, anyone. But the barman could pass for her grandfather.

'I get off in half an hour,' he said meaningfully.

Jennifer said, 'That's nice.'

'Would you like to meet up later?'

'I-I-I…' she stammered again.

'I'm sure she'd love to, but we have plans later, don't we, darling?'

'Yes,' she said, unable to formulate any further response, relieved beyond belief to have staved off the barman's attentions, and delighted that Ben, for she was sure it was Ben, had come to her rescue. She twirled to face her rescuer, who said, 'I came to help you with the drinks.'

'Thanks.'

'Can't have you being set upon by the wolves.'

Jennifer smiled faintly.

When she had placed the last drink down in front of Henry, she discovered on returning to her seat, that it was no longer Lee on her right-hand side, but Ben. His proximity intoxicated her more than the vodka did. Jeremy, sitting on her other side, struck up a conversation with Ben about climbing. She sat back and listened to them, nodding every so often to indicate her involvement. Meanwhile, she tried to make sense of her turbulent thoughts. She felt a connection with this guy. There was a lot of positive energy flowing between them.

The men began talking about abseiling, when suddenly Ben turned to her. 'Have you ever abseiled, Jennifer?'

'I have, but not for years.'

'Did you enjoy it?'

'Loved it, but I was fearless as a seven-year-old.'

They all laughed, then Lee excused himself to go to the toilet.

'Bring back more drinks,' Jeremy shouted, before turning to speak to Maggie.

'So, would you abseil again?' Ben asked.

'P-p-perhaps.' Jennifer stumbled over her words. 'I don't exactly get the opportunity.'

'You make your own opportunities in life. If you want to go abseiling again, just say the word. I'm a qualified instructor. You'd be in safe hands.'

And Jennifer somehow knew she would be. Even though he was sexy as hell and causing her to experience all sorts of emotions she hadn't felt for years, her gut told her he would be a dependable, reliable sort of guy. *What am I thinking?* He's not interested in me. She fancied the pants off him, but he showed no sign it was reciprocated. And then she thought, why the hell shouldn't she go? For once, she would be spontaneous. Nothing ventured, nothing gained.

'I'd love that. When's the best time?'

Ben smiled and looked pleased she wanted to take him up on his offer.

'Anytime it's not frosty or icy, if you're a beginner, although once you get more adventurous, perhaps we can get you ice climbing,' he said, his eyes twinkling.

Jennifer wasn't sure about ice climbing, but he was certainly making her heart rate climb.

'So, when am I taking you?' Ben broke into her reverie.

Now, she wanted to say, but then she thought of her mother, so said, 'I don't have much free time,' at which his face fell and he said, 'That's too bad.'

Jennifer sighed and said, 'It's complicated,' then briefly explained about her mum.

'That's got to be hard on you.'

'Sometimes,' she admitted, 'but I couldn't live with myself if she had to go into care.'

Ben looked at her in open admiration.

'If you ever have a free window, give me a call.' He took a supermarket receipt out of his wallet and scrawled his mobile number on the back.

Lee's reappearance heralded the arrival of another

round of drinks. The easy intimacy had vanished and all seven of them settled into a big debate about travel and where the most worthwhile place on Earth was. Jeremy said the missionaries in Africa must have the worst job, but with the greatest rewards. The others all shot him down and said they didn't want to hear of any noble causes, they wanted his dream destination. This debate raged until they had to leave, due to the campsite curfew. When chance allowed, Jennifer glanced at Ben, and a few times she thought she caught him looking at her too.

They all trudged along, singing and linking arms. Jeremy had talked Ben into coming back to the campsite with them, rather than getting a cab back to his B & B in Ballachulish. Lee was a dab hand at the old campfire and Henry had promised them all sausage sandwiches. They sat chatting for an hour or so, but Jennifer began to flag despite enjoying herself. She made her excuses and headed for the Portakabin toilet at the other end of the campsite. About a third of the way across, she cursed herself for not borrowing Lee's torch. She couldn't see a damned thing.

Hands washed, Jennifer came out and banged straight into Ben. Quickly regaining her composure after her initial fright at a shadow looming out of the dark at her, Jennifer smiled at him and said, 'Sorry, but do you usually loiter around ladies' toilets?'

'No, but I saw you struggling on the way over and figured I'd bring you a torch.'

Jennifer was touched.

'Did you really come all the way over here to bring me a torch?'

'Not exactly. The torch was an excuse.'

'What do you mean?'

And in answer, Ben bent down and kissed her softly on the lips.

Zing. She tingled all over. He drew away from her and looked into her eyes. Evidently seeing there what he wanted, he kissed her again, this time not so softly, parting her lips, making her breath catch in her throat. She almost gasped with pleasure. His tongue tangled with hers and his arms moved up and down her back as she snaked her arms around his neck. Eventually, he pulled away from her again. 'I've wanted to do that all night. I couldn't wait to see if you took up my offer of abseiling.'

'So I see.' She chuckled.

'I wasn't too forward, was I?'

'I'm glad you were.'

'So, where do we go from here?'

In response, Jennifer drew him down to her again, revelling in his kiss. He hardened against her, igniting her own desire further. It had been so long since she'd been touched like this. Ben traced his fingers over an exposed part of her flat stomach and every one of her nerve endings kicked into overdrive.

'We'd better go back or I won't be able to control myself.'

'Me neither,' she breathed.

'When can I see you again?'

'We'll sort something out,' Jennifer said, determined that she would. Tonight had reminded her what life was all about.

Chapter Nineteen

When Jennifer returned with Ben, Maggie looked at her quizzically. Jennifer feigned innocence, but she could see Maggie wasn't deceived.

It wasn't long before they called it a night. Ben had made a point of sitting beside Jennifer, but talked to everyone else too, so as not to arouse suspicion. Maggie was one of the first to lope off to bed. 'See you in the morning, Jennifer.'

'Yes, night.' Jennifer didn't realise Maggie was trying to engineer for them to be left alone. When only the two of them remained, Ben whispered in her ear, 'I want to kiss you again.'

She whispered back, 'Do it then.'

So he did, but broke away quickly. 'Come with me.'

Not in the slightest bit apprehensive she followed him to a more secluded part of the campsite. As soon as they were far enough away, they fell into each other's arms and kissed until their lips were red and sore, but still they wanted more. They touched each other all over, hesitating at the intimate parts. Ben caressed her nipples through her bra, but didn't dip inside it, which made his touch all the more exquisite. She stroked his upper thighs, almost but not quite reaching his erection, which drove him wild.

'I wish I could make love to you right now, but I won't.'

In response, Jennifer kissed him softly on the lips.

They rearranged their clothing and lay cuddled together, stroking each other for a while, then agreed they'd better get back.

'I need to get up earlyish to get to work in Fort William. But can I have your number before we part ways?'

Smiling, Jennifer gave it to him.

All the way home to Ayr, Jennifer thought of Ben and his body against hers and hoped and prayed he would phone. She was just going to bed early, as she wasn't used to partying and staying up late, when the phone rang. Who was calling at twenty to eleven? Usually it meant bad news if someone called after nine.

'Hello?'

'Jennifer, it's Ben. Sorry to call so late, but I wanted to check you got back OK.'

'I did, thanks.' She was delighted he'd called so soon. They talked for over an hour and eventually Ben said, 'I better go. I've work in the morning. I'll give you a call when I'm in Glasgow and hopefully we can meet up, discuss that abseiling trip in more detail.'

'That would be great.' She could hardly keep the excitement out of her voice. 'Bye then.'

Jennifer was unable to will herself to sleep. She wasn't sure she wanted to sleep anyway. She'd rather think about Ben, remember every inch of him. Throwing back the duvet, she padded through to the kitchen and switched on the kettle.

She settled down in her armchair with a cup of tea and perused the list of competitions she hadn't yet entered – a Ford Ka, £3000 cash, a year's free shopping at Sainsbury's, a trip on the Orient Express, a ski weekend in Austria, champagne for life. She busied herself filling out the postcards and completed a further twenty applications before her yawns told her she would probably manage to sleep now.

'So, what's going on with you and Ben?' Maggie didn't even introduce herself when she phoned. 'You looked pretty close. Is romance in the air?'

'We-ll…'

'I knew it! You bitch! He's bloody gorgeous. It's about time you starting seeing somebody.'

'I'm not *seeing* him,' protested Jennifer, secretly wishing she was.

'Did he kiss you?'

'Well, yes.'

'Jennifer Abercrombie, you dirty stopout!'

'It was only a little kiss.' She crossed her fingers behind her back.

'Has he phoned?'

'Last night.' Jennifer couldn't prevent the smile that spread across her face.

'See. Oh! Romance really is blossoming. So happy for you.'

'Thanks, but nothing might come of it. I do like him though.'

'And he seems a really decent, friendly guy.'

'Yes, that too. So, what's the catch?'

'There isn't *always* a catch.'

'No, just usually.' *I hope there isn't this time.*

'So when are you seeing him?'

'We've not made any definite plans,' Jennifer said. 'Possibly the next time he's down, but I'm not sure what to do about Mum.'

'You'll find a way. *We'll* find a way, even if I have to come over and sit with your mum for a while. I'm sure mine would be happy to help out. It seems they had a good chat and they have a lot in common.'

Jennifer wondered how true this could be, given that her mother was bedridden and Maggie's mum remained very active. Perhaps they'd been discussing her mum's life before the onset of her condition.

'I'll see you next week then,' Maggie said before ringing off.

The door rattled when the postman put the letters through. Jennifer bent down to pick up the post: a postcard from Tuscany.

Hi, Jennifer. You would love it here. If things were different, I would invite you over right now. Date for your diary, 9th November is my book launch for my second book, Venetian Dreams. *Maria's helping me organise it. Please say you can make it. I have so much to tell you. Will email soon. Hols. X*

She missed Holly. They had worked together years ago and ended up living in the same street for a bit, but then Holly moved in with Tom, and as Holly travelled a great deal for work, they rarely saw each other. Of course, she had devoured her friend's first book. The razzamatazz of the glamorous book launch had appealed to her too. It had been the highlight of her year. And now Holly was in Tuscany researching for her third book. Excellent. It looked like there would be several book launches to come in the future. Smiling, she pinned the postcard on the corkboard in the kitchen and turned her attention to the remaining letters. An electricity bill, a couple of pieces of junk mail, asking if they wanted their upholstery cleaned, or a conservatory put in. A flyer from a supermarket, with the week's special offers and finally one she couldn't identify. Puzzled, she opened it, read it, and with her hand covering her mouth, she leaned against the kitchen wall for support.

Chapter Twenty
Ben – ARIES

Assertive, pioneering, competitive, courageous and impulsive. Natural athlete, drawn to physical activity. Like danger, risk and adventure. Good at motivating others.

Ben Donnelly rubbed his eyes and tried to focus. He'd slept badly. Unfortunately, he had to work, so he got up and headed for the en suite to shower. As he smoothed shampoo through his short dark hair, he kicked himself for drinking again last night. This had to stop. It had been four months.

Four months earlier

'Honey, I'm home,' Ben called as he kicked off his trainers. Kathryn was very proud of their home. She'd chosen everything in it, being a lady of leisure and also fortunately a woman of means, as Ben's paltry income from the hiking-goods store wouldn't have covered a quarter of the lifestyle she was accustomed to. Their house was more a stately home, yet there were only the two of them, Kathryn loath to give up her figure to have children.

Theirs had been a whirlwind romance. Ben, a volunteer with the Lochaber Mountain Rescue, had rescued her from the top of Ben Nevis, when thick fog impaired visibility so badly they had no chance of getting down unassisted. Kathryn had been very poised. But after their wedding, Ben learned she was nowhere near so gracious most of the time. Yet, despite her faults, he loved her. She was funny, charming, when she wanted to be, intelligent and could be good fun.

Kathryn, however, was also a very self-assured woman, who knew what she wanted. And she wanted Ben. Ben had been so busy the last few years, working and volunteering for the mountain rescue, that he'd never given much thought to a relationship. Initially, he had no idea she was wealthy, and when he found out, he was horrified. He was out of his depth here. He didn't do the tux and cigars deal.

Her parents, Edgar and Amelia, were very aloof and didn't deem him good enough for their daughter. Perhaps they were right; he certainly couldn't support her. Edgar had made it painfully obvious to him, not long after the engagement, that trying to pay for his daughter's lifestyle would be futile and that she had her own money. He also made no secret of his disapproval of Ben's lack of career structure. In addition to being on the mountain rescue's rota and working part-time in McGregor's Camping Supplies, Ben covered a few shifts in a pub. Edgar seemed to have forgotten that Ben had rescued his only daughter. In the beginning, Ben assumed Edgar was being open and friendly, trying to set his mind at ease about providing for his daughter. Until one day Edgar hissed at him, 'I'll buy you both a house, but I expect you to make a living for yourself. I will not have my daughter supporting you.'

Ben had been shocked. He'd never been branded a sponger by anyone and he was furious. But he kept his cool, and apart from the palatial residence his father-in-law provided them with, he didn't take a penny from him, working hard to cover their bills. He certainly covered all of his, although he couldn't quite stretch to Kathryn's Nicole Farhi and Gucci monthly bills, nor those for her Louis Vuitton bags, for which she had a penchant.

'Kathryn. Where are you? I've got a surprise!' Ben's six-foot frame took the stairs two at a time and he walked along the plush-carpeted corridor towards their bedroom.

When he opened the door, his wife was standing at one side of their bed, her hands patting something down. A smile creased his face, until he reached her and saw her stony, impassive one.

'You're early,' she said.

'I wanted to surprise you.'

'You did.'

Ben looked from his wife's face to the bed where she had been folding negligees into a suitcase.

'Are you going somewhere? Have I forgotten?'

'Yes and no. I'm leaving you, Ben. This isn't working out.'

'What? Why?'

'I've outgrown you. You have no ambition. I can't be married to that.'

Ben's chin dropped towards his chest. He couldn't believe he was hearing this.

'Please tell me you're joking. I thought we had a good marriage.'

'Well, that just about sums you up. You can't see what's right in front of you. You'd rather gad about on mountains than spend time with me. You never socialise at all, unless it's one of those dreadful fundraisers for your damned mountain rescue. I need some excitement, and quite frankly you're not giving me any.'

'But you know I hate the social circuit. I don't do hunting or black-tie dinners. We had an understanding.'

'No. You chose not to accompany me to functions because you couldn't be bothered. I wanted you there.'

'Well, why didn't you tell me? If it means that much to you, then I'll go.'

'It's not only that.'

'What else?'

'I could be here all year telling you. I should never have married you. I should have listened to my father.'

'Why, what did Daddy say?' Ben asked masochistically.

'I married beneath myself.'

'So why did you marry me?'

'Oh Ben, this is pointless.' She rolled her eyes and sighed.

'Why did you *marry* me?' Ben raised his voice slightly.

Kathryn drew herself up, any trace of emotion long gone.

'Oh, darling, you were my bit of rough, my way of getting back at my parents.'

She had never loved him. She had used him. Wordlessly, he left the room and went to pour himself a large whisky.

The front door closed. Once she had gone, he went upstairs to investigate. Some of her things were missing. He rifled through their wardrobes and bedside cabinets, then her dressing room, adjacent to the master bedroom and larger than most people's bedrooms. Many of her things still hung on the racks, including her fawn slip dress, the most expensive item he had ever bought her. Of course, he hadn't paid for the engagement ring. Her parents insisted they pay for it, as their daughter had appearances to keep up. Twenty-five thousand pounds, and it had become a meaningless bauble in less than a year. They hadn't celebrated their first anniversary yet. There would be nothing to celebrate now.

He wondered why she hadn't taken all of her things. Then he saw the Oxley-Finch embossed notepaper on the bed. Gingerly he picked it up, 'Ben. I am not unreasonable. You have one week to move out. Kathryn.'

Ben crumpled the notelet in his fist and sat down on the bed. Oh great, not only was he losing his wife, but also his home. He looked around him and realised this wasn't his home. None of it was his taste. He walked out of the room and down the spiral staircase. If this was no longer his home, he'd better get cracking and find a new one, as moving within a week would be no easy task, even though he didn't have much to take with him. He climbed up into his Land Rover, the only concession he had made to the gentrified living he had grudgingly accepted, and headed into town to buy the papers to look for a flat to rent.

Chapter Twenty-one

Freshly showered, Ben felt better. He needed to get a move on though if he didn't want to be late. Much as he was respected at the hiking shop and the assistant manager, he had been slipping lately, what with all the upheaval in his life. He wasn't exactly flavour of the month. It was also a three-hour journey and he had to fill up the car with diesel first.

'Hi, Ben. How you doing?'

'Not bad, Charlie, yourself?'

'I'm all right, thanks. A word of warning. Forsythe's on the warpath today. Two of the boys phoned in sick and it's been really busy.'

Ben's heart sank. Just what he needed. Not the most mild-mannered man at the best of times, John Forsythe had an acid tongue and took no prisoners. Ben squared his shoulders, easy enough, broad-shouldered as he was, and approached the staffroom with what he hoped was the correct amount of bonhomie.

'Ben.' Forsythe nodded to him when he strode in.

'All right, boss?'

'Not really. Those two wasters, Lewis and Terry, aren't coming in. Sick. Sick, my arse. More like hungover.'

Ben winced, reminded of his own hangover, which had dissipated somewhat on his way up from Paisley. Before he could reply, Forsythe said to him, 'You're no' looking so sharp yourself.'

Reading the barely concealed warning, Ben said, 'I'm fine.'

'Good, because with two down, I need all the help I can get.'

The day passed in a blur. Everyone was going camping this year, if sales were anything to go by.

'Thanks for hanging back, Ben. You may as well go.'

'No problem, Forsythe. See you tomorrow.'

'Aye, hopefully we'll have a full staff.'

Ben pulled into the car park of the B & B. He had a nice little deal. Friends had suggested Mrs Lochray sell up to one of the many people eager to join the booming B & B business in the Glencoe area, but she had resisted. This was where her Donald had come from, where he had died and where she would stay. She had been advertising for lodgers when Ben first arrived and no fewer than six people had mentioned this to him, so it had seemed that it was providence. Mary had later been convinced to use her other two rooms as B & B accommodation. Since then Ben had started doing jobs around the house and helping with the tourists. In exchange, Mary provided him with three meals a day and did his washing.

'Hi, Mary. How's your day been?' Ben asked, stamping his feet on the mat.

'Hectic. We've a new Finnish couple in room four. Presumably they haven't come here to ski, or they'll be sorely disappointed. You'd expect there'd be plenty of snow where they live.'

Ben smiled. Mary had a habit of adding some comment about her guests. She would try to figure out what they did and why they had come to Scotland, long before they volunteered the information.

Her children had long grown up and lived in far-flung corners of the globe: one in Ottawa, one in Brisbane and the youngest was in Cambridgeshire. So she regarded Ben as a surrogate son and he was happy enough to assume the role and let her mollycoddle him. He certainly hadn't received much TLC from anyone else in a while.

'We have a new family in for a week, the Morrisons, from York. Two little ones, three and five, Griffin and Harriet. Cute as can be, but that Harriet is a sly little minx and has her father wrapped around her finger.'

'I'll watch out for her. But now, I'm off to have a shower.'

'Right you are. Steak pie OK for tea?'

'Absolutely.' One of his favourites and another reason he loved living here. All of Mary's food was home-made. Kathryn had barely known how to pop bread in the toaster. It wasn't that he was sexist and thought women should cook all the time, but she never cooked and she was home all day, or shopping, whilst he slaved away. It didn't matter that she didn't need to earn a living. It was the principle.

Ben applied aftershave to his jaw and chin, wincing as his skin absorbed it. He felt good tonight. Maybe he would go to the Aonach Inn. But first he'd have some of that steak pie.

The Finnish couple were also at dinner and Ben chatted to them about fishing and Formula One, the only two things he knew about Finland, apart from that Helsinki was the capital. The talents of Mika Hakkinen and Kimi Raikkonen exhausted, Ben excused himself.

He picked up his wallet and called his mate John, a taxi driver who often dropped him at the pub, as his girlfriend lived in Glencoe village. John said he'd be there in five minutes. Five minutes in the Highlands meant about twenty minutes, so Ben went into the kitchen where Mary was busy doing the dishes. He gave her the week's lodgings money and then chatted with her as she handed him the plates and he placed them in the cupboard above his head. The sound of a car horn broke into their ramblings fifteen minutes later.

'Ah, early for once,' Ben joked. 'See you in the morning.'

'Bye, son,' she said to his retreating back.

'Aonach Inn, please, John.'

'As if I didn't know. Where else would you be going?'

'Are you trying to imply something?' Ben feigned hurt.

'Aye. That you're no' using my taxi company for anything else.'

'Where else would I go?'

'Ye've a point there.'

The drive didn't take long. 'See you later,' John said, and with a screeching of brakes he sped off to his girlfriend's.

Ben opened the low door which led into the main section of the pub. *It's busy tonight.* He was trying to figure out if he recognised anyone when a familiar face flew into his line of vision.

'Ben! Ben! Over here!'

His old friend, Jeremy. Jeremy patted him on the back then asked him how he was getting on.

'I'm fine, Jez and you? What you been up to?'

'Rescuing this one from being arrested.' He indicated Maggie. Turning back to Ben, Jeremy said, 'Are you on your own?'

'Yes, I'm supposed to be at home in Glasgow. I wasn't meant to be working up here this weekend, but I'm covering for a mate who's gone on holiday at the last minute.'

'Well, why don't you join us? Budge up, guys!'

Ben glanced around as Jeremy made the introductions. Maggie had quite a hard look about her, as if she could hold her own, whilst Henry had the air of a college professor, or perhaps a boffin. There were another couple of lads and two women, one of whom was like a shy little mouse, trying to hide. What did Jeremy say her name was? He'd been so busy trying to keep up with who was who, he'd missed it. But, Jeremy had certainly saved the best for last.

There was something about her. He didn't know what. She wasn't beautiful per se, skinny rather than slim and looked awkward, like a newborn doe. When he'd shaken her hand, there had definitely been something, not fireworks, but a spark. He tried not to stare at her as Jeremy rambled on. He didn't want to be rude, but he couldn't give him his full attention. Usually, he enjoyed Jeremy's anecdotes, but he couldn't concentrate and provided clipped responses to most of his questions. He was still half lending an ear to Jeremy, half trying to home in on the other conversations, when a decidedly feminine voice said, 'Anyone for another?'

There were murmurs of assent and people reciting what they wanted.

'Ben, what are you having?'

He chose the glib approach. 'What are *you* having?'

'I-I'm having vodka and Coke,' she stammered.

'Make that two.'

She almost ran down the pub away from him. *Hmmm, what to do? What to do?*

The fact that she'd seemed nervous gave him hope that perhaps he wasn't the only one who'd experienced a little frisson from their handshake. He waited a few moments, hatching his plan, until she reached the front of the queue. As soon as the barman spoke to her, he interrupted Jeremy, saying, 'Scuse me a sec, Jez. I'll just give her a hand with the drinks.'

'What? Uh, Jennifer, sorry, I should have thought of that.'

'No problem. I'll go.' Ben was delighted. Jeremy had unwittingly aided him, by mentioning her name.

He stood behind her. She hadn't yet registered his presence. He was just in time to hear the barman say, 'I get off in half an hour,' and Jen's polite, noncommittal response of, 'That's nice.' The barman persisted. 'Would you like to meet up later?' Ben didn't know whether to thank him or be angry, as Jen stuttered, 'I-I-I...'

Ben stepped in, looked the bartender in the eye and said, 'I'm sure she'd love to, but we have plans later, don't we, darling?'

'Yes.' She turned towards him and the smile she gave him lit her face like the glowing embers of a fire.

'I came to help you with the drinks.'

'Thanks.'

He wasn't sure if she was thanking him for coming to help with the drinks, or for getting rid of the barman's unwelcome attentions.

'Can't have you being set upon by the wolves.'

She smiled weakly, but Ben was encouraged. He motioned for her to walk ahead of him and they carried the drinks back.

Whilst they were at the bar, Henry had swapped seats to sit beside Jeremy, so Jennifer and Ben were now sitting together. Ben was annoyed when Lee started talking to him, across Jennifer, about climbing. It was a bit rude; Lee was almost acting as if Jennifer were invisible, but he figured he should show willing and participate properly in the conversation; otherwise Jennifer might think he was a complete moron. So he chatted amiably enough, with Jennifer on the fringes of the conversation. Lee asked him about the Munros he'd bagged. He'd climbed seventy out of the two hundred and eighty-four. Then the conversation moved on to adventure sports.

Ben said, 'Have you ever abseiled, Jennifer?'

Jennifer seemed startled to be included, then said, 'I have, but not for years.'

Lee excused himself to go to the toilet and at Jeremy's request agreed to get the next round in. Taking advantage of their being alone together, Ben coaxed the details out of her. Perhaps he could persuade her to go abseiling. She explained about her mother, and after talking it through, he gave her his number in case she fancied trying it again.

Lee arrived with the drinks just then and the moment was lost. As the evening drew to a close, Ben wished he didn't have to go home.

Chapter Twenty-two

'We're all at the campsite. Come back with us. We've got sausages and burgers,' Jeremy said.

'I'm working tomorrow,' Ben replied. *This could be my chance with Jennifer though.*

'C'mon. I haven't seen you for ages.

'OK, you've twisted my arm.'

After calling John to update him, Ben stooped slightly to avoid banging his head on the low lintel and entered the pub. He headed towards the table where Jeremy was shrugging on his jacket and the others were downing the remainder of their drinks. Jennifer had started walking towards the door with Maggie, when she looked over, holding his gaze for a fraction of a second longer than necessary. His smile started at the corners of his mouth and reached all the way to his eyes. A long cream scarf lay on the floor, and dragging his eyes from Jennifer, he bent down to pick it up. 'Is this yours?' He held it out to her.

'Thanks. I didn't realise I'd dropped it.' She was silent for a moment.

The others were making for the door. Maggie was chatting to Jeremy.

'Are you joining us at the campsite?' Jennifer asked.

'Yes. Jez has said I can kip in his tent.'

'Well, we'd better get going then.' She held the door open.

He took it from her and said, 'After you.'

As they walked in the pitch darkness, Lee started singing 'Dancing Queen'.

'If you must sing, Lee, make it something more appropriate,' said Susan.

'But I like "Dancing Queen",' wailed Lee. Nevertheless the song soon changed to 'The Irish Rover', followed by 'Long Tall Sally', then 'Flower of Scotland'. Lee's repertoire wasn't very varied, nor was his singing much good.

It didn't take them long to arrive at the campsite. It was cold for June, but the heavy rain that had been forecast hadn't come to much and it was dry now. Just as well they had gas burners and stoves though. Meanwhile, Susan fetched some wood from one of the cars. *They're well prepared.* He huddled inside his puffy jacket, glad he'd chosen to wear it. He glanced over at Jennifer. She was lucky she had quite a few layers on: a green lined cagoule, a microfleece and possibly a T-shirt too, but it really wasn't sufficient for this type of outdoor activity. She was clearly a beginner, whereas the others wore proper walking garb. As soon as Jeremy had the fire going, Jennifer positioned herself nearest to it. Ben wanted to wrap his arms around her and keep her warm.

'Ben,' Jeremy shouted across to him, disrupting his thoughts. 'Give us a hand with these sausages.'

Ben grinned and took the two bags of food which Jeremy thrust into his hands then set about readying them for grilling.

'Oh, it's some place this!' said Ben. 'You get invited over for supper and end up having to make it yourself!'

Around the campfire everyone laughed. Maggie handed round cups of tea for those who didn't fancy whisky.

They chatted for a while, eating charred sausages and burgers.

'Why won't men cook in a kitchen, but when it's a barbecue, they fight over it?' Susan asked.

'Hear, hear,' said Maggie.

'That's not fair. What about Jamie Oliver?' asked Lee.

'He's cute,' said Susan.

'I meant professionally.' Lee rolled his eyes.

'He's changed my perception of cooking,' said Maggie.

'You mean, you actually cook now?' said Jennifer.

'Yes, but I have to follow a recipe.'

'I'm more of a find an onion, a tomato and two eggs and then make a three-course meal out of it,' said Jeremy.

'Aye right!' said Lee.

'No, seriously, although I do have a little help from Jamie Oliver.'

They all laughed at this. Jennifer heaved herself up from her cross-legged position. 'Maggie, where are the toilets?'

'Those Portakabins, by the campsite entrance.'

'OK, back in a minute.'

Ben watched her go, then realised this was an opportunity to get her on her own again and earn some brownie points at the same time.

'Lee, can I borrow your torch?'

'Sure.' He fished it out of his pocket and flipped it over to Ben.

Ben shone the torch in the direction he'd seen Jennifer

venture off in. It was pitch dark and the moon was almost completely hidden. He knew it was Jennifer's first time here and that there were a few potholes near the entrance and countless ruts. He didn't want her going over on her ankle. He reached the toilets and heard running water.

'Oh my God, you scared me,' she squealed, when she came out, head down, and almost walked slap bang into Ben. 'Sorry, but do you usually loiter around ladies' toilets?' A smile twitched at the corners of her lips.

'No, but I saw you struggling on the way over and figured I'd bring you a torch.'

He was rewarded with another smile. 'Did you really come all the way over here to bring me a torch?'

Ben hesitated. He didn't want to appear too keen, yet his instincts told him just to be honest.

'Not exactly. The torch was an excuse.'

'What do you mean?'

She wasn't making this easy. Once more he dithered, and then figuring nothing ventured, nothing gained, he bent down and kissed her. The kiss became more involved, and when they finally drew apart, he said, 'I've wanted to do that all night. I couldn't wait to see if you took up my offer of abseiling.'

They didn't exchange many words after that. With a promise to take it further later and so as not to arouse suspicion, they brushed themselves down and headed back to join the others. Lee raised an eyebrow at Ben, but apart from that no one said anything.

Soon Maggie made a move for her tent. Jennifer didn't immediately follow. The others drifted off one by one and Ben and Jennifer were left alone. After a few hurried words, they scuttled off to the other end of the campsite for some privacy, where they spent an enjoyable hour together chatting and kissing. Before Jennifer headed off to her tent and Ben to Jeremy's, he made sure she gave him her phone number. Ben slept fitfully, unable to get Jennifer out of his head.

Chapter Twenty-three

At seven thirty, Ben had to get up and thumb a lift back to Ballachulish to get to work in time. He went via the B & B to freshen up. Once at work, his day passed slowly. The only event of note was the turn for the worse in the weather. The heavy rain, forecast for the night before, was bucketing down now and the wind was gusting.

He decided to call his sister. 'Gaby. How you doing?'

'Been better.' She sounded depressed and angry.

'What's up?'

'I can't go into it right now.'

'So there *is* something up. You're not ill, are you?'

'No.' He heard her sigh.

'That's a relief. So, what is it?'

'I can't tell you, you wouldn't approve.'

'You haven't joined a cult, have you?' Ben joked.

'No.'

'WeightWatchers?'

'Ha ha.'

'Are things OK with you and Oscar?'

'Not exactly.'

'Oh, now we're getting to it. What's wrong?'

'He's working ridiculous hours. We hardly ever see each other.'

'Have you spoken to him?' Ben asked her, wishing he'd called her once he'd arrived home.

'Yes, of course I have, but he keeps saying it's for our future.'

Ben could almost see his sister making air quotes. 'Just tell him you need to spend a bit more time together.'

'I'm sick of suggesting it. He says I'm nagging him.'

'It's obviously upsetting you, sis. You need to make him listen.'

'I suppose, but I shouldn't have to do all the work in our relationship. It takes two.'

'No, you're absolutely right.' Suddenly aware that discussing such personal matters whilst at work might not be the best plan, Ben said, 'Listen, let's talk about this later. I'm at work at the minute. Will you be in tonight?'

'Where else would I be?' Gaby replied.

'OK, I'll call you later.'

The call with Gaby had left him worried. She had never sounded so off before, certainly not regarding her husband. He'd take Oscar for a beer and have a few discreet words with him.

He made another few calls, one to his mate Barry and one to the officer in charge of the training he was to give later in the week. It was four thirty; only another half hour and then he could head back and call Jennifer. His mobile vibrated in his pocket. Forsythe. Forsythe was a rescue team leader. It was one of the reasons he was so understanding about Ben leaving mid-shift to help out the MRT.

'Incident Stob Choire Claurigh. Multiple persons, multiple injuries. Confirm availability.'

Ben texted back that he was on his way and drove over

to the MRC in Glen Nevis.

Forsythe was already briefing the team.

'Stob Choire Claurigh: 4.27 p.m., multiple persons, multiple injuries. We have the approximate coordinates. It doesn't look easy.' They all knew the drill. They'd been there hundreds of times and had seen some horrific injuries, including the occasional death.

'Party of six, travelling one behind the other. The rope linking them together snapped. Four injured: one unconscious, one suspected broken leg and the other two have major contusions. RAF is picking you up in ten minutes.'

'Any potential difficulties?' asked Ben.

'They're underneath an overhang,' said Forsythe.

Great. How is the chopper going to reach them?

The radio crackled into life. 'RAF Fort William, Muldoon. Over.'

'Go ahead, Freddy. Over.'

'We should be touching down in a few minutes. Over.'

'We're ready. Over.'

'Roger that. Over and out.'

The team got their kit together and congregated beside the new helipad. A few minutes later the helicopter swooped down. They'd no sooner climbed aboard, jackets billowing behind them from the force of the downdraught, when the helicopter took off again. Ben relayed the grid reference to the pilot and they headed towards Stob Choire Claurigh. The driving rain made visibility poor and the storm forecast for the day before was in full swing. They neared the coordinates, but couldn't see the party.

The storm swirled all around them, buffeting the helicopter. It was imperative they find the walkers and fast. Although their information indicated they were beneath an overhang, which would afford some shelter, they wouldn't escape the full force of the wind. They switched on the infrared heat detector.

'There,' shouted Stan. 'A hundred feet below us.'

Sure enough, six red dots appeared on the imager. Freddy brought the chopper down, but couldn't quite bring it low enough, as there was another peak below him.

'Stan. Bring the stretcher.'

'Freddy, pull us in as close as you can.'

Freddy banked the helicopter slightly.

'Ready, Andy?'

Andy operated the winch, lowering them to the overhang. Fortunately the wind didn't rise any further, or they would have had to turn back; they couldn't afford to become casualties themselves – rule number one.

'Stan, you next.' Andy secured the winch to Stan's harness, tightening the collar onto the carabiner to secure it.

Stan dug out the pulley system and readied himself to help the pulleys support Ben's weight as Ben lowered himself down the overhang. They worked quickly and soon reached the party.

'You have no idea how relieved we are to see you. Thank you,' said an older man.

Ben nodded an acknowledgement, and assessing the situation, he identified an unconscious middle-aged man and a young chap who had broken his leg. Ben gave the others blankets and told them to shelter. Ben assembled the plastic stretcher and with assistance, lowered the older man onto it. He then secured him to allow him to be safely hoisted upwards. Stan operated the pulley, the stretcher across Ben's lap. Ben braced his legs against the mountainside, ready to protect the stretcher from listing. Finally, they reached the top, where the chopper sat about three hundred yards away.

Next they brought up the two women, who were in shock and badly bruised, but could walk. Andy took them to the chopper, leaving three people below. The man with the broken leg was fast losing consciousness; when they'd first arrived, he'd been howling. It was never a good sign when the injured became more docile.

'I need one of you to help with your friend.'

'I'll do it,' volunteered one man.

Ben inflated the splint and, the patient secured, lay the stretcher across his lap. Once the last man was up top, they sprinted towards the helicopter.

'Get in, get in. I don't know if I'll be able to take off,' Freddy yelled.

After a few thwarted attempts, Freddy managed to lift the helicopter into the air, although the wind was still blowing them about. Ben and Andy tried to warm the injured passengers, but they were unable to rouse the unconscious man.

'Freddy, ETA at Belford?'

'Ten minutes.'

The paramedics were already running out with trolleys when the helicopter landed.

'Over to you,' Andy said, as the medics put the injured men on trolleys.

'This one's still unconscious. We've checked his obs.'

Ben helped the medics, whilst Andy filled them in on the status of the patients.

It was nine o'clock by the time Ben arrived at the B & B.

Worry lines etched Mary's face. 'Ben, thank goodness. I heard you were called out.'

'We're all OK. I'll be much better after a shower though.'

'Right, I'll put your soup on. It's home-made chicken soup. Is mince, potatoes and doughballs OK for you?'

'That's great. I'll heat it up myself. You've had a long day too. Get yourself off to bed.'

'Not until you're fed and watered. Can you believe this weather?'

The rain was coming down hard still, thundering against the windows, but once Ben headed for bed, it would have taken a force nine gale to keep him awake.

Chapter Twenty-four

Ben stepped into the shower and closed his eyes, letting the water wash away the strains of the day. He hadn't thought about Jennifer for hours. When he was out on the mountains, it consumed him entirely and he was exhausted. However, far from wanting a drink to help him relax further, he wanted to call Jennifer. He wondered if it was too late to phone and he couldn't keep Mary waiting. She usually went to bed around nine; she was an old woman after all. Dressing quickly, he jumped down the stairs, two at a time and entered the dining room.

'There you go, son.'

'Thanks, Mary.' The soup tasted delicious. It always reminded him of his childhood, coming home on a winter's day, his mother setting a bowl of soup before him. The warming meal and the coal fire were his two favourite winter memories and Mary provided both. His soup demolished, he set about devouring the mince and tatties she laid before him.

'You're hungry today, son. Would you like some home-made apple pie?'

Sorely tempted, as Mary's apple pie was to die for, Ben declined. 'No, I'm fine, thanks. That was lovely. I'll clear the dishes. You've done enough.'

'OK, son. Goodnight.'

Ben scooted through to the living room and dialled Jennifer's number. He felt happy just hearing her voice. They talked for an hour or so. He told her about his day and his landlady and she told him about Maggie and the protests and about giving up her career to care for her mum. When he rang off, he told her he'd be in touch to arrange that abseiling trip.

Content and exhausted, Ben went to his room and picked up the *Da Vinci Code*. Everyone had been raving about it for ages. By the fourth line he was asleep.

Next morning, Ben realised he'd forgotten to do the dishes. He threw on his dressing gown and hurried downstairs. It was six thirty. Mary was already up, drinking tea, reading the first edition of the *Daily Record*. Ben knew without glancing at the dining room table that Mary had cleaned up after him.

'Morning, Mary. Sorry about the dishes. I passed out last night.'

'Don't you worry, what else have I to do?'

Apart from prepare for guests every day and run around after them? Nothing. But he said nothing, as her question was rhetorical. She always played down how hard she worked.

It only dawned on Ben, a few days later, as he drove back from Inverness, that he hadn't called his sister back. He finally phoned her around ten, but the phone rang out. He called again at ten thirty. This time Oscar answered.

'Hey, Oscar. It's Ben. How you doing?'

'Not bad. You?'

'Can't complain. I've been in Inverness the last few days.'

'Oh right. Yeah, I've had a long one myself. Just got in.'

'Ah, I tried about ten, but I got the machine. Is Gaby in?'

'No. She's out with a friend.'

'Can you tell her I'm really sorry I forgot to call earlier in the week? I thought maybe we could go for lunch on Sunday.'

'I'm working. Gaby might be up for it though. I'll get her to call you back.'

'Things OK between you two?'

'Yeah, never better. I mean, Gaby moans about the hours I work, but you can't have the nice house, car, two holidays a year and not make any sacrifices.'

'S'pose not,' said Ben, although privately he wondered whether his sister cared about any of that. 'Anyway, perhaps next time you're free, we can go for a beer.'

'Yeah. See you.'

'Bye.' Ben hung up. Oscar didn't think Gaby and he had any problems, but his sister had sounded odd the other day. He'd make a point of seeing her at the weekend. Now, however, he needed to think about his own love life. Much as he wanted to take Jennifer abseiling, he couldn't wait until then.

At lunchtime on Friday he called Jennifer.

'Hi, Jennifer, it's Ben.'

'Hi. How are you?'

'Fine. It's been a really busy week.' He told her about

the TA training in Inverness.

'Sounds like fun.'

'Yes, but at whose expense?'

Jennifer laughed. 'I'm sure you held your own.'

'Just. You'd swear some of them didn't want to be there and the TA is meant to have *enthusiastic* pupils.'

'I bet you're a great teacher.'

'Hmm. You wouldn't think that if you'd seen them. Listen, sorry for the short notice, and you might have an issue finding someone to sit with your mum, but would you like to do something this weekend?'

'Well, I'd love to, but I'm not sure I can make arrangements in time. Can I ring you back later?'

'Sure.'

'What did you have in mind?' Jennifer asked.

'It depends on when you're free. The only time I can't do is Sunday lunch, as I'm hoping to see my sister.'

'You have a sister?'

'Yes. Gaby.'

'How old is she?'

'Twenty-seven.'

'You can tell me all about her when we meet up.'

'Do you fancy X-Scape, where they have the climbing walls and the ski slopes?'

'Oh that sounds really fun. I've never skied before. I almost went to Austria once, to Kitzbuhel, but then Mum got ill and I had to cancel.'

'The best time for it is Sunday evening. If you can't do Sunday evening, try Saturday, and if you can't do either, we could go for a coffee or have breakfast at a little café I know. I don't mind.'

'OK. Thanks for being so understanding. I'll see what I

can do.'

They chatted briefly and then Ben said he had to go. The police were behind him and his Bluetooth headset needed recharging as the phone was beginning to cut out on him. Relieved, but unsurprised when the police passed him and headed down towards Ferguslie Park, Ben concentrated on the road.

Ben woke around nine thirty. For once he hadn't set the alarm. It had been a long week and he had needed the lie-in. He showered and put the coffee in the cafetiere just as the newspaper which he had delivered every Saturday plopped onto the mat. He retrieved *The Times* and retreated into his living room, still in his bathrobe. Ah, sometimes it was nice to be single, especially when you were anticipating a hot date. He put his coffee cup on the glass table. It was bliss not to be moaned at for not putting it on a coaster.

He slid out the supplements, extracting the special offers for support tights and best ever two pairs of slip-on shoes for an amazing ten pounds, as well as the house insurance, medical insurance and bank loan leaflets. Putting them to one side, he picked up the main newspaper. He was just reading an engrossing article about wildlife when his mobile rang. Jennifer.

Ben casually answered the call, as if he'd been doing something all-consuming when the phone rang and hadn't looked at caller ID before answering.

'Ben speaking.'

'Hi, Ben, it's Jennifer. How are you?'

'Good thanks, not long up. I'm having a cup of coffee and reading the papers. You been up long?'

'A couple of hours. I'm usually up early to get Mum to the bathroom and make breakfast.'

Ben tried to carry on from that as naturally as possible, although he couldn't help pitying her and quickly changed the subject. 'Right. So, do you have good news?'

'I think so. Either Maggie or her mum will come and sit with Mum on Sunday night.'

'Fantastic. Should I pick you up from the house?' He wasn't sure if she'd have an issue with that because of her mum, but no, that seemed to be OK.

'I'll pick you up at five. We can go to X-Scape for a few hours and grab a bite afterwards if you have time.'

'I'll probably need to be back no later than eleven, but we can sort that out tomorrow.'

'That's great and gives me an idea.'

'Good, well, I'll see you tomorrow.'

'See you later, Jennifer.'

Ben tried Gaby after Jennifer hung up. The answering machine picked up so he tried her mobile. No answer. He left a message suggesting they go for lunch on Sunday and asked her to call him back. The rest of the day passed slowly, nothing much to do, except housework and relax, but no pressure. The phone rang around ten thirty.

'Hello?'

'Ben. It's Gaby.'

'Ah, the wanderer returns.'

'Something like that,' his sister muttered.

'Is everything OK?' Ben was concerned.

'Yes. Why wouldn't it be?' Gaby snapped.

'Gaby, have you got PMT or something? You don't usually bite my head off for asking how you are, and if you remember, when I last spoke to you, things weren't all right.'

'I'm sorry. I'm just tired. What time do you want to do lunch tomorrow?'

'About one at Arta? I'm going out tomorrow night, so I need to be free again around half three.'

'Glad you could slot me in,' said Gaby, but this time there was no sarcasm in her voice.

'I'm looking forward to seeing you, sis.'

'Me too. Night, Ben.'

'Night.'

Chapter Twenty-five

Ben arrived early. It was always a nightmare trying to park in Glasgow, but he managed to get a space in Ingram Street. Gaby had come in on the Underground, so was already there. She stood up, kissed him on both cheeks and hugged him. Was it his imagination, or did she hold on to him a bit longer than usual? When she released him from her bearlike grip, he stepped back and studied her. She looked a bit peaky. Had she lost weight? Could she be anorexic? Was he worrying about nothing? Something was definitely bothering her.

They shared a pleasant lunch. The tapas bar had many dishes which were exquisite and moreish. They had the usual *patatas bravas, gambas a la plancha, calamares* and *tortilla del dia.* They ordered two of some dishes, as, being tapas, the portions were small. Ben tried to wheedle out of his sister what was wrong, but to no avail. Whatever had been bothering her was either no longer an issue, or she was hiding it well. He told her about Jennifer.

'Just watch yourself, Ben. You know how you get into things too quickly,' Gaby warned him.

'I know.'

'Take it slowly. It hasn't been long.'

'I know.'

'Does this girl know that technically you're still married?'

Ben looked surprised. 'No. Why would I tell her? It's in name only.'

'Yes, but Ben, you'd be amazed how a woman views a wife, separated or not.'

'But that'll just spoil our evening.'

'Believe me, if you don't tell her now, you're storing up trouble for the future.'

'Do you think so?'

'I guarantee you.'

They chatted about everyday events, although Ben thought afterwards that really they'd talked more about him. Gaby had an uncanny knack of deflecting attention from herself. He'd wanted to eke out of her what the problem was and yet instead she'd milked him for information. *How do women manage it?* After lunch, he offered her a lift home, which she refused, saying she had some errands to run.

'Take care, won't you.'

'I will, you too.' She turned and marched away towards Buchanan Street Underground. Ben walked over to Ingram Street to retrieve his car and hurried home to freshen up for his date with Jennifer. He couldn't really get dressed up. They'd be climbing walls and skiing down slopes. He'd already borrowed salopettes, gloves and the like from Forsythe, whose eldest daughter was about the same size as Jennifer.

Ben arrived at Jennifer's house at four fifty-two. Eight minutes early. He didn't know what to do. Women didn't like men being early, as they invariably weren't ready. He debated driving around for a bit or pulling into the next street and sitting there for a few minutes, but just then Maggie appeared at the window. He parked the car and checked his hair in the rear-view mirror. Thank goodness he always kept the inside of his car clean, if not the outside, which was always filthy from driving up and down the A82.

Jennifer opened the door just before he got the chance to knock.

'Hi. I'm ready.'

'OK. Let's go then.' She obviously wasn't going to invite him in. She didn't trust him enough yet to meet her mum and he understood that. With some concern, he wondered if she'd trust him even less after he told her he was still married. When would be the best time to tell her? She looked radiant, even in a pair of faded blue jeans, brown leather ankle boots, an off-white wool roll-neck jumper and a blue felt coat. Now was not the time.

When they arrived at X-Scape, Ben insisted on paying. He knew Jennifer didn't have much money and it was pretty expensive, but he figured it was money well spent. They practised on the climbing wall first so Jennifer could get used to the type of equipment she'd hopefully be using in the future: crampons, pitons, ropes and grabbers. She seemed to be having a good time and he loved the sound of her tinkly laugh. Ben taught her how to snowplough, showing her how to put her skis together towards each other in an A shape.

'I can't stop!' Jennifer spluttered, as she zoomed down the slope towards him, after her first unofficial lesson. Laughing, she careered into him, as Ben stretched his arms out to her, his legs at right angles, to better absorb the impact, but he still went flying backwards. They both collapsed in fits of laughter, once they got their breath back.

'Oh, that was brilliant.' Jennifer beamed at him. 'I haven't had so much fun in years.'

Ben examined her more closely. She was flushed, face scarlet from the cold or exhilaration, and she looked beautiful.

'Do you want to do it again?'

'Absolutely.' She grinned.

An hour later Jennifer was exhausted, but trying not to show it, so Ben decided to put her out of her misery.

'You hungry?'

'Starving.'

'Do you want to grab a pizza or something?'

'Sounds good.'

They changed, gathered up all their ski clothes and headed out. The pizza place was just across the road and glancing at his watch, Ben realised it probably made sense to go there, rather than waste precious time driving around Glasgow searching for a restaurant. Besides, they weren't exactly dressed for fine dining.

'Pizza Hut OK for you?'

'Yes. Let's go. I could eat a horse.'

Ben chuckled at this. He liked a woman with a healthy appetite. Kathryn only ever seemed to eat lettuce, celery and carrot sticks. Occasionally she would push the boat out and have some grilled chicken, but that was about it.

They were seated at a table for two and ordered some garlic bread to satisfy them until their main meal arrived. Ben joked, 'Well, if we're going to be kissing later, so long as we both reek of garlic, that's OK.'

'Yeah, but if we were to wake up next to each other in the morning, it wouldn't be such a good idea.'

Ben raised an eyebrow.

'I mean, because it oozes out of your pores next day,' she stammered.

Ben smiled. 'I know what you meant.'

They ordered, lasagne for Ben and *fettuccine Alfredo* for Jennifer. They chatted throughout the meal, dissolving into hysterics every now and then. *She's so dainty, although she can clearly look after herself.* He wanted to be able to help her, take care of her. She'd been caring for her mother for so long, but who looked out for Jennifer? They talked about their respective families and he felt angry at her brother and sister who had left her to cope with their mother alone. Jennifer deserved a life too. Somehow he didn't mention Kathryn and then it was time to take her home.

They kissed in his car before leaving the complex. He felt like a giddy teenager again, but he was a grown man and kissing wasn't all he wanted to do. He wanted to take her back to his place, but knew that was out of the question. They drove back to Ayr, where Ben dropped her back in Mill Street, at the flat she shared with her mother. Suddenly self-conscious, on her behalf, about kissing in front of her house, and in view of the neighbours, he restrained himself to a rather chaste kiss.

'I'll see you soon. I had a great time.'

'Me too. Thanks.'

'Thanks for dinner.' Jennifer had insisted on paying, even though he knew money must be tight.

'Thanks for the company.' Ben gazed deep into her eyes, trying to engrave her image into his mind.

Jennifer skipped up the path, put her key in the door, waved to him and was gone. Shaking his head, but still smiling, Ben drove away. He must be a saint. He'd wanted to make love to her so much. On his journey home, he realised he never did tell her about Kathryn. Damn! He'd tell her next time.

The weeks that followed were blissful for Ben and Jennifer. Although they couldn't quite establish a routine, they met each other at least once a week and Ben called her at least three times a week. They had dinner at Sarti's in Bath Street, lunched at Café Mao in the Merchant City, took the ferry to Arran and climbed Goatfell and they finally went abseiling, firstly at a quarry just outside of Glasgow, to practise. Jennifer was apprehensive but exhilarated at the same time, but Ben knew she trusted him implicitly. This was what he did. This was what he was good at. She loved descending, bouncing off the quarry walls, and for someone who'd initially seemed so scared, she was completely fearless, just as she told him she'd been as a child.

'So where did you go abseiling before?' Ben asked her, one day a few weeks later, as they sat sipping coffee in Princes Square.

'Perthshire, somewhere, I think. I was too young to remember where exactly.'

She regaled him with funny tales of the camp she had been at, but although he was interested, his attention drifted. He'd received an invitation to a friend's wedding, and he hoped to take Jennifer as his plus one, but was still working up the courage to ask her. It would be held at Culcreuch Castle in Stirlingshire, the perfect location for an overnight stay. He prayed she'd be able to make it and they could finally make love in the romantic setting of the castle. He'd already reserved a room with a four-poster bed, the nicest room after the honeymoon suite. Yes, it was presumptuous, but he wanted to be prepared and God knows it was overdue. He sensed she was ready and he had been since day one. Eventually, he returned to the present.

'So how come you abseiled? It's not a usual pastime for a seven-year-old.'

'I suppose not. I was the youngest. It was a community thing. You were supposed to be at least ten, but I was only seven.'

'Was it an Outward Bound programme?'

'Sort of. I'm not sure if it was called that back then, but we did archery and air-rifle shooting and canoeing and all sorts. It was great fun.'

'Air-rifle shooting? At seven? You're full of surprises.'

'I'm not quite so adventurous these...'

Ben gestured at her to finish what she was saying, but she seemed to be staring over his shoulder, her eyebrows furrowed. Ben turned around to see what was wrong and the force of the blow snapped his head straight back. At first he didn't know what had hit him, but then he heard her voice.

'You complete bastard!' Kathryn's voice cut through him.

'What the hell do you think you're doing? That's my boyfriend you just slapped.' Ben smiled inwardly on hearing Jennifer defend him.

Kathryn looked Jennifer up and down as if she were something she had scraped off her shoe. 'No, you little slut, that's my husband, but you're more than welcome to him.' She glared at Ben and stomped off.

'Kathryn! Kathryn!' Ben called after her. 'Wait!'

Suddenly realising how this must look to Jennifer, and holding his already swollen jaw, he turned to explain about his crazy, soon to be ex-wife, seriously wishing he'd followed his sister's advice. But Jen was gone.

Chapter Twenty-six
Oscar – TAURUS

Loyal, stable, conservative, practical. Patient, affectionate and good natured. Temper erupts dramatically if pushed too far. Home-loving. Jealous and possessive. Not fond of change, reliable and committed but inflexible. Very attuned to the physical world, appreciate great beauty. Good with money.

'I'm heading over to Byres Road,' said Oscar to his secretary, Janine.

'Are you coming back or should I close up?'

'No, I'll be back. Can you make sure the schedules for the Robertsons and the Johnstons go on the web today?'

'Got it. See you later.'

'OK. Mari, you're on late tonight, aren't you?'

'Yes, till seven.'

'OK. I'll be back before then.'

Oscar opened the door and the bell chimed. He hated that bell, but it was company policy at National Estate Agents. He clicked his BMW open, then checked he had everything before setting off for Byres Road to meet the client.

Oscar had been with National Estate Agents for ten years. He was now as high up as he could go without taking a regional manager role and he didn't want to do that at National. He witnessed what it had done to Max. The part Oscar enjoyed best about his job was dealing with the customers. Max dealt with National's employees. Oscar's ultimate aim was to open his own estate agency, but in the meantime he'd have to settle for being top dog in the branch he managed. It made him uneasy sometimes, that his wife, a fund manager at an investment bank, made more money than he did. He knew it shouldn't matter in this day and age, and he didn't really want to act like a dinosaur over it, but it still irked him that she earned a good thirty thousand a year more than he did and although he drove a top-of-the-range BMW, she had an Alfa Romeo.

Gaby was a remarkably confident, headstrong woman, which was one of the reasons he'd fallen in love with her. She wasn't like any of the girls he met in clubs. Gaby had been a completely different challenge. She knew her own mind and was the most independent woman he had ever met. She was also very intelligent, graduating with a First from Cambridge in History and Business Management. She could happily converse on a variety of topics, from the Shah of Iran, to chemistry. Often Oscar felt dim by comparison. He loved his wife, he truly did, but she was at the pinnacle of her career and everything she touched turned to gold, whereas he was treading water. Thinking like this made him hate himself. He didn't mean to be disloyal, and to make matters worse, Gaby never brought up her higher salary.

Parked outside the block of sandstone flats, Oscar locked

his BMW and focused on the task in hand. Properties in the West End virtually sold themselves. The Kilbrides had moved out two weeks before as they were relocating down south and BT, the employer, had put the flat in National's hands. As the University of Glasgow and the Western Infirmary were in the immediate vicinity, it stood to reason the property would sell quickly.

Oscar liked to arrive before the clients to make a few last-minute checks, ensure the property was warm enough, if the owners were no longer living there, or air the rooms if it were the height of summer. Entering the flats, he stopped on the second floor and opened the storm doors so the decorative inner door with its green and yellow leaves in stained glass could be seen as soon as viewers came upstairs. The entry hall was spacious and square, with feature cornicing and a high ceiling. The long galley kitchen with pearwood units was to the right. Cobalt mosaic tiles, granite worktops and brushed stainless-steel appliances added to the kitchen's attractiveness.

The vast lounge boasted large bay windows and the rose centrepiece complemented the cornice around the ceiling edges. The brand-new bathroom encompassed bidet, bath and shower. Oscar loved old houses, and they had so much more room in them, not like these poky little boxes developers tried to palm off nowadays at incredibly inflated prices.

The master bedroom was square and benefited from the same high ceilings as the other rooms. The second bedroom was also a generous size and had fitted wardrobes. The impression throughout was light and airy. The flat would go for well above the asking price of a hundred and seventy-five thousand pounds, despite current market conditions.

Oscar was mulling these thoughts over when the intercom buzzed.

'Hello?' he answered.

'Hi, it's Yvette and Iain Riordan.'

'C'mon up, second floor.'

Oscar went out to greet them. Rule number one – always enter a room after the client. It makes it look bigger.

Oscar introduced himself. He'd left the inner door closed to allow them to see the stained-glass window.

'Oh, that's beautiful,' said Yvette.

Oscar subtly stepped backwards into the tiny porch so the Riordans could appreciate the full size of the hall. His mobile vibrated in his pocket as it had been doing all day.

Oscar presented them each room, pointing out the various features and benefits. The Riordans cast appraising glances over each room.

'Does it have parking?' Yvette asked, and Oscar knew he had them hooked.

'Yes, two resident spaces.'

'Good. Will it be going to a closing date?'

'Yes. In the West End virtually everything goes to a closing date. It'll probably be about two weeks away.'

'So, have there already been offers?' Iain asked.

'Yes. We've just been trying to get a hold of the seller to set the details regarding the closing date. Anyway, I'll let you two have a look around on your own.'

Oscar stepped out into the hallway to listen to his voice messages, whilst the Riordans explored the flat.

'You have a new message,' his voicemail informed him. Oscar sighed.

'Message one, received Tuesday at 12.46 p.m. – "Oscar, it's Janine. BT has agreed the closing date of the twenty-second for Byres Road. Speak later.'"

Good. Something concrete to tell the Riordans.

'Message two, received Tuesday at 12.58 p.m. – "Oscar, it's Gaby. What time will you be home tonight? I might got to the gym. Call me back."'

'Message three, received Tuesday at 1.12 p.m. – "Oscar, it's Max. I need the projected figures for this month by Thursday."'

'Message four, received Tuesday at 1.17 p.m. – "Oscar, hi, it's Mari. Just to let you know the Armstrongs have signed."'

Oscar pocketed his mobile and strode back into the flat. 'So, what do you think?'

'We love it. We'll talk to our lawyer about putting in an offer.'

'Great. Also, I just picked up a voicemail saying the closing date is going to be the twenty-second.'

'OK,' Yvette said.

'Is there anything else you'd like to know?'

'No. I think that's it.' Yvette glanced around as if engraving the flat in her memory.

'Great. Here's my card. Let me know if you need anything.'

They thanked him and Oscar showed them out. As he closed the door, his mobile vibrated again. Janine.

'Hi. I got your message.'

'Good. Are you still in Byres Road?'

'Yes, why?'

'I've a lady who'd like to view it.'

'Can she come now?'

'Let me check.' Janine asked the client if she could go straight away.

'Yes, she's coming now.'

'Remind her it's second floor, right. I'll keep an eye out for her.'

Oscar washed his hands and ensured he was still presentable. It was amazing how dishevelled you became in this job, and presentation was everything. At thirty-seven, a good eight years older than his wife, he was still trim, but the overtime he put in didn't allow him to get to the gym as often as he'd like. He still had a full head of hair, even if it was more grey than brown these days. Oh well, it brought out the colour in his eyes, so Gaby told him. All in all, he wasn't in too bad shape, although the business lunches he took corporate clients to didn't help. He spent a lot of time entertaining corporate accounts. Sometimes it felt like whining and dining. At five feet ten, and thirteen and a half stone, he'd be happier if he could shed that additional stone. He checked his reflection in the mirror, adjusted his glasses and ensured he had nothing stuck between his teeth.

The second viewing completed, Oscar locked up the flat and set off for Pret à Manger to buy a much-needed chicken wrap. He had a meeting at three o'clock at the University of Glasgow with the head of relocation and the finance director. He was always on the run, but that was part of the fascination of his job.

'So, to summarise, I think over the two-year period we could save you ten to fifteen per cent,' Oscar said. If they weren't impressed by that, he didn't know what he'd do.

'Yes, that could be of interest to us,' the finance director eventually said. 'We will, however, have to discuss this with other colleagues.'

'Of course,' said Oscar. These guys were old school, stuffy and expected to be treated with respect. You couldn't enjoy a bit of light-hearted banter with them. He thanked them for their time.

After the meeting, he was exhausted, but had to go back to the office to talk over the forecasts with Mari.

'Hi, Mari. How's it been?'

'Usual. Too many punters in the branch, not enough staff, phone ringing off the hook. Did Janine tell you about the new signings?'

'She told me about one.'

'Well, we have the Armstrongs and then the Wildes who we spoke to last week, when they were originally thinking about letting. Four-bed detached with very large garden in North Kelvinside.'

'Oh good. That was quick. What changed their mind on letting?'

'They saw how much the property will probably sell for.'

'Ah, works every time. Listen, have you started work on next month's figures?'

'Yes. It looks like my department will be about ten per cent up on last month. The McDougall sale on the Newton Mearns property helped.'

At eight hundred thousand pounds, Oscar thought it probably had.

'Good, well you know how it goes. We keep slogging it out until the end, see what we can milk out of the cash cow. Dear God, sorry for sounding like Max!' Oscar ran his hands through his hair.

'Don't worry. We won't slack off, not yet, but if we get to the twenty-eighth and we've made target, I'm not going to push those last two days.'

'Let's see how it goes,' he said noncommittally. 'You going to be much longer?'

'No, I'm just finishing off.'

'OK. I need to go and work on those figures. See you in the morning.' Oscar went into his office and closed the door.

Oscar stretched. He had been poring over the figures for ages, but he thought he was finally getting somewhere. Another half an hour should do it. He glanced at his watch. Oh no, it was five past nine, Gaby would be cracking up. He dialled home.

'Gaby. Hi, I'm really sorry. I've just noticed the time. I'm still at the office, but I'm leaving now. I'll be home in twenty minutes. Have you eaten?'

She had. 'OK, well, I'll grab a Chinese on the way home. See you soon,' he rang off.

'Chicken breast curry, chopped, fried rice and prawn crackers, and can I have a wonton soup, as well, please?' Oscar looked out of place in the Chinese takeaway he'd stopped at. He'd been thinking about the stats and had driven straight past The Golden Fleece, his usual haunt. As he waited, he picked up a newspaper, rather than look into the eyes of the local teenagers. Some of them were rather menacing-looking, either punch drunk, or off their faces on drugs.

'Number sixty-seven,' the Chinese girl shouted.

'Right here.' Oscar exhaled gratefully. As he reached the car, he was relieved to see that it was still intact. He made a mental note not to go back to that particular takeaway.

Chapter Twenty-seven

'Hi.' Oscar planted a kiss on his wife's cheek. 'How was your day?' he asked, setting down his takeaway. He opened the fridge and poured himself a large glass of milk to accompany his meal.

'Do you want half of this, G?' he called through to his wife.

'No, but I would love some hot chocolate.'

'OK.'

Five minutes later he handed Gaby her drink and sat down with his plate on his lap. 'I'm starving.'

'I was too. I couldn't wait. I was at the gym for an hour and a half.'

'That's OK. I told you not to wait. You know how I lose track of time.'

'Yes, I know.' Something about his wife's tone wasn't right.

'You OK?' he asked her.

'Just tired.'

'Do you want a massage?'

'No, I'm going to bed soon. I'm heading down to London, remember. My flight leaves at half six, so I need to get up at half four.'

'I'm sorry, I forgot.' Oscar reached over and squeezed

his wife's leg. 'Are you back tomorrow night?'

'No. I'll be back about eight on Thursday.'

'I'll miss you,' Oscar said automatically.

'Me too,' said Gaby as they snuggled up on the sofa. 'I'm shattered. I'm going to head off to bed.'

'OK. Night.' Oscar kissed his wife on the lips as she moved off the sofa.

Gaby in bed, Oscar switched on the TV and watched *Newsnight*. He woke up with a groan around one thirty. Damn, he'd fallen asleep on the sofa. He went upstairs to join Gaby in bed for the three hours before she had to get up. Tiptoeing into the bedroom, he banged his foot against the wooden bedstead.

'Je-e-e-sus!' Oscar cursed under his breath then slipped off his clothes and sneaked into bed, but his swearing had woken Gaby.

'What time is it?'

'Half one. Go back to sleep.' Oscar cosied in against her. A few minutes later he was sound asleep.

Oscar woke at half six, patted the space beside him and then realised Gaby wasn't there. Damn, had she said goodbye and he'd been too sleepy to notice? He didn't think so. He padded downstairs to put the coffee machine on. On the fridge was a Post-it from Gaby: 'Didn't want to wake you. Wish you'd have the same consideration occasionally. I've tossed and turned all night. Gaby.'

Ouch! She wasn't happy with him. Gaby didn't sleep well. You couldn't have a job like hers without losing sleep. He'd make it up to her, buy her some lilies.

The traffic was abominable. An hour later, after sitting through twenty minutes of roadworks and waiting for the police to clear an accident, Oscar arrived at the office. *Thank goodness for Bluetooth.* He must have fielded about twenty calls already and his day hadn't officially begun. Janine was the only one there when he arrived. It was 8.04.

'Hi, Janine.'

'Morning.'

'Any coffee going?' Oscar gave Janine his best puppy-dog eyes.

'Yes. I just made some. Here's the mail.' She handed him a pile of letters.

'Thanks.' Oscar retreated into his office, sat down in his swivel chair and looked out the window at the bustling streets below. He opened his mail: a couple of invitations to events and some RSVPs Janine would have to answer. To maintain their profile, he attended all events they were invited to. Today he had a lunch with one of the newspapers. For once he wouldn't be paying the bill, as he was the client.

National had the biggest spread in the property section, about twenty per cent larger than their nearest competitor. It was therefore only fitting that their discount should be commensurate with the volume of business they put their way. He had a meeting with a developer at ten, who wanted to discuss an agreement for the hard-to-shift houses on their various developments. The credit crunch had hit the housebuilders particularly hard. After lunch, he had another meeting. Hopefully he'd be finished by five and could go to the gym. If he was lucky, he could do an hour there, have a twenty-minute swim and a sauna before it closed. That was his grand plan, but first he had to prepare for his conference call with Max.

Oscar looked through the commercial properties they'd brought on in the last week, collated the stats and called Max.

'Hi, Max, it's Oscar. How's tricks?'

'Great, thanks. You?'

'Good.' Max never really wanted to hear how you were. He wasn't interested in his staff and their personal problems, except when they spilled over into their work lives.

'So, do you have the numbers?'

Oscar rattled them off.

'Yes, well, that all sounds good, but how close are we to signing the agreement on the south-side hotel?'

'Tomorrow.'

'Make it happen, Oscar.'

'I will.'

'Hi, Oscar. How the hell are you?' Jim Rogers from the *Property* greeted him.

'Good thanks.' He'd known Jim for years. A waitress appeared with some menus.

'I love this restaurant. Small but perfectly formed.'

'I'll agree with that.'

They ate lunch, chatting about personal stuff, not yet touching on business. As the waitress brought their coffee, talk turned to the matter in hand. Jim was looking for more commitment from National and was hoping Oscar could put in a good word for them with Max.

'To be honest, Oscar, he's a bit of a hard man to get through to, your boss. He covers what, sixty branches, and for some reason, National in Edinburgh are doing an awful lot more business with the *Scotsman* than we're doing over here in Glasgow. Any idea why?'

Oscar shrugged. 'I don't know. Have you spoken to the branch managers?'

'Some of them, but I don't have the same rapport with them that I have with you.'

'I can only imagine he's been offered better rates, although last time they quoted me, it wasn't worth the hassle of changing.'

'Well, can you ask around?'

'Sure. Anyway, about *our* business. I'm giving you a heads up that when the stats are confirmed at month end, I'll probably be passing you more business, but, I'll be looking for a discount.'

'Sounds reasonable,' Jim said.

Jim settled the bill and they walked to Oscar's car. After Oscar dropped Jim at Kelvinhall Underground. He headed over to Cathcart for his afternoon appointment. The meeting was briefer than he'd expected, as the finance director wasn't available, called out of town at the last minute. *Nice of them to let me know*, Oscar thought, but actually it worked out better, as the second-in-command was much more accommodating. Oscar was happy at having achieved so much. Finished at a decent time for a change, he drove to the gym.

Done. Five miles. Oscar felt great, invigorated. What a pity he couldn't have more of a routine. His visits were sporadic because of his hours. He felt good about himself, alive, not mired in the drudgery of everyday life. Sweat glistened on his arms. He'd driven himself hard. He headed for the rowing machine, stopping only to grab a little polystyrene cone, fill it with water and take several gulps. Twenty minutes of rowing and his loose grey T-shirt was soaked through. Walking back towards the free weights area, he heard a voice call out, 'Oscar!'

He turned and saw his sometime acquaintance, Matt Foley, beaming at him.

'Good, Matt, you?'

'Yeah, can't complain. Still working at Endsleigh.'

'Right.'

'Listen, you doing anything later? A few of us are going to Quigley's for a pint.'

Oscar debated for a second and then thought, why the hell not? Gaby was in London. 'Yeah, sure. I'll meet you up there. I'm going to do some weights, then have a quick sauna.'

'Hey, you want me to spot you?'

'Yeah, that would be great.'

The two men then counted the reps the other was doing out loud. When they finished, Oscar said cheerio to Matt and went into the changing rooms to don a towel. He lay back on the wood, allowing the heat to relax him, taking away his post-workout aches and pains. He must have drifted off, as he woke with a start when the door opened.

'Evening.'

'All right?' Oscar replied, the limit to the most conversation men will make in a sauna with a guy they don't know. After a few minutes Oscar decided he'd had enough. Time for a well-deserved beer.

Chapter Twenty-eight

'Oscar! Over here!' Matt waved an arm at him, then held up his empty glass. 'Mine's a Stella.'

'A pint of lager shandy and a Stella, please,' he asked the barmaid.

'Coming right up.'

He thanked the girl and headed to where Matt was sitting, all the while trying not to get his drinks spilled by jostling arms.

'There you go. Anyone else want one?'

'No, you're all right,' chorused the others.

'Matt just drinks faster than an alcoholic at the top of his career,' piped up one. They all laughed.

'C'mon, Oscar, give us a song!' Matt slurred a few hours later.

'I don't know any.'

'Aye you do.'

'No, really, I don't.'

'What about Bryan Adams' "Summer of '69"?'

'That wasn't Bryan Adams.'

'Aye, it was.'

'No, it wasn't. It was Bruce Springsteen.'

'No, it was Bryan Adams.'

'It disnae matter who sang it, d'you know the words?'

'No.'

'Well, what do you know?'

'I know "Born in the USA".'

'Well, that *is* Bruce Springsteen.' So, after renewed calls for Oscar to sing, he gave his rendition of the hit. The others shrieked out the chorus. People at other tables turned to look their way, amusement written on the faces of some, disbelief on others.

'Matt, I'm pissed,' Oscar said, trying in vain to stop himself from stumbling, as they walked along the road, trying to flag down a bus.

'Ah know, me too,' Matt said cheerily. They'd been the last to leave. There was no question of their driving. Oscar hoped he remembered in the morning that his car was parked on the bridge behind the pub. Otherwise, its absence could come as a shock.

'Where's the nearest chippy? I'm starving.'

'There's one in Byres Road,' Oscar said, 'Beppe's.'

'That'll do.'

They criss-crossed the street, from Dumbarton Road to Byres Road and meandered along, supporting each other as they went. They couldn't stop laughing.

'You'd think we'd been smoking hash, wouldn't you?'

Oscar could barely contain himself. 'I know *and* I've got the munchies.'

'That always happens to me when I've been drinking.'

'Maybe eating before drinking would be a good idea.'

'Yes, that sounds like good advice,' Matt said, solemnly saluting Oscar and almost falling over a bin in the process.

'Who put that bin there? What about a poem? Ode to a

bin? Do you know any poetry?'

'Do I stuff!' Oscar was indignant.

'Women love it. You can't beat a bit of Keats.' And Matt proceeded to saunter up Byres Road, reciting Keats at full volume. He then launched into Rabbie Burns' 'To a Mouse' until they reached Beppe's fish and chip bar and dissolved into a fit of the giggles again.

'Right, what you having?' Beppe's Italian accent was quite pronounced, even after many years in Glasgow.

'Two fish suppers.'

'They'll be another five minutes,' Beppe said as he went to prepare them.

'We'll jus' sit here and admire the view.' And with that they were off again, as they looked out upon the now quiet street, empty apart from an old tramp, walking along, talking to himself.

'That'll be us one day,' Matt said.

'Oh the things we aspire to,' Oscar said.

'Taxi!' Matt walked out in front of the taxi, waving his arms to make it stop, forgetting he was still holding on to his fish supper. Chips and a piece of fish flew out of the paper.

'Damn, I've lost half my dinner.'

They got in and the taxi driver, who turned out to be Lithuanian, said, 'You can't eat in here.'

'We'll be really careful,' said Matt.

'Close it or I not take you. You make me have to clean car again.'

'OK, OK.' Matt scowled and wrapped his fish 'n' chips up, cupping his hands round what was left of them.

The idea was to drop Oscar off and then Matt, since Matt lived in the city centre.

'Oscar, I could go a drink. Have you any whisky in the house? I fancy a nice wee Lagavulin.' Oscar knew he had plenty, as they entertained occasionally.

'I'm sure there'll be something.'

'Keep the change,' Oscar said to the driver, as Matt fell out of the cab.

Oscar turned on the lights, but found them too bright. Turning them off and walking further into the house, he reached the living room and clapped his hands twice. The two standard lamps came on.

'Oh, I like that,' said Matt. 'Very classy. Right, where's the drink?'

'I'll get it.' Oscar headed through to the dining room, where the drinks cabinet was inlaid into the coffee table. It was really neat, hidden from view and a real space saver. He raised the lid and pulled out a few bottles. There was no Lagavulin, but there was a Bunnahabhain. He didn't think Matt would complain.

'Oh, now you're talking,' said Matt, taking the glass from Oscar's outstretched hand. He'd found the remote and put on the TV.

'I love basketball. American sports are so much more exciting, don't you think? They take themselves so seriously.'

There then followed a question-and-answer session regarding all manner of sports ranging from darts to ice hockey, snooker to potholing.

'OK. Who won the 1999 Davis Cup?' Matt asked.

'Oh, that's easy. Australia.'

'Yeah, I knew that too. Next. Who are the only women to have ever won the Grand Slam?'

Oscar liked tennis and had religiously watched Wimbledon since boyhood. He knew Steffi Graf had won Wimbledon in 1988 and he was sure only one other woman had won all four major tournaments in the same year, but what was her name? Damn!

'Have to hurry you,' Matt said annoyingly, toying with his remaining chips.

'I know this. Her name was Connolly, Marjorie, Miriam, no, no, Maureen Connolly. In the fifties.'

'Well done. Which year?'

'Dunno. Fifty-four, fifty-five?'

'Nearly. Fifty-three. So, only one woman has won it?'

'No. Two. Steffi Graf in eighty-eight.'

'Correct.'

Matt's tone meant there was at least one other. Oscar racked his brain, nope; no one came to mind. Sixties, nope, seventies, didn't think so, eighties, no way, nineties definitely not, all the way up to present day, no.

'In the seventies?'

'What year?'

'I don't know,' Oscar spat out, exasperated. 'But it *is* the seventies?'

'Yip.'

'Gimme a clue.'

'It's a big clue, but the only one I can think of,' said Matt. 'Her surname was double barrelled.'

'Oh, oh, I know this. Margaret, damn, it was early seventies.'

Matt nodded vigorously.

'Nope. It's not coming to me. Oh! Court something.'

'Nearly,' Matt said, 'but it's something Court, not Court something.'

Realisation dawned and Oscar jumped up, whisky spilling over the edge of his glass. 'Margaret Smith Court!'

'Correct!'

'OK, my turn.' Oscar started once he'd sat down again. 'Who won the Monaco Grand Prix in 1977?'

'Jeez, you're going back a bit. I like Formula One, but it's not something I'm up on.'

'Too bad. Anyway, you chose the seventies for the last question, so it's your own fault.'

'Was it us?'

'What do you mean?'

'Was it a British team that won?'

'I'm thinking driver, not team,' Oscar clarified.

'OK, was he English?'

'No, but he spoke English.'

'Well or badly?'

'Native tongue.'

'Oh, oh, that South African dude, Jamie…'

'No.'

'No, not Jamie, Jody, Jody Scheckter,' Matt announced, pumping his fist in triumph.

'Might've been,' replied Oscar.

'It was. He won it the year after Niki Lauda.'

'Yes, you're right, but did you know that Niki won it the year before that too?'

'Yup.'

They covered more sports than Oscar was even aware he knew of. Whisky glasses were filled and refilled, until Oscar woke up, glass in hand, lying on some scatter cushions. They were a tad wet from the whisky which had sloshed out of his glass. The display on the DVD player seemed to be mocking him in its brightness. He didn't feel too bright himself. As he heaved himself up, he almost fell over the prone form of Matt, who was lying arms out as if making a snow angel, snoring his head off. The room stank of stale booze. It was half past five. Oscar had to go to work in under two hours. What to do with Matt?

Deciding to forget about Matt temporarily, Oscar shuffled into the en suite. He turned on the power shower and searched for a fluffy bath sheet to dry himself when he got back out, if he ever got back out.

Oscar tried to bring himself back to life. Now he re-membered why he didn't do alcohol. He couldn't handle it. He flew out of the shower cubicle and hurled down the toilet pan. Sinking to his knees, he threw up, again and again, until nothing remained of last night's greasy fish supper. He felt like shit. Back in the shower, he tried to put his brain into work mode, but it wouldn't go. It was melted. His tongue felt like pond algae. He wanted to brush his teeth, but felt so nauseous, he honestly thought he'd throw up again.

After about half an hour, he decided he had to get out of the shower. He stumbled around the bedroom, really having to concentrate to remember what he was doing. Why was he in his sock drawer? He already had socks on. Oh, he meant to go into the wardrobe to look for a tie. He put back the T-shirt that he had pulled out.

It was a good while before he felt presentable. On the way back to the lounge, he fell over one of Matt's shoes. How on earth did it get into the hall? Then he remembered they had been bowling with shoes and empty beer cans. They only had eight pins though, as they had mainly drunk whisky, but that hadn't ruined their enjoyment. He looked around the detritus in the living room and at Matt, who hadn't moved a muscle. He left him a note and a spare key, saying, 'Matt, pls put through letterbox when you leave. I've got to get to work. Feel free to have a shower and some brekky. Good catching up. Oscar.'

With any luck the walk to the office would wake him up.

Chapter Twenty-nine

Fortunately, the morning sped past. Oscar's team sensed he needed time to himself. He was just starting to return to some sort of normality around lunchtime, when his mobile rang. Gaby.

'Hi, honey. How are you?'

'Don't you hi honey me! What the fuck is going on?'

'What do you mean?' Oscar asked.

'I come home early…'

Oscar didn't hear the end of the sentence. He knew this couldn't be good. The lounge was a mess. He hadn't cleared up, because Matt was still asleep.

'I can explain.'

'Explain! Explain why there's some guy I've never met in my shower?'

Ah. Timing wasn't the best for the shower, Matt. 'That was Matt.'

'Matt who? What the fuck is he doing in my shower?'

'He's a mate. I hadn't seen him for ages–'

Gaby didn't let him finish. 'So, you haven't seen him for ages and I find him in our shower! Oh, and since I thought it was you, I opened the cubicle to surprise you. Instead, some other guy's tadger was looking out at me. And for the record,' Gaby yelled, 'it was far bigger than yours.'

Ouch! Take that one on the chin, Oscar, she's just angry.

'I wasn't expecting you back early,' came his lame response.

'So when the cat's away, the mouse will play, is that it?'

'We just had a few beers.'

'Eight to be precise and a full bottle of whisky.'

'Well now, that's not fair, Gaby, there *was* a little out of it already.'

'I don't *care*,' she roared. 'And you left this guy in our house? Someone you haven't seen for ages? He could have robbed the place.'

'He wouldn't do that.'

'You let me walk in on a complete stranger, in my own bloody shower, in my own damned house!'

'Well, yes, now you put it like that, I can understand why you are upset.'

'*Understand* why I'm upset? You had better believe I'm upset. The whole house stinks of stale alcohol and sweaty men. Is there something you want to tell me?'

'Like what?'

'Are you gay?'

'Am I what?' Oscar spluttered.

'Gay, you know, homosexual, batting for the other side, lover of men,' Gaby continued.

'*No, no, no and no!* Are you crazy?' Too late, Oscar realised he shouldn't have said crazy.

'Crazy? Yes, that's me, crazy bitch. I'm not the one who gives our spare key to a total stranger. Anyway, I might be mad, in fact you can bet I'm mad, but I'm not crazy.'

She was sounding crazier with every passing second, Oscar thought.

'I'm sorry. I didn't mean to embarrass you.'

'Sorry is not going to cut it, Oscar. I am sick of this. You don't spend any time with me, but you can go out and get hammered the second I am away. You don't take time off your precious work for me.'

'I didn't take time off work. I met Matt at the gym and then we went for a few beers and…'

'*I don't care.*'

She was being irrational now. Here was he, trying to make amends and he still couldn't see what was so bad. If she actually stopped and thought about it, her walking in on a total stranger in the shower was really very funny. In the past she would have thought that was hysterical. He didn't know what to say, so he let the silence hang between them whilst he thought of something intelligent or Gaby hit him with another tirade. Nothing. Then she slammed the phone down. Not good. Oscar called Gaby's number. Voicemail. He tried again, voicemail. On the third attempt, he left a message.

'Gaby. I'm sorry. I screwed up. I should have made Matt leave this morning, or better still left him at the pub. I'll be back early to clean up the mess.'

But he wasn't really sure what he was apologising for. He was sorry she'd found Matt in their shower in a compromising position, but not for going out. He had to let his hair down every so often, and it's not as if he was away shagging someone. He'd make it up to her. Flowers or a nice gift, but what? She had everything already. He'd get her a takeaway from Thai Garden. That was her favourite takeaway place. Pity he couldn't cook; that would have worked wonders.

He'd best crack on. Luckily he had no more meetings,

just prep for tomorrow's sales meeting. Boss man was coming up to flex some muscle. He'd work like a fiend, finish on time and then nip to the supermarket on the way home. He wondered if they sold lilies. They wouldn't do gifts though, unless he was going to buy her a CD or a book. What was he thinking? The grovelling required in this instance needed more than a ten-pound gift. Would Next deliver to the office, he wondered. He had to get these reports finalised. What to do, what to do? Alison. Maybe his sister could help? She would probably be far too busy, but he had to try.

'Ali? It's me. Where are you?'

'Hi, hon. How you? I'm in Glasgow. Why?'

'In town? Oh, thank God. I need a favour.'

Five o'clock came and Oscar shot out the door as if pursued by a Rottweiler. Alison had dropped off a beautiful chiffon top and complementing ruffle skirt, which he was sure Gaby would like and hoped would appease her. It was exactly the kind of luxurious material she loved. It wasn't quite Nicole Farhi, but he knew Gaby would appreciate it. It did, however, depend on whether or not she had forgiven him. He called her from the supermarket car park.

'What do you want?' she snapped.

'To talk to my wife. What have you done with her, you grumpster?' Oscar tried jovial and cheeky.

'Oscar, I'm not in the mood. I am still pissed off at you.'

'I know and I am sorry. Can I make it up to you?'

'That depends,' Gaby said.

'On what?'

'Well, it's going to cost you.' Gaby was smiling now.

He could hear it in her voice.

'A lot?'

'Yes.'

'Well, I'm passing Thai Garden and was going to treat us.'

'What?'

'It's a surprise. You like surprises, don't you?' he teased, knowing she loved them, or scratch that, she liked *nice* surprises, not nasty surprises, like finding strangers in her shower, starkers.

'OK, but that's not the end of it.'

'Great, see you shortly.'

Oscar was right on time. He was hardly ever home when he said he would be these days. Work was taking over. He searched for his keys. He didn't want to ring the bell in case Gaby was relaxing and he disturbed her, altering her earlier peaceable mood. Or better still, perhaps she was luxuriating in a bath of aromatic oils and was intending to make an effort tonight too, like they used to. Oscar grinned. Who knows where it could lead? The house was eerily quiet.

'Gaby,' he called. No answer. He was a little worried now. Had she gone out? Was this her idea of punishment? 'Gaby?' He dumped the bags on the marble worktop and moved from room to room. She wasn't downstairs, so he searched upstairs. She wasn't in the bath, more's the pity. He checked in their bedroom, but drew a blank. Bewildered, he called again. 'Gaby! Are you in?'

A slight sound came from the bedroom. Oscar walked back in. He heard a muffled sound again. The door to the en suite was closed. 'Gaby, are you in the toilet?'

'Yes,' came a small voice. 'I'll just be a minute.'

'Why didn't you answer me before?'

'I didn't hear you.'

'You didn't hear me? I've been shouting half the house…' Oscar caught himself. It wouldn't do to antagonise his wife, not when he was looking for forgiveness.

'Are you OK? You're not ill, are you?'

'No, I'm fine. I'll be out in a sec.'

'OK.'

It was a full ten minutes before his wife appeared in the kitchen. She looked as if she'd been crying.

'You OK?' Oscar put a reassuring arm around her shoulder and pulled her to him. 'I *am* sorry, you know. It won't happen again.'

'I'm fine. I just have a bit of a migraine coming on.'

'Oh no, that's awful. You haven't had one for ages.'

'I know. I think I'm just a bit stressed.'

'Come here.' Oscar drew her to him again. 'Let me look after you tonight. Plus, I have a surprise for you. Maybe this will cheer you up. Ta da!' He pulled out the gift bag.

'What is it?'

'It's a gift for my beautiful wife, to apologise for being a drunken prat and leaving his drunken mate in our shower. Not that I actually left him in the shower, you understand,' Oscar clarified. 'More like on the living room floor. Nope, that still doesn't sound good, does it?'

Gaby smiled. She opened the gift bag and pulled out its contents. Her face lit up. 'Oscar, it's beautiful,' she gasped.

'There's another thing in the bag,' Oscar said.

'Good. I deserve them.' Gaby shot him a look, but it was one of affection. *Good-going, the outfit did the trick. I must remember to buy Alison lunch.*

'Well, do I get a kiss?' Oscar feigned hurt.

'Of course.'

'Are you going to just stand there holding them, or are you going to put them on?'

'I might have to find something to go underneath,' Gaby murmured.

'Oh, I like that idea,' Oscar said. 'On you go. I'll put the food out.'

'OK.'

Oscar chuckled to himself as Gaby went upstairs. Worked like a charm. Now all he had to do was whet her appetite with the feast he'd picked up at Thai Garden.

'That was delicious,' Gaby said, setting her cutlery in the middle of her plate. 'I am absolutely stuffed.'

'I could make a joke there, but I'll wait until later.'

'Ha ha. You'll get your chance, but you'll have to wait. I can't move an inch.'

'You haven't drunk much tonight. Are you sure you're OK?'

'Would I have been able to eat all that if I wasn't?'

'Fair point. Do you want coffee?'

'Only if it's not instant.'

'I'll make up a cafetiere. The night is young.' He winked at his wife.

Oscar returned with two coffee mugs, sugar and milk on a tray and a steaming cafetiere of Brazilian roast, only to find his wife absent. Where was she now? She was always disappearing. Sitting down, he picked up a magazine. He didn't want to switch on the TV, as that would spoil the mood, but he was getting restless doing nothing. He didn't really do relaxing. Idly he leafed through the F1 magazine. He hadn't realised how engrossed he'd become in it, until he noticed he'd read ten pages. Where was Gaby?

'Gaby? Are you OK?'

Standing outside the bathroom door, he could hear retching.

'Gaby, open the door.'

'I'm fine,' said an obviously not fine Gaby.

'Have you been sick?'

Silence, then, 'Yes.'

'Oh shit, do you think it was the prawns?' Oscar dreaded to think that his fine idea of putting things right with his wife had ended up giving her food poisoning.

Oscar put Gaby to bed. She looked green. He brought her some water and propped up her pillows.

'Just you relax. Are you up to reading?'

'I think I'll go to sleep. I'm sorry I spoiled such a lovely evening. Thanks for making the effort.'

'No problem. Get some rest.'

Chapter Thirty

Where did the time go? It was weeks since Oscar and Gaby had spent some proper time together. It had been all meetings, viewings, and yet more meetings about meetings. He was so sick of it. More and more he wanted to start out on his own. Perhaps he'd run it past Gaby tonight. The clock showed seven o'clock. He really must head home now and see if Gaby was still up. She'd been in bed so early the last few weeks.

'Gaby!' Oscar called. Surely she wasn't in bed already, it was only seven thirty. No note. Strange. He checked throughout the house, but couldn't find any sign of her. Where was she? Anyway, now he was home, he'd have a cup of tea and forage in the fridge, see if there was anything tasty. He idly flicked through the TV channels, until he came to *Top Gear*. That'll do. He ventured into the kitchen to see what delights the Smeg held. The answer was nothing much. He'd certainly had no time to shop recently. Maybe he could make scrambled eggs, if the eggs were still in date. He wasn't sure he was hungry enough to find out. A couple of wrinkled tomatoes were holding the fort in the vegetable tray. Finding a lump of cheese, he decided to have cheese on toast.

He was just popping the bread into the toaster, when he was startled by a pounding on the front door. What the hell? Bang, bang, bang. Bang, bang, bang, it went a second time, before he made it to the door. Bang… Oscar threw the door open.

'What the bloody hell…?' He stopped in his tracks. A woman stood before him, her hair wild, her face swollen and tear-stained with mascara running in rivulets down her cheeks. Between sobs, she managed to get out the words, 'Are you Oscar?'

'Yes, I'm Oscar. Who are you?'

'I'm Angela.'

'OK, what can I do for you?'

'I'm Kieran's wife.'

'Who's Kieran?' Oscar was beginning to feel a mixture of annoyance and confusion.

'Kieran's the father of your wife's baby,' Angela blurted out.

'The what? My wife doesn't have a baby.'

'Not yet she doesn't.'

Oscar decided that absurd though this conversation was, he didn't want anyone overhearing the craziness coming out of this woman's mouth.

'Look, why don't you come in and we can talk?'

'Thanks,' Angela mumbled.

'Why don't we calm things down a bit?' Oscar said. 'There's obviously been a mix-up, mistaken identity or something. My wife's not pregnant and she's not seeing anyone else.'

'Are you sure about that?'

'Yes, a hundred per cent.'

'So, where is she now?'

'I-I don't know,' admitted Oscar. 'I just got in from work.'

'So you don't think she's with my husband?'

'Absolutely not. Why would you think that?'

'Because your wife and my husband have been sleeping together for months.'

'It's not possible. We don't have any problems.'

'That doesn't always matter,' Angela said wryly. 'Believe me, I thought we had the perfect marriage, until Kieran started crying tonight, told me he's leaving me and that he's got someone else pregnant.'

'But where does my wife fit into all this?'

'Gaby, isn't it? How would I have known your name was Oscar?'

'I don't know. Any number of ways, I suppose,' Oscar said, although he was fast realising that would have meant a whole lot of coincidences and he didn't really believe anything that was too far-fetched.

'Tell me from the beginning so we can iron out this misunderstanding.'

'There is no misunderstanding,' Angela howled in despair. 'Your wife has been shagging my husband and now she's pregnant.'

'There must be some mistake.'

'Does this look familiar?' Angela dropped something into his upturned palm. Oscar couldn't believe it. It was one of the gold teardrop earrings he had bought Gaby for their anniversary. There had to be some explanation.

'My husband and your wife have been having an affair and neither of us knew. Can you believe that?'

Oscar was fast beginning to wake up to the severity of

Angela's accusations.

'And what's worse is I've always wanted kids and he never did, and now I'm never going to have them.' Angela started crying, gut-wrenching sobs from deep inside. Oscar could empathise; he felt as if someone had delved right inside his soul and ripped it out. His wife had been unfaithful to him. His Gaby. *Not* his Gaby. Someone else's mistress. Not only had she cheated on him, she was going to have someone else's baby. Oscar knew how Angela felt, because he was in the same position. He had always wanted kids and because of Gaby's career, there had been no real hope of that anytime soon. Now she would have someone else's child. He started piecing things together. That's why she wasn't drinking. Now he came to think of it, he hadn't seen her touch alcohol in weeks. Maybe that's why she was always in bed so early. That's why she'd been locked in the en suite that day, vomiting. She had morning sickness! Oh my God. It was true. It all made sense.

He stood up abruptly. 'I need a drink. Want one?'

Angela stopped crying long enough to say, 'Yes, please.'

Oscar returned with two large glasses of malt.

'I was keeping this for a special occasion, perhaps the wetting of my firstborn's head, but it doesn't look like that's going to happen now. I suppose this *is* a special occasion, just not the sort I'd hoped for.'

He looked at Angela, who was drying her eyes, and held up his glass. She gave him a puzzled look to start with and then the ghost of a smile escaped her lips. 'Cheers,' she said, and they clinked glasses.

Over the next half hour, Angela told Oscar the whole sorry tale. Kieran had packed his bags earlier that evening. Oscar wanted to know if he and Gaby planned to run away together. His wife hadn't returned home, her mobile was off and his wife's lover's wife had turned up on his doorstep. Angela didn't know. Kieran hadn't clarified if he and Gaby were going to make a go of it. She still loved him, she told Oscar drunkenly, after the third large Glenfiddich.

'Would you take him back?'

'In a heartbeat,' she said, then burst into tears again. 'I'm pathetic I know, but I love him.'

'But how could you trust him again? I love Gaby, but I can't forgive what she's done. She's going to have his child! They've taken from us what we've always wanted – a family. And the worst of it is, they probably don't care or even realise the damage they've done. It's not just the being unfaithful, it's the loss of our being able to be parents anytime soon. Even imagining we do meet Mr and Mrs Right in a few years' time, we'll be in our forties. How old are you? Sorry, I shouldn't assume.'

'Thirty-six.'

'See. During the time it takes you to meet someone else, the old clock will have been ticking away, and of course you need to find someone who actually *wants* kids, live with them for a while, see if that works out, then buy a house, decide if you're compatible and then eventually figure out if you can have kids together.'

'Not always. Look at those two.'

'True. Selfish bastards.'

As the clock hands spun, Angela studied her empty glass. 'I think we've run out of whisky.'

'Never mind. I think we have some vodka somewhere.'

'Don't put too much tonic in it.'

They sat, rehashing the good times and the bad, the latter being the occasions when they now assumed their other halves had been together.

'I just don't understand. If they weren't happy, why not tell us and make a clean break?' Oscar sighed.

'That'll be Kieran's fault. It's a man thing. They never commit to leaving someone, until they're certain the new one is the right one. It's an unwritten rule. Men don't want to be on their own, no matter how much they might sometimes think they do.' She was slurring her words and her half-full glass was swishing around, a few droplets landing on the carpet.

'Really?' Oscar mulled this over. 'I hadn't realised we did that.'

'Oh yes, anyone will tell you. I've seen it happen to so many of my friends.' Her lip trembled and she gulped as if she had a tennis ball stuck in her throat. 'And now it has happened to me.' She burst into noisy sobs again as the tears ran unchecked down her cheeks. Eventually she tried to wipe them away, but continued to howl like an injured animal.

Oscar didn't know what to do. He wasn't used to being in this situation. He felt uncomfortable, but then, when she didn't stop, he patted her back. As soon as he made contact with her, Angela completely broke down again, releasing all her frustration. It seemed the most natural thing in the world to put his other arm around her back as she cried on his shoulder. They sat there like that for a few minutes, whilst Angela unloaded all of her grief, Oscar holding her.

Finally, her sobs stopped and she glanced up at Oscar and shot him a small smile of gratitude. Later, he would ask himself what had possessed him, but she looked so small, so vulnerable and so pathetic, it had felt natural for him to help heal another soul. He kissed her. Shocked, he drew back. Angela's eyes were wide, staring up at him, as if searching for a reaction in his. Whilst he was still unsure as to what it all meant, she moved towards him, possibly too fuelled by alcohol to care. She kissed Oscar, but this time they didn't draw apart. Their kisses deepened. Their breath grew ragged. They panted, perhaps with the enormity of what they were about to do. Oscar's hands slid underneath her blouse. Angela shuddered. She stroked the contours of his back. They tumbled to the floor and then they were pulling frantically at each other's clothes, as if everything had been leading up to this moment.

They had sex fast and furiously on the shagpile. How appropriate. They sat up, and Angela, shy now, tried to cover herself with her top, which Oscar thought was adorable. They shuffled together and Oscar let her lean her head on his shoulder whilst they relaxed. They sat in silence for a few minutes. Then Angela said, 'What do you…?' She froze. A car door had just slammed outside.

Chapter Thirty-one
Lucy – GEMINI

Quick-witted, changeable, talkative and versatile, sometimes crafty and mischievous. Highly developed intellects and place greater value on learning than emotional or practical issues. They get bored easily and quickly want to move on to the next challenge and can often seem shallow or fickle.

'Oh bugger, bugger, bugger,' Lucy ranted. She was just stepping into her ice-blue Audi TT, when she snagged her stockings on the sill. She didn't have time to go back upstairs and change. Scowling, she slammed the car door shut. She'd have to change her stockings when she got to the airport. Her flight to Heathrow was due to leave in an hour.

Once the plane had taken off, Lucy picked up the sheaf of papers she had taken out to peruse during the flight, in preparation for her upcoming talk and began to read, 'Myocardial Viability post PCI'.

Lucy had studied and spent her junior years between the University of Glasgow and Glasgow Royal Infirmary, before moving on to do her SHO elsewhere. Returning to the university in her early thirties to do research, she had subsequently remained. She was good, no, great at what she did. Highly competitive, she sold herself well. It was difficult as a woman to become top in her field, but that was her objective. When her professor retired some time from now, she wanted his job, and travelling the world showcasing her skills as an eminent cardiologist added more strings to her bow.

On the ground at Zurich, an hour later than expected, due to the delay of her interconnecting flight, Lucy waited in baggage claim, checking her emails. She had a meeting at four o'clock. It was already three and her bag hadn't yet trundled off the carousel. As the last passengers moved away, dragging their case behind them, Lucy resisted the urge to stamp her foot in frustration.

Lucy's colleague, Lukas Bäcker, who worked in the cardiology department at the University of Zurich, had offered to pick her up. Lucy had told him it wasn't necessary but he had insisted.

'Lukas! How nice to see you.' Lucy offered her cheek for the obligatory three kisses. She had called to advise him she was running late.

'Lucy, my dear.' Lukas kissed her and took her case. 'How have you been?'

'Good, thanks. You?'

'It's going well.'

They chatted throughout the journey to the hotel. When they arrived, the porter took her luggage and after she had checked in, Lukas said, 'Would you like an aperitif?'

'Sure.'

'Fendant OK?'

Lucy smiled and nodded.

Lukas placed his order with a passing waiter and then returned his attention to Lucy.

'Right, about this paper...'

They had known each other since university when he had been on exchange for a year. He was one of the few people of her own age in a similar role to her. They had never been romantically linked, which was probably why they were still friends. He resembled Carl a little, with his very fine, sandy hair and wide-set, piercing blue eyes, and like Carl he had something special about him, but he was slimmer and taller than Carl. Even though they didn't see each other from one year to the next, they knew they could call if they were coming to town and spend some time together, without any awkwardness.

They whiled away a pleasant couple of hours, catching up on each other's lives.

'Oh, did I tell you? I've actually extended my stay by a few days. I'm going to Saas Fee,' Lucy said.

'No, you didn't. You're very lucky. The Valais region is one of the areas where you are virtually guaranteed snow.'

Lucy was an excellent skier but she hadn't been to Saas Fee before and wanted to pick Lukas' brains. 'Have you been?'

'Yes, many times,' he said. 'My family has a lodge there. Where are you staying?'

'Some spa place a friend recommended. Schweizerhof?'

'It has a very good reputation. It is quite remote and has an amazing view of the glaciers.'

'Yes, that sounds like it.'

Now that she'd had a few glasses of sparkling Fendant,

she was mellowing. The refreshing white wine was just what she needed. She was trying to get into the spirit of her holiday in advance. After two or three days in Valais, perhaps she'd go to Tuscany to surprise Holly. Meanwhile, she still had her lecture to get through tomorrow. Oh well, it was only an hour and a half. Then she'd listen to a few talks and leave for Lucerne. She had always wanted to go there. She'd never holidayed in Switzerland before, although she'd been to Geneva and Zurich many times. Having skied in Austria, in Zell am See and Kitzbuhel, she expected Switzerland would be similar: snow-capped peaks, blazing sunshine and pristine villages with immaculately kept ski lodges, as well as some pretty impressive après-ski action.

She decided to call it a night and Lukas accompanied her to the lift.

'Fifth floor,' she said, when his finger hovered over the buttons.

'Breakfast at seven thirty?' he asked.

'Sounds good.'

Lucy stood, calm and poised behind the lectern. She watched as around two hundred of her peers filed into the theatre to listen to her present the results of her research into Myocardial Viability post PCI. Inserting her flash drive, she booted up PowerPoint. When the buzz died down, she began.

The presentation took a little longer than expected as she had been asked plenty of questions, which she took to be a sign the delegates had been interested. She stayed for a paper by a friend of Lukas' on angiography, but when the conference drew to a close, she made a quick exit to beat the traffic.

It took Lucy just over an hour to reach Lucerne, as the roads were surprisingly quiet. A friend had recommended she stay at the Art Deco Hotel Montana. Online, it had seemed very pretty with a fabulous view of the lake. Positioned at the top of a hill, its bright yellow façade with the Swiss flag flying above and 'MONTANA' emblazoned in large white letters struck the right chord with her and she knew she would like it. After quickly changing, she dumped her bags and went out to explore.

Lucy headed down the steep slope beside the hotel, noting the immaculate gardens and spotless pavements. The view from her balcony had been better than expected. It was idyllic, very romantic. With an uncharacteristic burst of affection, she wished Carl were here. Unfortunately, her boyfriend was becoming incredibly boring about his restaurant, bleating on about it constantly. She wondered what he would do once his fantasy was complete. Initially, he had seduced her with his cooking, but their relationship was stagnating. They didn't do anything together any more. He was always at his damned restaurant.

As she strolled down the hill, she took in the other buildings and the people around her. She turned right onto Carl Spiegler Quay and meandered along towards the station. It was quite large, home to several good restaurants.

She wandered down towards the older part of town, crossing the Spreuerbrucke, a rather odd-looking zigzag bridge, which turned at right angles halfway across. It was so clean and fresh in Lucerne. The air, even though it was early summer, felt empty of pollutants. It was bliss to kick back for a while. She took in the paintings dotted along the inside of the bridge one called *The Dance of Death,* particularly caught her attention, with its skeletons and Grim Reaper. Dozens of them adorned the inside and it almost looked like the skeletons were inviting her to dance with them. *There's my culture injection for the day.*

Lucy sauntered off the other end of the bridge and headed down Pfistergasse. A smiling waiter greeted her at the second place she came to. She ordered the local beer then settled back to admire the view. She liked to listen in to others' conversations when she was on her own. A pity she understood practically nothing.

Just as the waiter was bringing her Eichhof beer, she heard a man speaking in heavily accented English. She resisted the temptation to turn around. His voice was soft, despite his stilted intonation. He sat down at the table to her right. At just short of six feet, light brown hair, slim built but with definition to his shoulders and upper body, from what she could make out over his suit, he had caught her interest.

Lucy knew she cut a striking figure, tall, slim, with her natural blonde, almost white, poker-straight hair, she looked like she should be strutting her stuff on the catwalk.

She concentrated on her body language; all it took was the right signals, the look held a fraction of a second too long and he'd be putty in her hands. She wasn't wrong. He had just put his mobile into his jacket, when he noticed her. After a moment's hesitation, he approached her.

'Excuse me, do you speak English?'

'Yes,' she replied.

'Do you have fire?'

'Fire?'

'For smoking.'

'Ah, you mean a light?'

'Yes, sorry, light, fire, I get them confused. It is the same word in French.'

Ah, so he's French.

'I'm sorry, I don't smoke.'

He grinned at her and said, 'Nor do I. Would you mind if I joined you?' She liked his style so indicated the chair opposite her.

His name was Marc. At twenty-nine, he was quite a bit younger than Lucy, but that didn't bother her. Marc continued to talk about himself. Although he was gorgeous, she wasn't interested in the minutiae of his life. He was a salesman, in town to meet some clients. He was leaving tomorrow, as was she. They had dinner. She chose a light salad and a seafood gratin. Sex was on the cards. The indicators were there. She'd touched his arm once or twice when they were laughing and making jokes. He'd stroked her fingers, when his hand happened to rest on the table, touching her own.

When the waiter asked if they would like dessert, Marc said, 'Perhaps later,' as he looked her in the eye and asked for the bill. When the waiter had left, he murmured, 'Would you like to come back to my hotel?'

'Do I get dessert?' asked Lucy.

His lips turned up at the corners. 'Oh, most definitely.'

Chapter Thirty-two

Breakfast at the Montana was a grand affair. Lucy helped herself to turkey breast, ham and Swiss cheese. Supplementing that with freshly baked bread and some watermelon, and after her regulation two cups of coffee, she felt ready to leave for Saas Fee. She decided to call Carl en route. Unsurprisingly, she hadn't called him last night. She had crept out of Marc's hotel at two, no note, no guilt.

Happy and sated, she set off on her excursion through the Alps. Saas Fee was south of Lucerne, heading towards the Matterhorn. Although the majority of her journey was spent on the motorways, she was still able to take in the beauty of the rivers, lakes and mountains. Window down, letting the breeze drift in, as she cruised along, she let the tranquillity wash over her.

Lucy reached Valais, passing through the municipality of Stalden and the villages of Zen Eisten and Saas Grund, before finally taking her first glimpse of Saas Fee. It stood proudly two thousand four hundred metres above sea level. There was a whole host of mountains she could ski down. She didn't think she'd been anywhere before where she had so much choice. The main place for après-ski was Mekka Allalin, next to Mount Allalin. Although she had a good level of overall fitness, it had been almost a year and a half since she had skied and she harboured some concerns that she might not be fit enough. But she was determined to give it a go.

As she drove into the village, she saw the signs for the central car park. Saas Fee was car free. You had to either reach the hotel by electro-taxi or have your luggage transported by handcart, which the hotel provided. This was the option she had chosen, so she headed out front to meet the representative.

The hotel was centrally located, but in a quiet area, the way she liked it. It lived up to its brochure pictures. She was looking forward to some hard skiing, lots of après-ski and the occasional spa treatment. A young man with floppy hair and distressed jeans was changing money at the reception desk. Pounds. British. As he moved away, she stepped up to the desk and the receptionist's attention turned towards her.

Flopping down on the bed, she kicked off her shoes and admired the breathtaking view. The glaciers were all around her. She wondered which of the impressive mountains was Monte Rosa. The one with the jaggiest peak and no snow right at its very tip was Rimpfischhorn. Tomorrow she would find out. She needed to hire some ski equipment too. Right now though, she wanted to find out where to get some après-ski without going up the mountain.

Lucy took the lift down to reception.

'How may I help you, madam?'

'Can you recommend some bars and restaurants, please?'

'Yes, madam. If you are looking for somewhere fun,

Popcorn in the Hotel Dom. If you wish somewhere quiet–'

'No,' Lucy interrupted her. 'Fun is good. Where is the Hotel Dom?'

'You cannot miss it. It is right in the centre, opposite the church.'

Thanking her, Lucy pottered along until she reached the church, whose tower against the glacier background left her speechless. Looking left and right and then remembering there were no cars, she crossed the street to the Hotel Dom.

After ordering a beer, Lucy found a seat. It was pretty busy, even in late afternoon. She had expected everyone still to be on the slopes. The age group was quite mixed, which surprised her, as from the way the receptionist had described it, she had assumed it would be a younger crowd, but no, there was an elderly couple ensconced in the far corner. She noticed a young couple, barely out of their teens, who couldn't keep their hands off each other. *Get a room.* As her mind wandered, so did her eye. Her gaze fell on a familiar face: the guy from reception. Lucy reckoned he was in his twenties. He had nice eyes, little bit of stubble, a bit scruffy, but cute with it. He was wearing khaki combat trousers with pockets on the knees and a cream Aran jumper was slung around his neck. Mmm, he wasn't bad. Just as she was giving him a thorough going-over, he glanced up.

Shit. She didn't like being caught out. He smiled at her. She tried to appear nonchalant, but couldn't pull it off. *Lucy, will you never learn?* She studied her drink.

'Hi. Do you speak English?' He stood beside her.

'Sometimes.'

'Ah, you're Scottish.'

'It's that obvious?'

'Yep.'

She was staring at him. She was relieved when he interrupted her stupor to ask if she wanted a drink. Looking at her full glass, she said, 'I'd love one.'

His eyes crinkled, he shot her an earth-shattering smile and went to the bar. He returned a split second later. 'Sorry, I forgot to ask, what would you like?'

'Gluhwein. I could do with being heated up,' Lucy replied.

She waited to see if her double entendre would catch hold in his young mind. He grinned and said, equally flirtatiously, 'I think we can accommodate that.'

His name was Robbie and he was from the Midlands.

'Where are you from?' Robbie asked.

Lucy said, 'Bearsden.'

'So, near Glasgow then?'

Surprised and impressed Lucy said, 'Yes. How did you know that? I didn't think anyone knew where it was.'

'Well, you see, I'm not just anyone.'

'Who are you then? What do you do?'

'Seventh son of a seventh son.'

'No way, you're not a seventh son.'

'No, you're right, I'm a student.'

'Of what?'

'Of life.' He smiled at her and raised his glass. 'Cheers.'

They chatted easily and were arguing good-naturedly about the best ski resorts in Europe, when Robbie bent over and kissed her. The kiss deepened until they were in danger of being accused of inappropriate behaviour. Breaking off, Lucy said throatily, 'Not here.'

'Yeah, let's go,' he agreed.

Nothing had been said, but their legs steered them towards the hotel. They were almost jogging when abruptly, Robbie stopped. He looked into Lucy's eyes with such a penetrating gaze that she thought he could see right to the heart of her. A second later, they were all over each other, kissing frantically, in the failing light. Her breathing ragged, Lucy finally pulled away. She took his hand and they practically sprinted to the hotel.

They fell over the threshold, mumbled a hello to the receptionist, who eyed them with curiosity, and tried to put their passion on ice as they passed her. Robbie searched for his room key, but Lucy said, 'No, come to mine.' She had a four-poster and the room was practically designed for sexy encounters like this one. She opened the door and they fell upon each other. A button pinged off as Robbie's furious fingers worked to undress her. Lucy tugged at his belt and it fell to the floor. Within seconds, they tumbled onto the bed and succumbed to what had been inevitable since the moment they met.

Afterwards, Lucy lay thinking about how good it had been, not great, it was never fabulous the first time. You needed to know someone better before their body responded perfectly to yours. Although she hadn't orgasmed, she had been close several times and she had enjoyed it. So much so, she wouldn't mind a repeat performance.

The second time was better. It lasted ages. She loved that: languorous, lazy sex after the first frenetic burst. They took their time, exploring each other's bodies. She orgasmed, which surprised her. When the church clock struck ten, Robbie said, 'I'd better get going.'

Miffed, Lucy said, 'Right.'

As Robbie dressed, Lucy realised she didn't want him to go but couldn't ask him to stay.

'I'll see you on the slopes,' he said, and kissed her. 'You take care.'

The door closed and Lucy sat there fuming. 'You take care.' Who says that to someone they've just screwed? She was beside herself. On the one hand she was mad, on the other, confused yet exhilarated, as he'd said he'd see her on the slopes. Did that mean he wanted to see her again? *Damn.* Springing out of bed, she raided the minibar, to see if there was anything of use there. Good, gin. That's what was needed right now, to help sort her head out, although she wasn't sure what sort of perverse logic that was.

She sat on the swivel chair at the bureau and wondered what had just happened. Why had this guy needled her so much? Sure, the sex had been great, but she'd had great sex before. It had never made her want to see someone again as desperately as she wanted to see Robbie. What if, for him, it had been a one-off? What if she didn't bump into him again? She'd never had these feelings of insecurity before. She was always so self-assured. What did that mean? Sighing, she scoffed the last of the crisps, poured herself another enormous G&T and settled back under the rumpled covers.

His smell, his body, his aftershave lingered. Her brain whirred into overdrive. She picked up a novel and started to read. Sleep wouldn't come for a while yet.

Next day Lucy had a slight headache. Nausea rose in her stomach as she pushed her breakfast around her plate. She looked around the dining room again. No sign of him. She wondered which mountain he would ski. Was he alone? Laying her toast to one side, she returned to her room to change.

'Today, we are going to Mount Allalin,' said Jonas, their guide. Lucy had signed up with a tour company so that she wouldn't be skiing on her own. You needed someone to buddy you. Wistfully she wished it were Robbie. Following Jonas, they set off for the Alpine Express.

It really was a long way up. The scenery was stunning. *No wonder it's called* the Pearl of the Alps. There were some red runs up at Allalin that she could practise on before moving on to the blacks.

When they reached the top, she slid around a little in her skis, trying to get used to them. 'Miss, what is your name?' Jonas asked her.

'Lucy.'

'One of our party is arriving late today. I will be your buddy until then.'

'OK.'

They swished back and forth down the first red run. *Wow, this is exhilarating.* She really should make more time for this type of release. The air was so incredibly pure. She zipped back down and around until she reached Jonas. She was a good, competent skier and knew it, but he was superb.

'Ah,' said Jonas, as she returned to the starting point, 'our missing person. Hello, Robbie.'

'Hi, Jonas. You been up long?'

'One time down this run. Let me introduce your buddy. Robbie, this is Lucy. Lucy, Robbie.'

Startled, Robbie said, 'Hi,' and to Jonas, 'We've met.'

Embarrassed, Lucy shot him a warning glance. Stumbling over his words, Robbie said, 'We're in the same hotel.'

Jonas' gaze flitted between Robbie and Lucy, as if trying to work out what he'd missed.

'OK. Robbie, Lucy. I leave you together and we meet at Mekka for lunch at midday.'

'Fine,' both of them said.

Giving them a strange look, Jonas dug his poles in, pushed off and was soon out of sight.

They stood in awkward silence, which Robbie finally broke by saying, 'When I said, I'll see you on the slopes, I didn't realise you would take me literally.'

Lucy shrugged. He didn't seem overly enthusiastic. Maybe she was expecting too much. He was a man. They weren't very good at showing how they felt. 'How's your skiing?' Robbie broke into her thoughts.

'Good.' Lucy was defensive.

'Great. Let's get going then. Ready for a black run?'

'Sure.' She raised her chin defiantly. She was nowhere near ready, she'd only just done her first red, but she wasn't ready to admit it.

He led her to the start of a black run and then disappeared, flying through the alpine landscape. Lucy pushed off and holding her poles loosely at her sides, glided down the mountain, until someone skied straight across her.

'Aargh,' shrieked Lucy as she stumbled, frantically trying to get out of the way of the idiot in front of her who had caused her to pull up so sharply that she hadn't been able to keep her balance. Unamused, she got to her feet. She wasn't hurt, just pissed off. She continued down the slope to where Robbie was waiting, with a 'what kept you?'

look on his face.

'Some idiot cut me up,' she explained.

'Male skiers, they're as bad as women drivers, too much testosterone going around.'

'Women drivers have too much testosterone?' Lucy asked, shaking the snow from her hair.

'No, male skiers. It was just an analogy.'

'Analogy. Big word.'

'Well, I am a student after all.'

'Yes, a student of life. You said.'

'Well, yes, that and Medicine.'

Lucy stared at him. 'Medicine? You're a med student?'

'Yes,' said Robbie. 'No need to act so surprised.'

'Where are you studying?'

'Glasgow Uni.'

Lucy stumbled as nausea clawed at her insides. *Glasgow Uni. Jesus.*

'Why?' asked Robbie.

'I'm a cardiologist.'

'Really!'

'Yes, really. I also lecture at Glasgow University.'

'You're joking. How come I've never seen you?'

'I lecture first and fourth year.'

'I'm in third year. Small world.'

Too small, and damned inconvenient. He might be one of her students next year and she'd slept with him. She'd messed up here and no mistake. *Best to make light of it. The damage is done.* Also, the sex *had* been good. The cogs were turning inside her head. Would there be any harm in continuing with it? As she stood looking at him, whilst he took in the ramifications of her bombshell, her whole body tensed.

'So, you're going to be teaching me next year?'

'It's possible.'

'Well, we'd best get to know each other then, hadn't we?'

'We already know each other,' retorted Lucy, the double entendre not lost on either of them.

'I'll be looking for some pointers from you,' replied Robbie with a smile.

'I thought I'd already obliged.'

'You're not worried, are you?'

'What? That next year you're going to be my student?'

'Yeah.'

'I've been in more comfortable situations.'

'Come on, get over it. What's the problem?' Robbie asked. 'Hear that?'

'What?'

'Nothing, absolutely nothing, so there's no problem, apart from the fact that we're not yet having fun. C'mon!' He slid down the slope and Lucy followed him, her mind racing. To hell with it; she'd let matters take their course and just enjoy herself.

Chapter Thirty-three

By the time they stopped for lunch, they were out of puff. Lucy was fit, but she'd forgotten just how different an exercise skiing was. Her muscles were bound to remind her in the morning. Robbie made it all seem so easy. They found their group and greeted Jonas, who indicated some seats a few spaces away from him. That was good; that way they wouldn't have to make polite conversation. If things became too stilted, she could talk to the others, but if events panned out OK, she would be alone with Robbie again. They tucked into a hearty rabbit stew and the conversation flowed.

'Hey, guys. Are you coming to the toboggan race?' Jonas asked upon reaching them. Robbie gave Lucy a challenging look, daring her to refuse. Never one to be outdone, she beamed at Jonas and said, 'When does it start?'

As Jonas provided her with the details, Robbie stood in the wings. It was only afterwards, when they were alone again, that he said, 'So, are you OK with me steering?'

Frowning, Lucy said, 'Thanks, but I can manage my own skis.'

Robbie laughed. 'No, not your skis, the toboggan.'

'Sorry?'

'It's a two-person toboggan. Are you OK if I drive?'

Damn, she had misunderstood. She'd thought they'd be racing each other, and she didn't know if she wanted him in such close proximity to her, if she didn't know how the evening was going to end. He still hadn't shown if he was interested in a re-enactment of last night. Curbing her indignation, she replied, 'That's fine.'

'Good, should be a good night. Plenty of schnapps. You do realise most people are completely pissed when they do these races?'

Yeah, I'm going to be one of them.

The rest of the day was spent up and down red runs, black runs, on T-bars, on every ski lift in the vicinity. It seemed natural that they would have dinner together. She still didn't know if it was as a friend, or lover. They chatted easily together, the earlier awkwardness long forgotten.

'Are you looking forward to the race?' Robbie asked.

'Should be a laugh.'

'I did it last year.'

'Did you win?'

'The idea is to survive, not win!'

She hoped he was joking.

'Anyway, we'd best get going. It starts soon and I don't have nearly enough schnapps in my system yet.'

'The rules are, there *are* no rules,' boomed the voice of the organiser. 'First to finish is the winner. Good luck, everyone. Go!'

'Hold on tight,' Robbie urged Lucy as they ran and jumped onto the toboggan. Lucy couldn't believe how fast they were going. She was glad of her hat as the temperature was much lower than during the day, plus her hair was whipping around her face.

'Watch out,' Lucy screamed, as a low-hanging branch almost lifted them out of the toboggan. It was pitch dark. She could barely see her hand in front of her face as they hurtled down the mountainside, blind.

'Woo-hoo,' yelled another team as they sailed past, but they were going too fast and didn't make the corner. Lucy and Robbie passed them on the bend, as the others clambered back onto their toboggan. *This is brilliant.* She wanted to drive but instead huddled into Robbie's slim frame and concentrated on not falling off, turning her body when he turned his, providing momentum for steering around the corners. Ahead of them she heard excited screams. It was like a rollercoaster, with all the bumps and loops. At least there was no real danger of falling off a rollercoaster. Seconds later, she discovered the reason for the screams. They were fast approaching a very steep gradient. No sooner had she realised it, when they went careering down it. What a rush! They overtook a few toboggans and then suddenly they hit a tree root and went soaring through the air.

'Oof,' said Lucy, as she landed on the ground with a thwack.

'C'mon,' Robbie yelled at her. 'Get on.'

Scrambling back on, she pushed forward. Their speed increased again, faster and faster. They burst through the finish line. Tenth. Not bad.

'When's the next one?' said Lucy, grinning.

'Oh, that was great, but this is just as good.' Robbie relaxed in the bar.

'Mmm,' Lucy agreed with him. 'We deserve a beer.'

'Absolutely.' They clinked glasses.

After a while, Robbie said, 'Do you want to go back to the hotel?'

'Yes.'

Uncertain what would happen once at the hotel, Lucy was relieved when they stepped into the reception area and Robbie solved the problem for her.

'Fancy a nightcap?'

'Why not?' She headed towards the bar.

'No.' He took her hand. 'I meant, just the two of us.'

As Lucy digested this, he smiled at her and said, 'If that's OK?'

'Yes, but it'll need to be your room. I drank my mini-bar dry last night.'

'I don't really want a nightcap.' He looked her straight in the eye.

A few hours later, after not only highly satisfying sex, but much cuddling and chatting, Lucy said reluctantly, 'I better go.'

Robbie's brow furrowed. 'Why?'

'Well, I thought you'd want your space.'

'I do.' The corners of Robbie's mouth turned up. 'This is my space and this–' he indicated the other side of the bed '–is yours.'

She stared at him, unsure what to say.

'If you want, that is.'

'OK, I'll stay.'

'Till morning?' Robbie quirked an eyebrow.

'If that's what you want.'

'That's very much what I want.'

The next few days passed in a fog. They skied a lot, ate well and spent the nights under the covers. They hadn't talked about what would happen when they returned to Scotland, but instinctively Lucy knew they would keep seeing each other. Maybe it was just an infatuation, but she had never felt such a pull before, like an invisible force attracting them.

The last night came around. Robbie was heading home in the morning; Lucy was driving to Tuscany. Holly had been overjoyed when Lucy called to say she was coming. As Lucy and Robbie lay in bed, a hush fell over them and she knew it wasn't that they'd run out of things to say. After an interminable silence, Robbie said, 'So what happens now?'

Lucy decided it was time to be upfront. 'Robbie, I'd like to see you again when we get back, but it's complicated.'

'What do you mean?'

'I have a boyfriend.'

'I guessed that.'

'You did?'

'Yes. Look at you. You're gorgeous, successful, funny and fun. Why wouldn't you have a boyfriend?'

Lucy took all of these compliments on board and was taken aback when Robbie said, 'I'd still like to see you.'

She was being offered the best of both worlds, so she said, 'OK.'

'Good. Can I have your number then?'

Lucy chuckled. 'Don't you think we've done this the wrong way around?'

'Sorry?'

'Aren't you meant to ask for my phone number, then we sleep with each other?'

Robbie laughed. 'I suppose so, but since we got the logistics arse from elbow, can I have it anyway?'

'Of course.' She smiled at him as she wrote down her number.

'Great. Do you mind if I sleep here tonight?'

'I'd be gutted if you didn't.'

'Let's get some sleep,' Robbie said, as he wrapped her in his arms.

As Lucy packed her things into her car, she reflected on the past few days. She was looking forward to seeing her sister. Holly had been in Italy for a few weeks writing her latest book and appeared to be enjoying herself immensely. Tom hadn't sounded too good last time Lucy spoke to him on the phone. She wasn't sure if he was pining for his fiancée or if something else was troubling him.

It would be a long drive, just under seven hours. Thank goodness for air conditioning. Lucy had a quick look at the map to see if she could spot a place for lunch. She glanced at Holly's address – Bibbiena. Parma or Modena for lunch then. She opted for Parma. Turning on her radio, she hopped in the car, cast a last look at Saas Fee and set off. She was glad to be leaving on such a glorious sunny day. You definitely gained a different impression of a place if the weather was horrible. As she drove she sang along to Queen, Duran Duran and The Rolling Stones, tapping the steering wheel in time to the music.

'Hi, Carl. How are you? Sorry I haven't been in touch.

There was no reception in Saas Fee,' Lucy lied. 'You'll never guess where I am. I'm in Parma, munching the best ham Parma has to offer, with olives, sun-dried tomatoes and a glass of Chianti.'

'Lucky cow!' said Carl.

'I know. Anyway, tell me what you've been up to.'

Carl was moaning that she could have used a pay phone, when she cut in, 'Carl, you know I don't *do* phone boxes. Tell me how things are with you. How's the restaurant?' She listened half-heartedly to Carl prattle on about minor disputes with suppliers and builders. His grumps and groans out of the way, he moved on to the positives, before turning his attention to Lucy.

'Anyway, how was the skiing?'

'The skiing was great. The weather has been fabulous. The runs were scary, the snow was perfect. The whole thing has been a wonderful break. Just a few days with Holly now and then I'll fly back from Rome. Are we going out for dinner?'

'Yes, I thought we could go to Sarti's.'

'Sounds good. You booking it?'

'Makes sense, since you're away. Some of us have to stay behind and earn a crust. Geddit? Crust? Restaurant?'

'Yes, I get it,' Lucy said. 'Look I need to go. I told Holly I'd be there for dinner, so I better make tracks.'

'OK. Drive safe and don't do anything I wouldn't do.'

'Of course,' Lucy said sweetly, thinking thank God he didn't know the half of it. Finishing her wine, she paid the bill and set off.

Chapter Thirty-four

'Holly! Look at you. You're so tanned. You look incredible.'

Her sister hugged her and said, 'Thanks. You don't look too bad yourself.'

They jabbered on for a few minutes before Lucy noticed someone behind Holly, waiting to speak to her.

'Guido. Come and meet my sister Lucy.'

Guido's eyes were popping out of his head. Lucy tried not to smile. She was, after all, used to this kind of attention. She went to shake Guido's hand, but he put his hands on her shoulders and gave her two kisses. The next minute, Sig.a Tagliaferri appeared, highly excited. Addressing Holly, she said, '*Questa è la tua sorella?*'

Holly nodded and Sig.a Tagliaferri said, '*Ma che bella ragazza che è. Guido, prendeti i suoi bagagli, subito.*'

'She says you are very pretty,' Holly told her.

Lucy said, 'The only word I caught was *bella*. I gathered that was a good thing.'

Whilst she was talking, Guido picked up her bags and rushed off, before his mother had time to shoo him away. Bending forward and kissing Sig.a Tagliaferri, Lucy said, '*Piacere.*'

The Tuscan woman's eyes widened. '*Ma, anche Lei*

parla italiano! She launched into fast-flowing Italian. Alarmed, Lucy swung round to her sister so that she could explain. Holly grinned and told Sig.a Tagliaferri that *piacere* was one of the very few words Lucy knew. Sig.a Tagliaferri eyed Lucy and then announced that she was happy Lucy had made the effort.

'You see,' whispered Holly. 'They like it when you try to speak their language.'

Sig.a Tagliaferri made as much a fuss of Lucy as of Holly. Likewise, Emilio, when he returned from town, gave her a most enthusiastic welcome. The boys offered to show her around, but Holly said she wanted to give Lucy the tour, as she hadn't seen her for a while. After dinner, Lucy and Holly sat under the pagoda, catching up.

'So, any gossip?' Lucy asked. 'What about those two?'

Holly reddened.

'You have not!!'

'They'd have liked to, but no, nothing's happened between us.'

Lucy sensed her sister's hesitation. 'Then what?' she asked, expert at sniffing out a secret.

'I kissed someone,' Holly said.

'You did?' Lucy was taken aback. 'Who?'

'Dario.'

'Is he another brother?'

'No. It's a long story.' Holly sighed.

'Take your time,' Lucy said, refilling their glasses.

Lucy was surprised by what her sister told her, but also excited. Although she liked Tom, she didn't think he was a match for Holly. She had pursed her lips and bit back a bitchy comment when Holly announced their engagement.

'What are you going to do?'

'I don't know. He just disappeared at that wedding.'

'Well, at least you know where he lives.'

'I think I'll chalk it down to experience and get on with my life.'

'Oh, come on. It's not as if you slept with him.'

'Thank God,' said Holly.

'Really?' said Lucy. She arched one eyebrow and winked. 'Are you sure?'

Holly laughed. 'You're incorrigible.'

'So you're going to do nothing about it?'

'What can I do? I have to think about Tom. I'm getting married, remember?'

'Oh yeah.'

'C'mon. You could be a bit more enthusiastic. I know you don't think much of Tom, but he's good for me and reliable and loving.'

'Get a Labrador.'

'No. I have to forget about it. It's for the best.'

'Your loss. Sounds like a goer.'

'Lucy!'

'Well, he does.' Lucy was remorseless.

They settled down to talk about other things and Holly said, 'C'mon, spit it out.'

'What do you mean?' Lucy asked innocently.

'Luce, I'm not your sister for nothing. It's got to be a man, or men,' said Holly wickedly.

'Actually, there was a rather nice French guy in Lucerne.'

'And?'

'Just sex.' She was dismissive.

'You should have been born a man, Luce.'

'You are joking, aren't you! Then I wouldn't have nice boobs and legs to die for.'

'You are completely shameless!'

'That's me,' Lucy agreed. 'There was another, in Saas Fee.'

'And?'

'Robbie. Twenty-one. Medical student.'

'Twenty-one? You'll be taking them out of prams next!'

'Thanks a bunch.'

'But seriously, twenty-one. When you lost your virginity, he was still in nappies!'

'Ha bloody ha. Anyway, he doesn't know that and what he doesn't know can't hurt him.'

'How old does he think you are?'

'Thirty-one.'

'Thirty-one.' Holly spat out her wine. 'You're nearly thirty-eight.'

'I know that and you know that, but my age is only given on a need-to-know basis.'

'At least you put yourself in your thirties for once.'

'Well, there was a bit of a complication.'

'What complication?'

'I might be his tutor next year.'

'Oh, you have got to be kidding. He's not at Glasgow Uni?'

'Oh yes, he is. Damn, I'd make a really good dame in a pantomime, wouldn't I?' said Lucy.

'Your whole bloody life is a pantomime, Luce! What the hell are you going to do? How could you be so stupid?'

'Nothing,' she replied.

'What do you mean?'

'I like him, a lot. He likes me. We're going to keep seeing each other.'

'Are you nuts? This could seriously damage your relationship with Carl, but it could also ruin your career. Reputation is everything in Medicine, you know that, and it's not quite the same thing, no matter how much you pretend it is, a doctor screwing her student.'

'I don't see why not,' Lucy said defensively.

'That's always been your problem. You always want to have it all.'

'Life is there to be lived,' Lucy shot back.

'You're messing with people's lives here.'

'I can take care of myself. C'mon. I came here to visit my little sis, not for a lecture.'

Sighing, Holly said, 'You're right, let's not talk about it any more.'

They changed the subject and were soon laughing and joking, as Holly told her about the wedding she'd been to. Lucy filled Holly in on the toboggan race, glossing over the fact it was Robbie she had been with. They spent a happy evening together, knocking back Chianti and nibbling gorgonzola.

The sisters enjoyed a relaxing few days pottering around Tuscany, but all too soon, Lucy had to drive to Fiumicino to catch her flight.

'You look after yourself,' Holly said.

'I know what I'm doing, sis. I'll see you when you get back.'

Chapter Thirty-five

The flight was on time. Lucy arrived into Glasgow Airport at half nine. She was distracted as she walked through Arrivals and banged straight into someone.

'Sorry.' She looked up to apologise, only to find Carl in front of her, his arms outstretched.

'I wanted to surprise you.' He lifted her off the ground and kissed her.

Drawing breath, Lucy said, 'You did that all right.'

'Nice surprise?'

'Very nice surprise,' Lucy said, linking hands with him and dragging him towards belt three to look for her suitcase.

'Turn here,' Lucy said abruptly to Carl.

'Here? Why?'

'Just do it!' Lucy said authoritatively.

'Please,' she added when she saw Carl's wounded look.

'Right here? Lucy, this is a dirt track.'

'I know.'

'There's nothing down here.'

'I know.'

'So why are we going down here?'

'OK, stop.'

'OK. What now?' Carl was confused.

Lucy started pulling at his trousers. 'I can't wait till we get home.'

'You horny little devil.' Carl laughed as he unzipped her skirt, his fingers running up her thighs.

'Well, that was unexpected,' Carl said when they arrived home.

'Nice surprise?' Lucy smirked.

'Definitely. Surprise me like that as often as you like.'

'I'll keep it in mind.'

'Do. Drink?'

'Rioja.'

'Me too.'

Setting the glasses on the coffee table, he kissed her softly.

'Now for the more leisurely version.' He started caressing her again, and things were just getting interesting when Lucy's mobile rang. Instantly she stiffened.

'You're not due back yet.' Carl groaned. 'Leave it. Please!'

Afterwards, Carl went off to refill their glasses. Lucy took advantage of his absence to check her phone. Robbie. Hastily, she read the text.

'How u? Get back OK? Can't wait 2 c u. Wen u 3? R xx.'

Adrenalin pumping, she deleted it. Tomorrow would be soon enough to reply as she wasn't careless enough to do it with Carl around. Yet she felt reckless. She'd just screwed her boyfriend twice and she was already caught up in the excitement of seeing another man.

Lucy was desperate to see Robbie, but didn't want to

appear too keen. He called her on Wednesday. She replied on Thursday afternoon saying she was free on Monday. They agreed to meet in the south side. Robbie's flat was relatively close by, but more importantly it was far enough from the city centre and the West End, so their tryst would go undetected.

They met in a pub on Clarkston Road. She arrived intentionally ten minutes late. He was drumming his fingers on the table. *Does he think I've stood him up?* When Robbie saw her, his face lit up and he stood up and kissed her on the cheek. She knew he was restraining himself, as they were in public. They looked at each other and read so much simply from each other's expressions.

'We're leaving,' Lucy said.

Wordlessly, Robbie picked up his jacket and followed her.

'Where are we going?' he asked.

'Anywhere we can be alone,' growled Lucy.

'Any ideas?'

'Do you know the Muirend Hotel?'

'No.'

'It's the closest place I can think of.' She shut out of her mind that it seemed a little sordid.

The receptionist looked at them oddly when they checked in without any luggage. They tore up the stairs, kissing and fumbling. They didn't notice anything about the room. It was enough that they found the bed and then they were lost in each other again, all thoughts of the outside world gone.

Over the next few months, they returned to the Muirend Hotel many times. It began to bother them that they couldn't stay overnight. Carl was at a critical phase with the restaurant. The run-up to Ryan's wedding and his father's seventieth, both of which had also kept him very busy, had alleviated the possibility of discovery. Lucy was starting to begrudge the time she spent apart from Robbie and the feeling was mutual. Although she was still cautious of their being seen together, they started to take more and more risks. Sex had become a secondary factor in their relationship, as Lucy and Robbie opened up to each other, sharing their hopes and expectations for the future.

The start of term was almost upon them, when Robbie would in all likelihood become Lucy's student. He was already her student, Lucy thought, the irony not lost on her. She was distancing herself more and more from Carl and made excuses not to have sex with him. He seemed glad, tired from the long hours he was working. Did she love Robbie? She thought she did, but he was so much younger than her. He was so laid-back and fun. She hated having to keep things secret. Mind-blowing sex and room service wasn't enough for them any more.

Robbie stroked Lucy's back as they lay in bed together. 'Luce?'

'Mmm.' She sighed contentedly.

'I want to spend the night with you again.'

Turning to him, she said, 'You know I can't.'

'Not tonight. I'd like us to plan a weekend away. Can you think about it?'

'Of course.'

Lucy was busy with work; she had been lucky after her holiday as she hadn't had any other lectures to do outside the UK for some time. Now, however, the circuit was recommencing. Her US tour would take in Duke University in North Carolina, the University of South Dakota, Harvard and the University of Texas, Galveston, among others. It was an intensive tour and she knew she would be exhausted when she got back, but more than anything, she didn't want to be apart from Robbie. She'd decided to tell Carl she had a conference down south the weekend before she left. She and Robbie were booked into Stobo Castle in the Borders. They would eat well, maybe do a little mountain biking at nearby Glentress, but most importantly they would be free to be a couple. No more hiding.

On the Friday morning, Lucy finished slinging her luggage into the boot of her TT and padded back into the flat. 'Bye, Carl. I should be back around ten on Sunday.'

'OK, have fun,' Carl said from the shower.

'I'll do my best.' Lucy almost felt guilty.

Lucy had arranged to pick Robbie up at Buchanan Street Bus Station. She had been dying to go to Stobo for ages. She was particularly looking forward to spending quality time with Robbie, but also simply enjoying being at the spa. It was expensive, and at first Robbie had baulked at the cost, but Lucy had waved it off, saying she didn't expect him to pay for it.

'Hey, you.' He clambered into the car and kissed her.

She smiled at him. 'Ready?'

'You bet.'

Lucy had booked a suite. It was heaven. Rich claret-coloured cashmere walls in the bedroom, with two, seven feet by five feet Italian hand-painted his-and-hers beds. A dressing room, decked out in American black walnut, nestled just off the bedroom. Matching flat-screen TVs hung in the bedroom and the palatial bathroom, where a cream limestone circular bath stood in the centre. They looked at one another and Robbie started unbuttoning his shirt.

'Let's see the rest first,' Lucy begged.

'Ooh, the floor is lovely and warm.'

'Underfloor heating,' Lucy explained, taking in her surroundings.

'Now, about that bath.' Robbie nuzzled her ear.

'Right, we can't lie around here all day,' said Lucy. 'There's pampering to be done.'

'What do you want to do first?'

'It's all booked. We're free for another half hour and then we have treatments lined up, so we can be done simultaneously.'

Robbie raised an eyebrow.

'Dirty mind you have there, boy.'

'Ooh, this is fantastic. Yes, there, just there. Robbie, isn't this the best?'

Robbie groaned as the masseuse manipulated his shoulder. 'Yes. Yep, that bit's always in knots.'

Tomorrow they would make use of the leisure facilities,

but today they wanted to relax and maybe have a walk before dinner.

'This wine's gorgeous,' said Lucy.

'I know. It's difficult to work out what's the best, the food or the wine. Not all students feast like this, you know.'

'I wouldn't have thought so. How's your crayfish roulade?'

'Divine, madam. How is one's roast tomato and mozzarella salad?'

'Rubbish. I could have made it better myself.'

'Really?'

'No, of course not, I can't cook, I just wanted to see the look on your face.' Lucy laughed, putting one hand to his cheek and stroking it, the other pinching a piece of Robbie's crayfish.

'Bitch!'

'Lucy?'

Lucy turned and wasn't quick enough to disguise her look of horror. One of her neighbours was standing in front of her. Lucy's hand flew to her side.

'Veronica, how lovely to see you.' It wasn't.

'Yes, you too. I'm here with my sister. It's my birthday,' she said.

'Happy birthday.' Lucy tried to keep her voice steady.

She made small talk with the older woman for a few minutes and then Veronica said pointedly, 'I'll see you and Carl when I get back.'

Robbie looked at Lucy for an explanation. 'Luce?' But Lucy was lost in thought.

'How could I have been so stupid?' she said under her breath. 'Shit!'

'What's wrong?'

'She's only the nosiest busybody you could ever meet and she lives three doors down from us *and* loves Carl.'

Robbie seemed to be digesting this. 'OK, so what are you going to do?'

'I don't know. She'll tell Carl she bumped into me at Stobo, when I'm meant to be at a conference in Hampshire.'

Robbie was silent.

'There's only one thing we can do. Leave. Now,' said Lucy.

'But we still have one more day.'

'We'll have to do it another time. C'mon.'

'But we've been drinking.'

'I've only had two glasses.' Lucy pushed her chair out and left the dining room.

'I can't believe that old bitch,' Lucy fumed, as she sped along the country lane.

'She knew exactly what was going on.'

'What if she doesn't tell Carl?'

'She will, vindictive old cow. She's spread rumours with less substance.'

'What are you going to say to Carl?'

'I don't know, but I…aargh!' Lucy screamed, as a deer bounded out of the undergrowth. She swerved, but it wasn't enough. With a sickening thump the deer hit the windscreen and she lost control of the car.

Chapter Thirty-six
Carl – CANCER

Caring, emotional, sensitive, resistant to change, home-loving. Family is all-important to them and they seek security. Withdraw into themselves. Find it difficult to be objective and are easily crushed by criticism. Worry too much.

Carl stepped out of his car and was heading towards the restaurant, when he heard a voice calling him.

'Carl! Over here!'

Turning, he saw the foreman from Tom's company waving at him. As he trudged over the muck towards the construction site, he caught sight of Lucy's brother-in-law-to-be. Tom owned the building company that was overhauling the old restaurant for him.

'What is it, Alex?' Carl asked.

'Just wanted to show you your foundations.' He grinned. 'We're through.'

'Really?' Carl was amazed; they'd said at least another week.

'Yeah, we managed to break through quicker than expected.'

'So what's next?'

'We have to review the foundations and then we'll need to sit down and see what your next priority is.'

It was a daunting task trying to organise all the trades-men and Carl was relieved he was working with Tom's company. His previous business venture hadn't taken off, and it had all been down to unreliable workmen. Thinking back on it now, Carl shook his head and turned to Alex.

'Do you guys have enough work for today?'

'Yeah, we need to take all this stone away.'

Carl wanted to take away the extension, as it wasn't in keeping with the beautiful exterior of the building. He'd rather have a smaller restaurant than a larger, hideous one. He intended The Steadings Strathblane to be the centre-piece of the village.

Carl had spent an incalculable amount of time deciding on the look for his restaurant. He wanted it to be relaxed but still upmarket. Locals should feel they could pop in for a light supper. There would be different eating areas, with lunches held in the brasserie whilst the restaurant would be à la carte. He had also added a small snug to the plans. It wouldn't be a proper bar, although guests could drink with their meals. His target market wasn't men coming in for a drinking session until dinnertime. The snug would be like those he'd seen in the Highlands: dark grey stone, roughly hewn walls and a roaring log fire. However, instead of uncomfortable wooden benches, his would house ruby red armchairs interspersed with mahogany coffee tables and chocolate leather sofas, and quality newspapers and classy magazines would be provided. The people in this area tended to be monied and *they* were his principal target market.

The floor would be oak, some of it remaining from the original structure. The restaurant would be Scottish in theme, but without any concession to tartan, and a few tasteful prints would be dotted around the snug. The brasserie would be bright, with terracotta and cream fabric wall hangings. Carl also wanted to include some period pieces, an old barometer maybe, or an eighteenth-century clock, as well as pictures of Scotland's great inventors.

It irked Carl that children nowadays often didn't know their own history. It was a shame, which meant it was left to the family to pass on the knowledge. Carl was lucky. He had a very large, extremely close family. Carl was fourth, after Fraser, Agnes and Ryan. He was followed by Hilary, Flora, Gillian, Grant and Izzy.

Carl roamed around the main dining room. It would be predominately cream and vermilion, and he was aiming for clean, understated lines. Nothing but the best for The Steadings. It had a real country feel to it and rightly so, as a century ago, it had formed part of a merchant's mansion.

At college Carl had studied Cookery and Business. Cooking was his first love, but fortunately he also had a good business head. The failure of his first venture had simply been bad luck. His natural flair for cooking had been first discovered helping in his parents' pub. The Jedburgh Tavern did a roaring trade and Carl was anxious to prove to his father that his business could be as successful. Carl had used his father as a sounding board when his previous business had failed and now hoped to prove himself to girlfriend Lucy and perhaps coax her to settle down. Lucy was wild. She liked to be able to spread her wings at a moment's notice. Next week it was Switzerland.

They really needed to make a concerted effort to spend some time together before she left. It had been crazy recently, trying to get everything organised for the restaurant.

His mobile rang.

'Carl, it's me.'

'Izzy, hi.'

'Listen, have you done anything about Dad's seventieth?'

'Not yet.'

'Do you remember that place we stayed in near Onich?'

'Yeah.'

'Well, it would hold all of us. It would be different from just having a meal. I've checked, we can book just for the weekend and the rates are reasonable between all of us.'

'Listen, Izzy, I'm really busy but I'm coming down tonight.'

'OK, I'll see if the others are free.'

He'd achieved a lot today, Carl reflected, as he dialled Lucy's number. Voicemail.

'Luce, I'm going down to my parents' for a bit. Izzy has some idea for Dad's seventieth.'

It was always difficult to get hold of Lucy as she was constantly busy. She earned a fortune but was never home. If they wanted to have kids, they'd have to stop working so much. At thirty-seven, Lucy wasn't getting any younger, and he was thirty-nine. He wanted to be able to kick a football around with his son, or go down the flumes at a theme park with his daughter. He didn't want to be creaking around with a Zimmer frame. And they'd need a house, not the three-bedroom flat they had in Bearsden.

When he'd bought it, it had been the area to live in, but a third-floor flat wasn't suitable for children. Carl wanted kids and lots of them.

His mobile rang.

'Carl Summers speaking.'

'Carl, it's Tom.'

'All right?'

'Just wondered if you fancied a pint later.'

'We-ell…'

'Oh, go on. I'm on my own, with Holly away.'

'OK, but it'll need to be later. I'm going to Jedburgh.'

'See you in The Bruce at eight?'

Carl wondered what that was about. He liked Tom but they didn't socialise together much unless Holly was around.

'I don't know why you lot bothered moving out,' Mrs Summers chastised them. Sheepishly, Carl, Izzy, Grant and Flora looked at their mum. Only Izzy had called. 'Sorry,' they muttered.

'Consideration, that's all I ask.' Their mum wasn't quite the battleaxe she made herself out to be; she simply liked to fuss.

'I like the car, Grant.' Carl changed the subject.

Grant grinned. He'd just bought an Audi R8. A stockbroker in the City, he had no kids, no girlfriend worth mentioning and was into boys' toys.

'You can take it for a spin later if you like.'

'Really?' Carl perked up, then remembered he was meeting Tom. 'Oh, maybe another time. I have something on later.'

'Dinner's ready,' their mother called. They all clattered

through to the dining room.

'Where are the wee ones, Flora?' Carl's father, Gordon, asked.

'With their dad.'

'Ah.' Gordon chewed his meat. 'You know, I like to see them now and again.'

'Dad, they're never out of here!' Flora burst out. 'Bryce never sees them.'

'Well, if you'd let us look after Katie and Jacob, instead of childminders, I'd get to see my grandchildren.' Gordon huffed.

'Actually, the reason we're here is so we can all spend more time together,' Izzy said.

'Oh?'

'That's right,' Carl joined in. 'Izzy's been researching your birthday do.'

His father smiled at his youngest daughter fondly. 'So what is it this time? Paragliding, white-water rafting, scuba diving?'

'No. It's a place called Ardrhu House...' Izzy filled them in whilst Carl watched the others, gauging their reaction.

The response was favourable and in the absence of their other siblings, the motion was carried, since they were already behind in booking somewhere. Izzy appointed herself as correspondent to the absent family members, with the exception of Fraser, the eldest, who lived in Queensland and was coming back for their father's birthday celebrations. The rest of the siblings were dotted around Scotland. Izzy and Fraser didn't get on; the age difference probably didn't help. Fraser had left home before Izzy could even walk. Carl would email Fraser.

'Hi, Tom. Sorry I'm late.'

'Don't worry. I've been watching the snooker.'

They chatted about the restaurant, but Carl knew that could have been done on-site. *Something's troubling him.* He left the pub an hour later, none the wiser as to what was eating Tom. Maybe he was missing Holly.

As he parked, he noticed Lucy's Audi was missing. If he'd known she wouldn't be home, he could have stayed at the pub.

Carl sank into his recliner and flicking on the TV, channel-hopped until bored, then drifted off.

He woke up when Lucy's key turned in the lock. Disorientated, he saw the digital clock read 2.39. Lucy was creeping up the stairs when Carl's voice broke through the silence.

'You don't need to tiptoe. I'm in here.'

'Carl! Don't do that to me!' Lucy's hand flew to her cleavage. 'You almost gave me a heart attack,' she slurred. Hiccupping she sat down on the sofa beside him.

'Were you waiting up for me?' she asked. He was unsure if she was flattered or annoyed, so decided to forego any brownie points and tell the truth.

'Actually, no. I fell asleep. I thought you were going to be here. What time you working tomorrow?'

'Nine.'

'You'd better take a taxi. C'mon, let's get you to bed.' He guided his huffing, drunken girlfriend upstairs.

Chapter Thirty-seven

Next morning, Carl slipped out of bed without waking Lucy. She'd need the extra hour's sleep, after the state she'd been in. He had an appointment with his bank manager, but wanted to peruse his paperwork beforehand. After padding downstairs, he made coffee and took it through to his home office. Everything seemed to be on track. The bank had lent him the money, but with rather stringent conditions. He pushed the papers aside, remembering he'd agreed to email his brother. Carl had a good relationship with everyone in his family; perhaps it was because he was the middle child: nine years younger than Fraser, nine years older than Izzy. Ryan and Izzy were closest to him. That reminded him; as best man, he really ought to start thinking about Ryan's wedding. It had worked out well for Fraser, who was coming home for six weeks encompassing their father's seventieth, his brother's stag night and wedding.

It took Carl longer than expected to compose his email and he realised he'd run out of time. Ryan would have to wait too. The wedding was only a few months away. He hadn't even thought about his speech and was hoping to enlist the help of someone who'd done it before.

Carl stared at his reflection in the mirror. He couldn't

bring himself to go all out and wear a suit. He gave himself a shake; it was only his bank manager. He scribbled a note to Lucy. 'Can we have dinner together tonight?'

'Hi, Carl. Got your note. Yes, I can be home for dinner. If you're good, I might take care of dessert,' Lucy purred as he drove along Great Western Road. Carl could feel himself getting worked up. Lucy did that to him and then, when they did get it together, very occasionally, all his expectations were exceeded. It had been a while; he had been so caught up in everything else: the restaurant and his family's events, but then, Lucy's schedule was hectic too. He was relieved Lucy was free tonight as they didn't spend nearly enough time together.

'Hi.' Lucy flounced into the hall, swinging her Gucci bag onto the table. Carl came towards her, apron on and utensils in both hands.

'Evening.' He kissed her gently, but Lucy was having none of the softly-softly approach. Her hands slipped down to his thighs and Carl groaned. He wanted to make love to her right now, but he had gone to all the trouble of making them a banquet for dinner. Lucy was in playful mode. Releasing him, she nipped to the bathroom, whilst Carl finished off preparing their main course. He was just dishing up, when she appeared resplendent in a black basque. Carl, lost, took one look at her and turned the gas off.

'I'm knackered!' Carl grinned, sweat glistening on his upper body. It was always a marathon with Lucy. She was insatiable, but now he was starving.

'You hungry?' he asked.

'Uh-huh.'

'Shall we have dinner then?' he asked, tracing his finger along the curve of her bottom.

'It's not dinner I'm hungry for.' Lucy eyed him wickedly, and laughing, they reached for one another again.

'You are one bad girl, Lucy Jameson.' Carl chuckled.

Two hours later, Carl did what he could to salvage dinner. They lay spent on the sofa, Lucy's blonde head on Carl's stomach, and chatted about trivial things. No family or work. Carl knew Lucy wasn't taken with his family; they were too interfering for her tastes. Although close to her sister Holly, she couldn't relate to Carl's troupe living in each other's pockets. Their careers were worlds apart and Carl guessed Lucy was fed up listening to him go over every detail about the restaurant.

'I am so looking forward to this ski trip.'

'Yeah, it's been a while since you've been on holiday,' agreed Carl. 'In fact, it's been a while since *we* went on holiday.'

'Carl, we've only been on holiday twice.'

'Really?'

'Really.' Lucy sighed.

'Well, we'll need to rectify that. Once the restaurant's up and running, let's go somewhere exotic.'

'Like where?' Lucy faced him, her eyes lighting up.

'What about Maui?'

'No, full of Americans.'

'Well, what about that place we talked about before?'

'In the Maldives?'

'Yes.'

'Moofushi Island,' said Lucy. 'That's not a bad idea. We should visit the Maldives now before global warming puts them underwater forever.'

'Good point. I'll look into it. When do you want to go?'

'That's more up to you, isn't it? The restaurant?' Lucy clarified, when Carl stared at her blankly.

'Oh yes. Maybe end of January?'

The next week came all too soon. Although Carl wasn't around much when Lucy was home, her absence affected him deeply. Even her asleep in bed beside him was enough sometimes. For once, Lucy was up before him, as she had an early flight.

Carl luxuriated in the shower, then started on the wedding plans. He had the speech to write and more imminently the stag night to organise. They had opted for a day at Knockhill Racing Circuit followed by a night out in Edinburgh.

A few calls later and thirty-five guys had signed up. Most of them would do the rally experience, but Ryan was car mad. He appreciated the beauty of the machines and was never done talking about brake horsepower. Carl had suggested chipping in a few extra quid to let Ryan have the Ferrari experience. The stag do would be a riot, just the thing to take Carl's mind off the restaurant for a bit. His heart, body and soul were being poured into it, leaving him no headspace for anything else. Hopefully, once it was ticking over and he had some decent staff, matters would improve.

Carl missed Lucy. He left her several messages, but hadn't spoken to her in days. Maybe she hadn't got his messages. Even so, she might have called *him*. Carl sighed. He knew Lucy; she only thought about the here and now. She'd be thinking solely of her ski trip. It wouldn't occur to her he might worry. OK, so she was Miss Well-Travelled, but you couldn't be too careful.

Over the next few days, Carl kept himself busy. He went to lunch at his parents' again. Izzy, Flora, Ryan and the kids were there.

'How's Lucy enjoying her trip?' Flora asked.

'Fine,' Carl said.

Izzy piped up, 'You haven't spoken to her, have you?'

His baby sister knew him too well. Sometimes they felt more like twins than brother and sister. He was annoyed with Lucy for not phoning him. He also guessed that Izzy was about to get on his case and he wasn't in the mood.

'Not now, Izzy.' Carl sighed.

Izzy raised her hands in defeat. 'It's your life, Carl.'

Carl was glad when Ryan came back in and they started talking about the stag do. They were staying at the Sheraton off Lothian Road. Carl had booked treatments for them and as a joke had booked Ryan in for waxing. Wait till his brother found *that* out.

The next day, Carl was driving to Strathblane when his phone rang. 'Hi, Carl, how are you? Sorry I haven't been in touch. There was no reception in Saas Fee.'

You'll never guess where I am. I'm in Parma, munching the best ham Parma has to offer, with olives, sun-dried tomatoes and a glass of Chianti.'

'Lucky cow!' said Carl.

'I know. Anyway, tell me what you've been up to.'

'Weren't there any payphones? He wasn't impressed by Lucy's response that she didn't 'do' public phones. She was in Italy, en route to see Holly. The conversation didn't last long and it left him dissatisfied.

Chapter Thirty-eight

The mock-up menu was back from the printer and Carl was delighted with it. The actual paper would be like that used for good wedding invitations, stiff as a board. It had scalloped edges and would nestle inside a leather-bound cover, embossed with gold lettering bearing 'The Steadings', the phone number, email address and website. All Carl had to do now was dream up the menu.

Carl parked in the nearest thing resembling a parking space in what remained of his car park and surveyed the buildings before him. The builders were making progress. Another few weeks and they would be ready to start putting in fittings and furnishings. He headed for his office, as he was interviewing serving staff. He didn't want to risk all the good people being snapped up by other establishments hiring Christmas staff next month.

The interviews were a mixed bag; he discounted the retired woman who wanted very specific hours, but the other two he would keep under his belt. A quick look on Google kick-started his speech-writing crusade. He was unsure if he should do anything risqué. His mother might disapprove, although the newlyweds would take it in good spirit. The last wedding he'd gone to, the best man had taken off his waistcoat, turned around to toast the bride and groom and shown the assembled crowd a blown-up poster of the groom at university, bollock naked in a drunken stupor. It had raised a lot of howls and was one of the best speeches he had ever heard, but he remembered that the elderly relatives had been appalled. On second thoughts, he'd better not risk it.

'Good evening, everyone. Before I start, let me just say that the formative years I spent in the groom's company means he played as much of a part in developing my sense of humour as anyone. So, although I have tried to make this speech as funny as possible, please blame Ryan if it's not.' (Laughter.) He'd stolen this from a website.

He discounted another offering on the website, suggested for weddings where Highland dress was worn.

'Just in case the bridesmaids were wondering, nothing is worn under my kilt – in fact, I'd go a step further and say everything is in perfect working order.' No, Lucy would kill him. The male members of the bridal party would be wearing kilts; Ryan had decided on Hunting Stewart.

'Ryan, out of all my brothers, is the only one to have asked me to be his best man. That might be because I was about ten when Fraser got married, but all the same.' (Laughter.) 'There's one photograph that we've never really been able to show Jackie before.' Carl would either hold it up or project the image of Ryan, aged one, his face covered in chocolate, wearing a filthy bib, a yellow dummy stuck in his mouth and not a stitch on.

Carl read over what he'd written. Perhaps he should ask the other members of the family what they'd like to hear about. A few more clicks of the mouse and then the website blocked him, asking him for payment before it would show him further examples. Damn, was nothing in life free?

Carl's stomach grumbled. Locking his office, he climbed up the hill to the shop to get a sandwich. He was almost at the top when his phone rang.

'It's me,' Izzy said. 'Just calling to say that's us booked up for Dad's birthday. I take it you'll be down on Sunday?'

'Yes.'

'Good, 'cos I want to discuss what we need to take with us. OK, must dash, my four o'clock's here.'

On impulse, Carl decided he would go to the airport to meet Lucy. She walked out of Domestic Arrivals and was so distracted she banged straight into him. He kissed her, then wrapped his arms around her, not wanting to let go. Each time she went away, when she returned she was distant, and he felt as if he had lost her and had to start over. Even now, he sensed reluctance in her. 'I wanted to surprise you,' he told her.

'You did that all right.'

'Nice surprise?'

'Very nice surprise,' Lucy assured him.

Lucy had some extra-curricular activities planned for them, so they arrived home quite late. Deciding it was his lucky night, Carl initiated round two. Lucy's phone rang at a critical moment and he urged her to leave it.

Carl was at Glasgow Airport earlier than expected for Fraser's flight. The past few weeks had disappeared and the wedding was now only ten days away. Inside the airport, Carl walked upstairs, past the money exchange and the postbox and waited for them to emerge from Domestic

Arrivals. He didn't have long to wait. Fraser and Maisie, sporting matching mahogany tans, were two of the next passengers through. His brother, reserved as ever, didn't hug him, preferring instead to clasp his hand.

'Good flight?' Carl asked.

'Not bad, although we did have some screaming kid kicking the back of our seats for the last two hours. Bloody parents.' Carl detected an Aussie twang in his brother's voice.

'Fraser!' Their mother ran out the door and showered her eldest son in kisses. When they pulled apart, she beamed at him, and then greeted Maisie, in a slightly less exuberant fashion. The rest of the family soon tumbled over the threshold to greet them.

'Fraser.' Izzy acknowledged her brother with a dip of her head.

'Good to see you, Izzy.' His sister gasped as Fraser clasped her to him. Carl raised an eyebrow. Fraser must be mellowing.

'I'll be back tomorrow about eight,' Carl said to Lucy.

'Have a good weekend,' she said, as he slung his rucksack over his shoulder and closed the door. Things had been a bit strained between them recently; not even their proposed holiday had drawn them together. They never seemed to be home at the same time and Lucy was spending more time at work, although she was travelling less. Mistakenly, he thought that meant he would see more of her. But she pointed out that she needed to catch up with other, long-neglected matters. He was beginning to feel envious of those other matters. *He* felt neglected. Anyway, now wasn't the time to be maudlin. They were off to Knockhill to enjoy themselves. Thirty-six men regressing to childhood for the day.

An hour later they arrived at the racing circuit. The other minibus had arrived first, so Ryan, Fraser and Grant came across to greet them, followed by a gaggle of Ryan's friends. Apart from Gary and Grant, who had opted for the racing car, everyone was doing the rally experience.

They resembled a swarm of buzzing bees, with the constant drone of their chatter, as they headed over to the track. Their instructor explained about checking in and getting suited up. Ryan would have his rally experience early and then his Ferrari experience as the culmination to the day. Some of the group became a tad nervous before their turn, others were brimming over with nervous excitement. The instructor talked them through the various techniques, how to cope with oversteer and how to manage weight transfer.

Finally it was time for the high-speed runs. As Donald flew round the track, nearly careering off a few times, the instructor muttered, 'Hope he learns to control that.'

'My turn.' Fraser approached the car.

'He's not as careful as I thought he'd be,' said Carl, as Fraser finished, flushed, close to Donald's time.

'Ryan, you're up,' cried Fraser.

'Now, Ryan, be careful. I promised Jackie you wouldn't come back in bits,' Carl joked.

'Don't worry. I'll be going up that aisle next week if it kills me.'

'That comes once you're married,' one of the lads put

in. They all laughed.

Ryan shot round the track. 'Thank God *you're* not racing him, Grant. Did he hear what we said about remaining in one piece?' Carl asked, as Ryan almost took out a barrier.

'When's his Ferrari 360?'

'He's already done his instruction. We just need to wait for his lap.'

Ryan was blinding in the Ferrari. He shot past them at, they calculated, one hundred and sixty miles per hour.

'Woohoo!' Ryan said. 'That was incredible! Can I do it again?'

'If you've got another few hundred notes to spare,' said Adam.

They piled into the minibuses and swigged beer from their carry-outs. In just over an hour the bus deposited them at the Sheraton. Carl had the booking information.

'Summers party, please,' he said to the receptionist.

'Fifteen twin rooms and two family rooms?' she confirmed.

'That's us.'

'So, meet here in half an hour?' Carl asked.

'That enough time for you to blow-dry your hair?' Ryan ribbed Calum.

'Cheeky git.' His friend dug him in the ribs. 'Don't you have nose hairs to trim?'

The receptionist moved away and appeared to be trying to hide a smile.

Chapter Thirty-nine

'Are we right?' Ryan asked.

'Are we all here?' said Fraser.

Ryan counted. 'Yep, let's hit the road.'

They headed past the Usher Hall and down Spittal Street into the Grassmarket. It was heaving. The rule was one drink per pub, so they ploughed their way through The Last Drop, the Black Bull, the Beehive and the Grassmarket Bar, by which point they were no longer thinking about the names. They made their way up towards Princes Street and amazingly crossed the road without mishap. They wandered up Hanover Street and nipped into a bar near the Assembly Rooms. They hadn't hired a stripper, instead choosing to pay a visit to one of Edinburgh's male-orientated establishments, Allsorts. Charlie told Carl that they could call for a ride, pardon the pun, and the lap-dancing club would send someone to come and pick them up.

'There are thirty-six of us,' Carl reminded him.

'Well they better find a big bus.'

'Fair enough.' Ryan shrugged drunkenly.

Ten minutes later they were in taxis heading for the club. Carl felt weary already; this wasn't his scene, but how could he argue with thirty-five blokes?

'Phwoar, look at her,' Charlie said. 'I wouldn't mind a piece of that.' He indicated a blonde dancer wearing the tiniest black thong Carl had ever seen and a tasselled top which barely covered her nipples. A few of the guys paid for dances. Carl felt uncomfortable. He knew he should be blokey, but it just wasn't his bag. He left the room and found himself a quiet spot to call Lucy. Machine. 'Hi, it's me. Sorry, it's a bit late. You're probably in bed. I'll call you tomorrow.'

Re-entering the club, Carl found a dark-haired girl gyrating over his brother's lap. Ryan was taking it in good fun, although Carl knew he wasn't remotely interested. The same couldn't be said of some of Ryan's friends, whose eyes were out on stalks and whose hands lingered dangerously close to the dancer's buttocks.

Six oversized taxis transported them back to the hotel. They had knocked back quite a bit of alcohol and the kitty was bare. They shushed each other as they traipsed into the Sheraton, like troops returning from war. They weren't in a much better state than broken soldiers. Peter had been sick over Ivor, who wasn't best pleased. They'd had to give the taxi driver an extra fifty pounds to pay for cleaning up his cab. All in all it had been a successful stag party. The sorry little band made for the lifts and staggered up to bed.

Miraculously, they all made breakfast. They had all had the munchies last night, but were too drunk to go foraging for food in the middle of the night. Yet, at ten thirty, they crawled out from under their stones and sat down to a full Scottish. Carl listened to the chatter around him. He felt delicate, but not as bad as the majority, from the groans he could hear and the bloodshot eyes he saw.

'What time are the massages?' Ryan asked.

'One o'clock onwards. You're having a couple of extra appointments.'

'Fair enough. What am I getting done? A pedicure?' Ryan put on a silly French accent. 'Or an Indian head massage?' He tried and failed to put on an Indian accent.

'Wait and see,' Carl said enigmatically.

'I am *not* getting waxed,' Ryan yelled.

'Yes, you are. We didn't tie you up naked, cover you in tar, pour chicken feathers over you and leave you attached to a lamp post, although that was my preference,' Carl said, 'but this is what the guys have agreed is your stag forfeit.'

'Where are the chicken feathers?' Ryan muttered.

'Stop being such a wimp,' Grant said.

Reluctantly, Ryan followed the beautician inside.

'What I'd give for a glass?' Charlie said, pressing his ear to the door.

'I am not having *that* done,' shrieked Ryan.

'Oh yes you are, Ryan,' Charlie shouted through the door, 'and we're going to inspect it later, so you'd better get it done, or we'll think of something worse.'

'What exactly did you ask them to do?' Fraser was curious.

'Back, sack and crack,' Charlie replied nonchalantly.

'Whaaat!' Fraser spat out his mineral water.

'Yep. That should give Jackie something to smile about.' Charlie grinned.

Fifteen minutes later, Ryan walked rather gingerly through the door to join them. 'I hate you. I hate you all. I wish I'd gone on my stag with my worst enemies.'

'We thought it would take your mind off your hangover,' Charlie said.

'Hangover?'

'See, it worked.'

'C'mon,' Carl said. 'Now the fun part.'

'I thought that was last night,' Alan said.

'Well, yes, of course, but a Swedish massage is not to be sneezed at.'

'After what you bastards put me through, I want two Thai girls suspended from the ceiling by ropes jumping up and down on my back.' Ryan huffed.

'That was fantastic,' Ryan said. 'I feel as if I have been pummelled into submission. I got an Indian head massage too and you lot can pay for it.'

'No problem.' Charlie smirked. 'Must be about a pound a head. Could we wax you again if we all put in a pound, say when you get back from honeymoon?'

'No, you bloody well cannot,' Ryan roared.

Carl was last to be dropped off. Lucy's car wasn't in the car park and the lights were out. Atypically, he was glad of the solitude. When Lucy was away, he had plenty of peace, but tonight he needed it. He wasn't used to drinking heavily. Bloody hell, he was turning into a pipe-and-slippers man.

'I'll see you tomorrow, Luce. You'll be OK with Jayne and Richard?'

'Yes, don't fuss.' Jayne was one of the few people in Carl's extended family whom Lucy got on well with. They were staying in the Dalmahoy Golf and Country Club, the wedding venue. To Carl's mother's dismay, there would be no church wedding.

'OK, bye.'

'Now, Ryan, your mother and I want you to know that this will always be your home. That said, I hope you never need to use it.' The rest of the family laughed as their father finished his short speech.

'You're only the third to get married,' their mother said. 'I'm not sure what I'm meant to do about the rest of you.' Again they all laughed.

'No, seriously,' she said.

The cerulean sky was devoid of clouds. It was why Ryan had picked a late summer wedding. A marquee was set up outside for the pre-wedding drinks, in the event that the weather was fair. Otherwise, they'd retire inside to one of the suites. Handmade song sheets lay on the chairs for the guests. Jackie's niece and Flora's daughter were flower girls and Flora's son was pageboy. They thought they were so grown up. Collectively, they appeared innocence itself, but everyone knew better.

Carl wondered if he'd ever be doing this. People got married all the time. It was the same with having kids. Everyone always thought it was no big deal, but it *was* a big deal, if you believed in all it signified. Carl smoothed down his shirt after helping Ryan on with his kilt and secured his skean dhu in the right place. He laced up his shoes and ensured his socks were at the right height. After checking the rings were in his sporran, he scrutinised his big brother. They looked nothing alike; Ryan was six feet and lanky with brown hair, going a little grey now, whilst Carl, as a restaurateur and chef, was never going to be skinny. 'You ready?' Carl smiled at his brother.

'Never more so.'

Ducking into the car, Ryan reached into his sporran and threw silver coins out of the window for the kids in the street to scramble after. It was over an hour to the hotel from Jedburgh, but Ryan had wanted to spend his last night as a single man in the family home. Ryan was strangely quiet. Carl wondered what was going through his mind.

'You nervous?' Carl asked.

'Just thinking.'

'You're not having doubts?' Carl was alarmed.

'No.'

Jackie was beautiful. Five feet three inches with an elfin face and long, naturally curly blonde hair whose waves framed her face. Her blue eyes sparkled and Carl smiled. *That's the way a bride should look on her wedding day.* This woman was so right for his brother. Her ivory strapless dress was dusted in tiny beads and her adorable flower girls held up her train.

The ceremony commenced. The air buzzed with excitement and hope. When the couple exchanged their vows, Carl passed the rings over trance-like.

The bride and groom were soon among their guests and now all Carl had to worry about was his speech. He'd cast a cursory glance over it a few times recently, but hadn't quite perfected it, always expecting to ad lib on the day. No great public speaker, he needed a drink to calm his nerves. As he headed for the bar, shaking hands with all who intercepted him, he was a man on a mission. It would be a few hours before he was called upon again in an official capacity.

In the end the speech went well. Carl forgot a few things and had to refer to his notes, but the champagne flowed and everyone enjoyed themselves. After dinner, they were free to roam around, and he managed to spend a bit of time with Lucy before the matron of honour and then the bride asked him to dance.

The photographer snapped shots of the various couples. Lucy was resplendent in an above-the-knee red chiffon dress with a scooped décolletage. It was sleeveless and floaty. Her hair was piled on top of her head and fastened with a trio of small jewelled clips, showing her slender neck. She had an almost otherworldly air about her.

'Carl, you look as if you've seen a ghost.'

'I'm fine,' Carl said, drinking her in. One day he hoped it would be them. 'Let's dance.' He held out his hand. Coquettishly, Lucy lowered her lashes and took his hand in hers.

Chapter Forty

'Brrrrrrr,' trilled Carl's alarm. He groaned and turned over. Lucy was still beside him. He wondered if she had taken the day off. That was the problem being your own boss, you could choose when to take time off, but you never did.

As he stirred sugar into his coffee, Carl noticed the holiday brochures he'd picked up, lying on the table. He scribbled a note to Lucy asking her to ring him.

Carl sat at his desk composing the menu. He wanted the courses to complement each other. Not too vast nor too restrictive. Carrot cake with lime mascarpone. There. Carl surveyed his efforts and was quietly pleased with himself. He felt he'd struck the right balance. In the brasserie, he would simplify the wording. It wouldn't do to flummox customers.

The flooring was being laid today. Just what Carl needed. After locking himself in his office, he printed out acceptance and rejection letters for the recent interviews he'd held. He needed to get some fresh air. As soon as the guys started hammering, he'd make a sharp exit.

By late afternoon, he had perked up. He decided to take Lucy out for dinner. He hadn't been to Pecorino for ages.

'Hello, is Giovanni there, please?' Carl asked.

'Speaking.'

'Giovanni, it's Carl. How you doing?'

'Carl, my old friend. I am well. You?'

'Busy preparing for the restaurant opening.'

'Fantastic news. I hope to hear all about it soon.'

'I realise it's very short notice, but do you have a table for two tonight?'

'Carl, for you, of course. What time would you prefer?'

'Eight o'clock.'

'Eight o'clock it is.'

'Thanks a lot, Giovanni. Hopefully, we can have a chat after dinner.'

'Absolutely. I am here until closing tonight.'

'See you then and thanks again.'

'Bye, Carl.'

'That was delicious, Giovanni, as always, even if we do come here less than we'd like to.' Carl sat back, hand over his stomach to indicate he was stuffed.

'You still owe me a drink,' Giovanni reminded Carl.

'Yes, we must do that. Anyway, you're invited to the restaurant opening on thirtieth November.'

'Ah, St Andrew's Day. I will put it in my diary,' Giovanni said.

'How was your food?' Carl asked Lucy.

'Mmm, lovely.' This was praise indeed from Lucy. 'Those porcini mushrooms were unbelievable. My risotto never tastes like that.'

Carl spluttered. 'Lucy, you don't cook risotto.'

'Well, if I did cook risotto, it wouldn't taste like that.'

'You can say that again,' Carl muttered.

'We should go out for dinner more often.'

'We should go out more often full stop,' said Carl.

'Yes, we should.' Lucy sat her glass of wine back down. 'I flicked through those holiday brochures. My heart's set on Moofushi.'

'It looks really peaceful, doesn't it, but apparently there's building work going on.'

'That doesn't sound good,' Lucy said. 'I don't fancy paying two thousand pounds each to go and lie on a building site.'

'Me neither.'

'Why don't we just go with one of your other options then?'

'I'll look into it.'

A week later, Carl was at the travel agency trying to book his second choice in the Male Atoll. There was more to do there, but it was another five hundred pounds each.

Holiday finalised, Carl headed to Princes Square. He had decided he wanted to buy his dad a dress watch; it was his seventieth after all. It was turning out to be an expensive day.

Carl arrived at the restaurant just as the furniture van rolled up.

'I see things are coming along nicely here.' The driver nodded his head towards the restaurant.

'Yes, we're a little behind schedule, but I'm confident all will be ready for the big day.'

'Carl. It's me. What did you get Dad?' Izzy asked.

'A watch.'

'Oh good. I bought him golf stuff. I wanted to check we didn't get the same thing.'

'What golf stuff?'

'How should I know?' his sister replied. 'I know bugger all about golf. Sticks, clubs, whatever. I think one's a driver, though.'

'Oh right. Well, I'm sure he'll like them. You did check he doesn't have this "stuff" already?'

'Of course. Listen, Flora and I have sorted out the food and drink.'

'Well, we'll bring a case of wine and some champagne.'

'Ooh, I am looking forward to this party. What does Lucy think?'

'She's, em, looking forward to it too,' Carl managed to spit out.

Izzy laughed. 'Carl, you are such a liar. You know she'll hate every minute. She hates families, especially ours.'

'That's not true. She just doesn't do families, except Holly. And she and Mum don't exactly get on, do they?'

'No, in fact, I'll help keep them apart. Deal?'

'Deal.' Carl was relieved. He had been wondering how to minimise the animosity between the two. It was his dad's celebration, after all.

'Luce, you ready yet? We're late.'

'Coming.' Lucy pouted as she glided down the stairs. She was dressed down today in a white T-shirt, a pair of cargo pants and hiking trainers. Even so, she was beautiful. Her hair was pulled back in a ponytail and her face was make-up free.

They reached the Green Welly just before noon.

'It's a long time since I've been here,' Carl's father said. 'It's all changed.'

Carl agreed. He hadn't been up this way for a few years. 'Hurry up,' he said, indicating the tour bus, which was busy depositing its fifty-strong army of pensioners.

They carried bacon rolls and bowls of soup over to a group of melamine tables. It wasn't a fancy restaurant, but it was the place to come, particularly in winter, for some heart-warming food. Lucy didn't look too impressed, but a glance from Carl warned her not to say anything in front of his mother, who was known for her acerbic tongue where Lucy was concerned.

The others soon poured in and Florence and Harry shrieked in delight upon seeing their assembled relatives. The adults queued whilst the little ones hopped up on their grandparents' laps. Duly fed and watered, they set off again.

As they swung into the grounds of Ardrhu House, their parents gasped. It was impressive. The grey stone baronial mansion looked positively stately, with its extensive grounds and its turret.

'I'd love my bedroom to be in a turret,' Izzy breathed.

'It's so romantic,' Flora murmured.

Flora and Izzy went to see the owner whilst the others milled around. The girls returned shortly afterwards dangling the keys. Everyone wanted to see all of the rooms, so they trailed through each building and finally keys were handed out, once they agreed who would take which room.

'What did you think of the conservatory?' their mother asked.

'It's fantastic,' said Carl. 'Very angular.'

'Yes, I can see us sitting in there in the evening.'

'I love the Jacuzzi suite,' Jackie said, looking at Ryan.

Their parents had offered the room to Jackie and Ryan, as newlyweds. The excitement was evident on Jackie's face. Carl guessed they'd slip away under the pretext of needing an early night. They agreed to meet in the dining room in half an hour and headed off to get settled in.

An excited babble awaited them in the kitchen where Flora and Izzy were unpacking the shopping. Foie gras, asparagus, goat's cheese, venison was piled into the fridge. They'd spent a fortune, but it would be worth it. Carl had helped compile the list, although he'd left buying it to the girls, well aware he would be heavily contributing to the cooking. He placed the wine he'd brought with him and some chocolates on the worktop.

'We've put Dad's cake in our fridge,' Izzy whispered.

'Good. What's for lunch?' he asked, tearing open a packet of ham and nibbling a slice.

'Hands off.' Flora smacked his hand away. 'We're making lunch. If you want something now, have an apple.'

'Gee, thanks,' Carl moaned.

'It won't be long.'

Over lunch they made plans for the weekend. They were keen to explore the local area. On the outskirts of Onich, some of the younger crew fancied bagging a Munro.

'We're meant to be spending time with Dad,' Flora said disapprovingly.

'We have plenty of time. If you want to go walking that's fine. Your mother and I have plans too.'

'That's right,' their mother piped up. 'I'd quite like to go to Inchree Falls.'

'Fair enough,' said Flora. 'I don't mind watching the kids if any of you are keen to take Grant up on his hill-climbing offer.'

The grounds took his breath away; acres and acres of land spread out as far as the eye could see. A hedge maze lay off to the left and there was even a little ornamental pond, where a few ducks bobbed along.

'Look, a tennis court,' shouted Izzy.

'Izzy, you don't play tennis,' said Grant.

'So? I might start now.'

'I don't know about you, but I'm here for a rest.' Flora yawned.

'Lucy, you'll play, won't you?'

'Why not?'

Carl was taken aback. Lucy didn't usually have much time for Izzy. She really was on her best behaviour this weekend.

They passed the day peacefully in some cases, noisily in others. It was lovely, their being together, yet doing their own thing. Izzy and Lucy were playing tennis; Carl's parents were sitting outside absorbing the infrequent rays of sunshine; the children were scrambling over the play equipment, with Flora keeping a watchful eye on them; and the other adults were relaxing on chairs, reading or listening to music. Carl lay back on his chair and started to read his new detective novel. He didn't often get time to read and soon he'd need to make a start on dinner.

'This looks amazing,' Carl's father said, looking down at his medallions of beef in a Marsala sauce, with parsnip mash. They'd started with smoked salmon and they were finishing with home-made chocolate tortes. Whilst Flora had helped Carl, Lucy had lounged in the sitting room, not lifting a finger. She came through every so often, refilled her wine glass and returned to the sitting room. Carl sighed. He supposed it was his penance for her being here. She didn't do these things easily. Maybe he should cut her some slack, but she could at least help a little; everyone else was mucking in.

After dinner, the mints came out, then the cheese and port and Trivial Pursuit. Flora put the kids to bed around ten and then the adults really began to unwind, sharing stories with each other, the pressures of everyday life ebbing away. Even when they were at their parents' house it wasn't quite the same ambience. They were invariably coming from or going somewhere and only had a couple of hours, except at Christmas. Being on holiday was different, special. Carl relaxed fully into the evening and reached for another bottle of wine.

Chapter Forty-one

Birdsong woke Carl next morning. That and the sun pouring into the bedroom through the vast Gothic arch window. He peered at the clock: seven thirty. If they were going to go up the mountain, they'd best get a move on, as they needed to be back before five to start making the birthday dinner. He nudged Lucy. 'Luce, it's half seven. You coming on this walk?'

'Uh.' Lucy buried her head under the covers. 'Yes, s'pose.'

'Get up then, c'mon.'

'Give me five minutes.'

Carl washed quickly. No point showering since they were going hillwalking; he'd have a good scrub later. He roused those siblings who'd expressed an interest in hillwalking, and after a few gulps of tea and some hastily prepared toast, they set off. *At least it's a good day, not overly warm, but then it is still early.*

'I think we can do it in about six hours,' Grant said.

'C'mon,' Fraser said. 'The sooner we start, the sooner we get back.'

Buachaille Etive Beag's Stob Coire Raineach stood at nine hundred and twenty-five metres. It was a gruelling walk and the unforgiving sun beat down on them for most of the day. Fortunately, Izzy had remembered to bring sunscreen, which they were all relieved at, as they didn't want to be in their father's birthday photographs looking like pillar boxes.

'Yay, I've done a Munro,' Izzy whooped, dancing druid-like around the cairn. Carl passed sandwiches around, whilst Grant poured some soup out of the vacuum flask and Lucy distributed chocolate.

'This is the life,' Fraser said, as his eyes took in Rannoch Moor and the Aonach Eagach.

'Yup,' Ryan agreed. 'Look at that view. It's incredible.'

'We'd best head down,' Grant said. Reluctantly, the others agreed. When you were up here, Carl thought, you lost all sense of time.

'Happy birthday to you, happy seventieth birthday to you, happy seventieth birthday, dear Daddy–' they all hammed it up, grinning at each other '–happy birthday to you. Hip hip hooray, hip hip hooray.'

'Now, Dad, we figured seventy candles might bring about a heart attack with the effort of trying to blow them all out.' Flora smiled at her father. 'So we thought seven would be sufficient.'

Her father looked at her and then each of his children and the other assembled family members. Drawing breath into his lungs, he then blew out all of the candles in one go, with a little help from Florence and her cousins.

'Don't write me off just yet,' their father warned, as he moved back to allow Flora to cut the cake, the kids jumping up and down beside him.

'Me next,' cried Finlay.

Cake consumed, they retired to the sitting room with

their coffee and liqueurs. Flora and Izzy had gone to a lot of effort to ensure it was a memorable experience, not just for their father, but for the whole family. Whilst Izzy had been mountain climbing with her brothers, Flora and Jackie had been decorating the room with balloons and banners and photographs of all the family.

'We have a surprise for you, Dad,' Flora announced.

'More surprises? That was a lovely dinner, Carl.' His father patted his arm affectionately. 'That Beef Wellington has to go on your menu. It was delicious.'

'Thanks, Dad.' Carl smiled. Even as a professional chef of many years standing, a comment like that, from his father, still meant the world to him.

'So, what's this surprise then?' their father asked.

Lucy was busy rigging up a laptop to the TV. Carl pressed the remote control and the first image flashed across the screen. Carl's commentary commenced.

'This is Dad, aged six months.' A grainy black-and-white photo of a pale, chubby baby with a large gummy smile appeared.

'Dad, this is you, at two years.' A picture of a baby with a chocolate-covered Babygro came into view.

'Dad starting school.' A photo of a little boy with knobbly knees, a grey school cap and a dark wool jersey with the prerequisite short trousers.

'Dad winning his first game of football at St Machan's, aged seven.' The slides continued as tears glistened in their father's eyes, as he revisited his past.

When Carl had introduced the last slide, of them all together the day before, Gordon wiped his eyes and said, 'Where did you get all those photos? There are some I haven't seen for years and others I've never seen.'

'We did a lot of digging.' Flora put her arm around

their dad. 'And we trawled the local newspapers' archives.'

'Thank you. I'll treasure this forever.'

His children smiled at him.

'Oh, that reminds me,' Flora said. 'Presents.'

'Me first,' Florence said.

'Thank you, hen.' Her grandfather tore off the wrapping paper, whilst Florence told him that this present was from her and her cousins. Initially, Gordon was bemused, as he wasn't quite sure what it was.

'It's a digital photo frame, Grandpa. Look.' Florence switched on the device, and instantly, pictures of his grandchildren flooded the screen. Carl saw his father was tearing up, so to save him the embarrassment, he handed him his gift next.

'Thanks, son,' his father said to him in gratitude. 'That's a lovely gift, boys and girls. Grandpa will put that in his living room so he can see you all the time.'

'It's from me and Lucy.'

'Oh, son, that's lovely. It's awfully expensive-looking though.'

'It wasn't too dear, Dad, and you're only seventy once.'

The gift-giving continued. The last one opened, their father said, 'I'd like to be seventy again next year. Look at all these gifts. You've all been very generous. Thank you again for organising this trip. It means a lot to me and your mum.' He eyed his wife fondly and she smiled.

The celebrations continued, champagne flowed, truffles were eaten and as the evening progressed, they moved on to whisky. After a few more Bunnahabhains than was advisable, pleasantly sozzled, Carl headed for bed. He wasn't the first to call it a night, nor the last, but he had to drive tomorrow and wanted to be fit for it. It was already three thirty. The kids had been hounded off to bed at eleven, and since then, the adults had deteriorated into having a sing-song and the occasional impromptu dance. Throat sore from singing, Carl had decided to bow out. Lucy, however, remained. She was busy chatting with Jackie, so after a quick kiss on the head, he said he'd see her later. By that, he meant, in the morning, as he was quite sure once he hit the pillow, nothing would wake him.

'I'm so glad to be home.' Carl slumped in the recliner.

'Yes, me too,' agreed Lucy. 'Do you want a cup of tea?'

'Yes, please and a bacon sarnie, if I'm not pushing my luck.'

Lucy stared at him. Carl grinned. He never asked her to make anything, unless he'd put new batteries in the smoke alarm. He was hopeful she could manage to prepare coffee and bacon though.

'Coming right up.'

Carl reeled from the shock. Bliss. He could just lie here and enjoy the rest of his Sunday.

'Here you go.' Lucy nudged Carl with a plate bearing two bacon rolls, liberally covered in brown sauce.

'Oh thanks, Luce. You're an angel.'

'No problem. Listen, I'm going over to see Elisa.'

'OK. I'm just going to veg here, maybe watch *Top Gear*.'

'Right, well, see you later.' She patted his chest and went to grab her coat from the coat stand.

'Enjoy,' Carl said, before wolfing down his first bacon roll.

The next night, Lucy was at body combat and Carl was taking advantage of the peace and quiet to catch up on some paperwork.

'Hi,' Lucy called to him from the hallway.

'Hi. How was your class?' Carl asked from his position under the en suite sink, which had sprung a leak.

'Good, thanks.' Lucy came into the bedroom. 'What's up?' She stood in the doorway, suffused in a healthy glow, whilst Carl was covered in drips of water and dust.

'It's leaking.'

'Not good. I'll leave you to get on with it. Do you want some wine?'

'No, thanks.'

'Right. Can I use the water downstairs?'

'Yes.' Carl grunted as he tightened the nut.

When Carl came back downstairs, Lucy was texting.

She glanced up. 'Oh, I have a conference this weekend I forgot about.'

'Pity. I thought we could have gone to Il Pescatore on Saturday.' Carl was marginally put out but tried to hide his disappointment. 'Never mind, it'll keep.'

'Great.'

'How's The Steadings coming along? I can't believe it's only six weeks until it opens.'

'I know. I can't wait.' Carl tried not to let his surprise at Lucy's interest show. Maybe she was simply making an effort. But since she was asking… 'I'm nearly there, Luce. Each room looks amazing. The colour schemes are perfect, exactly as I envisaged.'

Lucy made a non-committal sound which Carl took as a sign to go on.

'All the menus are done and all the provisions have been ordered. I only have a few minor details to sort, and we're actually ahead of schedule.'

'That's really great, Carl. I'm proud of you.'

Carl's heart lifted. Her validation meant a lot to him.

'I'll see you late Sunday,' Lucy said to Carl.

'Have a great time.' Carl kissed her.

'It's a conference, I'm not *meant* to enjoy myself,' she said.

'OK, well, enjoy the food. They always feed you well at these things, don't they?'

'I suppose.'

'Give me a call when you're at the airport.'

'Will do.' She kissed him lingeringly on the mouth and then left.

Carl's weekend had been blissful so far. He'd cooked, had a few glasses of wine, listened to a bit of music, he'd even cut the grass, but basically he had chilled out. He had even managed to read a bit more of the John Grisham he'd been trying to get into for ages.

Now he lay on the couch, drinking Rioja and munching on crostini he'd made as a late-night snack. He'd just put on *Die Hard* and plumped up two cushions behind him when the doorbell rang.

Two Strathclyde Police officers were standing in front of him when he opened the door.

'Is everything OK?' he asked.

'Carl Summers?'

'Yes. That's me.'

'Can we come in, sir?'

'Yes, of course. Is everything all right?'

'I'm afraid there's been an accident…'

Chapter Forty-two
Maria – LEO

Generous and warm-hearted. Protective of those close to them, especially children and those who are weak. Strong and surprisingly sensitive. Excellent organisational skills. Make bold plans.

'David, stop pushing Amy!' Maria shouted at her son in frustration. David could be a right little devil. He was seeing how far he could push her. He'd been following his little sister around like a second skin all day, so much so that when three-year-old Amy turned around, her brother bumped into her. Maria could tell Amy was getting annoyed. *It won't be long before* she's *pushing* you *around, buster.*

'Amy, come here so I can put your jacket on. David, get Amy's red hat for me, please.'

Obediently her son did as he was told.

'You like red, don't you, Amy?'

Her daughter, perched on Maria's knee, said, 'Don't like yellow.'

'No, you don't like yellow. What's yellow the colour of?'

'The sun,' said David.

'That's right. Good boy. What else?'

'Mr Wilson's car.'

'That's right too.' Their neighbour had a yellow Micra.

'Big Bird yellow,' Amy cried.

'That's right. Big Bird is in *Sesame Street.*'

'Mum,' David asked, 'is Sesame Street near Isaac's house?'

'No. It's in America.'

Frowning in concentration, David asked, 'Is that in England?'

'No. England is next to Scotland. America is across the big sea.' Technically it was an ocean, but Maria felt now was not the time for explanations. On reflection, perhaps she should have clarified matters, otherwise how would he ever learn? She was a firm believer in teaching coming from the home. As a single parent she felt this responsibility even more keenly. She'd never be accused of leaving teaching to the teachers. School certainly wasn't what it was when she was a pupil but she *was* grateful for Amy's nursery place. Coupled with David being in primary one now, it gave her five mornings of sanity a week.

Maria counted herself quite lucky. Their three-bedroom house in the village of Kings River, near Glasgow, was five minutes' walk from the nursery and primary school. Maria knew she had made the right decision moving here from the city, which could be rather lonely. David's conception was the result of a lapse in judgement. His father had no intention of sticking around. Then, whilst pregnant, she'd met Stuart, who was warm, kind, funny, took the bins out, put the toilet seat down and even bought her flowers occasionally. Before David was born, he asked her to marry him. She said yes and they were married when her bump had subsided. Stuart was delighted when David came into the world, not caring that David wasn't his natural son. He was Maria's birthing partner and had tears in his eyes when he held his son for the first time. He'd always expected to be a father, just not that quickly.

The first few months were hard; sleepless nights, a crying baby, Maria trying to work part-time from home, yet still breastfeeding. All her energy had left her and Stuart was run ragged too. No more socialising with his mates at the pub. When he came home from working in his garage, he was no sooner across the threshold, than Maria put David into his arms. She was wrecked. She'd grab a twenty-minute nap before dinner, whilst Stuart cooed at David. He blew raspberries on his tummy, tickled him and jumped up and down pretending to be a gorilla – anything to amuse him.

Six months after David was born, Maria discovered her period was late. She couldn't be pregnant surely. She was still breastfeeding and they always used condoms. So Maria nipped into the chemist and bought herself a pregnancy testing kit. The test was positive. She made an appointment with her doctor, to have him confirm it, but she already knew. Did she already feel different, or was she imagining it? The doctor congratulated her. Maria asked Stuart to be home on time. She picked David up from her mother's and ensured that their little family unit was intact for Stuart's arrival.

Stuart was over the moon. Although he considered David to be his son, Maria knew what it would mean to him to have his own child. They didn't tell anyone for the first twelve weeks, preferring to be cautious, but after that, you couldn't hold Stuart back. It had been easy to hide the pregnancy initially, as no one expected Maria to drink whilst she was breastfeeding David. Although their friends and families were taken aback at the two pregnancies so close together, they were happy for the couple. Stuart showered Maria and David with gifts, was even more affectionate than usual and talked about buying a house in the countryside. Their two-bedroom flat in Shawlands was lovely, but impractical with two young children. They spent hours poring over schedules, whilst Stuart ticked off the criteria for the location. Since they wouldn't be planning to move again anytime soon, good schools were a must, as was decent public transport.

One day Stuart came home from work, bursting with excitement. He'd found the perfect place. Fifteen miles from Glasgow, a village of seven hundred people, with a shop, a pub, a village hall and a primary school. Maria agreed that it sounded good, but had he checked out houses for sale there? Could they afford it? Well, that was the catch. As everyone loved living there, it was rare for people to move. So, they waited.

A few weeks later, Stuart called Maria to ask her to check out a property which had come up for sale.

'It's within our price range.'

Maria brought the website up. It was beautiful. Three bedrooms, large back garden, dining kitchen and a spacious, airy lounge. Without hesitation, Maria said, 'OK, make the appointment.'

Stuart rang back a few minutes later. 'We can see it tonight at six thirty.'

Stuart had said he wouldn't be late, so at quarter to six,

Maria dialled his mobile. No answer. When six o'clock came, she called again. Still no answer. Damn, now they were going to be late. She'd kill Stuart. By quarter past six she was beginning to worry. At six thirty she headed over to his garage to see what the hold-up was.

Driving at the speed limit, she made good time until she was slowed by heavy traffic ahead. 'Bloody roadworks.' Maria scowled. But this time it wasn't roadworks which was the problem. An ambulance flew past her, blue lights flashing, and drivers hurriedly pulled their cars up on the verge. As the siren faded, the traffic gradually started to move again.

'Thank God.' But as she approached the crux of the hold-up, she felt uneasy. Something wasn't right. Slamming on the brakes, she got out, oblivious to the car horns honking behind her. A scream tore from her throat. Stuart's Volvo lay wrecked in front of her. The roof had been ripped off and there was virtually nothing left of the driver's side. An articulated lorry lay awkwardly beside it, relatively unscathed. Maria could hear the policemen telling her to calm down, but she couldn't stop sobbing and she barely managed to croak, 'It's my husband's car,' before she collapsed.

When she came to, she was wearing a hospital gown. Her father was holding her hand, tears streaming down his face.

'Oh, Dad, please no.'

Her father looked at her sadly.

'Was it Stuart?' She had to be sure.

'I'm sorry, darling.' Her father's voice broke.

Maria fainted again. When she woke up, her thoughts were of the baby.

'Is the baby OK?'

'The baby's fine. They put you here because you fell when you saw the car. When the police realised what you were saying and that you were pregnant, they weren't taking any chances. Then they called me.'

'I need to see him,' she said firmly. 'Where is he?'

'I don't know exactly. I'm not sure if they've taken him to the mor–' He couldn't finish.

'Dad, what happened?'

'Stuart's car collided with a lorry.'

'Dad, it was wrecked.' Stifling a sob, she asked, 'Did he die instantly?'

Her father held her close and said, 'Yes, he didn't suffer.'

Stuart was gone. Gone and now he would never see his baby, which was growing inside her.

The next few weeks passed in a blur. Her parents moved in with her. Maria barely remembered the funeral; Stuart's parents had handled it. Her mother insisted she ate properly as she was still breastfeeding and also had to think of Stuart's baby inside her. That spurred her on.

Chapter Forty-three

'Push, Maria, push,' commanded the midwife. Maria clutched her mother's hand, as a scream burst from her throat. As yet another contraction ripped through her she bore down again. She closed her eyes and saw Stuart's face, urging her on. Alternating between despair at Stuart not being there to witness this and joy at the imminent birth of her child, she gave one final push.

'It's a girl,' said the midwife.

'Amy,' whispered Maria.

'Would you like your mum to cut the cord?' the midwife asked her. Mother and daughter exchanged a glance and Maria's mother took the scissors from the midwife.

As Maria watched her mother sever the physical link between her and her baby, she fought back tears as she thought how proud Stuart would have been of the little bundle of perfection they had created.

The midwife swaddled Amy in a towel then passed Amy to Maria. Out of such pain, comes such joy. She wasn't thinking of the labour pain, but the pain of losing her soulmate. Compared to that, labour had been a breeze. Amy looked so like her father: same eyes, nose and chin, and would serve as a constant reminder of Stuart.

Six months later, Maria's father brought her a schedule for a house in Kings River.

'Dad, what are you doing?'

'The flat's too small for you and it would mean you were closer to us.'

'Dad, I can't move there. That's where Stuart chose.'

'And that's precisely why you should move there. It's what Stuart wanted, for your family.'

Maria looked down at her daughter, who was gurgling in her rocker. 'I don't know.'

'Maria, it's got to be worth a look. It's the same house.'

'What?'

'It came back on the market.'

'Isn't that too weird?' Maria asked.

'I prefer to think of it as fate. Will I book a viewing?'

In two minds, Maria relented.

They went to see the house. Very little had changed since the photos Maria had seen previously. Her father had advised her not to mention how interested she might be in the house, as the owner might accept a lower offer to hasten the sale. Although she'd done OK from the insurance policy Stuart had put in place for them when they married, she would still need a small mortgage. The south-side flat should fetch a decent price, but Kings River was a much-sought-after locale.

The house was perfect. When the estate agent went downstairs to give them some privacy, Maria had cried on her father's shoulder.

'I think you should put an offer in,' her dad said.

Through a haze of tears, she agreed.

They'd lived here nearly three years now. Maria dedicated

herself to her family. Every now and then, she ventured out with friends, but she wasn't remotely interested in finding another partner. What were the chances of finding two soulmates in this life? She was the happiest she'd been in years. She loved her children intensely and often thought of her husband. Grateful to have such a level-headed father, she would have been lost without him.

'I want chocolate buttons, Mummy,' David cried, as he skipped along on his way to school.

'Fudge,' Amy said.

'If you're very good, you'll get a treat when you come home.'

'Want it now,' sulked Amy.

'Me too,' cried David.

'David, Amy, later. Understood?'

Meekly they mumbled, 'Sorry, Mummy.'

She might be overprotective, but she instilled discipline in her children. Would Stuart have done the same? she wondered. Sometimes she felt he would have been more lenient, but rather than be soft on them, as some sort of compensation for not having a father, Maria had chosen the opposite tack. She needed them to be tough for all the knocks life threw at them. They were allowed to watch one hour of television a day. Maria wanted to encourage creativity, to develop their imaginations. Rather than allow them to watch as much TV as they could stomach, they had to choose just one programme each. She spent a lot of time playing with them. Now her life was about her children and her work; her events company, Occasions, had prospered greatly in the last few years. Fortunately the children hadn't yet reached the stage of football practice, karate, ballet and piano lessons, so she was able to enjoy them whilst she was still the centre of their universe.

Maria ensured the children had everything, settled them into school, kissed them goodbye and returned home, via McAndrew's. The shop was an institution in the village; it first sold goods to the miners, when Kings River was in its infancy. Times had changed and both the railway line and the mines were long gone. The nearest train station was five miles away, although the village was on the main bus route. The shop sold everything the villagers could need at short notice and served as shop, bakery, butcher and post office. It was much larger than the original store opened in 1852. Although more expensive than the big supermarkets in town, the prices weren't so inflated that they drove customers away. On the contrary, people had been coming here for years.

Many people came to Kings River because they liked the idea of village life and had moved here away from the hustle and bustle of the city. Their children were also guaranteed to receive a good education. There were only fifty pupils at the tiny primary school and nine at the nursery. The four teachers, two classroom assistants and headmistress were a definite attraction. With the tranquillity of village life and removing themselves from the stresses of the city, people lived longer and the village was home to a burgeoning elderly population.

Maria moved around the shop. Ian McAndrew, the great-grandson of the founder, was busy with a customer, so Maria picked up a basket and trundled around the shop. Hedgehog bread for David, a few tins of soup; even she could cheat every so often. She added some tomatoes, lettuce, carrots and some goat's cheese, as well as the kids' chocolate.

'Hi, Maria. Just dropped off the little ones?' Ian asked.

'Yes. Now for some peace and quiet.'

'How's business?'

'Good, thanks.'

'Oh, my sister-in-law asked me for your details. It's her golden wedding anniversary in two months and she's just booked the venue and wants to arrange the invitations now.'

'That's great, Ian. Thanks.'

Maria was grateful for the recommendation. When her husband had died so tragically, and it being such a small village, everyone knew about her circumstances before she even moved in. There was no malice behind their whispered comments, and although she hadn't mixed with anyone initially and had been rather reserved, scarcely saying two words, it hadn't been long before the village had started to welcome and support her.

Within a few weeks of her introducing herself to Ian McAndrew, she'd received a request from a local woman to design a special Christmas card. Some silver wedding invitation and response cards followed. After that, the enquiries poured in. It kept her busy, temporarily taking her mind off her widow status and allowed her to work from home whilst her children were infants. When both children went to nursery, her father suggested it was time to branch out, so she'd quickly enlisted her sister and best friend's help.

Shopping unpacked, Maria sat down to write her to-do list.

<u>Mon</u>
Send sample card to printer for McKillops
Printers re cards for Hennesseys
Arrange meeting for Wed 14th Lighthouse Inn
Carriages re rehearsal dinner for Struthers
Renew employment insurance
Meet with McKillops

Maria decided that was enough to be going on with. After a few hours, she checked her watch and saw that soon she would have to collect the children. Although she worked from home, her mother took care of the children two afternoons a week. Today was one of Maria's afternoons and so work was put on hold again.

'Mummy!' Amy called, running towards her, face red with exertion. It was chilly today, even though it was summer. David had only started school two weeks ago. She couldn't quite believe her little boy was nearly five. She wished Stuart could have seen him. It had been very emotional for her, although David had strutted about the place in his new red jersey, black trousers and polished black shoes oblivious.

'Hi, sweetie.' Maria crouched down and hugged her daughter.

'I got a book, Mummy.'

'You have a book?' Maria asked.

'Yes. It has a gruffalo.'

'A gruff-a-lo?' Maria emphasised the word.

'Yes. Can we read it when we get home?' Amy asked.

'After lunch. Let's go and find David.'

They found him deep in conversation with a little girl.

'What's your name?' Maria asked, not recognising her.

'Angelika,' the girl said with a trace of an accent.

Ah, this must be the little Polish girl. She had heard that a family from Gdansk had moved into the village. The little girl was beautiful; pure white hair, big blue eyes, immense eyelashes and white, almost translucent, skin, with that amazing bone structure that only Eastern Europeans seem to have.

'Nice to meet you, Angelika,' Maria said. She already knew that Angelika's family lived in the street behind theirs.

'David, c'mon. Say bye to Angelika. You'll see her this afternoon.'

'Bye.' David took his mother's hand, but his eyes remained on Angelika.

David deposited back at school after lunch, Maria asked her daughter, 'Amy, where's your book?'

'Here it is, Mummy.' Amy plopped her Dora the Explorer satchel down on her mother's lap.

'OK. Let's see. *The Gruffalo.*'

Amy snuggled into her mother, fingers playing with her hair, as her mother read. After the fifth reading, Maria had had enough.

'OK, Amy, we can read it again tonight. Why don't you go and play with your dolls?'

'Don't want to.' Amy pouted.

Maria grimaced. She was like her brother in many ways. Unfortunately, although she had Stuart's temperament and could be very sweet, she'd learned from David how to remonstrate. Sighing, Maria said, 'Go and get a puzzle.'

Visibly cheered, Amy set off, dragging her bag with her. Maria didn't have time to constantly be tidying, so she trained the children well. It wasn't a big ask, but it helped. It never ceased to amaze her when she visited friends who had kids, whose houses were in complete chaos, with bits of trodden-in cornflakes on their floors. Then there were the dirty bibs, wipes and nappies; the latter thankfully clean, strewn around. She simply couldn't live like that.

Amy returned with the puzzle, a huge smile on her face. She dumped all the pieces out of the box.

'Igglepiggle!' she cried.

'Yes, that's Igglepiggle. Now, where's the other piece?' Maria asked.

Eyebrows furrowed in concentration, Amy pointed to a piece with blue in it.

Maria shook her head 'No, that's the sky.'

Amy found another blue piece, which also had a red section. 'Blankie.'

'That's right. The red piece is his blankie.'

She put the blue Igglepiggle and the half blue, half red piece together and smiled smugly at her mother.

'Now, where's Makka Pakka?' Maria asked.

Amy found a flesh-coloured piece of the tubby character and soon finished the puzzle then took it apart and started again. Whilst Amy was content to amuse herself, Maria jotted down items she needed to address. Their council tax needed sorting out, and she also had to go to the dry cleaner's in Kilburn, as she needed her suit cleaned for the wedding on Saturday.

Maria sat back on her recliner, added a few more items to her list, then picking up her cordless phone, padded through to the kitchen, closing the door behind her.

'Sandra. Hi, it's me. Any calls?' Maria listened as her assistant related a tale of woe about flower arrangements. She made notes as Sandra gave her a few bullet points and then added that Mr McKinstrie had left a message for her.

Alasdair McKinstrie III from Houston, Texas had Scottish heritage and therefore wanted to marry in a Scottish castle. Money was no object. They'd pared the options down to Dalhousie Castle, near Edinburgh, handy for guests flying in from the States; Duns Castle, in the Borders, with its Gothic architecture; and finally Edinburgh Castle. Maria didn't know if they would prefer the status of the latter. Certainly its location and presence dominating the city would impress. It was world-famous and instantly recognisable, but from a romantic perspective, she preferred Dalhousie Castle, with its library, secret bar, restaurant in the barrel-vaulted dungeon and period-furnished bedrooms.

Mr McKinstrie and Ms Geller intended visiting Scotland before choosing the venue, much to Maria's relief. She had gleaned that Cynthia Geller would be hard to please. It would be easier to get the measure of her when she was here and hopefully provide her with everything she needed to have the perfect wedding.

Maria completed her action items and made herself some tea. She glanced at the cuckoo clock on the wall, a gift from her grandfather, handmade in the Black Forest. It would soon be time for her to go and collect David. But first, she had to call the council tax office.

Chapter Forty-four

'Mummy, I want to go to Angelika's house,' David said as they walked home.

'Not today, David. We haven't met her mummy and daddy yet.'

David took the huff and pet lip out, arms folded, tried to squirm away from his mother.

'David, behave, or there will be no TV,' Maria said.

Reluctantly, David stopped his tantrum and reached his hand out to her. How wonderful it was to be a child, Maria thought, as they skipped home. Boys in particular had a fantastic capacity for forgetting slights, within five seconds of their happening. David had returned almost immediately to the sunny-natured little boy she loved.

'Right, David. Uniform off. Your play clothes are on the bed.'

Ten minutes later, David waltzed into the room. 'Mummy,' he complained, 'we're missing Dora.'

Maria flicked on the programme as Amy inched her way towards the TV.

'Amy, sit on the couch and watch,' said Maria. 'You're too close.'

Drawing her mother daggers, as only three-year-old

girls know how, Amy sat back, twirling her hair in her index finger.

Good, I might be able to make that call to the States now.

Maria ended the call to Alasdair McKinstrie to yells from the lounge, where Amy was standing over David, whacking him with a plastic spade.

'Amy, stop that!' She dragged her daughter away. 'Why did you do that?'

Amy didn't answer. 'OK, naughty step for you.' Maria took her daughter out to the hall and sat her on the bottom step. Bringing herself down to Amy's eye level, she told her why she was there and left. Five minutes later, ensuring her daughter apologised to her son, she left them to play again.

When Maria returned from making chicken goujons, she found them putting Mouse Trap together. David's tongue was hanging out slightly, whilst he concentrated, his sister wordlessly passing him the pieces. Maria promised them they could play it after dinner; as a result dinner was a quick affair. Amy tried to be sly, mushing hers up and dropping it under the table, but Maria noticed and told her she had to clean it up and if she caught her doing it again, she would go straight to bed.

'Mummy, I'm the green mouse. You moved the red one!' squeaked David.

'David, don't shout. Mummy made a mistake. Look, I'm putting Amy's mouse back.'

David was satisfied with this and twenty minutes later, it was Maria's unsuspecting mouse that was on the receiving end of the cage falling from the top of the post. The children looked at each other in glee.

'I won, Mummy. I got your mouse,' said David.

'Well done. Right, bath time.'

Amy ran away. David groaned.

'David, pyjamas, please.'

A docile David complied, whilst Maria went looking for Amy. She always hid in the same place – the walk-in cupboard. Maria tried not to laugh. When would children understand that hide and seek meant just that? You hide, someone looks for you. You don't reveal your hiding place when they get near, and you don't hide in the same place. Within twenty seconds, Maria was in possession of a wriggling, squealing Amy.

Maria loved when the children were freshly washed, hair still damp, smelling of baby shampoo. She dried Amy whilst David towelled himself, although Maria knew she'd still have to dry his back and ensure he was properly dry, particularly his fingers and toes. That boy must have been a seal in a previous life. He'd happily leave the house sopping wet. She towelled down her two children and then left them on the sofa with *The Gruffalo* for Amy, again, and *The Faraway Tree* for David, whilst she went to fetch their milk. Handing them their chocolate milk, she sat down between them to read their stories.

Amy was enthusiastic throughout the telling of *The Gruffalo*, but Maria could see her flagging before she reached the second page of David's book. She stopped briefly to throw a blanket over her daughter and then with a look of complicity at David, they snuggled together and she continued telling him about Moon Face, Saucepan Man and Silky.

David tried to press his mother for another chapter, but she was strict and, realising it was already late, told him it would have to wait until tomorrow. Maria carried Amy up to bed.

'Teeth, David.'

Groaning, David trudged off to the bathroom. What was it with little boys that they didn't like to be clean? That said, Maria remembered she had more problems bathing Amy than David. She put the night light on, tucked them in, kissed them goodnight and went downstairs to curl up with a book for half an hour.

Maria woke with a start. Damn, she'd fallen asleep on the chair. What time was it? Two o'clock? Bones creaking, she raised herself off the chair, turned off the TV and the lamps and went to bed.

The alarm seemed to go off just after Maria hit the pillow. It couldn't be seven o'clock. Two cups of coffee later, she felt much better. Today her mother looked after the kids. Maria simply had to take them to school.

Amy came downstairs, so Maria made her toast and egg soldiers and gave her a glass of milk, then went up to rouse her brother. They complemented each other well; Amy kicked and screamed to avoid having a bath and David made a major production of getting up. He slept very deeply; a hurricane could rip through their home and David would be none the wiser.

Kids dropped at school, Maria headed home for a few hours of uninterrupted work. First she transferred the cash into the children's trust funds and sorted her clothes for dry cleaning. She'd take them into town before the lunchtime rush. She stopped only to make a cup of tea and a sandwich, as although she'd given the kids breakfast, she'd completely forgotten to make any for herself. Wolfing down her sandwich, something she was glad the children weren't there to see, she grabbed her car keys and left for town.

Busy putting her purse back in her bag, Maria collided with someone as she came out of the dry cleaner's.

'Oh, I'm sorry,' she said. A split second later, she realised it was Angelika's mum. What a coincidence. 'You're Angelika's mum, aren't you?'

Maria couldn't decide if the reed-thin Polish woman looked at her warily or quizzically. Her mind went blank; she couldn't remember her name, although she'd thought about her only yesterday.

'Czeslawa,' she said, pronouncing it like ch in chestnut and replacing the W sound with a V. Maria thought she could figure out how it was spelled. Years ago, she'd worked with a Pole called Wieslaw.

Maria held her hand out. 'Maria, nice to meet you. My son David is in the same class as your daughter. Angelika, isn't it?'

Czeslawa nodded.

On impulse Maria said, 'Do you have time for a coffee?'

Czeslawa's eyes widened, but soon a slow smile broke out across her face and she said, 'Of course.'

They were only a few steps from Taylor's Tearoom, so Maria led the way, ducking to avoid the low ceiling as they entered. Indicating a free table, Maria said, 'What would you like?'

'Tea, please.'

'Would you like a cake?' Maria indicated the colourful array of cakes and pastries.

Czeslawa appeared unsure.

'Their honey and orange tea loaf is wonderful. My treat.'

Czeslawa accepted and Maria returned a few minutes later bearing a tray with two pots of tea and two slices of tea loaf. Czeslawa thanked Maria with a smile which reached all the way to her cornflower-blue eyes.

'So, how you do like living in the village?' Maria asked.

'Yes, very nice. Very happy here.'

Maria understood from those two phrases that Czeslawa's English wasn't fluent. 'Where did you live before?'

'In Livingston.'

'A nice enough town,' Maria said.

'But we living in Craigshill. Not a good area.'

Maria didn't know Livingston very well, but she had heard Craigshill wasn't one of its highlights.

'Kings River very nice village. It is safe for the childrens to play.'

Maria was glad she had brought up the subject of the children. 'Yes, I agree. In fact, I wanted to ask if Angelika could come and play at our house.'

Czeslawa beamed with happiness. 'Yes, would be very good. I think Angelika would like.'

'So, what does your husband do?'

'He builder. He work in Bearsden on new buildings. Houses too expensive there.'

Yes, Maria could see where she was coming from. Although Kings River was expensive, it was nowhere near as extortionate as Bearsden.

'School is good here?' Czeslawa had found her voice.

'Yes, Kirk Park is a great school. It helps that there are

so few pupils. They also have good facilities.'

'Facilities?' Czeslawa scrunched her eyebrows.

'Resources. For example, the sports equipment, the music room, the drama studio.'

'Ah, *obiekt*,' said Czeslawa.

'So, do you work?' Maria asked.

'Not yet. I start to look now we in Kings River. We stay here long time I hope.'

'What sort of work are you looking for?'

'Anything. Is difficult for foreigner to get good job here. Perhaps cleaning or work in supermarket.'

'Is that what you did back home?'

'No!' Czeslawa said, horrified. 'I was office manager. I responsible eight people.'

Maria thought how humiliating it must be for her to take on a more menial job.

'Do you want to stay here permanently or do you think you will go back to Poland?'

Czeslawa hemmed and hawed. 'I love Poland, but I like very much Scotland. My family still in Gdansk, and in Wroclaw, my brother. I hope maybe in ten years we go back and pay for house from money we make here.'

'You are very organised,' Maria said, smiling.

They chatted for a bit and as they were leaving, Maria asked Czeslawa where she was parked.

'Oh no, I not have car. Wojciech has car. I take bus.'

'Well, in that case, let me offer you a lift.'

'A lift?' Czeslawa clearly didn't understand.

'I will take you home.'

Czeslawa waved to her as Maria drove away and Maria decided she liked the Polish girl. She was too thin, but what there was of her was muscle. Maria, although by no means overweight, felt frumpy beside her. The girl's clothes were a second skin.

They had agreed that Angelika could come over on Thursday after school. When Czeslawa said she was looking for a cleaning job or something similar, Maria's first thought had been that she may be the answer she had been looking for, but then she realised that wouldn't work; she wanted this woman to be her equal, not her cleaner. A plan was forming in Maria's mind and she mulled it over as she made herself some camomile tea.

Chapter Forty-five

After her two-hour break, Maria buckled down and felt certain she'd caught up again. It was important, she felt, to have the flexibility which working from home and running her own business afforded her. Today she'd cultivated an important friendship. With the kids at her mother's for dinner, she could work on until six, when they'd be delivered in time for a bath and a story. Maria whizzed through her action items and then made a start on the washing and ironing.

'Mummy, look what Gran gave me,' burst in David. He was holding a bright yellow racing car in one hand and a remote control in the other.

'I've got a new Barbie,' Amy said, clambering onto the sofa to kiss her. Maria's mother smiled at the children's obvious pleasure at their gifts and sat down heavily in the recliner.

'You OK, Mum?' Maria was concerned.

'I'm fine, just a bit tired,' her mother confessed.

'If having these two is too much for you, let me know,' Maria said once the children were out of earshot. Her father, the designated chauffeur, had come in with the children's bags, and after acknowledging her briefly, was happily watching TV.

'No, not at all. You know I love having them. Amy has just been wild all day.'

'Do you want a cup of tea?' Maria asked. Her mother looked a bit paler than she was happy with.

'That would be great, but I can't stay too long. *Coronation Street*'s on soon.'

Maria hid her irritation. If it weren't for her grandchildren, her mother would live through that television. Her poor father; only two years until he retired. He never got to watch what he wanted, as his wife had the evening all planned out. If he were lucky, he was allowed to watch the occasional nature programme or movie, but the rest of the TV viewing was worked religiously around her mother's beloved soaps. The only time he managed to have a say was when he was at her house.

The children played happily with their new toys until their grandparents left.

'Right, guys, bath time.' She caught Amy round the middle, as she made to run past her.

'Oh no you don't.' She laughed at her daughter. 'C'mon, bath and then a story.'

Reluctantly, the children filed into the bathroom.

Soon the entire bathroom was like a swimming pool from the children sloshing water over one another with plastic beakers. Maria was soaked. But the kids enjoyed themselves and if it helped tire them out, then it was worth it.

As she tucked them in, she thought how exhausted they must have been. Both of them had fallen asleep during their stories. Tomorrow she'd have Amy in the afternoon after nursery, but right now she couldn't wait to get stuck into reading her novel again.

Next morning, after dropping the kids at school, Maria checked her emails. There was one from Tom, Holly's fiancé. He'd been her main contact since Holly went off to Italy to do research for her third book, set in Tuscany.

Maria wasn't arranging the whole wedding for them, but they had asked her to take care of the invitations, flowers, cars and kilt hire. Holly and Tom wanted to manage some aspects of their wedding, so they had approached venues about costs and menus offered, as well as using their own photographer and videographer, who was a media friend of Holly's. Maria wished more of her weddings could be as uncomplicated. No doubt she'd be receiving another call from the Fairbairns tomorrow.

The Jameson/Matthews wedding wasn't until spring, due to Holly's winter book tour for *Venetian Dreams*. Maria liked Holly. She had quite a few clients who gave her repeat business and Holly was one of them. They first met when she arranged Holly's thirtieth birthday bash and since then, Holly and Tom's engagement party, and she was now involved in the book launches. So, over the years, they'd socialised a fair bit. With a lump in her throat, she thought of how she'd met Holly when Stuart was still alive; she still thought of Stuart every day. They said time was a healer and although it didn't heal, hell, she didn't want it to 'heal', that would be tantamount to forgetting, she learned to live with it. Life was as good as it got without Stuart; she had two amazing children and she was financially secure.

Maria read Tom's email again. It was funny how different men and women were, even in something as simple as composing an email.

Tom's email:

Hi, Maria. We'll need a videographer after all. Can you suggest one and advise pricing, please? Tom.

Holly's last email on the other hand had started off by asking Maria how she was, how business was going, telling her about her travels and then after about three paragraphs, she finally reached the matter in hand. Although it obviously took her far longer to read Holly's email, she'd choose Holly's over Tom's emails any day.

The phone rang off the hook all morning. Maria knew she needed to address this staffing issue soon. She could call her mother and ask if she could take Amy, but her parents did enough for her and she didn't like to impose further.

When she picked Amy up from nursery at lunchtime she was still way behind. Again they found David with Angelika. Angelika was having dinner with them and Czeslawa would collect her about six. Angelika and David though had other ideas; they wanted to go now.

'No, sweetheart. You have school this afternoon. Angelika will be coming home with us after school,' Maria said.

Saying goodbye to Angelika, they headed home for lunch.

After lunch, Amy and Maria dropped David at school and went into Kilburn. The problem was she always ended up getting more than she came for when she came into town. She'd nipped into the tearoom and bought a lovely sponge cake to welcome Angelika, something light, not an E-number festival. Since she was here, she decided she may as well do a supermarket run and stock up on cleaning goods.

She completed her supermarket shop in record time.

'Mummy. I need a pee pee,' Amy tugged her arm.

She'd almost forgotten her daughter was there; she'd been so well behaved. 'Can you hold it just a minute?' she said as she paid for her shopping. Shoving her hastily packed bags in the trolley, she pushed it with one hand, grasped Amy's hand in the other and walked towards the Customer Toilets sign. A few customers let her go before them, when they saw Amy hopping from foot to foot.

'Mummy, I need a poo as well,' Amy said loudly. Maria was glad she was inside the cubicle, as she could hear titters on the other side. Amy was always mortifying her.

'Mummy, I want to watch Bob when I get home,' Amy said.

'That's fine.' Maria would have promised her anything at that point. Her discomfort increased further, as Amy started singing the *Bob the Builder* theme tune at full volume. Maria was cursing the builders of these toilets, as there was no window to use as an escape route. Finally, Amy was finished. Maria was scarlet and as she opened the door, a round of applause broke out.

'Well done, young lady,' one elderly woman told her. 'What's your name?'

'Amy,' she said proudly.

'Well, Amy, that was a great performance,' she said, grinning at Maria.

Maria, red-faced, hauled Amy off to the wash-hand basins before she combusted. As the door closed behind her, she heard shrieks of laughter from within.

Angelika and David let Amy play with them, which

warmed Maria's heart. Amy made them copious amounts of tea from her tea set and plied them with plastic fried eggs and sausages. When Maria brought out the very real cake, Angelika's eyes lit up.

Chapter Forty-six

'Hi, Czeslawa, come in.' Maria ushered her indoors.

'Mummy, I don't want Lika to go,' complained David.

'We'll have a cup of tea whilst you finish playing.'

'Thanks, Mummy.' He scampered off.

'Would you like some tea?' Seeing Czeslawa hesitate, she said, 'I'm making some anyway.'

'Yes, thank you.'

Maria returned a few minutes later with two cups of tea and the remainder of the sponge cake. She remembered that Czeslawa took her tea black.

'Oh, I forget,' Czeslawa said. She pulled out a box of Matchmakers from her bag. 'This for you. You bring me home other day and you ask Angelika here. Thank you.'

'You didn't need to do that.' Maria was touched. 'But thanks.' She hesitated a second then decided to dive right in. 'You know you told me you were an office manager?'

'Yes?'

'Well, I wondered if you might like to come and work for me.'

'You have company?' Czeslawa's eyes grew wide.

'Yes.'

'What is business?'

'My company mostly deals with weddings,' Maria

began, trying to keep her language relatively simple. 'Now the company is bigger. We deal with most aspects of weddings: flowers, photography, hotel, church.'

'Sounds good. But–' she broke off, before continuing '– what you think I can do?'

Maria had thought this through over the last few days. If Czeslawa accepted her proposal, she could help with admin until her English improved, which was bound to happen quickly, once she was using it daily.

'Well, although you wouldn't be office manager, as the company's not big enough for that and we all work from home, I was just about to place an ad with the job centre for an admin assistant. Would you be interested?'

Czeslawa's smile lit up her whole face and her eyes sparkled. 'I interested. Please tell me more.'

Maria outlined what she would expect from her, again trying not to overcomplicate things; she could explain in more detail once she started. It wouldn't do to overwhelm her.

'And you happy to offer me job?' Czeslawa seemed unable to take it in.

'Yes.'

'I not know yet what to do, but if show me, I learn fast.' Czeslawa stopped. 'There only one problem.'

'Yes?'

'My English,' Czeslawa said anxiously.

'I've thought about that, and I suggest that once you start working for me, you also go to English classes. It will make you more confident.'

'I good at languages,' said Czeslawa. 'I speak Russian, German and French, just no good English.'

'It's not a problem. I am prepared to hire you now and

hope classes and speaking English daily will bring your language skills on quickly.'

'Very good. We have deal.'

Maria could see the young woman's eyes held a question. She imagined it would be regarding salary, so she jumped in and started telling her what she could afford. Czeslawa seemed very happy at that.

'Thank you, Maria. This means lot to me. Wojciech will be so happy. He not want me to take inferior job.' She hugged Maria fiercely and then breaking off, she said, 'Angelika would like David come play at our house next week. Is OK?'

'Of course.'

An ecstatic Czeslawa left, promising to return on Monday to meet the others. Maria felt as if she had done something really worthwhile. It wasn't right that Czeslawa should be reduced to cleaning toilets; she should be able to put her skills to use.

Kids in bed, Maria emailed her team and asked them to be available on Monday at ten o'clock to meet a new employee. She'd barely pressed Send when her mobile rang. It was Sandra.

'What new employee?'

'What are you doing still working at this time?'

'Oh, I had a bit of an incident today and had to bow out early, so am making up for lost time tonight. What new employee?' Sandra asked again.

Maria filled her in.

'You are so impulsive, woman!'

Maria wasn't sure if it was a slight, but she didn't let Sandra rile her. She wasn't sure if Sandra was miffed at her for not discussing it with her before hiring Czeslawa, but if she was put out, Maria would sweeten her up on Monday. Czeslawa wasn't arriving until ten thirty and Sandra was always ridiculously early. Maria would be lucky if she were home from dropping the kids off before Sandra knocked on the door. She explained her reasons to Sandra, not that she felt she had to justify herself, it was her company after all, and Sandra seemed suitably mollified by the time she hung up.

Maria was exhausted. She had run herself ragged all day and now she was at the rehearsal for the McKillop wedding. All of the key players would be in attendance. Everything was in order so there should be no hiccups tomorrow.

Maria was dressed in black boot-cut trousers and a pink V-neck blouse. She could see the groom and another man striding down the aisle towards her. As the other chap resembled the groom, she assumed he must be his brother and hence the best man. A gaggle of girls then entered, led by the bride, and a couple of tots brought up the rear. The flower girls, she presumed. The minister arrived and the rehearsal began.

Good. That went without a hitch. Maria packed up her things. She always brought props for those who would be carrying things, flowers, a detachable Velcro train, that sort of thing, so that the participants could get a proper feel for it. OK, little Marisa had tripped over the train, but she felt confident she'd be all right on the day. Time to go home. Tomorrow would be a long day and she wanted to get the whole family to bed on time, since she'd have an early start.

The rain battering against the windows woke Maria up repeatedly during the night. As she shoved her head deeper into her pillows, she prayed for it to stop by morning. It didn't. When she got up at six it was still torrential. It should have been light by now, but the rain clouds blocked the sun's endeavours and a gloomy mist hung over the village. It could have been a November morning. Typical summer weather. She'd never understand why anyone booked a wedding during this time. May and September were far better months in her experience. Maria hoped that the old Scots saying would come true today, 'If you don't like the weather in Scotland, wait fifteen minutes.'

Kids despatched, Maria smoothed down her suit and retouched her lipstick, before swinging into action. The wedding was at eleven o'clock. Happy that all was on schedule, she set off for the venue.

As she entered the church, raised voices came from the sacristy. She quickened her stride, her heels echoing on the stone until she stood just outside. Pausing a second to listen, she heard a voice, the groom, she guessed, say, 'I can't do this.'

Maria's heart froze. This had only happened to her once before, and it was natural for the bride and groom to feel vulnerable and confused before the ceremony, but it still gave her the shivers to hear the doubts vocalised. As the best man tried to reason with the groom, she turned away, but stopped when the groom uttered the unthinkable.

'I have to tell her about Becky.'

'No, you don't,' a voice said.

'She deserves to know. Then she can decide if she wants to marry me or not. But she won't. She'll hate me and she should.' His voice was full of despair.

Emboldened by the lengthening silence, Maria knocked on the door. After a slight delay, the best man opened the door. He looked as if he'd aged ten years since last night.

'Hi.'

'Hi. I couldn't help overhearing.'

'Go away,' said the groom, almost in tears. Maria ignored him. She entered the room and closed the door behind her. Soon the guests and then the bride would arrive, so she needed to get this sorted now.

'You love Carrie, don't you?'

Angus nodded mutely.

'OK, so you've screwed up.'

Again, silent assent. 'But, that doesn't need to be the end of your life, or hers.'

'It doesn't?' Hope shone in his eyes.

'No. This Becky, does your fiancée know her?'

He shook his head. 'She lives in Liverpool.'

'Where we had the stag party,' the best man added helpfully.

'And this happened only on your stag night?'

'Just that one time,' said the groom.

'Well, Angus, you have two choices: you come clean, your fiancée will probably hate you, at best she won't marry you and you'll have humiliated her and your families; or, you learn to live with your little indiscretion, marry the woman you love and never tell her. Ever.'

Angus stared at her in awe. Maria broke in again on his thoughts. 'When you think about it logically, you just want to assuage your conscience, but is that fair?'

He didn't reply.

'If you genuinely love this woman and what happened

was a one-off, then don't let it ruin your lives.'

Angus rose to his feet. 'Thanks. You're right.' He hugged her.

'You're welcome. Now, go and freshen up.'

They headed for the church toilets and Maria exhaled heavily. She would only rest easy when they were pronounced man and wife.

Ten minutes later the groom and best man were in their rightful places at the front of the church. Maria helped the ushers show guests where to sit. Every so often, she would make eye contact with the groom and the best man. The latter gave her the thumbs up sign several times and she breathed more easily.

The bride arrived and the flower girls toddled down the aisle without tripping. The service was beautiful, quicker than she usually liked for a church service, but in this instance, relief that it had gone ahead replaced disappointment at the rapidity of it. As the bride and groom walked back up the aisle as man and wife, smiling at friends and relatives, Maria kept in the wings. Angus' eyes, however, sought out hers and his expression of gratitude was clear.

Maria was surprisingly organised on Monday morning for the meeting. Sandra, true to form, was early. Maria confided in her staff – Sandra, Maria's sister Wendy, Isla and Ariadne – about Saturday's near miss. Wendy disapproved, but Maria silenced her by saying, 'You only get one chance at happiness.' No one would argue with that.

The doorbell rang and Maria went to answer it.

Czeslawa was shy at first and insisted on repeating everyone's name several times to ensure she had them right. Sandra asked Czeslawa how she liked her tea and Isla offered her a choice of carrot cake or coffee cake, which she'd brought from the bakery in her village. By the end of the meeting they were like long-lost friends and Maria knew she had done the right thing.

Chapter Forty-seven

'Maria, here is a list of messages for you,' Czeslawa said. It had only been a few weeks, but Maria had already noticed a vast improvement in her English. Czeslawa had chosen the intensive English course. She was very hard-working and Maria was pleasantly surprised by Czeslawa's progress and could see she was a very determined young woman. It was almost as if she were proving to Maria that she had made the right decision. After some initial hiccups, the other staff counted her as a valued member of the team. In fact, Sandra had even commented that she didn't know how she managed before Czeslawa came along. Praise indeed, as Sandra didn't bandy compliments around. With the amount of extra work they'd taken on recently, Maria knew they couldn't have coped without Czeslawa's contribution. In fact, business was growing at such a rate, a nice problem to have she knew, that she might have to consider taking on yet another person. She'd make a decision in a few weeks.

The three children had become inseparable and as a result, Czeslawa and Maria spent more and more time together. They had a lot in common: both were well read and liked quality literature, not necessarily heavy-going and dark, but something requiring a bit of thought; their tastes in music were similar and they had an aptitude for cooking.

A few weeks later, Czeslawa arrived a little upset, dragging Angelika with her.

'Maria, I am very sorry to ask, but I have a problem.'

'Are you all right?' Maria escorted them in out of the rain. 'What is it?'

'Can I borrow your car to pick my brother up from the airport, please? Wojciech is stuck in traffic and there is no time for him to get here and give me the car and because he is stuck, he cannot even go to the airport to pick Anastazy up.'

'Of course, and I'll look after Angelika,' Maria suggested, handing Czeslawa her car keys and wishing her well.

An hour and a half later the doorbell rang. As Maria opened the door, she startled, as she'd expected to see Czeslawa; however, Czeslawa was retying her shoelaces, so Maria was greeted by the sight of a six-foot-tall, dark-haired, stubbled vision wearing a black leather jacket and faded jeans.

'You must be Maria,' he said, smiling at her. 'Anastazy. My sister has told me all about you.'

Momentarily dazed, she then shook his hand. 'Nice to meet you. Come in,' she said, as Czeslawa straightened up.

Once ensconced in the living room, Maria offered them tea and they were chatting animatedly when they heard a scream from upstairs.

'Mummy, Amy's hurt her head,' David cried. Leaping up, Maria sprinted up the stairs with Czeslawa close behind.

'Oh my God.' Nausea churned Maria's stomach. Blood was pouring from Amy's head and she was very pale.

'What happened?' Maria took a deep breath to calm her raging panic.

'She jumped off the bed and landed on the edge of David's garage,' explained Angelika.

'Amy, Mummy's here.'

Czeslawa passed Maria a damp facecloth she'd taken from the bathroom. Maria dabbed at Amy's head whilst Czeslawa ushered the other two children out of the room, as they were screaming at the amount of blood.

Instinctively, Maria knew it wasn't a superficial cut. 'I'll need to take her to Yorkhill,' she said to Czeslawa when she returned.

'The children's hospital?'

'Yes.'

'I will look after David.'

'Thank you.'

They went downstairs and Czeslawa rapidly conveyed to Anastazy what had happened.

'I drive,' said Anastazy. 'You need to stay with your daughter.'

Czeslawa, David and Angelika watched them set off into the rainy night. As she sat in the back seat with Amy, Maria started praying.

Chapter Forty-eight
Antonia – VIRGO

Practical, no-nonsense. Talkative and communicate well. Not interested in idle chit-chat. Critical. Well groomed and tidy. Obsessed with detail, analytical, intelligent and hard-working. Good organisers and multitaskers. Perfectionists. Humble.

Antonia watched the girl she'd just dressed down beat a hasty retreat back to the relative safety of her pod and wondered why HR sent her people who didn't have the confidence to work in this environment. You couldn't have namby-pamby people working in a contact centre. It was all about being self-assured, competent and a little bit hyper. She glanced at her diary; she had a meeting with HR at twelve thirty and her team leaders at quarter to two. Whilst she tried to find someone for the vacant team leader slot, she had to fill in and do appraisals, which would take the rest of the afternoon. Sighing, she picked up her phone and called down to the canteen for a baked potato and a latte to be delivered to her office at half one. With approximately an hour to go through her one hundred and ninety-five emails, Antonia started sifting through those requiring attention.

Dear all

There will be a meeting of all directors and CCMs in the Dublin office on 21st August to outline the plans for the next fiscal year. Please see Judy as usual for accommodation and flights. This will be an all-day event, with a dinner on the evening of the 20th. Attendance is compulsory.

Best regards
Seamus O'Leary
Chief Executive Officer

Antonia picked up her phone and input the dates. Next email.

Hi, everyone

As you know the European Train the Trainers day had to be postponed. Here are some dates I have available for welcoming you to the Munich office: 22nd August, 29th August, 8th September.

Please reply by return with your availability. Course is two days. I need four members of staff to represent each call centre.

Thanks
Arnie

Flipping through her calendar, Antonia saw that the twenty-second would be out as she would still be in Dublin. The twenty-ninth worked for her, but the eighth was no good, as she was on holiday. It would be her forty-eighth birthday and she wanted a day to chill. She opened her calendar to look at her group's holiday planner. She intended to send Noel, Chloe, Rajit and Amanda, as they were good operatives and had the right disposition for training. Fortunately, none of them had requested holidays for those dates.

She banged out the following:

Hi, Arnie

Seamus has booked all the CCMs in Dublin for the 21st, so the 22nd is out. My team could do the 29th August. Please advise as I am blocking all annual leave until I receive your confirmation.

Regards
Antonia

Twenty minutes left before her meeting.

Hi, guys

Please provisionally block out on your calendar 28th and 29th August. It looks like these might be the dates for the TtT event.

Regards
Antonia

Short and to the point. Antonia browsed the rest of her emails, sending some quick replies and making notes in her diary for those which needed some research first. She hesitated before deleting company reports not directly involving her department. You never could tell when you'd need something and she didn't like to look stupid.

Antonia looked up and saw the time. It was twenty-five past. Time to get a move on. She was never late and loathed tardiness in others, as it insinuated they were infinitely busier than you.

'Hello, Gina, how are you?'

'Good thanks, Antonia. You?'

'Not bad thanks. Did I see Dougie the other day at *La Traviata?*'

'Yes, he was there with some colleagues.'

'Ah, right. The performance was wonderful, such passion.'

'Yes. I need to find out what the next opera is.'

'*Madame Butterfly* is coming in September.'

'Oh really? I haven't seen that.'

They settled down as Gina's colleagues joined them. They discussed performance management, recruiting and even potential redundancies in other departments. The latter was news to Antonia.

'We're keen to see where we can redeploy staff, so we'll be implementing a hiring freeze,' Gina said.

'Well, I must say this *is* a surprise. The business appears to be going well, really well if I'm honest.'

'Yes, but some of the finance functions are being centralised in Paris, so at least half of our finance and related personnel here will have to go.'

'What, and you think they're going to be happy being offered contact centre jobs?'

'We understand there may be some scepticism and we are looking at other departments where they can be reassigned. What I'd like to do is discuss with you, in say two weeks' time, some potential candidates for your department. Since we haven't told those who need to be shuffled or let go, it goes without saying this conversation is highly confidential.'

'Of course,' Antonia muttered, her hackles rising a little. She felt as if she were being dictated to and as if she were going to be lumped with unsuitable staff. She knew most of those in finance, or sales prevention as the sales team called them, and she couldn't think of a single one who could cut it in her department. It was very high pressure, as opposed to the relatively stress-free environment which those in finance were accustomed to. On the rare occasions when she ventured out for coffee, there was always a gaggle of finance girls round the drinks machine, sipping coffee and gossiping. No, she was not happy about this at all. Surely management could see that certain cost-cutting exercises simply didn't make sense for the overall good of their business unit? When the meeting ended, she left most dissatisfied.

Fortunately, her baked potato and latte were waiting for her. Twelve minutes until her next meeting. She scooped up some of her baked potato and scanned her Inbox. Damn, she'd forgotten they were doing this Outward Bound day. When was that again? She scrolled down. Early September. At Arrochar. Team building. Too much team building, not very much work getting done, she felt. There was also an email from her boss.

Subject: Impromptu meeting

Antonia

I need to see you in my office tomorrow at ten.

Gregory

His emails were even shorter than hers; sign of a busy person. In some industries, the higher up the tree you climbed, the less work you did and the more you delegated, not Gregory. He was very hands-on. He had responsibility for the entire Scottish operation. She didn't begrudge him the job; she was ambitious, but she knew her forte and heading up the organisation wasn't it. She'd been at Insureall for five years, but sometimes she wished she could be customer-facing again. Now her life was about making decisions. She told Gregory she'd see him at ten.

Time up. She strolled towards the conference room, her mind whirring. She had two hundred and fifty people under her care, including fifteen team leaders. She knew all the staff, including the newest recruits. Francisco Rodriguez, who started last week, originally from Valencia, lived in Paisley with his four children. He intended to be here three years and then move back to Spain. She'd heard that often enough. Most of the foreign nationals they recruited remained longer than expected. Only the Poles were now starting to buck the trend and return home, due to the stronger zloty, weak pound and the glut of work in Poland. How could she carry on as normal knowing what she knew?

When Antonia reached the Skye Room, her team was already assembled. She liked to be last to arrive and was unamused when any of her team was late.

'Hello, everyone. How's it going?' Antonia was friendly, but her team knew not to reply in detail. She wasn't here for a chat.

One of the team leaders handed her a copy of the agenda. The nine women and four men who currently made up her team listened carefully.

'OK, before we start on the agenda, I have something to say.'

Her team looked back at her expectantly. They would know what she was referring to, as news travelled fast in a call centre, but they wouldn't know the ins and outs. One of the team leaders had been fired this morning and Security had escorted him from the building.

'We had a rather unpalatable incident earlier today. As you probably know, Geoff is no longer with us. I don't know if you know why, so I'll fill you in. He was downloading pornography.' Antonia glanced at each member of her team. Many looked shocked whilst others bore the masks of those who knew but did nothing. Antonia missed nothing and made a mental note to have the IT department check them out too.

'As you know, Insureall has a no-tolerance attitude towards downloading pornography and therefore Geoff was instantly dismissed, despite being here seven years.'

She waited for this to sink in.

'I'll circulate a memo reminding everyone about the use of email. The memo will also explicitly mention accessing pornographic sites, although it's unclear how Geoff managed to get past the firewalls. That is being looked into. I need you to be extra vigilant regarding each member of your teams. If any of your team is involved in such an activity, you will be held responsible too. It's a team leader's business to know everything about their team. OK, let's turn to the agenda.'

Agenda
Key Performance Indicators
Recruitment
Statistics
Salary review
Conversion rates
New products

New scripts
AOB

'Most of you have done your KPIs. I've done Melanie's team, since we still haven't replaced her. We're now going to have to find two new team leaders. I'd rather recruit from within, so I would welcome suggestions for potential candidates.'

A hand shot up at the back of the room. 'Yes?'

'I think Anne Marie McGuinness might be ready. She's been here eighteen months and is desperate to get up the ladder. She's good in training too. Patient.'

'OK, let's put her on the shortlist. Anyone else?' she asked.

Another hand shot up. 'Yes, Zoe Lesley. She's young, but hungry and very eager. Her conversion rates are fantastic, and I think she would be a very enthusiastic team lead.'

'OK, good.'

A few more possibilities were unearthed and then they moved on to discussing the KPIs. At Insureall this was not synonymous with pay increases, so staff provided real feedback. All in all the process had been a success. They passed on to statistics. The team leaders, generally speaking, were responsible for improving the statistics, which included call handling times, number of calls handled and waiting time. The first thing Antonia did whenever she left her office was look at the overhead screens indicating the status for the day.

The conversation soon turned to the pay increases. The company was doing well and pay rises had already been agreed for various departments. Antonia now meted out to her team leaders the various percentages they were able to offer to their staff.

Antonia then regaled her staff with details of a new product – flood insurance. It wasn't a big thing up here in Scotland, with more requirement for it down in England, but some coastal areas and the islands were occasionally affected.

They rattled through the rest of the issues and Antonia finished by asking the most competent team leaders to split cover of Geoff's team between them until she could come up with another solution.

Antonia returned to her office and busied herself preparing the performance management data. It was difficult appraising people you didn't know much about. What she *could* glean was from their personnel files, but it wasn't always enough.

She scanned through the categories.

Achievements
Attaining goals
Relationships
Objectives for coming year
Comments

She looked at the first team member's name and notes. Hugh Preston, twenty-eight, at Insureall for three years, two months. Why wasn't he a team leader? Antonia wondered. She knew it didn't suit everyone; not everyone wanted the responsibility and she could understand that, but just to be a call centre operative at twenty-eight? She read further. Ah, he was still single. No kids. His stats seemed OK. His conversion rates were fine and he managed the department football team. He was simply unremarkable.

Antonia moved on to the next one, Lucille Carter, twenty-four, single, with a two-year-old son. She made use of the company crèche. It was one of the major assets the company offered and often kept staff loyal to them. Reduced childcare costs and no additional commute to drop them off. Lucille had started with them last year and seemed to be enjoying it. Her figures were well above average and she had already asked about becoming a team leader. Her name hadn't come up at today's meeting as her team leader had left three weeks ago, so wasn't there to speak on her behalf. Antonia added Lucille to the shortlist.

As she scanned the next batch's credentials, a rap came at her door.

'Come in,' Antonia said.

Hugh Preston shuffled into her office. She noticed his shoes were scuffed and his tie wasn't straight. *Laziness. He'll probably still be a call handler next year.* She invited him to sit down and the appraisal began.

Chapter Forty-nine

At six o'clock, the last person left Antonia's office. The first part of the process complete, Antonia would instruct one of the secretaries to type up the notes. Antonia was pleased to see she was right about Lucille, who had the right amount of enthusiasm and common sense; she would make a good team leader. Antonia had raised the bar on each of the appraisees' objectives for the coming year and included some additional personal development goals. She was asking them to have some ambition; it seemed they were used to an easy ride.

'Goodnight, Bill,' she said to the security guard.

'Goodnight, Mrs Bacon.'

In the car, Antonia called home. Clara, her fourteen-year-old daughter, answered.

'Hi, Mum. Where are you?'

'Just leaving. Is your brother in?'

'No, he's just gone out. Dad said he'd be home in ten minutes.'

'Yes, I know. Did Felix say when he'd be back?'

'No, I think he was going over to Jamesy's. As long as he's not here bashing his drums, I'm quite happy.'

Her mother knew what she meant. No amount of

soundproofing their loft could completely shut out the racket Felix's band made.

'OK, I'll be home in half an hour. I'm just going to nip to Tesco. Have you to eaten?'

'Just some crisps.'

'Clara!'

'I was hungry.'

'Yes, well, there is a smoothie maker that you insisted we buy.'

'I know, but there aren't any strawberries.'

Sighing, Antonia added them to her shopping list.

Antonia arrived home as Jack pulled into the driveway.

'Hi,' Jack said, coming over and kissing his wife. 'I stopped by Waterstones to see if there were any new releases that you might like.'

'Were there?'

'Well, there was a new Lee Child for me.'

Antonia rolled her eyes at him.

'And a nice psychological thriller for you,' he added.

'Just as well.' She got out of the car, accepting the Lisa Jewell book he handed her. 'Ooh, my favourite.'

Draping an arm round his wife, Jack led her into the house, where they went into the kitchen and found Clara making toasted cheese.

'Hi, Clara.'

'Hi, Dad. Good day?'

'Not bad.' Jack hugged his daughter. She was definitely a daddy's girl. Her relationship with her mother was friendly, but lacking that special something. Felix on the other hand wasn't the most gregarious, and at seventeen and doing his A levels, he was moodiness personified. He was rarely at home, but was meant to stay home on the evenings Clara was back before her parents. *They used to be so close when they were little.* She studied a holiday snap of her children taken near Cannes a few years back. But when Felix turned sixteen he metamorphosed into a grunting, sullen youth. At least he wasn't doing drugs; she hoped. He had his head screwed on. He just forgot it sometimes.

'No dance class tonight?' Jack asked.

Clara shook her head. 'Cancelled. Teacher's got laryngitis.'

'You don't dance with your throat, do you?'

'Daaa-ad,' Clara moaned.

Jack turned to Antonia. 'What's for dinner?'

'Chicken breasts with honey mustard topping, carrot batons and baby potatoes.'

'Accompanied by a reduction of balsamic vinegar…' Jack laughed as his wife flicked him with a dishtowel.

'I don't know what you're laughing at. There's a dishwasher needs unloading. I'm on strike until the kitchen's cleaned.'

Jack's face fell. 'Clara?'

Clara held her hands up and started to back out of the room. 'No, Dad, I'm not doing it. I have homework.'

Antonia hid a smile.

'I'll make it worth your while.'

'Five.'

'Five?' her father spluttered. 'To load a bloody dishwasher?'

Instinctively he reached for the swear box and put a pound in it.

'That'll give me another ten goes.' He grinned. 'Two.'

Clara walked into the hall.

'Three, but you have to do the dinner things too.'

'Deal.' Clara strode back into the kitchen and plucked the five-pound note out of Jack's hand. She raced upstairs, and a few minutes later, when she came back and started unloading the dishwasher, her father said, 'Where's my change?'

'Oh I don't have any. I'll need to owe you it.' She smiled sweetly.

Antonia suppressed a snort. Her daughter really had her father where she wanted him.

Over dinner, Jack filled Antonia in on his day. He'd taken advantage of the forty-five minutes until dinner to answer some calls and check his emails. He was prosecuting a big medical negligence case next day. It could have a huge impact not only in Scotland, but in the UK. Alexandru Daicoviciu was an illegal immigrant who had received emergency medical treatment at a Glasgow hospital. Unfortunately, a nurse there managed to inject him with the wrong type and dosage of painkiller and he died. It was Jack's job, on behalf of Alexandru's family, to prove that the health board had been negligent and try to get the jury to find for the prosecution.

'I mean, personally, I don't think our health board should have to pay damages. Yes, it's a tragedy, but accidents happen and with underfunding, staff shortages and nurses being able to administer drugs now, is it any surprise? Nowadays there always has to be a scapegoat.'

Antonia cut into her chicken and listened. Jack continued, 'I mean, I don't have anything against immigrants, if they have something to offer the country and they don't just intend to come here and bleed the system dry, but he wasn't even legal and now potentially his family could receive hundreds of thousands of pounds in damages, never mind what the court case itself actually costs the taxpayer,' he said indignantly.

Antonia mostly agreed with him, although her heart went out to the man's family. He had a young son and his wife was pregnant again. Now their children no longer had a father. Alexandru had been in Britain trying to gain legal status so that his family could have a better life. But she knew where Jack's frustration stemmed from: the government didn't inspire confidence that they were managing Immigration, and services were overstretched. She looked at her husband fondly. He was a Tory through and through. They were poles apart. He, born into an upper-middle-class family, whilst she had been born into a working-class one, her father a bricklayer and her mother an operative in a bottling plant. It was unthinkable that their family would do anything but vote Labour.

'Oh, I meant to say, I've been given two tickets to *The Mousetrap*. I know you've seen it, but do you fancy going again?'

'Lucky you. You missed it when I went. It was fantastic, but tell you what, why don't you ask Clara? I know she hates opera, but she would probably be up for a good play.'

'That's a great idea. Maybe I can exchange it for dishwasher-unloading services in future.'

'I wouldn't count on it,' said Antonia.

'It's worth a try. Worst-case scenario, I get to spend quality time with my daughter.' He smiled and refilled their glasses.

They had no major plans socially for the next few days. Jack would be busy with the case for the next few weeks at least. After a little more catching up on their day, Jack excused himself to work through the final details of his opening statement. Wearily, Antonia placed the dirty dishes beside the dishwasher. Her daughter had to earn her money after all. She retired to the lounge to watch a movie but drifted off soon after.

'Bye, darling, remember I'm eating out tonight.' Jack pecked her on the cheek, his skin, freshly shaven, smooth against her cheek. 'Have a good day.'

Antonia picked up her briefcase, set the alarm and got into her car.

When she arrived at the centre at eight thirty, it was still relatively quiet. She unlocked her office and sat her briefcase on her desk then booted up her computer. As the Windows symbol scrolled and then disappeared, she opened her briefcase, took out her planner and slid her briefcase under the desk. She had a little time to catch up on emails before her meeting with Gregory. Launching straight in, she read,

> *Antonia*
>
> *I'm going into hospital on the date of the TtT event. What do I do?*
>
> *Chloe*

Damn, Antonia had forgotten Chloe had this coming up. She hadn't told her the date before. She'd have to take her to task about that. If she asked her European colleagues to change the date now, she'd look stupid. It might be easier to replace Chloe. She wouldn't be happy, but there was nothing she could do.

Subject: RE: Train the Trainers Day

Arnold

The Polish team will be ready on 29th.

Marina

Antonia was in a bit of a bind now. Next email. There were quite a few replies to Arnie's original email.

Arnie

We will be happy to attend on 29th August.

Jean Philippe

As Antonia scrolled through her emails, she found another four acceptances for the twenty-ninth. *Well, that's torn it. I'll have to tell Chloe she can't go.* She sat, drumming her pen on the desk, wondering whom she could send in Chloe's place, then battered off,

Chloe

Need to see you when you get in.

Antonia

Antonia checked her diary to see what she had on after Gregory. Amazingly, she had a relatively free morning and spent the next five minutes trying to work out why. With a jolt, she remembered she was meant to be seeing one of Felix's teachers at eleven o'clock. Damn, she hadn't put it in the diary. She didn't have any idea how long she'd be with Gregory and it was a good twenty minutes from here to St Aloysius. There was nothing for it. She'd have to call the tutor and admit she'd forgotten. After two rings a secretary answered.

'Good morning, St Aloysius College, how may I help you?'

'Good morning. This is Antonia Bacon. I'd like to speak to Mrs Teviot, please.'

Antonia heard pages being rustled and then the woman said, 'I'm afraid she has a class at the moment.'

'Oh, well, I'm supposed to have an appointment with her at eleven and I'm going to be a bit late. Could you give Mrs Teviot the message, please?'

Phew, at least that was done. She hated breaking arrangements. As she started working out her afternoon schedule, she saw she was meant to be meeting Louise in Princes Square for lunch. Damn, she'd forgotten that too. What was wrong with her? Well, at least since she would be up at St Al's, she wouldn't have far to go, although driving and parking in the city centre at lunchtime simply didn't bear thinking about. She was surprised that Louise hadn't texted her. Their plans were always made so far in advance, that her best friend tended to send her a text the night before to ensure their catch-up was still on.

Chloe popped her head around the door. What Antonia liked about Chloe was she was very outgoing, and whilst she was respectful, she didn't kowtow. She treated the cleaners the same way she did Gregory. She'd never be ingratiating to get ahead, which made telling her she was off the course even harder.

'Hi, Chloe, take a seat.'

Chloe obliged, smoothing down her skirt.

'I have some bad news.'

'Is it about the course?' She was on the ball, this girl,

Antonia would give her that.

'Yes. I'll come straight to the point. I have to replace you.'

Chloe's face fell.

'I know it's disappointing, but unfortunately all the other call centres can only send their staff on the twenty-ninth.'

'I could cancel my hospital appointment,' Chloe said desperately.

Antonia's heart sank. Chloe wanted to be one of the super trainers so much, she'd actually forego important surgery to be able to attend the course.

'Chloe…' Antonia began.

'No, you're right, that's a stupid idea, I need the operation.'

Antonia nodded. She knew that Chloe had some sort of gynaecological problem, but she didn't know the intricacies of it.

'Chloe, there will be other opportunities, and that's not a platitude. We'll be offering another course in December and you'll definitely be on that one.'

'OK, thanks, Antonia. I appreciate that,' Chloe said dully.

Chapter Fifty

'Hi, Gregory. How are things?'

'Wonderful, Toni. Wonderful.'

It was the one thing about Gregory which grated; no one had called her Toni since primary school.

'Is it just us?' Antonia asked.

'Yes, sit down. I'm seeing everyone separately.'

Antonia fidgeted on the black leather chair, causing it to squeak. She felt like a little girl in the headmaster's office. Gregory wasn't even that much older than her. A shock of white hair, and a weather-beaten face, criss-crossed with lines, belied his fifty-five years. He looked late sixties. But maybe that came from being at the top, and the accompanying lifestyle.

Steepling his hands, Gregory said, 'Antonia, I know you had a chat with HR about staff redistribution.'

'Yes, I did.'

'And they mentioned the hiring freeze?'

'Yes.'

'Well, what they didn't tell you is, if the proposals go ahead, Corporate want to dramatically downsize this centre over the next three years, with the aim of closing it within five.'

The blood drained from Antonia's face. She hadn't seen

that coming, although perhaps she should have. In recent years, when competitors were defecting to India and the Czech Republic, Insureall had steadfastly remained in the UK. Their ad campaign was centred around local call centres, not having to call another continent. That would have to change.

'Where's the work moving to?' she blurted out.

'Cape Town.'

No surprise there then. India was getting more expensive and there were too many complaints about customers not understanding what was being said. Analysts had discovered that Brits found the South African accent more empathetic, easier to understand, and the insurance companies and banks wanted to keep their customers happy.

Antonia waited for Gregory to continue, but he remained impassive.

'So, what now?' Quietly furious, she wouldn't give him the satisfaction of knowing how much the news had upset her.

'Well, over the next few weeks, we'll hold meetings to decide which departments will be transferred and when, and to understand if Corporate want any business kept in the UK.' He paused and then said, 'Toni, it's long term, not just our office, Birmingham and Milton Keynes too.'

Is that supposed to make me feel better? Even more people were going to lose their jobs, if not now, then over the next few years. At least some would have the chance to prepare for it.

'What kind of timescale do we have?' she asked.

'Realistically, in six months we expect to make the first redundancies.'

'Which departments?'

'Almost all. Yours most definitely, but my gut instinct tells me they will keep a token presence in the UK, although not necessarily in Glasgow.'

'No, more likely it'll be Milton Keynes.' Antonia couldn't keep the bitterness out of her voice.

She wasn't really worried for herself. No doubt they'd keep her on until the transfer was complete, so that gave her a couple of years, but she worried about her staff. 'So, what now?'

'Nothing. Just bear it in mind. I'll be talking to the other managers today. You have to go on as before.'

'Anything else?'

'No, that's it.'

As Antonia entered her office, she saw her voicemail was flashing red.

'You have two new messages.'

'Hi, Antonia. It's me. Just checking we're still on for lunch. Twelve thirty at Zizzi's. See you then.'

In spite of the grimness she felt inside, Antonia couldn't prevent a smile escaping. She knew her friend inside out. She played the second message.

'Mrs Bacon, this is Geraldine Teviot from St Aloysius College. If you are able to make it before eleven thirty, I can still fit you in. Thank you.'

Relieved that at least something was going right today, Antonia called her straight back to confirm she could make it.

'Geraldine Teviot. Do sit down, Mrs Bacon,' said the elderly schoolteacher, extending her hand. She was very bright-eyed for someone who should probably have retired several years ago if the way she shuffled around the room was anything to go by. She placed her hands in her lap and didn't trouble herself with referring to any notes. Antonia could see she was old school and probably kept it all in her head.

'I wanted to speak to you because I am rather concerned about Felix.'

'In what respect exactly?'

'Well, he used to be an A student, but lately his work has been slipping.'

'Oh?' Antonia's eyebrows scrunched together.

'Yes. He seems distracted. Are there any problems at home?'

'No, none.'

'Well, could you have a word, please? As things stand, if he doesn't improve, I may have to fail him in Chemistry and Physics.'

I'll bloody kill Felix. When she thought of all the advantages he had, this posh school for a start and the hockey matches he always wanted a lift to. He was grounded. No more slinking off to spend time with his band.

'Can I ask how long his marks have been deteriorating for?'

'About two to three months. It started before the examinations.'

She wondered why the school hadn't contacted them before now. Mrs Teviot, however, evidently saw the question about to form and said, 'Sometimes the stresses of school life get to young people, boys in particular. They are not as mature. They withdraw into themselves for a short time or rebel, but when the problem persists, we address it,' she said like Confucius delivering a nugget of wisdom.

Mrs Teviot stood up and Antonia realised she was being dismissed.

Antonia had circled and circled, trying to find somewhere near Princes Square to park, but it was impossible. Eventually, she'd slung the car in the car park next to Central Station. It cost a fortune, but needs must. Trotting across to the entrance to Princes Square, umbrella held low over her head, she was about to go up the escalator when she heard Louise shout, 'Antonia!'

She turned and saw her friend come out of The Pen Shop, laden with shopping. They hugged, and kissed each other on the cheek, then took the escalator up. A waitress showed them to an outside table and although they could hear the wind and rain above them, it was mild, so they sat at the balcony table and ordered drinks whilst they scanned the menu.

'I know what I'm having,' Louise said.

'Louise, *I* know what you're having. You always have the same.'

'Well, I can't help it. I love it, so much so, I've had to learn how to make it. Fusilli with courgettes, peppers and mushrooms.'

'I think I'll have the *spaghetti alle vongole*.'

'Ugh. I hate clams.'

'Hey, that's my lunch you're talking about.' It took a lot to put Antonia off her food, although Felix playing up at school was still preying on her mind.

They sipped their mineral water and Louise filled Antonia in on the latest events.

'I have something enormous to tell you,' Louise breathed.

Antonia smiled. Her friend was one of the most melodramatic people she knew. 'What?'

Louise held her breath for a moment and then exhaled. 'We're going travelling for a year.'

'You're what?' Antonia gaped. Louise? Louise didn't really do travelling, Granted, now she and her neurosurgeon husband had retired, early, they didn't have a great deal to tie them down, but her friend was such a homebody. She'd had her boys late in life and since meeting their father twenty years ago, hadn't worked. She'd always wanted to be a stay-at-home mum and fortunately her husband's generous pay packet meant she didn't need to work. He had travelled a lot when the kids were young, which wasn't much fun for Louise, but now she would have her chance to explore the world too. But knowing her friend as she did, she couldn't quite compute the idea of her going abroad for a fortnight, never mind a year.

'Yes, we're going round the world, backpacking. We start in September.'

'I can't believe it. Backpacking!' That was the part Antonia had most difficulty with.

'I use the term backpacking loosely, as we'll be staying in hotels not hostels, but essentially we'll be backpacking. I can't wait.'

Louise filled Antonia in on all the places they would see. It all seemed meticulously planned and Antonia couldn't dampen completely her pangs of envy. What wouldn't she give sometimes to just jack it all in, at least for a while. Even three months would be sufficient. Talk of Louise's impending trip took up most of their lunch, leaving Antonia no time to think about Felix.

'You'll miss Holly's launch,' wailed Antonia. She was

fiercely proud of her niece, her sister's daughter, and the more pleasant, in her mind, of the two siblings. She found Lucy a bit full on most of the time. Perhaps they were too alike.

'I'm sorry about that, and I'll miss their wedding too.'

That hadn't occurred to her. This was going from bad to worse.

'I *am* very excited for you though.' Antonia patted her friend's arm. 'I'm just going to miss you so much.' She suddenly realised how true this was. Sure, she and Jack were close but it wasn't the same. Her oldest and dearest female friend would be adrift for a year. She knew she was a grown woman, but even so, she couldn't stop a sense of foreboding from descending over her. She had other friends, but some of them were more acquaintances than friends, and they all had their own lives to lead. Louise was the only one, who in spite of her family commitments, was consistently there for her.

'I'm going to blog,' Louise said cheerfully.

'Blog?' Antonia had always viewed the online diaries as distasteful, airing your feelings and business online. It was this era of reality TV programmes that had fuelled this. Perhaps though, it would be the only way of catching up with Louise whilst she was away.

'Yes, I'm doing the blog as a permanent reminder for us once we get back. It also means the kids can see where we are and what we're doing, not that we'll tell them everything.' She winked. 'And we don't have to email our friends and family with the same news. They can simply log on to the blog.'

Louise was so poised. When did her friend, a housewife all these years, get ahead of her technologically? Antonia wondered.

She'd barely tasted her lunch, a pity, as it was one of her favourite places to eat, when the alarm on her watch went off.

'I need to go.' Signalling the waiter over, she gave him her credit card.

'My treat,' she said to Louise, leaning back and draining her glass. 'It's not every day you reveal something of this magnitude.'

'I suppose not.'

They parted with a promise to call each other later in the week and then Antonia set off to retrieve her car.

As Antonia drove back to the contact centre, she mulled over the morning's events. This downsizing news was an incredibly large secret to have to keep. But these things had a way of getting out. It wouldn't be long before the Chinese whispers filtered down and the imminent redundancies were out in the open, but the rumours wouldn't come from her.

Chapter Fifty-one

'Felix,' Antonia called upstairs when she got home. 'Get down here, now!'

I'm turning into my mother. What had happened to her belief that when she had her own kids, she would treat them differently? Maybe her parents hadn't been so wrong after all.

'Yeah?' Felix grunted when he entered the kitchen, his eyes wary.

'Sit.' It was not a request.

Felix scuffed over to the table and pulled out a chair.

'I saw Mrs Teviot today.'

'Uh-huh.'

'And stop talking like that! Do you think your father and I pay a fortune to send you to private school for you to talk like an ape?'

'Apes don't talk.'

'Don't backchat me, Felix. I'm not in the mood. I want to know what's going on.'

He shrugged.

'Your grades have gone from being excellent to Mrs Teviot possibly having to fail you.'

Silence.

'Fine. Your father will talk to you later, but in the

meantime consider yourself grounded until I see an improvement in your marks and–' she held up her hand to block his interruption '–that includes the concert you have coming up.'

'But I've already paid for my ticket.'

'I don't care. Upstairs and get your science books out, if you want to ever leave this house again, or alternatively let me know what's going on and why your grades have slipped so dramatically.'

Felix stared at her for the longest time and then wordlessly went upstairs.

Fine, if that's the way he wanted to play it, so be it. She hadn't even got to the part about no allowance for two weeks.

Antonia started making their evening meal, and once the chicken pie was in the oven, she grabbed one of her recipe books and went through to the lounge. They were having a dinner party on Saturday, this time for friends. She liked to have plenty of time to prepare. Fortunately, she wasn't working on Saturday, so she would have the whole day to get everything ready. There would be eight of them. Clara was having a sleepover at one of her friends' houses. Felix would have been out, but now he'd be stuck in his room, unless of course he decided he wanted to share before Saturday.

'Hi.' Jack swept into the room, making Antonia jump. She'd been so immersed in Saturday's menu she hadn't heard the car.

'So, how did the first day go?'

'Good, I think. Opening statements are done. You know how it is. I fret about it the night before. I want it to be perfect, but as soon as I get up there, it just flows.'

Antonia knew. She sat her glass down on the pewter coaster and tried to work out whether to tell her husband about Felix yet. She opted to let him eat in peace and unburden himself about his day. After dinner, before he retreated to his office, she'd tell him. She didn't think Felix would show his face until he was called anyway.

They ate in companionable silence. Clara was having dinner at her friend's house. If Jack was surprised that Felix didn't join them, he didn't show it. Either he was used to his son's idiosyncrasies or he had his mind on the case.

Antonia cleared the plates, loaded the dishwasher and went into the living room to find Jack relaxing with a magazine. He had kicked off his slippers beside his chair, magazines were strewn all over the coffee table and his tie lay discarded on the sofa. She checked herself from tidying up and sat opposite him, plumping up the cushion.

'Jack?'

'Yes?' He regarded her closely, no doubt aware that his name said in that tone wouldn't portend good news.

'I went to see Felix's teacher today.'

'Why?' Jack folded the magazine over at the page he was reading and dropped it on the coffee table.

'His work's slipping.'

Jack raised his eyebrows.

'Badly,' added Antonia.

Jack looked downright pained. 'Felix?' He gestured upstairs.

'Yes. I tried to talk to him, but he clammed up. I've grounded him until his marks improve or he tells us what's going on.'

'Is that why he wasn't down for dinner?'

'Probably. Anyway, could you have a word?'

'Sure. Wonder what the problem is.'

Antonia wondered too.

Half an hour later, Jack came back into the living room, hands in his pockets. 'He won't tell me. Something's wrong, I can sense it, but he's keeping shtum. I asked him if he was being bullied and he looked at me as if I was something he'd scraped off his shoe.'

Antonia didn't know whether to be relieved or not. Did that mean that whatever the problem was, it was worse or better than being bullied? What could they do if he wouldn't tell them?

The next day Antonia was particularly snappish at work. She prided herself in being one hundred per cent professional, but she was human and she had off days the same as anyone else. She checked her messages. Nothing from her son. Was he just being a typical teenager? Would it all blow over? She hoped so. She'd been lucky when he was a young teenager. He hadn't become an unruly mass of raging hormones on the eve of his thirteenth birthday. This was alien territory for her. What if he had got in with a bad crowd? Maybe he owed money. What could it be? The phone ringing returned her to the present.

'Hi, Antonia, it's Holly. How are you?'

'Holly! What a lovely surprise. I'm great, thanks,' said Antonia, neglecting to mention her errant son. 'How's Tuscany?'

'Oh, it's wonderful. You'd love it here. You should come and visit. Lucy's just been.'

'Has she?' Antonia tried to disguise her lack of astonishment. Lucy always landed on her feet, and it didn't surprise her that Lucy had made the most of having a sister in Tuscany whom she could descend upon. Poor Holly was always in Lucy's shadow. Not quite as stunning, but infinitely more pleasant.

'Yes. We had a fabulous time and I've been to a wedding.'

'Lucy too?' Antonia was intrigued. She couldn't imagine any man would be safe with Lucy around.

'No. It was before she came.'

'Ah. And how are preparations coming along for your own wedding?' There was a brief silence before Holly answered and Antonia wondered at the hesitation.

'Ticking along. Yes, left Tom in charge whilst I'm away, and of course I keep in touch with Maria by email.'

Antonia tried to recall who Maria was. Holly knew such a lot of people. Then she remembered that was the wedding planner's name.

'Well, that's great. Were you phoning for a chat or do you need help with something?'

'No. I was just phoning to see if I can talk you into coming to visit me. It's so lovely here.'

Antonia was delighted that her niece had thought of her, but at the back of her mind, something was brewing. She couldn't quite put her finger on it, but there was definitely something.

'I'd love to, darling, but I'll need to see. What's the nearest airport?'

'Florence, but if you want to go with the low-cost airlines, you're talking Pisa or Rome. They're both about a three-hour drive.'

'Three-hour drive. Well, I'd need to come for more than just the weekend then, for it to be worth the hassle,' she said not unkindly.

'Even better,' said Holly.

'I'll speak to Jack, but he's busy with a case at the moment, so I think it will just be me.'

'Fantastic. More time for us to have girly chats.' Holly always said the right thing. 'Anyway, best go. I know how busy you are.'

'Thanks for phoning, Holly. Maybe I can get out next month.'

'Look forward to it. Bye.'

As Antonia put the phone back in her bag, she realised she'd have to get to the bottom of the Felix situation before jetting off anywhere. She was due a break though. It had been ages since their trip to New Zealand, and they'd only managed the odd weekend to the lakes since then, not enough to sustain you when you worked as hard as they did. Besides, if Louise could go off gallivanting around the world for a year, why shouldn't Antonia go to Italy for a week?

The weekend soon came around and it was all Antonia could do to finish the housework before she started cooking for the party. Clara helped and even insisted on making dessert, white chocolate pots, simple but delicious. Jack was off playing golf, and Felix was in his room, studying, desperately trying to improve his grades so he could get out next month. He made no secret of how unfair he thought the whole situation, silent when he did venture downstairs, although he stomped around in his room and on the stairs to such an extent that his father came out and told him to cut it out or he'd be grounded for longer.

Antonia could hear him on his mobile, which she'd

forgotten to confiscate. That was too great a distraction for him to have.

She swept into his room and plucked it out of his hand. 'I'll have that, thanks. You can get it back when you let us know what's going on.'

'Mum,' wailed Felix.

'Enough.' She gave him a stern glance and he instantly backed down. Felix had been on the receiving end of his mother's tongue too many times and she knew it wasn't an experience he relished.

Antonia went to shower and change her clothes. The house sparkled. Her guests could have eaten their dinner off any surface in the house, they were so immaculate. It was a bonus about entertaining: you had to do a mountain of housework for them coming, but then the house was clean and tidy for a good while after that, in theory at least, not counting one messy husband and a slobbish teenage boy. Clara was like her, tidy to a fault. All of her clothes were sorted in her wardrobe, hangers facing the same way, coordinated by colour and season. Her shoes were still in the boxes.

Antonia luxuriated in the spa shower. It had been expensive, but it was worth it on occasions like this – when she'd worked hard all day, or on her day off – to feel as if she were being pampered. The jets sprayed out from six different holes and water swooshed over her body, relaxing her. Tilting her face upwards to the huge showerhead, she let the water cascade over her hair, face and shoulders. Squirting shower gel over her body, she rubbed it in slowly. She liked to take her time when getting ready for a dinner party, particularly when she was hostess.

After drying her hair, she used her straighteners to make it glossy and smooth, then painted her fingernails. *I don't brush up too badly for my age.* Dousing herself liberally with perfume, she finished off with a little spray in her cleavage. She donned cream trousers and a red blouse with matching camisole underneath; then stepped into cream Cuban heels. Gold leaf earrings and a pendant completed her ensemble and then she was ready. It wasn't often she dressed up like this, only when they had company or went to the theatre. Around the house she wore jeans or joggers.

Jack came in as she was applying mascara. He kissed her, told her she looked beautiful and left to shower. It was so much easier for men.

Antonia bustled around the kitchen, apron over her trousers, applying the finishing touches to the meal, whilst she awaited her guests. White wine chilled in the fridge, the Pinot Noir breathing on the worktop. Everything was ready. Then the doorbell rang. As Antonia went to answer it, first removing her apron, she smoothed her hair in the hall mirror as Jack came downstairs to join her.

'Hi, Carrie. Come on in. Malcolm, nice to see you again,' she greeted her best friend from her previous job and her husband. The men shook hands as the women received kisses and embraces. Jack passed their coats to Felix, who had materialised then disappeared to hang the coats upstairs.

Antonia had just invited them to take a seat in the lounge, where she would serve drinks, when the bell rang again.

'I'll get it,' Jack said.

Jack showed the guests in. Elvi was one of the teachers at the kids' school, but they had met through Carson, one of their friends from the gym. Guiltily, Antonia realised she hadn't been recently. Jack tended to go in the morning as he was usually up with the larks.

Ten minutes later, last as usual, came Patricia and Edmund. Pat was a friend of Antonia's from school. They saw each other three times in a month and then didn't see each other for two years. Yet they always drifted back together seamlessly, as if they'd only spoken yesterday, a symbol of true friendship, Antonia always thought.

Once all the guests were settled, Antonia served the canapés: little gem lettuces with cucumber, mint and chilli yoghurt; crostini with brie and grape; artichoke bites in puff pastry and finally Catalan toasts with sun-blushed tomatoes.

'These are lovely,' said Carrie.

'Have some more.' Antonia offered her the serving dish again.

Next, Antonia served the starter of aubergine terrine with mushroom duxelles. It hit the spot with her guests.

'I have to confess, Antonia, I wasn't sure it was my thing. I don't think I've ever had terrine before, although I've seen it on menus, but this is delicious,' Edmund said in his west coast drawl. Edmund had met Pat when she was in the States for a training course. After a short courtship, he'd chucked the job he'd detested anyway and moved to the UK.

'Thanks.' Antonia beamed at him.

After a short interval, Antonia served the main course. Tournedos of beef topped with mushrooms, roast potatoes done in goose fat and shredded Savoy cabbage. There was much ooh-ing and aah-ing as this was served up.

'I am never going to be able to move again,' Elvi groaned.

'Ah, don't sweat it,' said Edmund. 'Enjoy tonight, repent tomorrow and go for a long walk.'

They were discussing the best local places to go walking, when the doorbell rang. Jack raised an eyebrow at Antonia.

She shrugged. 'I'll go.'

The chatter continued as she closed the dining room door behind her. She opened the front door and took a step back in fright. A policeman stood in front of her.

'Mrs Bacon?'

She nodded. 'Is everything OK?' Clara was the only one out of the house, but she knew that she was safely at Giselle's. She'd called when she arrived.

'We need to speak to you about your son Felix.'

'Sorry, I didn't catch your name, Officer.' Antonia glanced back at the dining room door, behind which her guests were busy enjoying themselves.

'I didn't give my name. It's Archie Furnival and I'm not here on police business. Yet.'

Antonia must have looked suitably confused as he rushed on, pushing a young girl in front of him.

'This is my daughter, Jessica. She's made an allegation against your son, and I'd like to get to the bottom of it before I have to make it official, if you wouldn't mind.'

Wordlessly, she showed them into the hall.

Chapter Fifty-two
Jack – LIBRA

Diplomatic and refined. Intelligent, thoughtful and warm. Romantic, crave relationships and enjoy luxury. Have strong sense of justice. Good leaders. Peacemakers.

'The Daicovicius and Mr Manning are in reception,' Jack's secretary, Gloria, announced.

'Show them in,' Jack said. Thomas Manning, the Daicovicius' interpreter, had briefed him on the phone the other day. It was the first case of its kind to be brought against the NHS in Scotland. The Daicovicius' son had needed emergency surgery for a burst appendix. He was mistakenly administered the wrong drug and dosage and died shortly afterwards in hospital. It would normally be a clear-cut case of medical negligence, but there was nothing clear-cut about this case. Alexandru Daicoviciu was an illegal immigrant who'd managed to evade detection in the nine months he'd lived in Scotland, whilst he sought work and a way to gain legal status. His dreams of making a new life for himself and his family, who'd stayed behind in Bucharest, had ended in his death. Now his family wanted justice, justice and compensation for the wife and son he'd left behind. It was Jack's job to ensure they got it. It was just the sort of challenge he relished. Something which hadn't been done before.

'Pleased to meet you.' Jack held out his hand, first to the victim's father, then to his wife, then to the widow and finally to the interpreter. 'Please, take a seat.' Jack asked the interpreter if they knew any English. The father knew a little, but the women didn't speak any. Jack asked the interpreter to relay to the Daicovicius what he knew so far. Mr Daicoviciu asked the interpreter a barrage of questions. Mr Manning came back to Jack with, 'Did his son have any rights? Has a similar case happened before? Can they get help with the cost of taking his body home? Can they get compensation for his family? Will there be an interpreter in the court? Who pays for that?'

Jack answered their questions one by one. The Daicovicius had arrived two days ago, initially to arrange to take their son's body home, but the Home Office wasn't yet willing to release it, given its connection to the scandal. Both mother and wife had wept floods at this. Thomas Manning had been brought in to help the family with the language barrier. As it was so early in the proceedings, they didn't know when the case would be heard. Jack said he would be in touch with the NHS and the Home Office about repatriating the body to Romania. He took as many details as he could from them about what Alexandru was doing here, when he'd been here, if he had lived in the UK previously, if so, where. He asked question after question in an attempt to build up a complete profile. Eventually, when he had exhausted all possibilities, he told them he would contact them shortly and Gloria showed them out.

Jack finished his note-taking and buzzed Gloria

through to retrieve the dictation.

'Can you type this up for me ASAP?'

'No problem.' Gloria sashayed back out of the room. Jack glanced at his diary to see what the rest of his day held. Ah, his least favourite case, the Lafferty murder trial. Dave Lafferty, eighteen, of Nitshill, Glasgow, was accused of stabbing to death a twenty-seven-year-old mentally handicapped man at a bus shelter in Edinburgh's Leith area, whilst his two friends watched. Apparently he had done it for kicks, one of his friends capturing it on his mobile. *The wonders of technology. Not only does it advance us for good, but also for evil.* What motivated these people to kill an innocent person? Could it be attributed to violence on TV? After years of programmers and film-makers saying no, now medical research was saying yes. Was it really all down to social factors? And what of the two who had looked on? They were appearing on less serious charges, but even if they were convicted, with good behaviour and parole, they'd be out in minimal time.

Sometimes the whole justice system made Jack weary. The charade the courts perpetrated wasn't justice. Too many crooks had excellent counsel who could get them off, especially the rich. The prisons were too full and the prison service was a shambles. Prisoners likely to reoffend were being allowed out into the community before the end of their jail term. If they happened to escape, the response was, 'our procedures and processes were followed.' It was a joke.

Dave Lafferty's parents were ordinary, blue-collar, working-class, good people. They hadn't much money, but they believed they'd instilled the correct values into their son. So, where had it all gone wrong?

Sometimes it was a relief to go home, throw off the cloak of the Law and lead a normal life like everyone else. Except it wasn't really like that. Jack spent hours locked in his study, answering emails, preparing for court, making calls and spending less time with his family. He had to make some changes. He worked to live, not the other way round. Maybe he should think about early retirement. But how to pay for school fees, the luxury holidays, plus their £600,000 home in Newton Mearns? He'd always intended to work until he was sixty-five, but now, it was worth re-evaluating.

Jack thought back to when he first met Antonia. She was very attractive and had such presence, which he found alluring. They didn't have much back then, as students. Although several years older than her, they'd both been at the University of Glasgow at the same time, as Jack had taken a gap year, back when it wasn't yet called that. Antonia had gone to university to read English and Russian a year earlier than usual, when Jack was in his final year. At that time there weren't as many business courses available. You went to university, unless you studied Medicine or Law, to gain an education, not simply to pass exams and get a job. He empathised with his children now. There was so much pressure these days, to do well, to get good grades, go to a top university.

For all the worldly goods they'd amassed over the years and despite the fact that they had an excellent marriage, could he really say he was happier now? OK, nothing was quite the same as the first flush of young love, but even with the addition of their two children, all the money they had now didn't make them any happier. In fact, they saw so much less of each other now, as they were always working. What *was* the point? Couldn't they just live with less stuff?

Jack worked late that afternoon. He didn't often have these maudlin lapses, but afterwards he always attacked work with renewed vigour. Of course, he knew why he was still here. He wanted to get scum off the streets, make the country safe for its citizens to live in, including his family. The cruelty, brutality and pure evil he witnessed just unnerved him sometimes. The legal profession had a reputation for being emotionless, but it simply wasn't true. They were just people at the end of the day, not immune to feeling. It was no different to a doctor or nurse's attitude in the face of sickness or death. It was their coping mechanism.

This case, with the mentally handicapped man, had sickened him. The man was defenceless. He didn't even know what was going on. The same anger surged in him when he prosecuted young men who'd murdered a ninety-year-old for her pension, or in some cases the fifty pences which were in her electricity meter. Society was changing and not for the better.

Looking at his Rolex, he saw it was six thirty. He'd call his golfing buddy, Oscar, see if he was free.

'Hello?'

'Hi, Oscar, it's Jack.'

'Jack! How you doing?'

'Good, thanks. You?'

'OK, sales are slow.'

It flitted through Jack's mind that Oscar had just characterised his well-being by how well work was going.

'You busy?' Jack cut straight to the point.

'I was just finishing off. Why?'

'Any plans for tonight?'

'Well, I *was* going to the gym, but I don't know if I can be bothered.'

'So how does a pint sound?'

'Great. It's been a long day.'

'Well, I'm at the office. How about I meet you in All Bar One in half an hour?'

'Sure. Best get finished off.'

'See you in a bit.'

As Jack opened the door to the pub, two young women burst out, already rather inebriated, giggling their heads off. Maybe more than drink was responsible for their light-heartedness. There was something vacant about the eyes, which might have been an indication of a narcotic.

He'd experimented with drugs himself in the sixties, everyone had. Nobody knew of the negative effects it could have, the depression and schizophrenia it could cause. He hadn't touched drugs since. Felix had probably tried drugs, but he couldn't see Clara doing it. He'd have to be careful she didn't get in with a bad crowd.

She was a good girl, very intelligent, and sending her to Craigholme, a private single-sex school, had been one of their better ideas. It was a pity they needed to go down this route, as neither he nor Antonia had attended private school, but with Education in its current state, they owed it to their children to give them the best possible start.

Jack dropped his briefcase on one of the wooden Rennie Mackintosh-style chairs. Dumping his raincoat on top, he headed over to the bar, keeping one eye on the table.

'Vodka and Coke, please.'

The barman returned with Jack's drink and wiped the bar with a damp cloth, before putting the glass on a beer mat. Jack handed the barman a fiver and told him to keep the change. He realised he hadn't let Antonia know he was going out with Oscar and she might be expecting him, even though he was often late. He pressed Home on his contacts list.

'Hello?' Clara said.

'Hi, sweetheart. It's me.'

'Hi, Dad. You looking for Mum?'

'Yes, thanks.'

'Just a sec.'

'OK.'

'Guess what, Dad?'

'The Pope came for tea?'

'Don't be silly,' his daughter said.

'Elvis has risen from the dead?'

'No!'

They often played this game, whenever Clara said 'guess what?' to him. She paused for dramatic effect and said, 'One of my poems is being published in a collection.'

'That's fantastic news.'

'Isn't it?'

'You must be pleased.'

'I am quite chuffed. In fact, I'm off to see what else I can come up with before I become an adult and have no imagination left.'

Jack chuckled and a minute later Antonia came on the line.

'She told you?'

'Isn't it great?' Jack said.

'Yes. A budding poet in our midst. Where are you?'

'I'm in the pub. Thought I'd catch up with Oscar to-night. I'm having one of my days.'

He didn't need to explain to Antonia what that meant. She hated when he was like this and would be glad he could let off steam with Oscar.

'Get a cab then.'

'Of course I'll get a cab. You couldn't have a highly respected member of the legal profession driving about the city centre over the limit, could you?'

'It wouldn't be the first time,' mumbled Antonia.

'I heard that and I hope you're not talking about me, madam.'

'No, just your colleagues.'

'That's all right then. I'll grab something to eat here.'

'OK, see you later.'

'Bye.'

As Jack closed his phone, he caught sight of Oscar approaching.

'How's it going?' He stood up to shake his friend's hand.

'Not bad. You look well, Richard.'

It was a standing joke for Oscar to address Jack as Richard as many people had pointed out he was a ringer for Richard Gere. Personally, he couldn't see it.

Oscar appeared rumpled and distracted, as if he'd already been out drinking, which Jack knew wasn't the case. *He's obviously working too hard.*

'What would you like?' Jack asked.

'Guinness, extra cold, please.'

'I'll be right back.'

Jack handed Oscar his drink and then, sitting down, pulled the chair closer to the table.

'So, what you been up to?' Jack asked after taking a sip of his vodka and Coke.

'Working. You know I hope to branch out on my own?' Oscar wiped away his Guinness moustache with the back of his hand. 'Well, I'm working on some pretty high-profile accounts, nurturing important relationships, so that when I do–' Jack noticed Oscar's use of 'when', not 'if' '– start up on my own, I have the contacts.'

'So, have there been any more developments on that front? Have you spoken to the bank?' Jack was curious, as he knew Oscar worked really hard and was passionate about estate agency, and although there were tighter rules and regulations these days, he believed that if Oscar did get a chance, he would make a success of it. He had never discussed it with him, but if Oscar managed to get the bank's backing, then Jack might consider investing in his company.

'Yes, but the less said about that the better.'

'Fair enough.' Jack raised his glass. 'Slainte.'

'Slainte!'

Jack decided now was not the best time to suggest a partnership to Oscar, for two reasons: there was a slow-down of the housing market and he had too much on his plate. Maybe in a few months.

'So, how's the family?'

'The same. Antonia's working herself crazy. Difficult to say who's working more.'

'Yeah, it must be hard for her. She told me you've lost your cleaning lady.'

'Yes, she's got a job in a call centre. What's the poor woman to do? Now, we're trawling the agencies, searching for a new one. I'm bribing Clara to do chores and Antonia's doing the rest.'

'What about Felix?'

'Felix is…Felix,' Jack said eventually. 'He's at a difficult age and becoming more withdrawn. I don't recognise the boy I used to take fishing, hillwalking and go-karting. Now it's all about this band he's in. I can't even remember their name, but it's awful, Mangled Dead or something.' Jack shook his head.

'Well, we all went through our wild stages. Didn't you?'

'Doesn't mean I'm happy when it's my own child.'

'S'pose not.'

'What about you and Gaby?' Jack asked, watching Oscar closely. 'You two not thinking of having kids?'

'Well, sort of, but Gaby's, you know, a hotshot career woman.'

'So was Antonia. So is Antonia, but we still popped a couple out,' Jack said.

'I know, but try telling that to Gaby. Anyone she knows with kids has changed beyond all recognition. It's all children's TV and "look, the baby smiled", when it simply had wind, or her friends come to the door to greet her, covered in vomit and smelling as if they haven't washed in a fortnight. It frightens her. Same again?'

'Yeah, vodka and Coke.'

'I'll be right back.'

'So, golfing on the twenty-seventh?' Oscar asked Jack, when he sat back down.

'Yes, Troon, isn't it?'

'Yes, tee off at nine.'

'Do you want me to pick you up?'

'That would be great. I can't wait, a rare day off.'

'No, nor can I,' Jack agreed.

When Jack next checked his watch, nearly three hours had passed.

'Oscar, I didn't realise it was so late. I'm going to have to run.' Jack drained his glass.

'No problem. I best get home too, see my wife before she goes to bed,' Oscar replied meaningfully.

They left the bar and walked up the street, in search of taxis.

Chapter Fifty-three

'Hi,' Jack whispered in his wife's ear as she lay dozing on the sofa.

Antonia flinched. 'What time is it?'

'Eleven thirty.'

'I must have dropped off,' Antonia said, covering a yawn with her hand.

'Do you want some hot chocolate?'

'No, I'd rather have a toddy. My throat's sore.'

'Hope you're not coming down with something.'

Antonia gave her husband a look. OK, she was right; she never came down with anything. She was indestructible in that department.

'Right, a toddy it is then,' Jack said. He was traditional with his toddies. Boiling the kettle, he sliced a lemon, added some honey and a generous measure of whisky, before pouring the water in.

Antonia accepted it gratefully. He sat on the arm of the sofa as his wife blew on the liquid, before sipping it.

'So, what's new with you today?' he asked.

'Just usual staffing problems, shortages, unhappy customers, that sort of thing.'

'Sounds scintillating.'

''Tis.'

'How about you and I go to bed?' Jack said, waggling his eyebrows and sneaking his hand under his wife's top, stroking the smooth skin of her stomach beneath.

'For goodness' sake, Jack, didn't I just say I have a sore throat?'

'Sorry. I'm going to have a shower,' he said, tugging off his tie and kicking off his shoes. Before he left the room, he kissed Antonia on the side of her cheek and padded upstairs to their en suite to have a cold shower.

Six hours later, Jack was up again. Waking before the alarm, he peeked through the blinds. A light drizzle was falling from the sky. Undeterred, he splashed his face with water, put on his running gear and quietly let himself out of the house. He loved this time of the morning. No one was around. Women didn't dare go jogging alone early in the morning any more. Jack did his best thinking at this time of day. He ran towards Eastwood Golf Club. People who lived round here didn't tend to get up until later. *Give it another hour and you won't be able to move for BMWs, Audi A6s, people carriers and 4x4s.*

He loved the silence. Even now, as he ran along the deserted streets, he could hear his own footfalls thudding on the pavement. A keen runner, he'd done a few marathons in his time, including the New York one when he was forty-two. No one could call him a slacker in anything he did. He felt better and thought better when he was fit. He tried to instil this into his family, but to no avail. Whereas Clara took dance lessons and rode horses, Felix was permanently attached to either a sound system or a laptop. Antonia didn't exercise much either. Although she had a full membership at the gym, she only made a half-hearted attempt to go once or twice a month. She was often away on business, and when she wasn't, she was taking care of their family. Guiltily, Jack wondered if perhaps he helped with the housework occasionally, she would make the time to go. Housework wasn't his forte though. Generally, if he cleaned something, it wasn't up to Antonia's scrutiny. He did cook sometimes, when they had guests, but he couldn't rustle up a meal out of the random contents of the fridge and certainly not in twenty minutes. He needed a good complex recipe which would take him two hours of preparation and three of cooking and taste exquisite. Maybe it was because he had so much pressure in other areas of his life that he wanted to feel as little as possible in his home life. He hated ironing with a vengeance. In fact, did Antonia even do that now? Didn't she sub it out to Pressed for Time or Laundry Basket or one of these other agencies? Was it bad that he didn't know?

Apart from investments, Antonia dealt with the day-to-day running of the family finances too. She paid all the bills, did all the shopping and dealt with any maintenance to the house. Perhaps he should broach the subject with her, about getting fit, or should he suggest they go for a walk on Sundays, start her off gently? Felix barely participated in their weekend life, and although Clara was sometimes around for meals, when she didn't have activities, she was often out, or having sleepovers with her friends. Jack missed the close relationship he'd had with Clara when she was little. She really was his princess.

He'd reached the halfway point and jogged up and down on the spot checking his time, before turning around and running back the way he'd come. He reckoned he could break thirty minutes this time, if he kept up his pace.

Lengthening his stride, he was home in a record twenty-nine minutes, forty-eight seconds. A sheen of sweat covered him from top to toe. Jack kicked off his trainers at the front door and padded upstairs, where he heard the shower running.

'Morning.' He popped his head around the bathroom door, almost frightening Antonia out of her wits.

'I didn't hear you come in.'

'Obviously not.'

'New time?'

'I knocked fifteen seconds off.'

'Well done. Are you going to shower next door?'

'Yes, kids up yet?'

'Don't think so. Do you want coffee?'

'Yes, thanks. Any chance of a bagel?'

'Just this once. Smoked salmon and cream cheese?'

'You know me too well.' Jack smirked before heading for the guest bathroom.

Felix wasn't up before Jack left, but Clara came down in her pyjamas.

'Morning, Dad,' she said, stifling a yawn.

'Morning, sleepyhead.' Jack smiled up at his daughter from his place at the table, where he was sipping coffee, *The Herald* spread out in front of him. Often he met the paperboy on the way back from his run, but not today.

'Is there any coffee left?' his daughter asked.

'Yes, I made a whole pot.'

Clara raised an eyebrow. 'You mean Mum did.'

'Caught.' Jack laughed.

Jack hadn't seen his daughter yesterday. She wasn't up when he left for work and was already in bed when he arrived home. *She's taken a real stretch. Soon she'll overtake her mum. Her height must come from me.* Clara looked more like him, whereas Felix, if he bore any resemblance to anyone, under all that hair, it was Antonia.

'Where's Mum?'

'Getting dressed.'

'Daaad?' Clara said. In this respect she was very much like any female Jack knew. She had a special way of dragging out a word, so you knew a request was coming up in the next sentence.

'Yeeeeees, Clara.' By now he knew the game.

She drew her father a look. 'Are we going on holiday this year?'

Jack hesitated. He knew the kids would go stir-crazy over the holidays if they didn't, but he was simply too busy and Antonia was inundated too.

'Maybe for the October week,' he replied, at which Clara's face instantly lit up.

'Where?' she asked, sitting on her hands. From experience Jack knew if she didn't, she would jump up and down with excitement, but she was too cool for that now.

'I don't know. I haven't thought about it.'

'Tell you what, why don't I get some brochures?'

So grown up. 'Where would you like to go?'

'New York.'

'New York?' Jack was taken aback. 'Why New York?'

'Well, there's the Guggenheim, the Museum of Natural History, Central Park, the Empire State Building and–'

'OK, I get it,' Jack interrupted her. 'What does Felix think?'

'Oh, I haven't asked Felix. He probably won't even go.'

'He'll be going,' Jack said, not daring to think what

could happen in their week-long absence. New York. Maybe that wasn't such a bad idea.

They could go to Carnegie Hall one night. They hadn't been to Broadway for more than twenty years, when they celebrated their wedding anniversary. Perhaps they could fit in a performance at the Met. He'd quite like to see *Tristan and Isolde*. 'OK, I'll try to talk Mum into it. But it's our secret for now.'

Once again Jack's day was full. He'd never been in such demand. He didn't know if that was good or bad. His conscience told him it was bad, as it meant there were more criminals. His bank balance told him it was good, but as he'd just mulled over the other night, was that really what was important? Well, no, but Clara wanted to go to New York and he couldn't blame her. Guilt overwhelmed him again, this time because the kids wouldn't have a summer holiday. He needed to spend more time with them. He often felt his profession was like the little Dutch boy who put his finger in the dyke to stop the water pouring through – a sticking plaster, nothing more.

Jack went over the paperwork in front of him again. It was odd that this case was being tried in the high court, although if it were left to him, all cases of causing death by dangerous driving would be tried there. Very few were, in fact, resulting in much lighter sentences. His client, whose brother was killed in the incident, was one of those few. James Brodie, eighteen, driving without insurance and whilst banned for speeding, had collided head-on with the Renault Espace which Alan Fairlie was driving when Brodie had strayed onto the wrong side of the road, at seventy miles an hour. Miraculously the other passengers were OK, although the son suffered a broken leg, but no other injuries, apart from a few cuts and scrapes. The ten-week-old baby in his car seat in the back was unscathed.

Chapter Fifty-four

'All right, Dad?'

Jack looked up from his phone. He'd just stepped out of the car and was walking towards the house. 'Not bad, son. Where you off to?'

Scowling, he said, 'Just out.'

'Right.' But his son had already gone. His question was meant as a polite enquiry, not the Spanish Inquisition Felix clearly took it for.

One of these days he would know how to deal with Felix. Antonia wasn't much better with him. When Felix was younger, Antonia and he had been close, but now he doubted anyone could get close to him.

Clara was home. 'So, how's my favourite girl?' Clara pretended to cringe, but he knew she was secretly pleased.

'Daadddd!' Clara said.

He grinned and mussed her hair.

'Watch the do.'

'So, what have you been up to today?' Jack asked as he put the kettle on.

'This and that.'

'This and that?'

'Yep.'

'So, how's about you tell me what this and that entailed?'

Sighing, Clara said, 'Well, after school, I read a bit of *Pride and Prejudice* and then tidied up. Mum's always tired when she comes in.'

Again, that stab of guilt. 'Tell you what, why don't we surprise Mum? Why don't we make dinner? What's your best dish?'

'Spaghetti carbonara,' Clara replied without hesitation.

'Spaghetti carbonara it is,' Jack said, taking off his jacket. He washed his hands and then said, 'What do we need?'

Clara counted out the ingredients on her fingers, checking as she went along, that they had everything.

The phone rang. It was Antonia. 'I'll be home in twenty minutes,' she told Clara.

'Make it ten,' shouted Jack, so she could hear. 'Dinner's nearly ready.'

'What's your father yelling about?'

'He says be home in ten. Dinner's nearly ready.'

'Dinner will be ready?'

'Yes.'

'Dad's making dinner?'

'Yes, but I'm helping him. We're having spaghetti carbonara.'

'Lovely. I'm on my way.'

'Can you set the table, Clara, please?' her father asked.

'OK.'

'Don't forget black pepper.'

Clara rolled her eyes.

'Sorry, you know what you're doing.'

'It needs black pepper and parmesan,' Clara said.

'Is Felix coming back for dinner?' Jack wondered aloud.

'Don't think so. He was going over to Tigsy's for prac-tice.'

'Who's Tigsy?'

Clara shrugged. 'One of the band?'

He'd have to keep a closer eye on his son. He didn't know who his friends were these days, but then, he was seventeen and who did know what their kids did at that age?

'Did he eat before he went out?'

Another non-committal shrug from Clara. His son had looked a little thin. He'd have to get a good look at him next time he saw him. He should make him get a summer job, although Felix wouldn't be thrilled at that suggestion. With the schools in their last week, no doubt all the summer jobs had been snapped up anyway.

Antonia opened the kitchen door, bundling five shop-ping bags through to the kitchen. She covered her hand with her mouth. 'Nice apron, Jack.'

'Hi, you lot.' She kissed first Clara on the cheek and then Jack on the mouth, making Clara groan and seek refuge in the lounge.

'Good day?' Jack asked.

'Better now. That smells great,' she said, as Jack dished up.

The three of them sat companionably eating their spaghetti carbonara and garlic bread, which Clara had popped in the oven as a welcome afterthought. They talked mainly about Clara and to a lesser extent Felix, it being difficult when he barely told them anything about his life, apart from a little about his music.

Jack and Antonia encouraged the kids to be independent and supported their interests, and fortunately they had enough money to throw at the various enterprises the children chose to undertake, within reason.

'So, could you dance to Felix's band?' Jack played devil's advocate.

'That dirge?'

'Now, now, Clara, you must appreciate your brother's gifts too,' Jack said.

'But they're terrible! They really are. They played a gig at Glasgow Academy last week and they were booed off the stage!'

'Really?' Jack exchanged a look with Antonia, whose eyebrows told him all he needed to know. He'd need to challenge his son at some point on where this was all going. This was an important year for him. A levels were coming up. Jack and Antonia were liberal, but to a point. They still wanted their kids to do well and if they were overly distracted, then they wouldn't hesitate to rein them in.

'So, are you going up to Hazelton tomorrow?' Antonia asked Clara.

'For a couple of hours. Laura's mum is picking me up.'

They owed that woman a medal. She was always running their daughter places.

'So, will you be mucking out the stables or just trotting around on Ginger?' Antonia asked.

'Both. Colette's got a new pony, Cosmo.'

'Cosmo?'

'Yes. It's a Welsh Cob.'

'Really?'

'Yes. It's black, male.'

'I'm surprised her parents let her get such a powerful horse. How old is she?'

'Thirteen.'

Antonia's eyebrows raised and Jack glanced between his wife and daughter, seeking enlightenment. He didn't do horses.

'Clara, could you clear the table, please?' he asked her, motioning with his eyes for her to skedaddle. His canny daughter caught on straight away.

'Sure, then I'm going upstairs to listen to my iPod.'

'I'll bring you up a cup of tea later,' Antonia said.

'Antonia, you coming through to the comfy seats?'

'I think so. Is there anything on TV?'

'Not sure. Actually, I wanted to talk to you.'

'Fire away.' Antonia made herself comfortable, plumped three cushions round about her and leaned on the arm of the sofa.

'Well, I've been thinking that we haven't had a holiday yet.'

'No, we haven't.'

'I know we've been busy, but my idea was perhaps during the October week, we could take the kids to New York,' Jack blurted out, before Antonia could take over the conversation, as she was wont to do.

'New York? We haven't been there for years.'

'I know, but now the kids are old enough to appreciate it, and there's so much for them to see and do. Even if they only recognise more places in movies they watch when we get back, it will have been worth it.'

'I need to check my calendar for October, but I don't see that being a problem.'

'Fantastic. I'll get Gloria to look into flights.'

'This is exciting. Gives us something to look forward to.'

'I know.' Jack leaned forward and gave her a hug. 'It'll

be great.'

As Antonia flicked the TV on, Jack excused himself, saying he needed to grab a jumper.

Jack padded up the stairs and knocked on Clara's door. No answer. Then he remembered what she'd said about her iPod, so he opened the door to find his daughter dancing about the room, headphones on and her iPod stuck in her jeans pocket.

'Clara.' He leaned down into his daughter's face. She almost screamed, as she had her eyes half closed, whilst she danced around, lost in the music.

'Dad! You almost gave me a heart attack!'

'We're going to New York!'

At that she did scream and jumped up and hugged him. 'Oh, Dad, that's fab. Wait till I tell Laura. She'll be so jealous.'

Jack released her and said, 'Don't tell Felix. I want to tell him myself.'

'OK.'

'Promise?'

'Promise.'

Jack returned to the living room and snuggled down on the sofa beside Antonia. She leaned her head on his chest, whilst his arms snaked round her waist, as they lay watching some reality TV show. Jack hated that sort of thing.

'Antonia, what are we watching?'

'It's the end of *Wife Swap USA*. *A Few Good Men* is coming on.'

'That's ancient.'

'I know, but I need to hear Jack Nicholson say, "You can't handle the truth" and besides, Tom Cruise is in it.'

Knowing when he was beaten, Jack relaxed, enjoying the heat of his wife's body.

'Didn't you find your jumper?'

'No, not sure what I did with it.'

'You could have taken another one from the drawer,' suggested Antonia.

'No, I wanted that one. It's OK. You're nice and warm,' he said suggestively.

'Jack. Later. Tom Cruise, remember? Priorities. If you want to be useful, get me some chocolate.'

Trying not to smile, Jack dutifully fetched the chocolate.

'Guess who called me again today?' Antonia said.

'Who?'

'Holly.'

'Holly? How's she doing?'

'Fine. She's enjoying Italy and everything's going well. She asked me again if I'd come over. I was thinking that maybe we could go, just the two of us, perhaps get my parents to watch the kids.'

'When?'

'In a few weeks.'

'I can't. I'm too busy. You go.'

Antonia's lips quirked upwards. She was angling for exactly that. He knew her too well. It would be good for her to spend some time with her niece.

'Are you sure?'

'Positive,' said Jack, turning back to his *New Scientist*. Antonia cuddled into her husband and Jack tried not to laugh. Did she think he was so dim that he couldn't see her plan? Well, they'd all got what they wanted today, he and Clara, New York; Antonia, Tuscany.

Chapter Fifty-five

Next day Jack was late getting away from the office. In two days he'd be in court and he still had to polish his opening remarks. The house was quiet when he arrived home, so he poured himself a glass of wine and sat in his study. As he sipped his wine, he allowed his thoughts to flow away from work to his enigma of a son. They had almost nothing in common. Felix wasn't much interested in the Arts and Jack couldn't bear to listen to that noise Felix called music. He wondered what he'd make of New York. Would he want to go? Perhaps he and Antonia needed to make a concerted effort to spend time together with the kids as a family, do things they would all enjoy. New York could be the start of it. Clara was certainly excited enough for all of them.

The door to his study opened. Felix.

'Mum said you wanted to see me.'

'I did. Come in.'

Felix shut the door behind him but didn't venture fully into the room.

'How would you feel about going to New York on holiday?'

'New York? With you?'

Jack smiled. 'And Mum and Clara.'

'Do I have to go?' Felix asked.

'You don't *have* to go,' Jack began, in a tone which indicated he would be disappointed if he didn't, 'but I thought you'd like the buzz of New York. Clara can't wait to go.'

'Yes, well, she's a girl. It's all shopping for her.'

'You know that's not true. Give your sister more credit.'

'How about you give me more credit?'

Whilst Jack saw Felix's point, he wasn't going to allow him to speak to him like that.

'Felix, I think you've forgotten who you're talking to.'

'Sorry, sir!' His son's voice dripped with sarcasm.

Where did he go wrong?

'Felix, where would you like to go?'

'It doesn't matter,' mumbled Felix.

'It does matter.'

'Nashville, Memphis, Graceland, listen to the blues on Beale Street, that sort of thing, but you–' he spat '–won't want to do that.'

This much was true, Jack thought, but that didn't mean he wouldn't do it for his son. Who knows, it might be fun. After a few minutes, Jack said, 'If we went to Nashville and Memphis for three days, would you come to New York?'

His son stared at him. 'You'd take me to Memphis and Nashville?'

'Yep.' Jack smiled. 'On one condition.'

Felix's face fell. 'I knew there'd be a catch. What?'

'You do the research, you find the hotels, you work out the itinerary. It's all down to you.'

Felix looked up at his father, his eyes alight. 'Deal.'

Over the next few weeks, Jack and Antonia were increasingly busy at work. Jack's case had begun in earnest and so he and his family flitted past each other. He couldn't wait for October to come when they could spend some quality time together. There had been a marked improvement in Felix's mood, almost as if someone had flipped a switch. *If getting to go to the Deep South does that for him, we can go more often.* On the rare occasions Jack had crossed paths with his son since their talk, Felix was full of plans and printouts and had booked the hotel. He'd arranged the internal flights from New York to Memphis and they'd decided to drive the few hundred miles to Nashville to see a bit of the South at its best. Antonia wasn't fussed; she was happy Felix was showing a bit of character. Secretly, although their musical tastes differed, Jack was looking forward to it and of course, there was Graceland, which even he was interested in seeing.

'Gloria, I have to be in court at ten. Is there anything urgent before I go?'

'I've left messages on your desk.'

'Thanks.' Jack let go of the intercom.

Jack strode into the courtroom, acknowledging Ted Harvey, QC for the defence and sat down beside his clients. Opening statements had gone well and Jack was more than halfway through his witness list.

The judge entered, addressed the courtroom and then the jury filed in. Jack knew he had to play to an audience, something Harvey was no stranger to either. Harvey was trying to portray his client as a poor, misunderstood young boy from a crumbling housing estate, with no prospects. Even if he were only slightly bending the truth, it was irrelevant. A man was dead, leaving a son without a father, a wife without a husband, all because Brodie was driving dangerously along the same road on that fateful night. Jack could see the defendant's mother in the assembled crowd, face grim. He felt for her. He was her son, but justice needed to be served.

The formalities over, Jack called his next witness. 'Prosecution calls Elizabeth Navarra to the stand.'

A responsible-looking woman in her forties, hair tied up in a bun, approached the stand and took her seat.

'Do you swear by Almighty God that you shall tell the truth, the whole truth and nothing but the truth, so help you God?'

'I swear by Almighty God that I will tell the truth, the whole truth and nothing but the truth,' said Elizabeth.

'For the benefit of the court, can you state your name, please?' Jack said.

'Elizabeth Navarra.'

'Ms Navarra, can you tell the court of your whereabouts on the evening of March twenty-first of this year?'

'Yes. I was on the A76, driving back from seeing my sister in Sanquhar.'

'What time was this?'

'Nine o'clock, quarter past?'

'Was it dark?'

'Yes.'

'Did anything unusual happen on the drive home?'

'I saw a Ford Mondeo collide head-on with a Renault Espace, just as I approached the Cumnock sign.'

'Was there anything out of the ordinary with the way either vehicle was being driven?'

'Objection!' shouted Harvey.

'Overruled,' said Judge Connelly. 'You may answer the question, Ms Navarra.'

'Yes, the blue Mondeo was on the wrong side of the road.'

Jack continued, 'Do you see the driver of the blue Mondeo in the courtroom?'

Elizabeth gestured to Brodie.

'So, the man sitting in the dock, James Brodie, was the man driving the Mondeo that night?'

'That's correct.'

'Did you stop?'

'Of course.'

'What did you do first?'

She thought for a few seconds, then said, 'I pulled my car up onto the verge and checked the Espace. There were several people in it. The windscreen was gone, the airbags had gone off on both the passenger and the driver side and I heard crying coming from the back. I later discovered this was a baby. The driver's head was at a funny angle and there was a lot of blood. The teenager in the back was unconscious.'

'What did you do next?'

'I looked over at the Mondeo and James Brodie was getting out. So I concentrated on the Espace.'

'Then what?'

'I called 999.'

'So you placed the call to the emergency services?'

'Yes.'

'What happened next?'

'I convinced the mother to get out of the car, although she was bleeding and shaken, and I took the baby seat out, but didn't take the baby out of it, just in case there was any injuries we couldn't see. I was scared to move him as he was so tiny.'

'Then what?'

'Then I spoke to the father, who was unconscious. He looked in really bad shape and I wasn't sure if doing anything would make it worse.'

'What about the other child?'

'I shook him a few times and spoke to him. I then told his mother he was unconscious but breathing.'

'Did you check Mr Brodie for any injuries?'

'No.'

'Why was that?'

'Another motorist had stopped and was talking to Mr Brodie, who said he was all right.'

'Did the deceased regain consciousness before the emergency services arrived?' Jack asked.

'No. I believe he died on the way to hospital.'

'Thank you, Ms Navarra. No further questions.' Jack sat down.

Ted Harvey QC took the floor and tried to needle the witness and plant the seed of reasonable doubt in the mind of the jury that his client hadn't caused the victim's death. A picture of confidence, he smiled at Ms Navarra and said, 'So, Ms Navarra, we have determined that on the night of March twenty-first, you were returning from Sanquhar after visiting your sister. Is that correct?'

The morning continued, with Harvey haranguing the witnesses in a desperate attempt to set his client free.

Jack rocked back and forth on his chair, trying to think of his next step. He'd come from court to the office, as he needed to think and here was where he thought best. He clicked his pen on and off repeatedly. Undoing his tie, he made notes on his plan of attack. It was obvious Brodie had caused Alan Fairlie's death. It was all the rigmarole surrounding the case that needed work now, the waltz that had to be danced.

'You OK?' Antonia asked Jack that night.

'Mmm.' Jack was evasive.

'Bad day?'

'You could say that.'

His wife hugged him and said, 'Jack, you can only do what you can. You do it really well. If anyone can get this guy put away, it's you. Just remember that.'

Smiling down at his wife cuddled into his chest, stroking the grey hairs there, Jack kissed her softly, and when she made a move to take things further, he didn't stop her.

'Remember I need you here by five. Everyone's arriving at seven thirty,' Antonia said.

'OK, I'll be back in time. Love you.' Jack hung up. He was playing golf with Oscar at St Andrews.

'That was some game.' Jack grinned at Oscar. It was a beautiful day and there was even some heat in the sun, unusual for the east coast.

'Yes, it was.' Oscar returned his grin.

Oscar had improved upon his handicap, but Jack had still beaten him. It hadn't really been decided until the seventeenth. Overall it had been a good game. Jack's short game was better than Oscar's, but Oscar could hit some serious long balls.

'That you, Jack?' Antonia called from the kitchen as the front door slammed.

'Yes.'

'Good game?'

Jack strode into the kitchen, where Antonia stood, hair swept up, a few tendrils falling loose around her face. She looked hot, in both senses.

'Yes, not a bad day, thanks. Sorry I'm a bit late. Traffic.' He didn't need to finish the sentence. It was a good two hours' drive from St Andrews to Newton Mearns. He wasn't lying, just stretching the truth. He declined to mention his shandy with Oscar. He'd wanted to talk about the business proposal he'd contemplated last time.

'I'm just going to put some jeans on.' He kissed Antonia, took her face in his hands and said, 'You're a good wife, you know.'

She rested her hands on his chest and said, 'No, dear. I'm a *fabulous* wife. You need to work on your compliments, especially when you've been in the Nineteenth with Oscar.' The shandy, she'd obviously smelled it on his breath. Damn. A few Tic Tacs would have sorted that out.

'OK, you win, *fabulous* wife.' He grinned.

'Go and get changed,' she ordered.

'Any chance of a glass of wine?' Jack asked, when he reappeared, wearing faded Levi's and a khaki shirt.

'It's in the bottle,' Antonia informed him.

'Where's the bottle?' Jack asked.

'In the garage, and whilst you're there, bring six bottles of red in for tonight. The white's already in the fridge.'

'OK, got it.'

Antonia was already dressed and applying her make-up

when Jack finally headed upstairs to get showered and changed into slightly more formal clothing for dinner. Shortly afterwards, the doorbell rang. Antonia beat Jack to the door, but as their friends entered, he passed their coats to Felix who took them upstairs. It wasn't long before the bell rang again and soon they were all in situ, glasses of fizz in hand for the non-drivers.

Dinner was magnificent. Antonia had excelled herself. When Jack had first met her, her cooking was dreadful; he'd cooked everything or they'd have subsisted on tinned tomato soup, but over the years, it had become a shared passion. Even if he said so himself, he was the better cook, when he got the opportunity.

The beef was done to a tee and he had been ravenous, but now he was replete. Antonia had just risen to clear away the plates and bring out dessert when the doorbell rang. They looked at each other, surprised at the doorbell ringing at this late hour.

'I'll go,' said Antonia.

Jack gathered up the plates and retreated to the kitchen. He was just going to chase up Antonia, ask her to come in and help him take the dessert plates through, when she came into the kitchen.

'Great, you can help me carry these. I've dished up,' Jack said, eager for some brownie points. He grinned at her, his face falling as he saw her ashen one. 'What is it?'

She opened the door wide and said, 'Come in and sit down.'

Jack watched as a pale young girl and a policeman entered the kitchen and proceeded to sit at the breakfast bar.

'What's going on?' Jack asked his wife.

'This is Archie Furnival and his daughter, Jessica. Jessica's made an allegation against Felix,' she said, her words staccato-like.

'What sort of allegation?' asked Jack, setting the bowls on the worktop.

'I don't know yet. I just asked them in.'

Jack was trying to think on his feet, but failing miserably.

'We have dinner guests, Officer. It's not really a good time.'

'I'm not here in an official capacity. Yet,' said the policeman.

This is surreal.

The policeman interrupted his thoughts, saying, 'This can't wait.'

'OK, right.' Jack's mind was whirling.

He turned to his wife and said, 'Antonia, can you please take dessert through and I'll handle this?'

'I want to know what's going on too,' his wife insisted.

'Well, can you go and tell the others we're having a problem with dessert and we'll be in shortly.'

'OK, I'll offer them more wine in the meantime, but don't discuss anything until I get back.'

The policeman and Jack stared at each other for what seemed an age, before Antonia returned. The girl's eyes had remained downcast.

'Right, what's going on?' Antonia asked, before Jack could say anything.

'Jessica tells me your son raped her,' the officer said matter-of-factly.

'What!' cried Antonia, horrified. 'That's not possible!'

'Antonia, keep your voice down.' Jack was quick to

think of their guests.

He could see Antonia was restraining herself when she asked the girl calmly, 'Why are you saying this?' But the girl remained silent.

'That's not all,' the officer said.

'What do you mean? Isn't your daughter's allegation bad enough? Felix wouldn't do such a thing,' Jack said vehemently. 'His only interest is his band.'

'All I know is my daughter has been acting very strangely since last Saturday night, closeting herself in her room, not eating and then today she told her mother, who couldn't even bear to come here, for fear of what she might do to your son, that she was raped. She named your son as her attacker…and she's pregnant.'

Jack's head spun and he thought he was going to be sick. He couldn't, wouldn't, believe it of Felix. 'My son's upstairs. I'm going to get him.'

The blood drained from the girl's already pale face and she shook her head vigorously.

'I don't think she can cope with that. It took everything she had to come here tonight. I just wanted to speak to you first, before we press charges.'

Dazed, Jack said, 'I'm a prosecutor. I know how the system works.'

Numb, he turned to the girl. 'This isn't right. You know this isn't right.' She wouldn't look at him.

'I'm going to speak to Felix and we're going to get to the bottom of this. Do you think you can stay here whilst I do that? I'm happy for you to see him after I've let him know what you're alleging, but since your daughter doesn't want to see him, I can't bring him downstairs.'

'That's fine. We'll wait.'

Jack turned to Antonia. 'Sweetheart, go and speak to the guests. Do what you think is best.'

Antonia had frozen, struck by disbelief.

Jack climbed the stairs with legs of lead. He hesitated outside Felix's door and then knocked loudly. No sound came from within. He turned the doorknob and saw him lying on his bed, headphones on, lost in his own world. As he walked towards the bed, Felix finally noticed him and removed his headphones.

'What is it, Dad?' Felix peered at him curiously, almost as if he was concerned for him.

'Felix, does the name Jessica mean anything to you?'

'Jessica who?'

'Do you know a Jessica?'

'Sure. There's one in my class at school, Jessica Adams.'

'Any other Jessicas?'

Frowning and clearly wondering where this was leading, Felix said, 'No, I don't think so, why?'

'Because there's a Jessica Furnival and her father Archie, a policeman incidentally, downstairs in our kitchen.'

'What's that got to do with me?' Felix's eyebrows scrunched up.

Jack took a deep breath then said, 'She says you raped her.'

'I what?' Felix had turned white.

Chapter Fifty-six
Czeslawa – SCORPIO

Energetic, deep, passionate, intuitive. Wilful and stubborn. Keen observers of people. Sensitive. Strong leadership qualities. Good analytical skills, incisive. Very career motivated.

Czeslawa helped her daughter into the van then her husband started the engine and they were on their way. They had only lived in Livingston a few months, but it felt longer. The two-bedroom flat in a depressing block in the Craigshill area was not the best place to live and they were anxious to escape it.

Many windows were boarded up and gangs of youths hung around on street corners. She didn't want Angelika growing up in that. So she was glad when Wojciech was offered a new job. They could get out of this place. The area was beyond deprived, with burnt-out cars and shady characters peddling drugs in the corridors of the flats.

As they left their old home behind, Czeslawa began to relax and she exhaled noisily, realising that she'd been holding her breath. Her husband raised his eyebrows.

She took his hand as Angelika jabbered away to them in Polish. She was six years old and quite the little chatterbox.

Her English was better than her mother's. Czeslawa hadn't been able to bring herself to look for a job in this area. She'd be scared to work in a corner shop in case she was held at knifepoint. When Wojciech was promoted to foreman, she was beyond relieved. He'd proven an accomplished worker, trustworthy and hard-working, more than could be said of the work-shy youths he worked alongside. Over dinner he would entertain her with tales of his workmates. It annoyed her that talk was often of the Poles taking jobs away from UK workers, many of whom didn't want to work, instead preferring to claim benefits and milk the system.

As they drove along the M9, passing lush green fields and rolling hills on one side and a sprinkling of villages on the other, Czeslawa caught sight of the towering chimneys of the Grangemouth refinery. A necessary blot on the landscape. Soon it was in the distance and the vista gave way to the undulating hills once more. Wojciech took the cut-off for the M80 and before long they were trundling over the country lanes to Kings River, their new home.

Czeslawa had only seen the house in a picture, trusting Wojciech to get it right. She'd researched the village on the internet and found it idyllic. She had a good feeling about this. Once they were settled, she would start looking for a job. The larger towns of Kilburn and Cumbernauld were nearby. She wanted to meet people. It was lonely on her own, with Wojciech at work all day. She loved her daughter dearly, but there was only so much she could offer her.

When they arrived in Kings River, it was the annual gala day, a festival for the whole community which also encompassed a local teenage schoolgirl becoming queen for a year, attending a feast of charity events and judging competitions. Angelika was excited to see the red and yellow flags strung from one house to the next and the banners on some doorways heralding the gala queen's home and those of her pageboy and flower girl. Czeslawa smiled at Wojciech. They would unpack later.

The gala day was in full swing. The queen's coronation would be at one o'clock after running events, as well as tug o' war and an egg and spoon race. A large queue streamed from an ice-cream van at one end of the football field. When Angelika saw children slurping *99* cones, she wanted one too.

Czeslawa slipped her hand into her husband's and they followed their daughter through the thronging crowds. There were stalls selling local produce, bring and buy stands, a tombola and face painting. Everything she'd expected a village fair to offer. Angelika ran ahead shouting, 'Look, Mummy, look, Daddy, they are painting their faces. Look, Mummy, there are carts.' Wojciech and Czeslawa smiled and made all the appropriate noises to Angelika's exclamations.

'Daddy, I want one of those teddies,' Angelika said, pointing to prizes at a hoopla stall.

'We need to start talking to her in English,' Czeslawa said.

'Then you'll have to learn English, and I'll have to improve,' said her husband, putting his arm around her.

'Mummy, can I run in the race?'

Wojciech and Czeslawa exchanged a glance, then Czeslawa said, 'Go on.'

'On your marks, se-e-et–' the starter blew his whistle '–go!'

'C'mon, Lika, you can do it!' her parents shouted, in Polish, which attracted a few stares. She finished second. Two minutes later, she took part in her first awards ceremony. They hadn't seen inside their new home yet, but their daughter had already won a medal, already a part of the community.

Angelika stared open-mouthed at the young girl with the golden curls, wearing the pretty dress, looking like a bridesmaid at a wedding. The official slipped the sash reading 'Kings River gala queen' over her head. An important-looking man, perhaps the local councillor, placed a sparkly tiara on her head and a bouquet of mixed blooms in her hands. The crowd cheered, then the marching band played a few numbers before the crowd dispersed, some parents being dragged to the face-painting stand, others trawling their children to the ever-popular raffle. After a pleasant two hours of wandering around, they decided it was time to go and meet their new home.

'It's beautiful,' said Czeslawa. It was a four-in-a-block terraced house, with a UPVC door, red tiled roof and pebbled walls. The long hall led to a kitchen on the left-hand side after an adequate bathroom, with new-looking three-piece suite. The lounge was at the end of the hall and very spacious, although had no real room for a dining table. The two bedrooms were on the right and she was pleasantly surprised at their size. She would be able to set up a little desk in the corner over there, with a computer. She hugged her husband. Angelika barrelled into her as she returned from racing around the house, eager to explore her new surroundings.

'Thank you, Wojciech. It's perfect.' They'd been lucky to hear about it. His friend's sister had previously rented it.

'Glad you like it. Shall we unpack?'

'Yes.' She answered him in Polish then remembered they should be speaking English. But it was hard, and they were proud and didn't want Angelika to forget her roots. Sighing, she followed her husband's footsteps outside to the van.

An elderly man came out to meet them as they manoeuvred a chest of drawers up the path. 'Hello. I'm your neighbour, George Kelso.'

Czeslawa wiped her hands on her jeans and said, 'Nice to meet you. Czeslawa.' She held out her hand to shake his.

He scrunched up his eyebrows. 'Ches-what?'

'Czes-lawa,' she emphasised for him. 'This is Angelika,' she said, proudly pushing her daughter forward, 'and this is my husband, Wojciech.'

'Watch ek? What kind of name is that?'

'Polish,' Wojciech said, smiling at the old man.

'Ah, I thought it was foreign. Well,' he said, looking them up and down, 'you seem all right. I'm sure you won't be any trouble.'

Czeslawa was indignant, but didn't want to upset her new neighbour so soon. Restraining herself, she said, 'You are right. We are not any trouble. Perhaps we see you later, but now we have to take furniture inside.' She turned on her heel.

'Well, he was charming,' Wojciech said.

'Oh, you know the type. Hopefully not everyone is like that. I like it here.'

'I have a good feeling about this place. It will be fine.'
Wojciech is always so optimistic.

A few hours later they slumped on the sofa, exhausted. At least their belongings were inside. It was dinner time and Czeslawa ached for *bigos*, but she'd have to wait until she had time to do some shopping as she didn't have all the ingredients for the stew. As Wojciech handed her a pan from one of the boxes marked 'Kitchen' and searched for plates, Czeslawa made potato and cheese *pierogi*. She hoped the cottage cheese was OK; it had been in the van longer than intended.

'This is lovely,' her husband said.

Czeslawa was so happy. They would overcome the man next door. Contented, she tucked into her *pierogi*, savouring the bacon which accompanied them.

Chapter Fifty-seven

The next day Czeslawa woke up early. It was six twenty. Too early to get up. She listened to the birds twittering in the trees. Realising she wasn't getting back to sleep, she sneaked out of bed and padded across the carpet to the door, which gave only the slightest creak as she opened it, and passed undetected into the hall. Breathing a sigh of relief, Wojciech worked six days out of seven and needed his rest, she went through to the kitchen to make herself some coffee.

Czeslawa sat in the living room, sipping her strong coffee, watching the world go by, despite the torrential rain. The village already showed signs of life; a couple of villagers passed by her window. Maybe she'd go and explore, see what she could forage for breakfast.

Wrapped up against the rain, Czeslawa arrived at the store, face red from the wind and wet from the rain. The bell trilled overhead when she entered and a man in his late forties smiled at her. 'Morning.'

She returned his greeting and glanced around the shop. She popped some flour, sugar and crusty bread into a basket, then added bacon, sausages and eggs. She'd make a Scottish breakfast. Finished, she headed for the counter.

'Hello there,' the big man greeted her warmly. 'I'm Ian

McAndrew, the owner. Are you the lady who has moved into number eleven, next to George?'

Czeslawa nodded.

'Well, I hope you'll be very happy here, and if you need any information on the area, let me know.'

Czeslawa understood most of what he said. Finally she found her tongue. 'My name is Czeslawa. Nice to meet you,' she said in her thick accent.

Ian repeated her name back to her. 'Czeslawa? Is that Russian?'

'No, Polish.'

'Oh, I should have guessed,' he said. 'There are a lot of Poles in Scotland now, but I think you might be the first in Kings River.'

There was none of the condescending tone George had used to them the previous day.

'So, how do you like your new home?'

'Very nice,' she said. 'The weather could be better.'

Ian laughed. 'The weather could always be better.'

Ian rang up Czeslawa's purchases as he chatted away to her. He was quite easy to understand, although sometimes she didn't know how to reply, but at least she was improving. She had been too scared to talk to anyone when they lived in Craigshill.

'Sorry, I need newspaper.' She studied the display in front of her, trying to figure out which would be the easiest.

'I'd recommend the *Sunday Mail*. The sentences are short and it's easy to read.'

'OK, I will take that one. I go home and read now to improve my English.'

'Good luck.'

Czeslawa lay on the sofa reading. Some of the language was odd, but Ian was right, the sentences were short. She struggled over many of the words, but understood more than she expected.

'Morning.' Wojciech yawned.

Czeslawa glanced up. 'Sleep well?'

'Like a log.'

'Mummy, are we going to God's house today?' Angelika burst into the room.

'Yes, after breakfast.' She'd checked out Catholic churches and found one in Kilburn. Today, their first full day, they would go to twelve o'clock Mass. That way they could relax and have a leisurely breakfast. Maybe they'd take Angelika to the park afterwards. Sunday was the only day Wojciech had free. Back in Poland, they would have joined Mama and Anastazy for lunch. Their family was very close-knit. On Saturdays, the girls would go cycling with Anastazy, whilst Mama prepared dinner. Once they were more settled, she would see what the surrounding area had to offer by way of activities.

The church was a concrete block, and inside, it was only marginally less gloomy. The cavernous chapel held over a hundred pews. Czeslawa checked her watch. It was eleven fifty-five. Dipping her hand into the font, she blessed herself as Wojciech strode ahead of them. Czeslawa watched her husband choose a pew and when she reached it, she genuflected and sneaked in after him.

Czeslawa took in the interior of the church. It was vast, with huge windows. It was such a stark contrast to the churches in Gdansk. They were buildings of beauty and grace. The altar was sparse and the white tablecloth bore only a few items, among them candles and goblets, presumably for the wine, although she'd heard you were rarely offered wine in Scottish Catholic churches. With any luck, there would be a Polish Mass near them soon.

The Mass was short by Polish standards. In three quarters of an hour, it was over. The elderly priest's mumbling had been difficult to understand. As they filed out, they came across churchgoers mingling with their fellow worshippers, now that the rain had finally stopped. The scene lightened Czeslawa's heart. So, the church was ugly, but the community spirit was there. Elderly people greeted each other whilst children ran around on the grassy knoll beside the car park, relieved to be out in the fresh air. With a final glance around, Czeslawa moved towards their eight-year-old Ford Fiesta.

'Mummy, can we go and explore?' Angelika asked as they ambled up the path to their new home.

'Yes, darling. Let's change out of our church clothes and then we'll go for a walk. I believe there's a park near here.' Angelika almost ripped her dress off, once inside, but her mother scolded her. 'Lika, you'll ruin it. Take it off properly.'

While Angelika perused the offerings in her wardrobe, Czeslawa tidied the living room. She didn't consider herself to have OCD, but she did like things to be neat, and she was proud of their new home.

'Mummy. I'm ready,' declared Angelika, who appeared wearing a cream skirt, a pink T-shirt and red and yellow Wellingtons.

'Lika. I don't think so. It's beautiful outside. Go and put on shorts and trainers. If you want to go on the slide at the park, you can't wear a skirt.'

Angelika seemed to think about this then skipped off to change.

Ten minutes later, they were ready for their second outing in the village. George was sitting on his doorstep, smoking his pipe. He greeted them gruffly.

'Hello, George,' Wojciech said. 'Lovely day now.'

Czeslawa hid a smile. Wojciech had chosen the right thing to say. The British loved talking about the weather.

'It won't last. It was raining at five o'clock.'

'I suppose not,' Wojciech agreed.

'George, can you tell me where the park is?' Czeslawa asked.

'Up on the hill.'

'Thank you. Perhaps we will see you later. Angelika, say goodbye to George.'

'Bye, Mr George,' Angelika said, clambering up the steps.

'Mummy, look!' Angelika sang as she hurtled down the chute.

'Be careful.'

Her parents watched as Lika played on the slide, the roundabout, which they were duty-bound to ride with her, and the see-saw, where they took turns at being on the other end. They laughed until Czeslawa thought they would burst.

Back home, Angelika played in the garden, whilst her parents took a well-earned rest.

'Would you like a beer?' Czeslawa asked Wojciech.

'Yes, please.'

Just then George came out to bring in his washing: large, lonely white underpants and brown socks, accompanied by a couple of vests, which presumably had been white in a previous life.

'Hello, George,' she called.

George grunted.

At least it's some sort of response.

He laughed at Angelika chasing a butterfly. He watched her as the butterfly flew away and she started digging in the dirt with her spade, overturning bugs and worms.

'Look, Mummy, this one wriggles.' Her daughter held out a woodlouse.

Czeslawa prayed her daughter would not bring her any further such treats and that she'd outgrow this fascination with creepy-crawlies.

At that moment, George said, 'Round here, we call that a *slater*.'

'Slater? Is that not a person who puts roofs?' asked Wojciech.

'Yes. It's the same word.' He turned back to Angelika. 'Would you like me to show you some more?'

Czeslawa turned away to stifle a laugh. What an attractive thing to suggest to a six-year-old girl. Well, if it helped bond with George, she was all for it. Angelika skirted the fence and headed towards George, who was pointing at a large stone. As she approached, he lifted it and about a dozen slaters scurried out.

'Ugh!' Czeslawa recoiled.

'I can do better than that.'

George asked Wojciech if it was OK for Angelika to follow him to the other end of the garden. Wojciech nodded, and as they walked, Angelika took George's hand in hers. The old man looked at her fondly. They came to a wooden structure with wire leading from it.

'What's that?' she asked.

'You'll see,' George said, smiling at her.

He opened the box.

'A rabbit! Mummy, Daddy, a rabbit!' Looking at George, Angelika asked, 'Can I pick him up? Is it a boy? What's his name?'

'He's a boy and his name's Goldie, and yes, you can hold him. Put your arms out like this.' George showed her how to cradle her arms then placed Goldie in them.

'He's lovely. How old is he?'

'Two.'

'I'm six. Daddy, come and see the rabbit!'

Czeslawa and Wojciech came to admire Goldie.

'He's beautiful,' said Czeslawa.

'Look how big he is,' said Wojciech.

'Would you like to see him play in his run?' George said, pointing to the wire fencing that ran twenty feet round the garden.

'Yes, please,' said Angelika.

They watched as Goldie scampered through the run, stopping here and there, to nibble some grass, his little white nose scrunching up. Angelika continued to question George long after her parents retired to their loungers and was still playing with Goldie when Czeslawa started preparing dinner.

'Angelika, dinner's ready,' Czeslawa called over the fence. George and Angelika appeared a few minutes later.

'Thank you, Mr George. I like Goldie very much,' said Angelika solemnly. The old man's face turned pink.

'You're welcome. Maybe I will see you tomorrow.'

'George, would you like to join us for dinner?' Wojciech asked.

'Oh, you don't want me intruding.'

'You are not,' said Czeslawa. She realised he *would* like to join them. She could see him already eyeing up the food on the table.

'It's nothing special. Simple Polish food. Meat,' she said, in an attempt to clinch it, 'and salad and potatoes.'

'Well, in that case, I would be honoured,' the old man replied.

George ate his *schabowy* with relish. He even had a beer with Wojciech. He told them about his wife, Marjorie, who had died of cancer ten years earlier. After that, he kept himself to himself. He had been a miner until he retired at sixty. His two children had emigrated, one to Canada, Elise, named after her grandmother, and Bernard, who had gone to New Zealand. Czeslawa detected a trace of bitterness in his voice. *Poor man.*

'Bernard doesn't have any children. Too selfish. Can't even keep a decent woman. Too busy living the high life and barely a phone call. He hasn't been back once. Twenty-five years now.'

The young couple exchanged a worried glance as George continued, 'Elise. A beautiful girl, just like her mother, petite with huge eyes and a heart of gold. She went to Canada and came back engaged. Of course we were happy for her, but they've only been back twice in the last five years. My grandchildren are all grown up now. Stevie, he's a dad now. I'm a great-grandfather and I haven't even seen her. Sophie. Elise calls regularly, but it's not the same as being able to see them and spend time with them.'

Wojciech and Czeslawa listened to the soap opera unfolding in front of them. How sad. Czeslawa hoped when Angelika grew up, she wouldn't forget her parents and move far away. It was one thing for children to fly the nest, quite another for them to disappear off the face of the earth. As if realising how sombre he had rendered the atmosphere, George changed the subject and asked about their life in Poland, but Czeslawa sensed it was an act, for their benefit. She and Wojciech fed him tales of Gdansk, Wroclaw and the countryside, and before she knew it an hour had passed.

George's glass was empty.

'More beer?' she asked him.

Shaking his head, George said, 'No thanks. I really best go.'

'Tea?' The British never refused tea.

Looking at his watch, George said, 'OK then, one cup.'

As Czeslawa and Wojciech lay in bed, spooned into each other, Wojciech whispered in Czeslawa's ear, '*Najdroższa*, we need to look after George.'

Czeslawa turned towards her husband. 'I agree. He's lonely. I think he relaxed with us more today.'

'Yes, he did, thanks to you inviting him to dinner.'

'I wanted to. It seemed the only thing to do.'

'Goodnight, Czeslawa, I love you.'

'I love you too, *moj najdrozszy*.'

Chapter Fifty-eight

Over the coming weeks, they settled into their new home. Angelika spent most of the time with her mum, or next door with George. Wojciech was working a lot, as he had to prove himself in his new position. Her husband was ambitious and anxious to make their move from Poland to Scotland work. Plus their aim was to save enough to buy a house when they returned to Poland.

As Angelika played, Czeslawa made their house into a home. She bought material and sewed pretty curtains for the living room. On the few sunny days they had, she sat in the garden. She felt blessed, as if it were a good omen for their new life. George continued to accept their invitations to dinner.

Whilst Angelika played and Wojciech worked, Czeslawa read the newspapers. As her English improved, she asked Ian's advice on the better newspapers to buy. She knew that the next step was to get a job. Now her broadband was connected, she could search for jobs online, and once Angelika started school next week she would have more time.

She came across dozens of websites offering jobs, which made it hard as she didn't really know where to begin. Her English wasn't of a high enough standard yet to go for interviews, and she didn't want to be turned down at the first hurdle. Picking up her bag, she called Angelika in from the garden and told her they were going to Kilburn.

In Kilburn, Czeslawa tugged Angelika along, threading her way through the pedestrian precinct, past elderly men seated on benches and mothers taking a break from pushing prams. She passed the travel agent and the greengrocer, the pharmacy and the newsagent, and finally, when she'd all but given up hope, she came across a bookshop. She was in luck; they had the book she was looking for. It was on offer, so with her meagre income she could just about afford it. Without improving her English she was unlikely to get a decent job.

Czeslawa decided it was time to find out what Angelika would need when she saw the outfitter's sign 'School Uniforms'. Venturing inside, she waited patiently as a woman with three school-age children in tow had them measured. When it was Czeslawa's turn, the matronly woman peered at them and said, 'How can I help you today?'

'My daughter's going to Kirk Park. Can you tell me what she needs?'

'She'll need two grey skirts, thick grey tights and several pairs of grey socks. Black plimsolls and shorts, two red jerseys and two red polo shirts.'

'OK. Can you give me prices, please, and do you have her size?'

After ascertaining what size Angelika took, the woman rattled through the prices. Gulping, Czeslawa ordered the uniforms and the lady handed her a receipt and told her to collect them on Thursday.

'How was your day?' Czeslawa asked her husband.

'Strained.'

'Strained?'

'There was some trouble.'

'Involving you?' Czeslawa's eyes grew wide.

'Yes, although I didn't do anything.'

'So, why did it involve you?'

'Because I'm Polish.'

'What?'

'Some guy started shouting about Poles taking their jobs.'

'That's terrible!' Czeslawa hugged Wojciech.

'Yes, and our boss gave him hell, but I've made an enemy. He's angry because my team is more productive. He's just a bad manager.'

'What happens now?'

'He's been given a warning.'

'Can he push you out of this job?' Czeslawa asked anxiously. They'd only just got here.

'No, but he can make life uncomfortable.'

'He wouldn't hurt you, would he?' A shiver ran down her spine.

'I don't think he's that stupid.'

'You've obviously had a dreadful day. Why don't I make us some nice *zrazy*?'

'I do love you, sweetheart.'

As Czeslawa seasoned the beef, Angelika read to her. She placed the bacon, cucumber, breadcrumbs and mushrooms inside the beef and then rolled it shut.

Soon after, they sat down to their meal, and when they were finished, Wojciech patted his stomach. 'That was delicious.'

As Czeslawa cleared away the plates, Angelika climbed onto her father's lap and started reading. Smiling, she left them to it.

When she returned from doing the dishes and tidying the kitchen, they were asleep. Lifting Angelika off her father's chest, she carried her through to bed, pulled back the blanket and sheet and placed her daughter underneath, then covered her again. It was seven thirty. Czeslawa went into the kitchen and made a cup of tea. She'd let Wojciech sleep. He was obviously worn out. In the meantime, she'd make a start on the *English for Beginners* book she'd bought.

The next few days were busy. Fortunately, Wojciech had no further problems at work. George and Angelika spent a fair bit of time together, since she was starting school on Monday. He even offered to look after her whilst Czeslawa went into town.

Finally the day arrived. Angelika couldn't stop jumping up and down with excitement and chattered non-stop. She wriggled as Czeslawa tried to tease the tangles out of her hair. Dressed in her little grey skirt, red polo shirt and black shoes, she was ready. Taking her mother's hand, Angelika waved to George and they set off.

The walk to school took five minutes, Angelika skipping all the way. When they arrived, Angelika made a beeline for the little library in the corner, where two other children were already sitting on beanbags.

Czeslawa introduced herself to Miss McKenzie, Angelika's teacher, who reassured her that she would be fine, and with a goodbye wave to Angelika, Czeslawa left. Her little girl was growing up. She would make friends no problem. Reluctantly, Czeslawa walked out of the school building and made her way home.

'Mummy!' Angelika shrieked as her mother crossed the playground towards her.

'Hi, darling. Did you have fun?' She pushed her daughter's hair back from her face.

'Yes. We played games and read books and I made lots of new friends.'

'That's wonderful.' Czeslawa's heart sang.

'I have a special friend. His name's David. He's five.'

'That's great. Is David here?' Czeslawa asked, looking round.

'No. His mummy took him home.'

'Ah. Well, maybe I can meet him another time. Are you hungry?'

'Yes, but can we go to the park after lunch?'

Angelika settled in well at Kirk Park. By her second week, she already acted as if she'd been there for months.

Since Angelika wouldn't be out of school until after three, Czeslawa headed into Kilburn to have her interview suit cleaned.

The bus deposited her in Main Street. She crossed the road and was about to push open the door to the dry cleaner's when a woman coming out barrelled into her.

'Oh, so sorry.'

'Is OK,' said Czeslawa.

The woman hesitated, then said, 'You're Angelika's mum, aren't you?'

Czeslawa smiled. 'Czeslawa.' She held out her hand. The woman introduced herself as Maria, saying her son David was in Angelika's class. So this was David's mother. Maria invited her for coffee and Czeslawa decided this was the way to make friends. Maria led them to a tearoom and asked Czeslawa what she would like. Czeslawa had five pounds. Everything was so expensive and she knew she'd have to be frugal until Friday, so she settled for just tea, but then Maria coaxed her into having a cake, announcing today was her treat. Czeslawa would return the favour some time.

They chatted about the children. Maria asked if Angelika could come to play later that week and Czeslawa was delighted. Angelika had a real friend here already. Czeslawa told Maria of her life in Poland. Although she struggled with some of the words, she enjoyed her conversation with Maria. She was reluctant to leave, but knew she had to get back for Angelika. As they left the tea room and Czeslawa started for the bus stop, Maria offered her a lift. Czeslawa had a warm feeling in her heart when Maria dropped her off. Perhaps Angelika wasn't the only one who could make friends.

Czeslawa waited until Angelika was in bed and then started to surf for jobs online. There wasn't a great deal available. Maybe it was a bad time of year. The pay was terrible when you considered how much things cost. She had to start at the bottom again. In Gdansk, she had been an office manager. Short of working as a cleaner, or a checkout operator, she didn't know what she could do, without any experience. A little deflated, she made herself some hot chocolate and sat down to read her book. Wojciech was in the bath. He'd been a little distant lately.

She hoped everything was OK at work.

On Thursday, Czeslawa spent the morning in the garden.

George sat on the step, watching her. 'How's the job hunting going?'

'Not good,' she replied ruefully.

'You'll find something.'

Czeslawa realised she had two friends now. All that was missing was a job, she thought as she walked down towards McAndrew's where she bought some chocolates for Maria as Angelika was having dinner there. It was the least she could do. Thank goodness she had enough food in the house as she was now down to her last two pounds.

At five to six, she put on her shoes and jacket and scribbled a note to Wojciech. It started to rain as she left the house and she hurried down the road to the address Maria had given her and knocked on the door. Maria's home was larger, more comfortable than theirs, but all Czeslawa could take in straight away was the children's excited chatter and their faces falling when they saw her.

'Mummy, I don't want Lika to go,' complained David.

'We'll have a cup of tea whilst you finish playing.'

'Thanks, Mummy.' He scampered off.

Whilst Maria made tea, Czeslawa took in the oak floors, the scalloped curtains and the intricate detail of the fireplace. There were no toys here, so the children must have a playroom or be playing in the bedrooms. The furniture was very pretty, much as she would choose herself, if she had the money. A thirty-seven-inch television graced the centre of the room. Maria returned bearing two cups of tea. She sat down and Czeslawa remembered the chocolates she had brought. Maria thanked her and as

Czeslawa sipped her tea, Maria said, 'You know you told me you were an office manager?'

Czeslawa agreed this was so. Maria's next sentence bowled her over. She was offering her a job. It sounded wonderful, an event-planning business. Initially, she would do admin for Maria. Czeslawa was speechless. She was really excited, but then, like a lightning bolt, a thought struck her. 'My English?' But Maria seemed to have the answer to that. She could attend evening classes in Kilburn. Czeslawa couldn't wait to tell Wojciech. She wanted to hug Maria. They hadn't been here a month yet and she was going to have a good, interesting job. Her prayers had indeed been answered.

Over the next half hour, they discussed what would be involved, plus terms and conditions. Then it was time to take Angelika home. Czeslawa thanked Maria and promised to return on Monday for a briefing.

'Wojciech,' Czeslawa shouted as she burst through the door. 'I've got a job.' She stopped and recoiled in horror as she saw the livid bruises on her husband's face and neck.

'What? Angelika, go and get ready for bed,' she said.

'But Mummy...'

'Now, please.'

Her daughter knew when her mother meant business and her smile fell from her face. Czeslawa was dismayed that Angelika's earlier euphoric bubble had burst, but she would sort that later. Right now, she had to take care of her husband.

She put her arms around Wojciech.

'What happened? Was it the same man?'

'Yes. Again, my team did a better job. The boss has

only enough work next week for one team. As my team performed better and also because of his recent behaviour, the boss decided he had to go.'

'Are you OK?'

'Yes, but it hurts. He said we Poles were dirty and dishonest.' Wojciech sniffed.

Czeslawa snaked her hands around his neck, trying not to touch the red welts.

'Have you gone to the police?'

'They came to the site. My team tied him up after he tried to throttle me.'

'So what happens now?'

'I'm pressing charges. What if he had really injured me? I have a family to think of and support.'

'Do we have anything to be afraid of? Does he know where we live?'

'No. I made sure of that. Thankfully, he lives in the east end of Glasgow.'

Czeslawa exhaled with relief but couldn't bring herself to break free of her husband's embrace. 'So, he has definitely been fired?'

'Yes, there were lots of witnesses.'

'Thank goodness.' She finally extricated herself. 'Have you eaten?'

'I thought I'd wait for you.'

'Pasta?'

'Sounds good.'

Over dinner, Czeslawa gave him the more positive news of the day: her job offer from Maria.

'Czeslawa, I am so happy for you. I know how tough it is to get a good job here and not be treated like an immigrant only able to do menial tasks. Congratulations.'

'Thank you.' She smiled. 'I've invited David over on Tuesday to play.'

'That is good. I know Angelika loves chatting with George, but he's in his eighties. It's good for her to have friends to play with outside of school. Two pieces of good news in one day. It's a good omen for the future.'

Czeslawa couldn't have loved her husband more in that moment. Despite being beaten up, he always saw the positives, and she was only glad she had been able to deliver some good news to counter his horrific experience.

Chapter Fifty-nine

Saturday was glorious. Contrary to popular myth, it didn't always rain in Scotland. The changeable weather was anathema to her, so she was delighted to see it being predictable for once. There wasn't a cloud in the sky. She'd been up early, had already hung out her washing and chatted with George before he'd gone into Kilburn, to the bookmakers. She was sunbathing when a voice called, 'Hello?'

She went round the side of the house. 'Hello,' she said to the postman.

'Hi. I have a package for Mr Kelso.'

'He's not in. Can I take it?'

'Sure. Can you sign here?'

Czeslawa scrawled her signature and handed him back the clipboard.

The package was from Canada, from his daughter. Czeslawa grabbed a pen and paper, wrote down the name and address and put it inside her diary.

Wojciech's boss had given him Saturday off to rest after his attack, and he was paying him for the day, which was generous. After a lie-in, he was up, yawning and hungry.

'Do we have any bacon? I fancy a Scottish breakfast,' he

announced.

'Go and have your shower and I'll make it. I thought we could go to the llama farm today.'

'Llamas are indigenous to Scotland?' he asked cheekily.

'Ha ha! Angelika's been banging on about it all week and it's such a nice day.'

'OK then. Right, I'm off to get washed.'

'Good, cos you smell,' she said.

'That said, I'm not in that much of a hurry. How about we revisit the bedroom first.'

'Now that's not a bad idea.'

The llama farm was a great success, as was the rest of the country park. They also scoffed the picnic of cold meats and cheeses, crusty bread and strawberries in next to no time. Czeslawa and Angelika played tennis on the lawn whilst Wojciech took the opportunity to listen to the football on his MP3 player. Then he and Angelika played tag whilst Czeslawa read. It was an idyllic day. When it grew late, they packed up their things and headed home.

George's light was on and Czeslawa remembered his parcel. She went next door and knocked.

George opened the door. 'Hello. Is everything all right?'

'Yes. This parcel came when you were out.'

'Come in.' He ushered her through to the living room.

She passed him the parcel and his face lit up.

'Thanks.'

'Did your horse win?'

'No, it was second, but it was enough. I had it each way.'

It meant nothing to Czeslawa, but he seemed happy, so he must have won.

'So what did you do today?'

'We took Angelika to see the llamas.'

'Ah, you went to Castletop Country Park.'

'That's right.'

'It's nice there. I used to go, long before there were llamas.'

'Well, see you tomorrow.'

'Yes, goodnight.'

As she opened the door to her house, a surge of pity rose within her.

Czeslawa woke up with a start. What was that? Paranoid, she thought of the man who had attacked her husband. Then she heard a low moan, coming from next door.

'Wojciech, wake up!'

The moaning continued as Wojciech rubbed the sleep from his eyes.

'I think something's wrong with George. Can you hear that?'

Wojciech listened and after a few moments, said, 'I think you're right. Let's go.' They threw on their clothes and ran downstairs. The hall clock showed five twenty-six.

They peeked through George's letterbox but couldn't see anything.

'George,' Wojciech called.

Again, that moaning sound met their ears. Czeslawa tried the door. Locked. She ran round and tried the back door; also locked. She sprinted back round, and as Wojciech's eyes met hers, she shook her head.

'Find something I can break the glass with,' he said.

She ran into their house and returned with a hammer. Meanwhile, she could hear Wojciech shouting, clearly no longer caring how loud he was, despite the early hour.

'George, are you all right?' No answer. Wojciech glanced at Czeslawa.

She nodded; they had to do this, even if they were wrong. Wojciech swung the hammer. It smacked through the front door panel and the glass fell out inside. Smashing the glass enough so he could get his hand through, he reached in and turned the lock.

'George,' he shouted. He turned on the lights and with Czeslawa right behind him, he moved from room to room. George lay prostrate on the landing, his breathing laboured.

'George, can you hear me?' No reply.

'Czeslawa, call 999.'

Czeslawa looked around for the phone then dialled 999 whilst Wojciech talked to George. When it started ringing and the operator asked which service, she requested an ambulance. She then managed in her very broken English, as she was pretty distressed at seeing George like this, to tell them the specifics. She explained he was in his eighties, but they didn't know what had happened and asked them to hurry.

Kneeling beside him, she said, 'George, the ambulance is coming. You're going to be OK.'

They talked to him until the ambulance appeared fifteen minutes later. He was still unconscious as the paramedics loaded him onto a stretcher. The commotion and the lights had woken Angelika, who stared out of the window, wide-eyed. Czeslawa went up to her as Wojciech called out, 'I'm going in the ambulance.'

They waited two hours before Wojciech called to tell her George had had a stroke. He would be in hospital for a while, but after that Wojciech didn't know. He would fill her in when he got home.

The news travelled round the village fast. Everyone praised them for their quick actions. A glazier had already repaired George's door, no charge. Czeslawa asked Maria if she could watch Angelika for a couple of hours so they could visit George. To placate Angelika, they told her the most helpful thing she could do was care for Goldie, so they put down fresh straw, cleaned out his cage and gave him some carrots and water before they set off for the hospital.

George seemed to have lost weight and aged since yesterday. She hoped nothing in the parcel from his daughter had caused the stroke. His family! His family should know. She wondered if she could find a phone number. Perhaps the police could help. All of these thoughts coursed through her mind as she sat by his bed, George staring unseeing into the distance.

'He wasn't even aware we were there,' she said to Wojciech when they left the hospital.

'Not yet, but these things take time. I don't know who else can visit him but us. Does he have any friends?'

'None that he's mentioned to me, but he knows every-one in the village.'

'Maybe it's worth seeing if people will extend their community spirit. He needs us, he needs our help.'

Czeslawa couldn't agree more.

The next day, Czeslawa started work. Maria opened the door and ushered her in, just as the team pounced on her. Isla, Sandra, Ariadne and Wendy, Maria's sister, introduced themselves, although Czeslawa had to repeat their names a few times before remembering who was who. She was nervous but glad Maria had placed her trust in her. She wouldn't regret it. After her initiation, which consisted of tea and cake, Maria gave her some tasks to do from home. Czeslawa filled Maria in on George's condition and mentioned her idea about asking other villagers to visit. Maria thought it an excellent idea and suggested the best course of action was to discuss it with Ian. He knew everyone and would likely have an idea of who had time to devote to visiting the old man.

Czeslawa had planned to visit George that afternoon, so Maria said she would pick Angelika up from school. Once Czeslawa got back, she fully intended to go over to Kilburn to enrol in the evening class, which started the following week. She could take Angelika with her. Hopefully, by next week George would be a bit better and a visiting plan would be in place. No doubt social services would get involved. She could have kicked herself; she meant to speak to Maria about contacting George's family. She'd check on the internet and discuss it with Maria later. First though, she would try to get her head round some of the work Maria had given her.

'The course is for those who have a basic understanding of English, but who need practice speaking and writing English. Are there any questions?'

Czeslawa's only question was 'How long before she was fluent?', but she daren't voice that. It was down to her. As the tutor outlined the costs and options, Czeslawa thought it made more sense to do the intensive course. Two hundred and fifty pounds was a lot of money, but she needed to improve her English quickly. Maybe Maria could give her a small advance on her wages. Excitement bubbled up within her. She was doing this. She was going to learn English properly and she would have a great job which she would be good at. Everything was going in the right direction. If George could be OK, that would make things perfect.

The car door slammed and Czeslawa ran to the door. It was Wojciech. His face was pale and dark circles ringed his eyes.

'How is he?'

'Not great. Still doesn't recognise me. Can't move his left side at all. Social services were there.'

'And?'

'They're planning for when he gets out, since he has no family here.'

'What did they suggest?' Czeslawa asked, the blood draining from her face. They couldn't take George away.

'It's too soon to say, but I did overhear them talking about him needing round-the-clock care and they mentioned Rosebank.'

Rosebank was a residential care home on the other side of Kilburn from Kings River.

'Oh no! That's awful,' gasped Czeslawa. 'There was a story in the newspaper the other day. They treat their patients like prisoners.'

'I know, but what can we do?'

'I don't know, but we have to do something.'

Czeslawa apologised to Maria for calling so late and then filled her in.

'No problem,' Maria said. 'Now, before we start on what to do about George, tell me how you got on with your language course.'

'I wanted to talk to you about that…'

Maria told Czeslawa she would pay for the course. She listened as Czeslawa clued her up on George's family predicament.

'I wonder how we can get in touch with his family,' Maria said.

'We may be lucky,' Czeslawa said. 'I took a parcel the other day for George from Canada. I am assuming it was from his daughter.' She read the address out to Maria.

'Just a sec. Let me Google it.'

Czeslawa waited on the other end.

'We're in luck. The phone number was listed. Now we can contact George's daughter. Surely no one could be so heartless as to leave their father here to rot.'

'I am happy to phone, but I afraid she not understand my English. Could you phone, please?'

'Of course. I'll phone now. Hopefully, someone will be in. It's about five hours behind in Quebec, so they may be at work, but if no one answers, I'll try again later. I'll call you right back.'

Czeslawa waited by the phone, trying not to bite her nails. Finally, the phone rang again.

'She was home,' said Maria.

'What did she say?'

'She was very upset. I told her about her father and how you found him and called an ambulance, and how social services are discussing putting him in a home. She was in bits, said she had to speak to her husband and then make flight arrangements. She said she'd let her brother know too.'

'Good.'

'I gave her my number and yours. I explained you were Polish and although you spoke English, you weren't very confident.'

'What did she say?'

'She said if you could understand her dad, you'd be able to understand her. I think she's going to phone to thank you. What you and Wojciech did might have saved his life.'

'I don't know,' said Czeslawa.

'Well, that's what everyone thinks.'

'Is it?'

'Yes, you're heroes. I heard someone saying in McAndrew's, "Yes, George is old, but imagine what would have happened if that new Polish family hadn't been there. He might not have made it."'

Czeslawa was stunned. Heroes? Anyway, hopefully, George's family would arrive soon and sort things out.

'Maria, until comes George's daughter, OK if I work flexible hours?'

'Of course.'

'Thank you. You give me a wonderful chance with good job and already on second day, I have to ask for time.'

'Don't worry about it. I know you'll get through the work. Most of it's answering messages and picking up emails. You can do that anytime.'

'Thank you, Maria. This is very important to me, your kindness.'

'You're welcome. Anyway, you must be tired. A lot's happened today.'

'Thank you. I will call you tomorrow.'

'Night, Czeslawa.'

'Goodnight, Maria.'

Chapter Sixty

Czeslawa slept fitfully and rose early. She made breakfast, read through her tasks and set to them enthusiastically. The business side was so interesting and she understood a lot more than she expected to. She sifted through the emails she'd been allocated to deal with and started making notes. A few points she'd need to clarify with Maria, but for the most part, the Events folder Maria had given her, which acted as the company's bible, was enough of a guide. The morning whizzed past and soon it was after two and she had to go and catch the bus.

The double doors leading from the waiting area to the ward were already open. Signs reminded everyone to wash their hands on entering and leaving the ward, to prevent the spread of virulent superbugs.

No one was at the nurse's station when she arrived. She'd go back and see someone after visiting ended. George's eyes were open when she reached his bed, and she smiled at him.

'Hello, George. You look better today.'

His eyes found hers and she could sense he wanted to say something, but his speech hadn't returned yet. She sat beside him and told him about Goldie and Angelika, school and her new job. She debated whether to tell him about his daughter, but decided against it, unsure what the shock might do to him. She'd never known anyone who'd had a stroke. As she was leaving, she straightened George's blankets and bent over to kiss him on the forehead. Her hand brushed his. She looked up and his face was full of gratitude.

'Wojciech will be here later, George. I'll see you tomorrow.'

Czeslawa fought back tears as she left the hospital. Thank God his daughter was coming. Imagine if his condition deteriorated. It made her think of her own father and wish she were back in Poland.

Czeslawa was putting Angelika to bed when the phone rang.

'I'll be back in a moment,' she said, kissing her daughter's cheek. It was late. Perhaps it was Maria.

'Hello,' she said.

'Is that Ches lava?' The woman pronounced her name as if it were two separate words.

'Yes.'

'My name is Elise.'

'Hello. Maria said maybe you call.'

'First of all, thank you for saving my father's life.'

Czeslawa mumbled that it was no problem.

'I just wanted to let you know that I'm at the airport. I'll be landing in Glasgow at seven thirty tomorrow morning. What hospital is my father in?'

Czeslawa told her and then said, 'Would you like that I come with you? Your father expects me.'

Elise hesitated and then said, 'I'd like that very much. You live next door to Dad, don't you?'

'Yes, but I am sorry, I don't have key.'
'Don't worry. I still have one.'

Czeslawa rattled through her work, eager to complete as much as possible before Elise's arrival. A black cab drew up just after nine thirty. A rather dishevelled, tired-looking woman of fifty or so, got out, accompanied by a man who was more Czeslawa's age. Czeslawa rushed out to help them carry their cases downstairs to George's.

Elise threw her arms around Czeslawa and said, 'Thank you so much. It was a blessing the day you moved here.'

Czeslawa gave a modest reply and then Elise introduced the man beside her. 'This is my son, Stevie.'

Czeslawa shook his hand. Whilst Stevie made tea, Czeslawa filled Elise in on her father's condition and suggested they might like to rest before visiting hours began at three.

'I think I'm too antsy to sleep,' Elise said. She looked at her son, who read her signal and made himself scarce. Emboldened by Stevie's absence, Czeslawa explained as best she could, not only George's condition, but also his situation and how he only had Goldie and now them to keep him company. She told her of his pain, but not his bitterness, at never seeing his family. Elise fought to hold back tears. Anxious to give her a moment alone and not upset her further, Czeslawa offered to make fresh tea. Elise gratefully accepted. On the one hand, Czeslawa felt sorry for Elise and for having to be so blunt, but on the other hand she didn't. If anyone should feel guilty, it *should* be George's family, for barely considering him over the years.

They stopped by the nurse's station. Czeslawa had already discussed Elise's potential visit with the staff nurse, who had thought it might be just the jolt he needed. She'd requested Czeslawa be there too. George was sitting up, watching TV. When Elise called 'Dad' in her Scots-Canadian accent, his eyes swivelled round, initially registering disbelief and then pleasure. He still wasn't able to speak, but he managed to croak a response. He glanced at Czeslawa, gratitude shining in his eyes.

'I took parcel for you Saturday. It was from Elise. I wrote address. Easy to find phone number on computer,' she explained.

George's lips moved, in what almost passed for a smile. It was time to leave George alone with his daughter. His grandson was waiting outside. One shock at a time, they'd decided. Elise could bring him in when she deemed him ready. They had a lot of catching up to do.

Chapter Sixty-one

Venetian Dreams Launch

'Sandra, down a bit. Left. No, too much,' Maria said as Sandra and Czeslawa slotted the *Venetian Dreams* sign into place. Holly had chosen the venue with great care. Glasgow City Council had been very reasonable with its rates to one of its most recent protégées. The City Chambers, built in 1888 was one of the most majestic buildings in Glasgow. The splendour of the building was the perfect setting for the glamour of the occasion. An eight-feet-high laminated billboard displayed details of the event. Waiters were dressed as gondoliers, and seating areas were in the form of gondolas. Staff offered guests the opportunity to really get into the spirit of the theme by providing them with Venetian carnival masks.

It had been an inspired idea to hire the banqueting room in the City Chambers. Gold leaf and filigree covered the walls. The area around the podium had been converted into a miniature of St Mark's Square, with a scaled-back version of the cathedral painted onto a 3D backdrop. A three-tier cake depicted the hotels overlooking the Grand Canal, complete with gondolas below.

Maria's company, Occasions, had been hard at work, contributing to the arrangement of the décor, and Anastazy had volunteered his services, to help Maria out, since it was such a huge undertaking. A dressing room had been set up for Holly within the City Chambers, so she could be on hand if required, but still look her best for the event. Holly had never met Anastazy before, but Maria had talked of him a great deal in the last few months. She'd grown very close to him, in the aftermath of her trip to hospital with Amy. Holly hadn't quizzed Maria on her relationship with him; she was just glad to see her friend so happy. Maria's children had always been a source of great comfort to her, but now she seemed to be learning to enjoy an adult relationship again.

Maria had told Holly she had been so relieved that the head injury Amy had received, despite being concerning enough to keep her in for a few days' observation, hadn't been too serious, although she had been frantic at the time. Anastazy had taken control of the situation less than an hour after meeting her, when she'd been at her most vulnerable, and had waited with her whilst Amy underwent tests. Once she'd been stitched back together and given the all-clear, Anastazy had calmly driven Maria back. They'd managed, over the coming weeks he spent in Scotland, to talk a lot, despite the language barrier. Hiring Czeslawa had been one of the best decisions Maria had ever made, and she was thankful for the day she met her.

Holly appeared in an amber empire-line dress, with a gold band hugging her ribcage. A few dark curls hung loose, framing her heart-shaped face, whilst two gold-leaf clasps held up the remainder. A touch of bronzer, an amber-coloured bangle jangling on her wrist and a string of tiny gold leaves hanging from her neck completed her autumnal theme. It was her big night and she was out to impress. Her heels click-clacked across the marble floor as she clipped across to Maria to ensure everything was ready. She was really looking forward to tonight and was glad that Tom, Antonia and Jennifer would all be here.

Her thoughts turned to her parents, and she hoped they were looking down on her with pride. It seemed selfish to wish her sister was there to offer her the moral support she craved, but she was crestfallen at her absence. She still couldn't believe it. Two months after the accident, Lucy was mentally still in pieces. Everything she'd known had been taken away from her. She'd been lucky not to get a prison sentence, after being convicted of causing death by dangerous driving. The General Medical Council hadn't yet ruled on whether she'd be struck off or not, but her reputation had been irreparably damaged. Carl had broken off all contact with her. Anyone could see she was on the verge of a breakdown. For usually big-hearted Carl to act as if Lucy didn't exist, to not even try to understand or forgive her, was what pained Lucy most. Holly knew Lucy had treated Carl badly, but Lucy was such a mess. Grief for Robbie overwhelmed her and she couldn't comprehend that he was gone. On the few occasions when she'd spoken to Holly and appeared to have any semblance of the old Lucy, she'd still been in a piteous state. One mistake had cost her Robbie's life and in many ways her own too. Lucy couldn't believe she was the reason he was gone, and she'd only realised after his death that he was the only man she had ever truly loved.

When Lucy visited Holly in Tuscany, Holly knew something was different about this guy she was seeing. Of course, Holly had never met him, but she had attended his funeral. Robbie's family had specifically requested Lucy stay away, but Holly had gone. Successfully passing herself off as a friend from university, she had seen his photo in the chapel of rest. He had been a very handsome young man. She felt sorrow at Robbie's life being cut short, yet protective of her sister, who'd always been there for her.

Her sister had already lost so much. Who knew how the GMC hearing would go? Guilty until proven innocent. The media hadn't been lenient with her either. A young, beautiful, talented doctor causing the death of a promising young student. She still didn't know how the papers had learned that Lucy had lied about being at a conference in Hampshire. Certainly Carl wouldn't have told them, although she knew there was no love lost between his mother and Lucy. When it came out that Robbie was a student at the university where Lucy taught, coupled with a few hotel staff coming forward and volunteering that they looked very much in love, it hadn't painted Lucy in a favourable light.

Lucy was holed up in a rented flat. Holly had suggested Lucy stay at hers, but she'd refused. She made a point of visiting Lucy regularly. Her sister had changed overnight. The oomph had been knocked out of her. No longer slim and beautiful, she was rake-thin, with dark shadows courting her eyes, and hollowed-out cheeks.

'Holly, your publisher's here,' Czeslawa said.

'That's my cue to go change,' said Maria.

Tom arrived with Carl and took in the impressive mosaic of the Glasgow Coat of Arms and the Japanese-style tapestry which hung on one wall depicting the city's past and present as he strode through the entrance hall of the City

Chambers. He glanced around for his fiancée then climbed the marble and alabaster staircase leading to the banqueting hall, all the while admiring the granite and marble pillars.

He accepted a drink from a gondolier, surprised that so many guests had already arrived. But Tom had turned up early to enjoy Holly's success. He was so proud of her. He knew she'd be thinking of her parents tonight. It hadn't been an easy time for her family lately. First her cousin Felix, then Lucy. Surely his and Holly's wedding in the spring would boost the family's morale? For now, he prayed that Holly's launch would do the trick and raise everyone's spirits.

Tom introduced Carl to Czeslawa and asked where Holly was. Czeslawa indicated a room off the main hall and hinted that Holly might have gone in there with her publisher. Unsure whether to disturb Holly, Tom lingered in the banqueting hall and admired the substantial efforts which had gone into making this Scottish literature's event of the year. No detail had been spared.

Carl stood chatting with Czeslawa and Sandra as they finished the preparations. The launch would start in thirty minutes. Czeslawa informed Carl that the publisher was simply early. At a loose end, Carl asked if he could help with any last-minute tasks. He wondered how many people would know about his situation regarding Lucy and Robbie. The media had swarmed around his house and his parents' for weeks afterwards, eagerly awaiting some titbit. Since he was the injured party, they expected him to spill his guts to get back at her. But it wasn't his style. What had appeared in the press had been injuring enough. A few eager journalists had turned up at the restaurant, but they'd soon been turned away by Carl's impromptu bouncers. In that respect the builders had proven invaluable. Carl wanted to be here for Holly. They had always got on well. Their relationship might have difficulty moving forward in the future, but for the moment, it was important to him to be here. Tom had told him Lucy wouldn't be attending and he'd drawn a sigh of relief.

When Czeslawa had put the finishing touches to her display, she thanked Carl for his assistance and summoned a passing waiter to fix him a drink. She excused herself and went to change. As she headed for the dressing room, she thought about how much her world had improved since Maria had become part of her life. She adored her job, her colleagues were lovely to her and were fast becoming like family. A born organiser, she couldn't have been placed in a better role than with Occasions.

Her daughter had adapted seamlessly to life at Kirk Park School and had made plenty of friends. Wojciech's altercations at work had ceased and he was progressing happily. His men respected him and his boss was pleased with the consistently good job his team made. Czeslawa couldn't be happier. Her course was going well too. Elise had helped her practise in the few months she'd been staying at George's, preparing for the sale of his home. Meanwhile her husband had found something suitable for George in their town, back home in Canada. His daughter had asked him if there was any real reason why he couldn't emigrate. When he examined her question carefully, he'd realised there wasn't. This way he could spend the rest of his life with his family, and even though Czeslawa and her family would miss him, there was no doubt this was the best solution for all concerned. She was delighted that George's family had finally appreciated how important he was.

Maria was applying mascara when Czeslawa entered the Ladies'. She smiled. 'Everything ready?'

'Yes. Anastazy is at the door, ready to receive the guests. I think we have about ten minutes.'

'You had better get changed then.'

'Yes. See you in a minute.'

Holly strolled back out of her temporary dressing room, glass of champagne in hand, flanked by her commissioning editor and entourage from Reisen Publishing. They made their way over to Tom and Carl, who had since reunited and were standing making small talk with Sandra. Introductions were made and then Anastazy announced over his walkie-talkie that the first guests had arrived.

As she walked towards the door of the banqueting hall, Holly thought about how much she wanted to savour this party. Of course it was important to her and her publisher that it was a huge success, but more than anything she wanted to revel in what she had already achieved. The previous launch hadn't been as grand an affair. She had been lavish this time, but she had also received an unexpected contribution from her publisher towards it, and she also had quite a few dinner speeches lined up over the festive season, which would net her some funds. She felt justified in hosting this bash. She'd earned it. Many people had been involved in making it a success and they deserved a good party too.

After the launch would come the opening of Carl's restaurant, then the Christmas season, then New Year and unfortunately a no-doubt dismal January, before spring arrived and finally her wedding. Guiltily, she realised she'd invested more time in the launch party than in the wedding arrangements so far, but that would change once this was over.

'Jennifer, you look amazing.' Holly kissed and hugged her friend, careful not to crease her fabulous outfit. The figure-hugging red dress, with a plunge neckline, would have looked sluttish on anyone else, but it gave her friend the air of a film star about to walk down the red carpet. It had been so long since she had seen Jennifer look anywhere near as smart. New lowlights in her hair gave her the wow factor. Holly stepped back to admire her friend and then hugged her again.

When she finally released Jennifer, her friend introduced Maggie, whom Holly had met once or twice. Even Maggie had made an effort. Her usually unkempt hair was sleek and shiny. Whilst her outfit didn't quite have the polish of Holly's or Jennifer's, it far surpassed what she usually wore. It just proves that anyone can scrub up nicely.

'This is Ben,' said Jennifer. Holly appraised Jennifer's boyfriend, liking him instantly. Dressed in a pale blue shirt, navy chinos, no tie and with his top button undone, he seemed very down to earth. Her friend had chosen well. Enthusiastically, Holly hugged him and kissed him on both cheeks.

'Nice to meet you, Ben,' she said. She led them into the hall and after they had put their carnival masks on, she signalled for drinks to be brought over. No sooner had she found them a place to stand and admire the décor, when activity at the door made her excuse herself to greet her latest guests.

'Wow, would you look at this place,' said Jennifer. She focused on a backdrop of the Grand Canal, where the houses simply disappeared into the water, one or two steps being all that separated the canal from the residences. She giggled at the gondolas. 'Let's try one of those out,' she said.

Ben smiled at her. Maggie rolled her eyes.

'C'mon then,' she said. Some guests would prefer to stand at the bar or at the many high tables dotted around the room, but Jennifer wanted to fully experience the launch the way she thought Holly had intended. She snorted as she almost fell into the gondola, even with Ben's assistance. Maggie wasn't convinced.

'Come on, Mags. Don't be a spoilsport.'

'This shows you how good a friend I am,' Maggie said.

The three of them sat in their four-person gondola, sipping their champagne. A gondolier passed by with canapés: bruschetta with a choice of sun-dried tomato, Parma ham or gorgonzola, which they readily accepted.

Shortly afterwards, Holly returned. 'Some writer friends. They're nice, but I'd rather hang out with you guys.' Glancing round, she said, 'Where's the canapé man? I'm starving!' She edged her way into the gondola, careful not to catch her dress and waved encouragingly to a waiter circulating with canapés. Tom and Carl approached just then and took the gondola next to them.

'I'd sit with you guys, but that would involve clambering back out of the gondola, and I've only just managed to get in,' Holly explained.

'No problem, Hols.' Carl grinned. 'No offence taken.'

'Love the décor.' Tom spread his arms out, indicating

half of the venue.

'Me too. The girls have done a great job.'

'So, you lot,' she said, turning to Jennifer and company, 'What's the goss? I haven't seen you in ages.' She settled back into the gondola, one arm resting on the wooden side.

'Well, we've been house-hunting, as you know. We've another few places to look at the day after tomorrow. Originally, it was meant to be tomorrow, but then I thought we'd probably be pretty hungover after tonight.' Jennifer smiled.

'Too right,' said Holly. 'So, have you seen anything you like so far?'

'It's hard to say. Obviously we need something that's big enough for us and Mum. We've been showing her schedules.'

'Where have you been looking?' Holly asked.

'Mainly in Ayrshire, but we've looked at places in Johnstone, Kilbarchan and Kilmacolm too.'

Turning to Maggie, Holly said, 'Are you still in the West End, Maggie?'

'Actually, I'm just about to move.'

'Oh yes, where to?'

'I've taken a post with the VSO, so I'm doing a year's placement in St Vincent.'

'St Vincent! Lucky you. What are you going to be doing there?'

As Maggie launched into how she would be teaching the locals about AIDS and its long-reaching effects and about how she would be educating them to be more sexually aware, the occupants of both gondolas listened intently. She was just getting into her stride, when Maria arrived to tell Holly a journalist from *The Guardian* was on his way up. Telling Maggie once again how lucky she was, but how admirable too, she left to greet the first of the media. *I hope she holds onto him.* Holly glanced back over her shoulder at Jennifer. *He looks like a keeper.*

Jennifer had given Holly the low-down on their relationship so far. They'd almost broken up, due to Ben's soon-to-be ex-wife causing a scene. It hadn't helped that Ben hadn't seen fit to tell Jennifer he was in the middle of divorce proceedings or that he was still technically married. But Jennifer had decided not to hold a grudge. Life was too short and she'd had very few chances of happiness in the last few years, so she wasn't about to let this one get away from her. If first impressions were anything to go by, Holly was glad her friend had persevered.

Holly saw the journalist from *The Guardian* from a distance away. A gondolier greeted him as he entered, and accepting the carnival mask offered him, he was just admiring his reflection in a handily positioned mirror, when she descended upon him.

'Marcus, how are you?'

He kissed her cheek. 'Great. You look magnificent.'

'Thank you. You don't brush up too badly yourself.' She smiled at him. 'Well, you're the first of the press to arrive, so you get extra marks for punctuality. Would *The Guardian* like an exclusive preview?'

'Definitely.' He linked his arm in hers and let her lead him to the other end of the hall, where she regaled him with anecdotes of her trip to Venice the previous year and told him book three would be set in Tuscany.

Maria had settled into the vacant spot Holly's absence had created in her gondola and was graciously trying to find out all she could about Holly's friends. She had arrived just as Maggie had been telling Holly she was going to do some voluntary work in St Vincent. How exciting. It wasn't even like going to work in Africa, where missionaries had been getting posted for years, certainly since she was a little girl attending Mass every Sunday and they were asked to pray for them. It was the Caribbean. Lucky sod. Holly hadn't mentioned too much about Maggie to Maria, as she was really Jennifer's friend, but apparently she'd had a tough time in the past. Things appeared to be looking up for her now.

'I can't wait to fly out next week. I've done most of the packing, although it's a bit sad that I can actually fit most of what matters in my life into two suitcases.'

'Jennifer's taking more than that on the cruise,' Ben piped up good-naturedly, ducking to avoid a blow from his girlfriend.

'That's not true,' she protested.

Ben grinned and Maggie simply said, 'I know what you're like. I bet your poor mum gets about ten per cent space in the cases.'

'Rubbish,' Jennifer said dismissively. 'Mum's even asked me to buy her some new outfits.'

'Is she looking forward to the trip?' Maggie asked.

'Like you wouldn't believe. She's worse than a child, but I don't grudge her a bit of it. She deserves it with everything she's been through. So do I,' she said as if as an afterthought. She told them all how it was manna from heaven, being given the lifeline from the travel company who arranged the competition she'd won. She was so ecstatic when she received the letter informing her she'd won the top prize. Concerned it might be a scam, she had read it carefully and checked that there was no, 'calls to this number will last approximately eight minutes and cost one pound fifty a minute' small print and then she called the London number. Only when the girl on the other end asked her about the dates and her travelling companion's name, did it hit her she couldn't go. Her mother needed round-the-clock care and couldn't possibly travel. She explained about her mother's situation and that she'd need to get back to them, and the girl had asked if she could put her on hold for a moment. A few minutes later, her supervisor came on the line and said there were full-time carers on board.

They were due to leave on the twenty-third of December for two weeks, cruising the Caribbean, and it was clear Jennifer couldn't wait, despite it meaning leaving the luscious Ben behind.

A waiter brought more canapés and the gondolas soon filled up with guests. As she accepted a goat's cheese crostini, Jennifer took in the waiter's black-and-white striped top, black trousers, red neckerchief and straw boater with red ribbon and suppressed a giggle. Holly had outdone herself this time. She really knew how to throw a party. Maria gave her a conspiratorial smile, as if she had guessed what was filling Jennifer with mirth. Once the gondolier had passed to the next boat, Jennifer leaned over and said, 'You've done a fantastic job. It's so decadent. So over the top.'

'I know.' Maria grinned. 'I love it. It's been one of the most fun events I've ever done.'

Czeslawa and Anastazy sidled up just then. 'Have you

seen Holly?' Czeslawa asked.

Maria shook her head.

'Last I saw her, she was with some journalist,' Tom said. 'I've barely exchanged two words with her all night,' he said mournfully.

'Oh, right. Well, Antonia and Jack are here,' she said.

'We'll let her know if we see her,' said Ben.

'I'll go and say hi,' said Tom, getting up.

'Hi, Antonia, Jack, Oscar,' Tom said, shaking their hands in turn. 'Holly's otherwise engaged, somewhere. How are things? I take it the kids aren't coming?'

'Yes, that's right. Things are fine. Jack and I popped in to see Lucy before we came over. She's OK, gutted to be missing this though,' Antonia said.

'Yes, she likes a good party. She would have loved this. Are the kids looking forward to the holiday?'

'They can't wait. I think it's all that's been keeping Felix going. Something to look forward to,' said Jack.

'Well, that's to be expected, with all that's happened.'

'Can you excuse me a sec, Tom?'

Jack headed to the bar, leaving Tom with Antonia. Their family deserving a holiday was the understatement of the century. It had been a trying year for them. Felix in particular needed a proper break, after defending the accusations of rape made against him. Formally charged, he'd had to go through the indignity of DNA and other tests, even though any real forensic evidence would be long gone and still wouldn't prove if sex had been consensual. Compounded with the Chinese whispers that spread around their middle-class neighbourhood regarding him, it was no wonder it had been such a low point for him. He'd lost so much weight he was almost emaciated. If you didn't know better, you would think he was a junkie, but that's what stress could do to you, when you were accused of a crime you didn't commit.

In the end he'd been lucky. The girl's story didn't add up. She was more pregnant than she'd let on. It came out in the forensic evidence that she'd already had at least one previous sexual partner. She'd finally broken down in court, in front of a disbelieving father and sobbed that Felix hadn't raped her. They'd had sex, but it was she who had foisted herself on him. She thought her father would kill her if she told him she was pregnant, never mind pregnant to a thug whom her father knew well and had always professed a dislike for. So, she'd set her sights on a nice middle-class boy. One her father could approve of.

The relief of Felix's family was palpable; however, the damage to his reputation was already done. The tabloids hadn't waited to find out if he was guilty or not. No, a middle-class, prosecutor's son? Of course they were going to chase that story. Jack had demanded they print a retraction, but it didn't make much difference. The seed was sown so Jack had arranged for Felix to be tutored at home for the time being. He was too raw to return to school. His hopes of going to university next year were fading fast, but ultimately it depended how well his mind recovered from the ordeal he'd been through. So far he wasn't coping well and Jack was hoping the holiday might be the turning point.

Jack returned to Antonia with their drinks, desperate to pull himself out of his maudlin thoughts.

'There you are.' Holly hugged and kissed her aunt and uncle then greeted Oscar, whom she had met a few times at parties at her aunt and uncle's.

'Glad you could make it. Grab a gondola whilst you can,' Holly advised them.

Since she'd been back in the country, Holly had been spending a lot of time with Antonia, as a result of the situations with Lucy and Felix. It was an unwritten rule that they wouldn't discuss those topics tonight. The past few months had been hard. Tonight was about celebration, and it showed. Holly had gone over the top with the décor but it lent a classy air to proceedings not a gaudy one. Antonia had previously confessed to Holly that Felix, relieved at the rape charges being dropped, had broken down and confided in her.

'Mum, she's the only girl I've ever slept with.' Antonia had told him not to worry about it any more. But Felix was insistent. 'Mum, you don't understand. She's the only girl I'll ever sleep with. Why did I have to pick her? I'm gay, Mum.' He had burst into heart-wrenching sobs that would stay with Antonia forever. His revelation wasn't common knowledge. Their family had been under the microscope enough recently, so she was waiting for the right moment to tell Jack. It hadn't arrived yet.

Antonia had taken a leave of absence from work. The timing couldn't have been worse given recent announcements regarding redundancies, but her family needed her, and for the first time in a long while, it took precedence. Jack and she had talked at length about his proposal to set up an independent estate agency with Oscar, in which Jack, naturally, would be a sleeping partner. But what was to stop Antonia working there? She would have a vested interest.

The property market had to recover sometime. Why not be ready for it? She was seriously considering it and she knew from the many talks they'd had with Oscar that he was biding his time at National.

The trio headed over to the gondolas adjacent to Jennifer, Ben and Maggie.

'Oscar, what are you doing here?' Ben said.

Oscar stared at his brother-in-law. 'I'm a friend of Jack's. Who are you here with?'

'This is my girlfriend, Jennifer. You remember I met her in Glencoe?'

Oscar trawled his memory banks, but drew a blank.

'Ah yes,' he said. 'Nice to meet you.'

Oscar and Gaby were making tentative moves forward with their relationship. After much soul-searching, he had given his wife another chance. She had cheated on him, but then again, so had he on her, even if it was after finding out she was pregnant with another man's child. It was almost tit for tat. They weren't living together again yet, but they were spending quite a bit of time together, trying to recapture the essence of their relationship. Oscar had been ready and willing to raise the child as his own, but it hadn't been necessary. Gaby had miscarried not long afterwards. They weren't sure whether to be saddened or glad.

Oscar had accepted that he needed to spend time with his wife, and as a result, had cut back his overtime at the office. They had talked at length about the future they might have. Whilst he could never forget what had happened, Oscar hoped he could forgive and was determined to try. Hopefully, it would make them stronger as a couple and maybe they would give each other the attention they needed now. He wondered how much Gaby had told her brother. His brother-in-law was affable enough with him, but he hadn't seen Ben since he and Gaby split up. It didn't appear as if there were any hard feelings there, but then why should there be? It was Gaby who had become pregnant by someone else.

During the course of their many discussions, late into the night in some instances, they had agreed that if they were able to sort things out, then they would try for a baby. But they were a long way from that yet.

How odd. Of all the places to run into Oscar. Gaby had given him the whole sorry tale, and he had been shocked. From the conversations he'd had with his sister in the preceding months, it had been obvious she wasn't happy, but getting pregnant by another guy took things to a whole new dimension. He really liked Oscar, but his loyalties naturally lay with Gaby, so he'd felt awkward about contacting Oscar, unsure as to the reception he could expect. And of course, he'd been busy with his own new circumstances.

Gaby had needed him, too, in the weeks after discovering Oscar naked on their lounge floor with another woman, the wife of the man Gaby had cheated on Oscar with. The irony of the situation wasn't lost on her, but it hadn't made it any easier. At least when she had lost the baby, Oscar and she were already trying to make a go of things. It brought home what a decent guy Oscar was that he'd been prepared to raise someone else's kid as his own. Ben didn't know if he would have done the same. People commented on his taking on Jennifer's mum, but that was different. He wanted to be with Jen and her mum came as part of the package.

Fortunately, Jennifer had been reasonable and heard him out when he'd finally made contact with her through Maggie, whom he'd initially thought would have been the path of most resistance. He'd explained matters to Maggie, as Jennifer wouldn't return his calls or messages. Mindful of her mother's condition, he'd stopped short of turning up at the door. Maggie had looked at him as if he were a complete moron when he'd finished cataloguing the whole mess for her. Her expression said he had created this whole unnecessary shambles. Telling the whole truth from the beginning would have saved a whole lot of hassle.

Holly had a lot to handle. The launch was a fabulous success so far, going by the numbers. She'd barely spoken to anyone for more than a minute or two. Her neighbours had arrived, some old friends from uni, a group of girls from the gym. She'd invited everyone and anyone she could think of. If nothing else, they'd all buy a signed copy of her book. Czeslawa was over by the signing stand, waving at her. Ah, another taker. *Here we go again.*

Tom was sitting with Maria when Anastazy found them and promptly flopped down in the gondola beside her, his hand resting lightly along its back as he caressed her shoulders.

'So, what do you think? Is it a success?' Anastazy asked.

'It's certainly bigger and better attended than the first one, but then she really has gone to town on this one. Look at this place.'

They both agreed that it was one hell of an event.

Tom watched the interaction between Maria and Anastazy. Was something going on between them? The Polish man seemed very comfortable in her presence, very casual. Maybe they were seeing each other. Intuition wasn't his strong point. He'd need to ask Holly, as his curiosity was getting the better of him. It was the first time he had met Anastazy or Czeslawa. Initially, he'd thought they were man and wife, but then noticed the family resemblance and soon dismissed that notion. Watching the preparations and the way they worked tonight, he had every confidence in using Occasions for their wedding. Ah, finally. Holly was heading towards him.

'Well, hello, stranger.' He smiled up at her, rising out of the gondola to give her a quick peck. 'Everything OK?'

'Yes, just mad busy. You guys OK?'

'Fine,' Tom fibbed. 'Just wondering where you'd got to. Love you in that dress.' He admired his fiancée's petite frame in it.

'Thanks.' Holly grinned.

'So what's the script with those two?' he whispered, gesturing towards Maria and Anastazy.

'Who?'

'The organisers,' Tom said.

'Oh, you mean Anastazy and Maria?'

'Yes.'

'Tom, do you ever listen to anything I say?'

'Not if I can help it.' He laughed as Holly gave him a playful push on the arm.

'Anastazy is Czeslawa's brother. He was over visiting her, and Amy, Maria's daughter, fell and had to be taken to hospital. Anastazy was her knight in shining armour who took her there in his chariot.'

'Sorry?' Tom was confused.

'She was shaken up because of the amount of blood pouring from Amy's head, so he drove. Since then they've been seeing a lot of each other.'

'So, does he live here?'

'No, but I think he's working on it.'

'OK,' said Tom, curiosity satisfied.

'So, what do you think of the launch?'

'I think it's amazing,' he said frankly. 'You obviously put a lot of thought into it.'

'I did, but it was so much fun, I enjoyed every minute of it.'

'I'm so proud of you, Holly.' Tom pulled her to him and gave her a hug.

'Thanks, but don't crush my dress.'

'Sorry.'

'I'd best go. More guests are coming in. See you in a bit. Have fun.' She squeezed his hand and was gone.

As he watched Holly stride off, he sighed with relief that he hadn't pursued things with Shirley. He loved Holly and couldn't wait to marry her. What had happened with Shirley a few months earlier had been an aberration. She was a lovely girl and if he hadn't already been with Holly, who knows, but he had hurt Shirley and he hadn't meant to. No wonder she had been mad with him. For a while, he wondered if she would cause problems for him with Holly. But on reflection he'd decided she wasn't like that. She was a decent woman. Tom despised himself for his betrayal and had resolved to more than make it up to Holly when he married her.

The voice of local DJ Glen Barnes burst out over the microphone. 'Everyone, could I please have your attention?

I'd like to welcome to the stage, one of the UK's most original travel writers, a woman who makes us want to literally follow in her footsteps, who brings the places she writes about to life, imbues the familiar with a sense of the extraordinary and who is here tonight to talk about her second book, *Venetian Dreams*. Please welcome Miss Holly Jameson.'

Holly shone as she climbed the few steps to the makeshift stage, which was in the form of the Bridge of Sighs. She coughed nervously, sipped from the water glass provided and then began.

'Good evening, everyone. Thanks very much for coming to the *Venetian Dreams* launch. I'm sorry I haven't managed to speak to everybody yet, but the night is young.' She paused as laughter pervaded the hall.

'I fell in love with Venice one December, when it was at its least smelly.' More laughter. 'So much so, that I am going back in February for *Carnevale* with my better half.' She nodded to Tom. 'I have always been captivated by the tradition of the masked ball and managed to swing us an invite, a miracle, as you have more chance of winning the lottery than getting one of those tickets. Only a select few have the privilege of receiving a much sought-after invitation, and I was delighted that I was able to wangle it. The devil is waiting on the other side for my soul.' Further laughter.

'It was utterly captivating. Then I just kept going back. If you can overlook the whiff of the Grand Canal in high season, it's well worth the trip. I found the most amazing places in Venice. Some bargain rooms to sleep in, in people's houses as opposed to the bank-balance-depleting usual suspects.' Holly glanced quickly at her notes to jog her memory.

'I found a chocolate shop, which made hot chocolate so thick, I was able to turn my cup upside down without it coming out. It was a meal, more than a drink. Absolutely sensational, but totally sickening, in a good way,' she added.

'I've been overcharged for gondola rides and not cared and been fleeced the following day and minded greatly. A lot depends on the gondolier and the weather.

'I've done all of the cultural things, been inside St Mark's Basilica, after being subjected to the security searches and endured the pain that is leaving your bags at a cloakroom on the other side of the square. I'd like to say I've chased pigeons in St Mark's Square, but I hate pigeons and birds in general flocking me, so I didn't actually participate in that notable pastime. Alfred Hitchcock's *The Birds* will do that to you. I have, however, visited the Palazzo Ducale di Venezia, better known in English as The Doge's Palace. The carved marble façade inside the courtyard of the Doge's Palace and the two most visible facing out onto the Venetian Lagoon and St Mark's Square are sights worth beholding. The Bridge of Sighs to its right is one of the most contemplative places I've ever been. There are countless more cultural sights to explore, but for me discovering a city is not only about visiting the tourist spots, but about unearthing those things only locals know about.

'I've spent a lot of time with the people who live there. What makes contemporary Venetians tick? Who are today's Venetians? How *do* they cope with *having* to get a water taxi to work? How odd would it be, if you had to stand at the top of your steps and wait for a boat to come along and spirit you away from your front door? It would be romantic for a while, but I'm sure you'd soon grow tired of it. No supermarket nearby either. Some of them have their own little boats, but more often than not they don't.

'The Venetians are a relaxed people. They are very proud of their lives in the Veneto. Many older Venetians don't speak Italian. Many of the younger generation still prefer to speak Venetian instead of Italian. Of course, at work, it's often more difficult, as they have to speak with other Italians, in Milan, Rome, Turin and beyond, and they don't speak Venetian. In other parts of the Veneto, traditions are being lost. Grandparents speak Venetian, whilst their grandchildren speak to them in Italian. This is a proud people. Remember Italy didn't become a unified country until around 1850...' Holly coughed and kept coughing, until she almost turned blue. The water didn't quite do the trick. She felt physically sick.

Her publisher took one look at her and said, 'I think that'll do, Holly. I'll wrap it up. You don't look well.' Holly stood gratefully aside, as her publisher spoke into the microphone.

'It's rare in travel writing that a true genius emerges. Of course, everyone is always looking for the next new thing, how to be different. Holly Jameson doesn't need to look for that. The embodiment of the aspirations we all have with regard to understanding other cultures and visiting new, undiscovered, exciting places, Holly blends with the culture, the people and the places. She adopts the place she is writing about. It becomes her new home and that shines through in her writing. You could imagine Holly and her family living there day in day out, as that's what she conveys to us. She provides far more than a tourist guide to the area, although she does give several off-the-beaten-track suggestions, for those wanting to explore more than simply the top ten sights of a city. I am certain that *Venetian Dreams* will be a huge success.'

As her publisher invited the crowd to applaud her, Holly continued to feel faint. She stared straight ahead at the source of her choking fit. Dario. As he leaned against a pillar, his gaze burned into hers. Holly stood rooted to the spot. Why now? How could fate be so cruel? Didn't he realise this wasn't the right time nor the right place? Every day for the first few months, she'd pictured him and then over time she'd thought of him less and less, allowing her to focus on her wedding, her future, her life with Tom. Now, the spectre of the recent past was back to haunt her. She knew she'd need to address these demons before she could move forward. But she didn't know what to do, nor did she know how to do it. This launch was too important to her. It was a celebration of her career, but also a catalyst to the next level. Book launches and signings would give way to daytime TV slots and a world tour perhaps, maybe even her own travel programme. It was of paramount importance that nothing jeopardised that. As she stood there, feeling more zombie-like by the second, she knew she needed to speak with him.

Dario propped himself against the colonnade and admired Holly. She looked even more stunning tonight than when he'd last seen her at the wedding. He'd come to tell her how he felt and wouldn't leave without doing so. He had arrived late on purpose so that he couldn't be ejected prematurely, and so far his plan was on track.

When Holly noticed him, her face had registered surprise, then alarm. Shortly afterwards, she'd vacated the lectern. What he didn't know was exactly how or when to approach her. It was imperative to get her on her own. Perhaps this hadn't been the best choice of place, but how else could he have contacted her and ensured she would meet him?

Czeslawa and Maria were waiting offstage for Holly, and they supported her back to her dressing room.

'Are you OK, Holly?' Maria asked. 'You're white as a sheet.'

Numbly, Holly managed to convince Maria that she was OK, just a little faint. 'Must be all the excitement,' she mumbled.

'Sit down. I'll make you a cup of milky, sweet tea, see if that helps.'

'I can't be gone long,' Holly protested, knowing that her publisher too would be daunted by her earlier display.

'Just a quick cuppa,' Maria insisted. 'Czeslawa, you stay with her. I'll go and make tea.'

'No, I'm all right,' Holly assured her.

'OK, I'll be back in a minute. Czeslawa, can you check with Anastazy just how many people we've had through and ensure there are plenty more books ready to be signed when Holly reappears?'

'Of course.' Czeslawa followed Maria out.

Holly sat forward in her chair. *Oh my God, Dario's here, he's really here.* What did he hope to achieve by coming to her launch? She couldn't even work out if she was pleased or not. Tom was here. Surely he'd thought of that. Perhaps he had already talked to Tom. What was she going to do?

She couldn't go back out there, to face him, but she had to. She had the press, her publisher and countless guests waiting for her. This was her career, her big night. Pondering what to do, she heard a knock at the door. Maria returning with the tea. Holly leapt up to open the door. As she walked away, she gasped at Dario's reflection in the mirror, looking back at her. Not Maria then.

'Holly. I am sorry to interrupt your launch, but I wanted to set things right between us. I needed to tell you how I feel.'

Holly could barely think straight. She took in the intensity in his dark eyes, his mouth, the muscles on his arms, which were showing through his thin jersey. Finally, she said, 'Well, you certainly took your time. I've been back for months. And what did happen to you at the wedding?' She crossed her arms.

'I'm sorry. I am here to explain. I am in Glasgow for a viticultural conference. It would have been foolish not to see you.'

'You pick the days.'

'I didn't know if you would see me. I am sorry about leaving the wedding without saying goodbye, but a friend of mine had a fit. He has epilepsy. I took him to hospital, but we tried to keep it quiet so that it wouldn't ruin the bride and groom's day.'

'So why didn't you contact me after that? You could have easily found out where I was staying.' Holly wasn't letting him off the hook so easily.

'I had to go to California the next day. I had no time to explain. Then, when I got back, I thought you would have forgotten me, so I gave it up as a lost cause.'

'I did too,' Holly said, her heart beating fast.

'But I couldn't give up on you entirely. I have…feelings for you, feelings which won't go away.'

'And what am I meant to do with that now, Dario?' Holly asked, all her frustrations of a few months ago boiling to the surface.

'I-I-don't know. I needed you to know how I felt.'

'And you chose tonight to do it? The most important event of my career and you thought it would be a good idea to come here and turn it upside down?'

'Well, now you put it like that, perhaps it wasn't the best choice, but I didn't know what else to do.' He clasped his hands together. 'Please believe me, it was not my intention to ruin your big night. I just wanted to see if we had a chance.'

Holly sat back heavily in her chair. She didn't invite him to sit. Emotion coursed through her veins. What did she feel? What did she want?

'It was one kiss, Dario. Relationships aren't created or destroyed on the basis of one kiss,' she finally said.

'The kiss wasn't the important thing, Holly. It's what it signified.'

'You're too unreliable. I barely know you, but already I know that about you.'

'I can assure you that I am not usually.'

'How can I believe that?'

'You have to trust me,' he said softly. 'That's the only guarantee I can give you.'

'I don't know if it's enough. Look, I have people to see. Maria will be back any minute. You have to leave.'

'Not now, Holly, please. Don't leave things like this. I'm staying at the Millennium, across the square. Come and find me when this is finished.'

'I don't know, Dario,' Holly said.

'Holly, you need to know, just as much as I do,' he said, as his hand grasped the door handle.

'But not quite as much as I do,' said Tom, eyes blazing, as he opened the door from the other side. 'What the hell is going on?'

'Nothing,' said Holly, averting her eyes.

'Holly, I heard everything. I want to know who he is and what's going on.'

'Nothing's going on. He's just a wine producer I met in Italy.'

'Holly!' Tom barked. 'You kissed him. Doesn't sound like nothing to me.'

Holly looked from one to the other, feeling backed into a corner. This was crunch time.

'What the hell is going on?' Tom turned to face Dario, face puce with anger.

'I think you should ask your fiancée,' Dario said as he strode from the room.

'I can't do this right now, Tom. My publisher is expecting me.' She ran from the room, dress rustling behind her.

Holly was rattled and flushed as she joined her publisher at the signing table. She pasted a smile on her face and somehow muttered the pleasantries required of her. The girl from the publishing house, assigned to sort out the autographing of books, handed her Post-its with names and dedications to put in the flyleaf, which she wrote on autopilot. Her heart was thudding inside her chest. Decision time. What was she going to do? She felt sick. She needed to confide in someone. She needed Lucy. But Lucy wasn't here. Maria.

Maria and Czeslawa were talking to Carl and Maggie. Jennifer and Ben were nowhere to be seen, or she would have asked Jennifer's advice too. Antonia was busy at the other end of the room talking to Oscar. As the signing queue dwindled, Holly tried to attract Maria's attention before Tom could catch up with her. Where was he anyway? She hadn't seen him since she'd left her dressing room. He'd probably stormed out and gone home. Oh well, she'd work out what to say to him later.

The last volume signed, Holly sped over to Maria. 'Maria, I need to talk to you,' she said through gritted teeth.

'What is it? Are you OK?'

'I'm fine, but I really need to talk.'

As they made their way to the Ladies', shouting came from the corridor. Holly sensed trouble, so changing course, she walked quickly to the door with Maria in hot pursuit. Out in the corridor, Holly couldn't believe the scene which met her eyes. Tom had Dario by the scruff of his neck, as Dario nursed a bloody nose. It looked swollen, possibly broken.

'Tom, what are you doing?' she yelled.

'Oh, what am I doing? What about you and lover boy? Did you think I wouldn't find out?' he roared.

'There is nothing to find out,' she hissed. 'You're causing a scene.'

'That's nothing. I've only just started.' Again, he launched himself at Dario, who tried to protect his face.

'No,' screamed Holly, inserting herself between them. Tom's blow caught her on the side of the head, knocking her flying.

Two security guards appeared and hauled Tom away,

but not before the press had snapped a few shots, complete with a prone Holly. Maria flew to Holly's side, calling for water.

'I-I-I, Holly,' cried Tom.

'Tom, I think you've done enough damage for one night,' seethed Maria. 'And you,' she said to Dario. She turned to Security. 'Can you get them both out of here, please?'

As Holly regained consciousness, she was woozy at first. 'What happened?' she asked Maria.

'It's OK now. It was an accident.'

'Well, this has certainly been more eventful than I expected,' said a journalist standing to the side of them.

'I've got my byline,' said another. 'Holly Jameson, you really are full of surprises.'

Lucy went out to fetch the newspapers. For once she wasn't the newsworthy one. Obviously there was little news in Glasgow the previous day, as her sister had made the front page in one of the main dailies. 'Lover launched at book launch!' cried one, referring to Tom punching Dario. 'Venetian Nightmares' was the cry of another. 'Italian Stallion' was the lower-class comment of a cheap tabloid. Holly was distraught, her career down the toilet.

'Not necessarily,' said Lucy. 'Should help sell more books. Apart from in my case, there's no such thing as bad publicity.'

'Oh, Luce,' wailed Holly, reading about the bust-up at the City Chambers. 'What am I going to do?'

'Sit it out,' her sister said. 'If I can, you definitely can.'

When the phone rang, Holly refused to answer it. Lucy, also loath to pick it up, for her own reasons, reluctantly accepted it was her turn.

'Hello?' she asked warily, half-expecting it to be a newspaper. 'Hi,' she said, once the speaker had identified themselves. 'Sure, she's right here.'

'It's your publisher,' she mouthed as she handed over the phone.

'Hello,' Holly said, unsure if she was about to have her contract curtailed.

'Hi, Holly. How you doing?'

'Been better.'

'Do you want the good news or the bad news?'

Taking a deep breath, she said, 'The bad news. May as well get it all over at once.'

'OK, the bad news is there is no bad news. The good news is Amazon have received a record number of advance orders for the book. Same story with the booksellers. Seems that your net worth went up overnight. Sensation sells.'

Consoled by the fact that her career apparently wasn't in tatters yet, she thanked her publisher and fibbing, agreed to tuck into the champagne. She hadn't heard from Tom, nor Dario. She'd gone over with Lucy a thousand times last night, what she wanted, what she felt. She still didn't know. There was only one way to find out. She needed to see them both, separately. She dialled Tom's mobile.

They arranged to meet in town. A neutral place. He had already bagged a corner table in the coffee shop when she arrived.

'Hi,' said Tom, giving her a weak smile.

'Hi,' said Holly, seating herself without making any

move to kiss him.

'So,' they both said at the same time.

'So,' said Holly, a second time. 'Where do we start?'

'Did you sleep with him?'

'No.'

'Did you want to?' he asked next.

'I don't know, maybe,' she replied.

'I have something to tell you…' He told her about Shirley and how the problems he'd been having with his company had led up to it. He had already told her he had set a private investigator on the trail of one of his employees for corruption and that finally he'd been arrested and would now be tried in court.

When he had finished, Holly paused as if trying to sort out her thoughts and then said, 'Don't you think this is all a sign?'

Stubbornly Tom said, 'No.'

'Tom.' Holly gave a sad smile. 'I don't think we're meant to get married.'

'Don't say that.' Tears welled in Tom's eyes. 'I love you.'

'Sometimes it's not enough. Would you have hooked up with Shirley if you loved me one hundred per cent? No. Would I have been remotely interested in Dario if I loved you as I should? I don't think so.'

'Holly, what are you saying?'

'I think we need a break to see how we feel.'

'You want to be with him, don't you?'

'No, Tom, that's not what I'm saying, but we need a few months apart. We shouldn't have any secrets from each other.'

'So you want to call off the wedding?' Tom asked.

'At the very least postpone it. Don't you think we should be sure?' Holly said.

Tom didn't trust himself to answer.

'I'll move into Lucy's in the meantime. She needs me anyway.' Standing up, she kissed him gently on the cheek. 'Goodbye, Tom.'

Dario was waiting in the conservatory of his hotel, sipping a cappuccino. He rose to kiss Holly when she approached, but she waved him away. She sat hands folded in front of her, body language not encouraging.

'Well, at least you are here,' Dario said finally.

'Yes, I'm here, Dario,' she said.

'Should I be happy?'

'I'm not sure.'

'Have you left Tom?'

She looked at his nose, which was still swollen and bandaged, the latter courtesy of the Royal Infirmary and said, 'Yes.'

Dario smiled, as much as his broken nose would allow. 'Then you think there are possibilities for us.'

'No.'

Dario's eyes widened. 'No? But you have left Tom.'

'Yes, because there is no point being with someone who is not the right person.'

'Tom is not the right person?'

'I don't know.'

'Am I?'

'I don't think so. Perhaps if we had met under different circumstances, at a different time, but since you came into my life, it has been chaos. I need order, not chaos.'

'We could fix that.' He stretched his hands across the

table to take hers in his, but she drew back.

'I think we missed our time, Dario. Maybe it could have been, but things are too complicated.'

'I like complicated.'

'Well, I don't. I came to tell you, it's over, before it begins. I'm sorry.'

'Holly, don't do this. Give us a chance.'

'Dario, I don't even know how I feel. I'm going to have a break from men for a while, see how things work out.'

He tried repeatedly to convince her, but Holly's mind was made up. She left soon afterwards, tears swimming in her eyes.

Back at Lucy's, Holly sat at the computer, opened a new Word document and typed 'One Hundred Paths Through Andalucia', then clicked on the BA website and booked herself a one-way ticket.

THE END

Note From the Author

Did you get your free short stories yet?

TWO UNPUBLISHED EXCLUSIVE SHORT STO-RIES.

Interacting with my readers is one of the most fun parts of being a writer. I'll be sending out a monthly newsletter with new release information, competitions, special offers and basically a bit about what I've been up to, writing and otherwise.

You can get the previously unseen short stories, *Mixed Messages* and *Time Is of the Essence*, FREE when you sign up to my mailing list at www.susanbuchananauthor.com

Did you enjoy *Sign of the Times*

I'd really appreciate if you could leave a review on Amazon or Goodreads. It doesn't need to be much, just a couple of lines. I love reading customer reviews. Seeing what readers think of my books spurs me on to write more. Sometimes I've even written more about characters or created a series because of reader comments. Plus, reviews are SO important to authors. They help raise the profile of the author and make it more likely that the book will be visible to more readers. Every author wants their book to be read by more people, and I am no exception!

Other books by Susan Buchanan

Have you read them all?

The Dating Game

Work, work, work. That's all recruitment consultant Gill does. Her friends fix her up with numerous blind dates, none suitable, until one day Gill decides enough is enough.

Seeing an ad on a bus billboard for Happy Ever After dating agency 'for the busy professional', on impulse she signs up. Soon she has problems juggling her social life as well as her work diary.

Before long she's experiencing laughs, lust and … could it be love? But just when things are looking up for Gill, an unexpected reunion forces her to make an impossible choice.

Will she get her happy ever after, or is she destined to be married to her job forever?

The Christmas Spirit

Natalie Hope takes over the reins of the Sugar and Spice bakery and café with the intention of injecting some Christmas spirit. Something her regulars badly need.

Newly dumped Rebecca is stuck in a job with no prospects, has lost her home and is struggling to see a way forward.

Pensioner Stanley is dreading his first Christmas alone without his beloved wife, who passed away earlier this year.

How will he ever feel whole again?

Graduate Jacob is still out of work despite making hundreds of applications. Will he be forced to go against his instincts and ask his unsympathetic parents for help?

Spiky workaholic Meredith hates the jollity of family gatherings and would rather stay home with a box set and a posh ready meal. Will she finally realise what's important in life?

Natalie sprinkles a little magic to try to spread some festive cheer and restore Christmas spirit, but will she succeed?

Return of the Christmas Spirit

Christmas is just around the corner when the enigmatic Star begins working at Butterburn library, but not everyone is embracing the spirit of the season.

Arianna is anxious about her mock exams. With her father living abroad and her mother working three jobs to keep them afloat, she doesn't have much support at home.

The bank is threatening to repossess Evan's house, and he has no idea how he will get through Christmas with two children who are used to getting everything they want.

After 23 years of marriage, Patricia's husband announces he's moving out of the family home, and moving in with his secretary. Patricia puts a brave face on things, but inside she's devastated and lost.

Stressed-out Daniel is doing the work of three people in his sales job, plus looking after his kids and his sick wife. Pulled in too many different directions, he hasn't even had a chance to think about Christmas.

Can Star, the library's Good Samaritan, help set them on the path to happiness this Christmas?

Just One Day – Winter

Thirty-eight-year-old Louisa has a loving husband, three wonderful kids, a faithful dog, a supportive family and a gorgeous house near Glasgow. What more could she want?

TIME.

Louisa would like, just once, to get to the end of her never-ending to-do list. With her husband Ronnie working offshore, she is demented trying to cope with everything on her own: the after-school clubs, the homework, the appointments … the constant disasters. And if he dismisses her workload one more time, she may well throttle him.

Juggling running her own wedding stationery business with family life is taking its toll, and the only reason Louisa is still sane is because of her best friends and her sisters.

Fed up with only talking to Ronnie about household bills and incompetent tradesmen, when a handsome stranger pays her some attention on her birthday weekend away, she is flattered, but will she give in to temptation? And will she ever get to the end of her to-do list?

Coming May 17 2022

Just One Day – Spring

Mum-of-three Louisa thought she only had her never-ending to-do list to worry about, but the arrival of a ghost from the recent past puts her in an untenable position. Can she navigate the difficult situation she's in without their friendship becoming common knowledge or will it cause long-term damage to her marriage?

When her friend Nicky's new boyfriend becomes best buddies with her husband, Louisa is delighted, until he begins to suspect there's more to her relationship with the new sous-chef than meets the eye.

Can Nicky convince her boyfriend that all is above aboard or does Louisa have to talk herself out of a jam?

A new addition to the family undoes the recent gains she has made in ticking things off her to-do list and finding balance in her life. With tensions running high between Louisa and her husband, will she manage to keep her family on track whilst her life spirals out of control?

For fans of Fiona Gibson, Miranda Dickinson and Jill Mansell.